RESTING BEACH FACE

SWALLOW COVE #4

DJ JAMISON

Resting Beach Face
By DJ Jamison

Copyright 2025 DJ Jamison
Published by Must Love Books LLC

Cover design by Morningstar Ashley

 Created with Vellum

AUTHOR'S NOTE

I'm so happy to finally share Cash and Declan's story! *Resting Beach Face* starts before *Knockin' Boats* ends, so don't be surprised if you see a few familiar events, but both stories can be enjoyed separately!

This romance is very close to my heart because Declan, like me, is a gray ace. For those not in the know, that means he's on the asexual spectrum. Gray aces typically feel little to no sexual attraction, or they only feel it in certain circumstances. Asexuality is a spectrum, so ace experiences can vary a lot. I wrote this book primarily from my firsthand perspective as a gray ace, but I also had a sensitivity read done. I hope I've done justice to Declan and all the gray aces out there.

Thank you for reading and opening your heart to all the expressions love can take on.

DJ

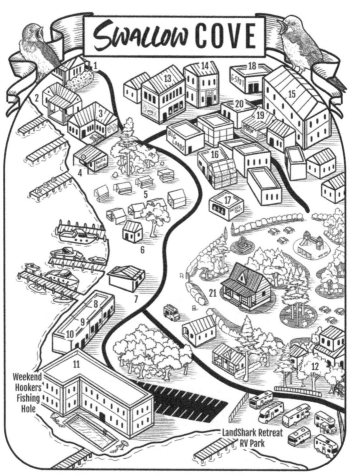

Swallow COVE

1. The Savory Swallow
2. The Rusty Hook Pub
3. Catch of the Day
4. Bait & Swallow
5. Outdoor Market
6. Swallow Adventures
7. Boat Rental

8. Dirty Dockers
9. The Drunken Worm
10. Tourist Trap
11. Swallow's Nest Resort
12. The Treehouse B&B
13. Little Clay Pot
14. Just the Sip

15. Silver Cove Assisted Living
16. The Dirty Hoe
17. Decked Out
18. The G-Spot
19. Tastes Like Grandma
20. Hot Buns Bakery
21. The Lake House

PROLOGUE

Cash

I slurped my spicy mango margarita—because I was manly enough to enjoy a good drink, regardless of its frilly packaging—and tried to focus on the pretty tourist beside me at the bar. Blond curls spilled down her shoulders, practically more coverage than her low-cut tank top provided. Her hazel eyes drank me in, gaze slipping up and down my body in a not-so-subtle invitation to get naked with her.

Tequila and bad decisions were flowing at The Drunken Worm. It was nearing midnight and the Tex-Mex restaurant had shifted from family fun to rowdy pickup spot. Laughter rang out loud and brash, drawing my attention to a table full of women in bikini tops and wraparound skirts, all sipping from fishbowl-sized margaritas large enough to drown a small child.

Amy—or Annie?—tugged my arm to regain my attention. "Hey, did you hear me?"

"Hmm?"

"I asked if you wanted to get out of here?"

She dangled an old-fashioned brass key emblazoned with a treehouse between us.

The logo of the Treehouse B&B.

Declan's place.

My mouth went dry at the sight of it. I shouldn't be excited to go there, right? Declan wouldn't be pleased to see me again. Two nights ago I'd hooked up with a guest named Raul, and things had gotten a little loud.

Declan had knocked on the door and told us to keep it down.

His forehead creased with a frown, but that meant nothing. Declan was always frowning. It seemed to be his natural expression. But that night, his eyes also narrowed, and he pinned me with a glare that told me he was pissed.

I was seriously messed up for liking a man's irritation so much, but damn, it'd been hot.

And if I couldn't have his interest, at least I could get under his skin.

"Well?" she asked. "What do you say? Shall we go have some fun?"

Fun? Was that what this was? I'd done it so many times I'd numbed myself to any spark of excitement. Hooking up with tourists was no longer about fun for me. It was about escape.

Escape from my house.

From my asshole dad.

From thinking at all.

I licked my dry lips, thinking about how Declan might react tonight. It didn't really matter, though. He'd notice me.

I wasn't sure why that was so important, only that it was.

"Okay, let's go."

We were a few blocks from the B&B—and I knew a shortcut across the park that saved us from passing by the old defunct resort or RV retreat.

Amy giggled nervously as she followed me between trees. "I hope you know where you're going."

"Like the back of my hand. I'm a local, remember?"

She grasped my arm, pressing in close, and I fought the urge to pull away. If I didn't want to sleep outside or go crawling to one of my friends and admit to just how bad things had gotten at home, then I needed to see this through.

Amy was a pretty enough woman. There was no reason to not do this.

Still, my stomach tied itself in knots. It was getting more difficult to slip from one bed to the next. Especially when none of them were the bed I really wanted.

The B&B loomed up in the darkness as we stepped from the trees. It was a two-story house with one wing hovering above ground—supported by a large oak tree that grew up through the center of it and exited the roof.

Amy led me to the front entrance, using her key to let herself in. A lamp sat on the check-in counter to the left of the door, casting a soft glow over the great room, where guests could lounge on sofas and chairs that looked like they'd come straight out of the 1970s. Declan really needed to redecorate.

It was late enough I might miss his scowl altogether. That was a shame.

Amy veered toward the staircase that led to the second floor. "I've got the treehouse suite," she said. "It's gorgeous. We can fuck out on the deck."

I cringed as her voice carried.

The door from the kitchen swung open and Declan stepped out, lips pressed together, brow furrowed. He wore a surprisingly adorable pajama set covered in SpongeBob characters and pineapple houses.

"What are you wearing?" I raked my gaze over him as he crossed the dining room, my smile widening with delight.

Sadly, the PJs were cotton and didn't cling to his chest and thighs the way his usual navy silk pajamas did.

"What?" Declan glanced down, a breath of displeasure escaping. Color darkened the back of his neck. "My niece gave them to me."

"Aw, sweet," Amy crooned, reminding me she was still there. "Sorry if we disturbed you. Cash and I were just on our way upstairs. Right, Cash?"

Was that right? I wanted to linger and tease Declan. Amy didn't interest me. But I had given her certain expectations...

"Right." I stepped closer to Declan, unable to resist one parting shot. "You know," I murmured. "The upside-down pineapple is a symbol swingers use." I poked his thigh where SpongeBob's house was floating upside down. "You never told me you were so adventurous, Dec."

His eyes widened as he sputtered a denial. I turned with a laugh to follow an impatient Amy up the stairs.

"Please keep it down," Declan called after us, so sternly it sent a little shiver across my skin.

Amy led me to the suite, unlocking her door and stepping inside. I followed, looking around even though I was already familiar with the king-size bed in the center of the room, the floor-to-ceiling windows, and the large soaker tub in the corner.

The lights were off, but moonlight poured in, silvering everything in a gentle glow.

Amy turned to me with a smile that surely worked on most men. "I thought we'd never get up here. The owner is such a stick-in-the-mud."

My reflexive smile tightened on my face. "Declan is a good guy."

"Oh, of course," she said, moving in close. Her hands rested on my waist, and she leaned up to kiss my neck. "He's just...you know...kind of weird."

I stiffened—and not in a fun way.

Amy didn't notice, too busy trying to feel me up. She slipped small, soft hands under my T-shirt. Not at all what I was craving.

Unbidden, an image of Declan rose in my mind. He wasn't a bear of a man by any means, but his hands were large and callused from all the gardening he did around the B&B grounds. One night when I'd pushed him too far, he'd taken my arm and walked me to the door. My biceps twinged, an echo of the bruising touch that had turned me on even more.

All the thoughts of Declan were helping my body respond appropriately, but Amy's touch was still all wrong.

Her words were even worse.

"Declan isn't weird," I snapped into the quiet space between us. "He's gorgeous and smart and...and I know he's a bit of a grouch, but it only adds to his charm. He's sweet under that exterior. He doesn't show it often, but..."

Amy pulled back from me, eyes wide. "Are you gay for him or something?"

Oh, nothing like a little bi-erasure to make this shitfest of a night better.

"No, I'm bisexual, Amy. Pansexual, really, not that you'd even understand the nuances."

She looked affronted. "My name is Annie, and I never agreed to that."

I barked a laugh. "You never agreed to my sexual identity? Well, good thing it's not up to you."

"You know what I mean. I'm not having a threesome with you and that...that..."

She waved her hand toward the door.

I rolled my eyes. "You should be so lucky. Don't worry. Declan has absolutely zero interest in you or me."

She crossed her arms over her chest. "I think you should go."

I sighed and raked my hands through my hair. Thought about whether I could still salvage my sleeping arrangement. If I grabbed her, kissed her, put my hands and tongue to work, I could persuade her.

I hesitated too long.

Amy gave me a shove. "Just go!"

"Okay, okay," I said, fending her off. "No need to get all violent and shit."

"Get out of my room now! I hope your weirdo is worth losing all this!"

She gestured to her body as if it were a prize—and granted, she was a lovely woman—but the idea that skipping a night with her was any great loss made me chuckle.

I ducked out the door just before a vase hit it with a crash.

Oops. Declan would not be happy about that.

I halfway expected him to be waiting outside with his disapproving glare and orders for me to straighten up. But the hallway was dark and empty. I slunk down it, torn about what to do next.

Declan was gone to bed, as were all the guests. I paused, eyeing the sofa in the living room.

I could just wait a couple hours to ensure my dad was out cold, then walk to our place on the other side of the park. The thought of sneaking past him snoring on the couch in the same stained tank top—the coffee table littered with cheap-ass Pabst beer cans—and climbing into my too-small twin to sleep in a house steeped in hate and regret did not appeal at all.

At least Katelyn wasn't there tonight. She was staying over with a friend. A tactic she often used during the summer, and good for her. I'd done that shit when I was in high school, too. Now that I was an adult, it was actually more difficult because my friends had all moved out of their parents' places and had their own lives. Even Brooks had unchained himself from the bar and was shacking up with that pretty Skylar.

I sighed and sank back against the cushions, my eyes growing heavy. Maybe I could just stay here a little while longer. I'd clear out before morning...

~

Declan

I rolled onto my right side, the faint ache in my lower back nagging me awake. I'd overdone it in the garden, trying to get my last fertilizing of the summer in before it was too late. I should have used the wheelbarrow, but I got impatient and lugged heavy bags around like I was twenty years younger.

Not that I'd been sleeping *well,* anyway. I huffed an annoyed breath and flipped my pillow to the cool side. I closed my eyes, but they sprang open a second later. I was restless. Uncomfortable. *Thirsty.*

I blamed Cash Hicks.

He had to stop rolling through here like a tumbleweed. I should be used to him turning up with his flavor of the night. I *was* used to it. In the beginning, I'd seen Cash as a minor nuisance. An immature fuckboy who was sowing his wild oats, but as long as guests wanted that sexual energy in their rooms, it wasn't my problem.

Then he turned that seductive smile on me. And, well...I'd have preferred that he didn't. For one, it didn't make any sense. What did he see in *me* when he was hooking up with half of the Swallow Cove tourist population? Secondly, I'd never been comfortable with things of a more intimate nature. My ex-boyfriend had called me cold, uptight, guarded. Take your pick.

But no matter how I shot down Cash, he always had a smile for me.

A smile that didn't *always* reach his eyes.

I threw back the blankets and got up, unable to ignore my bladder's urging even though it was nowhere near morning. Once that was done, my thirst renewed itself and I resigned myself to being awake.

I headed out of my private quarters to get a glass of water in the kitchen. I gulped cool tap water, sighing with relief, and started the trek back to my room. I could read for a while or maybe start a crossword puzzle to unwind...

A shadow moved in my peripheral vision. I stopped and turned. A man-sized shape slumped on the sofa in the great room. Had a guest returned drunk?

Hesitantly, I crouched down by the sofa and put my hand on his shoulder.

He exhaled softly—and though the idea of recognizing someone's breath seemed ridiculous, I instantly knew it was Cash.

"Hey." I shook him gently. "You okay?"

Cash turned over, his eyebrows drawn together and his lips parted, but his eyes still firmly shut. I had an up-close view of his objectively gorgeous face. He had nicely symmetrical features. His nose was straight and not too big. His lips were full but not too pouty. Stubble darkened his jaw. He really should shave more, but Cash seemed to like the scruffy look, and judging by how many people he took to bed, others did, too. There was a certain rakish charm to it that fit his personality, I supposed.

When his eyes were open, they were as bright as the Caribbean under his dark brows, and usually filled with mischief or humor. Though sometimes, lately, there seemed to be darker shadows there, lurking under the surface.

I shook him again. "Cash. Hey. You can't sleep here."

He started awake, sitting up so quickly I had to rear back to avoid a knock to the head.

"Wha..." He swiped a hand over his face. "Declan?"

"You can't sleep out here," I repeated. "Go back to Annie's room."

"Annie?" He looked confused for a moment. "You mean Amy? Er...no. Annie is right." He groaned. "Shit, I can't go back there."

"Why not?"

He smiled sheepishly. "I sort of got kicked out."

My stomach tightened. I didn't take Cash for the type of guy to cross the line, but I had to ask. "What happened? You didn't—"

"Of course not," he said, hurt flitting through his gaze. "I would never do that."

I nodded. "I didn't think so. Sorry. I had to ask."

He shook his head. "I just...I wasn't in the mood."

I raised an eyebrow. That had to be a first.

Cash read my expression. "I'm not just a walking sex machine. I have feelings too."

"I'm sure you do." I hesitated. "I can't let you sleep out here. The guests..."

He sighed. "Yeah, I didn't mean to crash. I was just waiting until—"

He stopped short.

"Until what?"

He hesitated, nibbling his full bottom lip.

"Cash," I said sternly. "Tell me."

A breath rushed out of him. "Just until I was sure my dad would be unconscious. We don't get along."

"Why haven't you moved out of there yet?"

Cash was twenty-four or twenty-five. Most people didn't

stay with their families that long, though Swallow Cove had limited housing available—especially affordable housing.

Cash's face tightened. "I would have, if not for my sister. She needs someone in her corner. My mother works crazy hours, and I contribute to the bills. It's not like I have a lot of better options other than a camper like Sawyer, anyway."

"I'm sorry to hear that."

He shrugged. "I find ways to avoid the house when things get too messy."

"Ways," I said slowly. "Ways like..." I gestured toward the stairs. "Like Annie?"

Cash's eyes clouded over. "I'll head home. Sorry for the inconvenience."

"It's three in the morning."

"It's fine."

"No." I stood. "Come with me. You can stay in my room."

His eyebrows shot up and a cocky grin spread across his face. "I thought you'd never ask."

"To sleep," I said firmly.

Cash followed me down the hall and into my private quarters that included a small sitting room, office, bedroom and attached bathroom. It was essentially a full apartment minus a kitchen. With the full house kitchen so close, it seemed silly to add in a kitchenette.

The B&B had been my aunt's pride and joy, and she'd loved cooking and always joked that she had no desire to do it in miniature.

I still wasn't sure why she'd left me the B&B in her will. I had fond memories of the place, of course, but I wasn't the most social butterfly. Still, Aunt Millie loved it, so I tried to love it too.

Tried being the operative word there.

"You can sleep on the couch. I'll get you a pillow."

Cash tucked his hands into his pockets. "Thanks."

I went to the closet and pulled out a sheet, a light cotton blanket, and a pillow. When I returned, Cash had taken off his shirt and was unzipping his shorts.

He was objectively gorgeous everywhere, then.

I averted my gaze as I placed the bedding on the end of the couch. "Do you need anything else?"

"Maybe just one thing."

I turned, and Cash cupped my face in his hands.

"A kiss?" He leaned in, eyes on mine. "If you want it?"

My heart thundered, catching me off guard. Did I want a kiss from him? From anyone? Normally, the answer would be an easy no. But something about this man, so casual with his affections and yet weighed down by worry, captured my attention.

But he was so very casual with his affections.

He probably believed this was a suitable way to thank me. Just one more way he was finding to avoid going home.

I didn't want to be that. Didn't want to be an excuse or a crutch or whatever the heck Cash's conquests were to him.

He inched forward, and I couldn't bring myself to move or speak. Not until his lips brushed over mine, so warm and soft. My breath caught, and for a moment, I could almost understand the fuss everyone else made about sex.

I stumbled back, shaking my head. "N-no. That's not why I said you could stay here."

His smile was small, a little questioning. "Would it be so bad?"

I pointed at the bedding and said sternly, "Go to sleep, Cash."

He chuckled. "Okay, but I'm not giving up on you."

"Lord help me," I muttered as I went to my bedroom. There was no chance I'd sleep a wink with a mostly naked Cash in the next room.

I curled up with a crossword until morning. Then I woke

Cash and told him I was going to Tastes Like Grandma to pick up biscuits and gravy for my guests. I only served a full, home-cooked breakfast on the weekends to save my sanity.

When he invited himself along, I didn't protest. Which was unlike me.

We ordered breakfast for ourselves while we waited for Rosie to whip up the larger to-go order, and I paid the tab.

"This is great," Cash said once we sat down with coffee and breakfast plates. "But you do know I can buy my own breakfast, right?"

"Well, I don't know how you do things, but when a man spends the night with me, he gets breakfast."

A surprised laugh burst from him. "Did you just make a joke? Really?"

"I'm not totally humorless," I grumbled.

He smiled. "Maybe not. Maybe there's hope for you yet." He leaned in. "You *could* have made me breakfast in bed, or better yet—"

I shoved a piece of toast in his mouth before he could say something suggestive.

"I want to talk to you about last night." At his expression, I quickly added, "Not anything with us. Just your situation."

He pulled the toast from his mouth. "My situation..."

"Yes. I want you to know you can stay at the B&B anytime."

"With you?"

"In one of the guest rooms. I'm rarely fully booked. There's no need for you to...find someone. Understand?"

His smile dropped. "Why?"

"Because you obviously need a place to go."

"I manage okay. It's not like I *can't* go home. I just prefer to avoid it sometimes."

"And you can avoid it at the B&B. Alone."

"But..." His brows drew together, and he leaned in over the

table. "Dec, are you making this offer just to be nice or because you don't like to see me with other people?"

"W-what?" I stuttered. "No. That's not it."

"Because you seemed like maybe you wanted that kiss last night. Why did you pull away?"

I stiffened, those words triggering a flood of memories. Every time a date would ask, *Why don't you want to kiss more often? Why do you say no so much? Why don't you want me as much as I want you?*

I snapped open the newspaper I'd purchased from the box outside the diner. "Just eat your breakfast. If you need a place to stay, you can have an *empty* room. That's all I'm offering."

"Got it." Cash plastered on a fake smile. "I'm fine, Declan. You don't need to worry about me. I'll steer clear of the B&B."

"I wasn't—"

"Let's just eat breakfast," he cut in. "I apologize for the inconvenience to you, okay? I should have gone home."

My lips pressed tight. I didn't want him to apologize. I didn't view his night in my quarters as an inconvenience—which was a surprise to me, too.

But I couldn't find the words to express that to him. Not without tipping us right back into his world of sexual innuendo and expectations I could not meet.

Cash and I spoke different languages.

So I nodded and fixed my eyes on the newspaper as if the articles within held all my attention when really my mind was far too full of the man across from me.

CHAPTER ONE

EIGHT MONTHS, 3 WEEKS, 2 DAYS WITHOUT SEX...

Cash

Bang-bang! The flimsy bathroom door shook in its frame, jolting me out of a steamy fantasy with a handsome stranger. He was tall, dark, brood—eh, who was I kidding? He was Declan.

Only this Declan didn't shut down the second my lips touched his. He pulled me closer. He whispered in my ear—

"Stop jerking off in there already and come out!"

Katelyn's screech snapped me back to reality. I poked my head out of the shower curtain to shout at the door. "Oy! Since when do you talk like that?"

"Since I'm about to pee my pants! Hurry up!"

There was a clatter of aluminum beer cans hitting the floor, then a snort and a grumble from Dad. He was passed out on the couch, and I'd like him to stay that way. At least until Kat and I were out of the house.

"Okay," I called quickly. "Give me a minute."

I glanced down at my flagging cock. "Sorry, buddy, no happy time for you today. Not even with my hand."

You could get laid anytime you want...

The thought crept across my mind, tempting. I was a grown-ass man. A single, unattached man. There was nothing to stop me from hooking up with anyone who was interested.

I twisted the knob to cold, dousing that thought in its tracks as I rinsed quickly, shivers overtaking the burn of arousal. Yes, I could find a hookup—but I already knew I wouldn't. I'd made a promise to myself. Not to be celibate or anything wild like that, but simply to have sex with someone only when I really wanted it. Only when I felt a spark and a connection.

The only trouble was...once I started paying attention? Well, I only sparked with one man. Too bad he didn't spark back.

I turned off the shower and did a quick rubdown with a towel before knotting it around my waist. Katelyn charged past when I opened the door, nearly knocking me off my feet.

"Get out," she ordered.

I cast a glance in the mirror. "I need to shave. Just—"

She threw a roll of toilet paper at my head, and I laughed. "Okay, okay, I'm going." I scooped up the toilet paper. "I'll just take this with me since you obviously don't need it..."

"Cash!" she called desperately.

With a grin, I tossed it back to her before stepping out and closing the door. I headed for my bedroom at the other end of the hallway, passing by the kitchen. Mom was carrying a trash bag that clinked enough I could tell it was full of Dad's empties.

She looked up from the pile of mail she was sorting into bills and junk she was adding to the trash bag. "Cash, honey, can you take this out? I've got to go."

She crossed to the hall and thrust the trash bag at me. I

grabbed for it with my right hand while holding up my slipping towel with the other. "Now? I'm kinda—"

"Yes, please!" She strode for the front door without looking back. "Love you!"

The door closed behind her.

"Naked," I muttered. "I'm kinda naked. But sure, taking out the trash."

I considered leaving it in the hallway, but something was dripping from the bottom. Best to just give Miss Mable a thrill. She was always peeking through her window or peeping over the fence, hoping for a bit of juicy gossip. With my family? She got more than enough. Sadly, it was usually the same old story over and over.

That poor Mr. Hicks, she'd say. He just hasn't been the same since that work injury to his back. He drinks too much to drown the pain, poor dear. And the yelling and the fighting? It's downright shameful. Poor Mrs. Hicks works nonstop and the good-for-nothing son, well, he *still* mooches off them. I just feel bad for the girl, little Kat. She's a good girl.

I opened the back door and went down the steps to put the trash into the bin. I nearly lost my towel when I lifted the lid.

"Oh my! Cash Hicks, what are you—"

I shot our neighbor a big grin. After all, *most* of what she said about us was true. Except for the bit about me mooching off my parents. I'd have left years ago if Kat didn't need me. I also paid some of the bills since Mom struggled to do it on her own with her housekeeping jobs—even taking overtime as often as she could.

"Morning, Mabel! Beautiful morning, isn't it?"

"Well, I..." Her gaze raked over me, she clutched at her non-existent pearls, and to my great delight, her cheeks pinked. "Why yes, dear, a *very* lovely day."

"Are you all right, Mabel?"

DJ JAMISON

She fanned her face. "Wh-what? Oh. Oh! Yes, just fine. Yes, indeed. You know, my granddaughter, Sadie, is visiting this summer and—"

"Sorry, Mabel, I've got to get ready for work."

I hightailed it back inside, a chuckle working its way up my throat. It was one thing to tease our nosy neighbor, but another to encourage a setup with her granddaughter. Still, maybe Mabel's impressions of me weren't *so* bad if she wanted to foist Sadie on me. That was progress, right?

Katelyn was in the hall when I came in. "What are you *doing?* We need to go!"

"The women in my life are far too bossy."

"We're just bossy enough," Kat threw over her shoulder with a smirk.

She took after me just a little too much.

I retreated to my bedroom to dress in my Swallow's Nest Resort uniform of khaki pants and a forest green button-up shirt. It was short-sleeved, but it would still suck during the hottest part of the day.

Thankfully, I'd spend most of my time in an air-conditioned hotel lobby. I'd had worse jobs. Far worse.

I popped into the bathroom to clean up my face. I didn't have time for a full shave, but I tamed my scruff to more of a designer stubble and used some hair wax to make my hair strands look artfully wavy instead of a bedhead mess. I wanted to look like I'd rolled out of a bed in a movie—not in real life.

"I'm heading to the marina!" Kat called through the door. "I don't want the Millers to leave without me."

"And let their poor Benny suffer all day without his love muffin?"

"Ugh, I hate you," she called without heat.

A few minutes later, the front door closed. I followed not long after, gaze sweeping over the sacked-out form of a man who had once been my father. It had been a long time since he'd been anything but a mess.

He lay on the sofa in a stained undershirt, a bag of Cool Ranch Doritos still resting on his chest. Drool trickled from one corner of his mouth.

The coffee table had been cleared and wiped down, but by tonight, Dad would have worked his way through a twelve-pack of that shitty Pabst again. I swear half Mom's paychecks went to enabling his addiction, but she never wanted to hear it when I talked to her about cutting him off.

"He's living with pain," she'd say. "We don't know what it's like. Just try to cut him a break."

But I'd been cutting him breaks for nine years. For a long time, I'd hoped things would change. That Dad would recover and come out of his funk. But at some point between years five and nine, I realized that I'd lost my dad the day of the boating accident that broke his back.

That man was gone, and he wasn't ever coming back.

I quietly closed the door behind me and cut across the street, between two houses, and through the park. As always, my gaze was drawn toward the Treehouse B&B and its lush gardens. Sometimes, I spotted Declan out digging in the soil or pruning roses. There was no sign of him this morning.

I didn't have a car, to save on expenses. Swallow Cove was small enough that I could walk most places without too much effort. Sometimes I went by my friend Sawyer's place to catch a lift to the resort with him. But today, I was meeting Poppy for coffee at Just The Sip, so I turned the other direction.

When I arrived, Danny was serving a young couple. The guy was blushing and stammering while his girlfriend laughed at him.

Danny's T-shirt read "Just The Sip" with a winky-faced emoji over the i. There was an image of a frothy drink with a *lot* of cream at the top and a puddle of coffee at the bottom. Beneath that, it said "Unless you want to swallow more!"

I snorted as Danny finished torment—er *flirting*—with the poor guy and I stepped up to the counter. "Nice shirt."

Danny grinned and tugged the hem forward so he could gaze down at his handiwork. "Isn't it great? I just got them made."

"It's very you, but does this mean I won't get to walk in here to see a new gay pun on your T-shirt every other day?"

"Oh, heck no. I must *express* myself as the amazingly gorgeous—and *available*—gay man I am. I mean, just imagine if my Prince Cumming walked in and he didn't know I was a desperate bottom just aching to sheath his sword."

I groaned. "Man, that was bad, even for you."

He laughed, eyes sparkling. "Can't fault a guy for trying."

I folded my arms on the high counter between us and made eye contact. I let my lips slowly tilt up in a smile that had never failed to make someone look twice. "Maybe you don't need to try so hard."

"Is that right?" Danny bit his lower lip as he looked me over. "Lord knows you don't need to try at all."

I grinned. "You're almost as tempting as your coffee."

"Just almost?"

"Sadly, I don't see a *Mocha me Moan, Danny* on the menu."

He wiggled his eyebrows. "That could be arranged."

Poppy walked up just then. "Good gravy, are you two going to flirt all day or are we going to actually get some coffee before you have to go to work?"

"Says the woman who's late."

"Well, I came over *on time*, but there was no sign of you, so I popped back over to the store to do a little more work. When I came back—five minutes ago, by the way—you were just too busy gazing into Danny's pretty green eyes to look my way."

Poppy ran a pottery shop, Little Clay Pot, next door with her dad.

I shot her a sheepish smile. "Sorry, we were just…"

"I know what you were doing," she said with a laugh. "You're both huge flirts and when you meet, there's some sort of gravitational force that makes you try to outdo each other."

I shrugged. She wasn't wrong. It was fun to flirt, and it was especially fun to flirt with Danny because he wouldn't take it as an invitation.

"Well, since Danny *isn't* on the menu yet, what can I get you two?" he asked, all business now.

"Hmm. I'll take the DP Cream," I said with relish.

It stood for double-praline cream, but Danny's names were always way more fun.

"Yummy. Hot or cold?" he asked.

"Ordinarily, I'd say hot, but uh…"

"Yeah, you need to cool off," Poppy said dryly. "And I'll take the flat white."

Danny often teased his customers into saying the full names —the Flat-On-My-Back White, in this case—but Poppy always got a pass.

"Can you whip up drinks for Brooks, Sky, and Grandma Kitty, too?" I checked the time on my phone. "If I'm gonna waltz in late, I need a peace offering."

"Sure thing."

Danny made our first two drinks, and Poppy and I took a seat while he made the rest.

I took a long draw from my straw, sighing as the sugary bliss washed over me. "This is almost as good as sex."

"I'll have to take your word for it," Poppy said.

She was ace and aromantic, and from what she'd told us, had no desire for a romantic or sexual partner.

"Don't you ever..." I stopped, chewing my lip, unsure if I should ask.

"What?"

I lowered my voice. "Tell me if this is too personal, but do you ever have physical cravings at all?"

She rolled her eyes. "I don't want physical intimacy with another person, but yeah, I still..."

She trailed off, but I got the picture.

"It's different for everyone on the spectrum, I suppose," she mused. "There's not any one way to be ace."

"Right." I cleared my throat. "I just wondered, because being horny all the time is fucking hard."

She busted out laughing. "I don't think it's the same, Cash. You're allosexual. You get it on all the time." She paused. "Or you used to, anyway. Is that what this is about?"

"It's not about anything."

"I mean, I've noticed that it's been a while."

"Shh. You'll ruin everyone's certainty that I'm a shameless man whore."

"I would have thought you'd want them to notice."

"If they haven't noticed yet, they never will. It's been eight months. Not that I'm counting."

She smiled sympathetically. "You are, apparently. But why —" She stopped. "This is about Declan, isn't it?"

"No."

That was only a partial lie. It was about Declan, but only because I was hung up on wanting him. Not because I expected anything to happen. That was obvious when he shut down the kiss at the B&B.

Mostly, it was about me. About deciding I was using sex to hide from my problems. That I was as reliant on it as my dad was on alcohol. And I'd be damned if I ever followed in his footsteps.

But going cold turkey wasn't easy. I'd fallen off the wagon once or twice, when I'd gotten a little too desperate for human contact. I missed sex, but mostly I missed being close to another person, sharing their warmth, their breath.

Feeling connected—even if only for a few minutes.

I didn't understand how Poppy didn't want or need that. But in a way, I envied her. She wasn't driven by hormones or loneliness. She found her contentment, her happiness within herself.

"Drinks are up!" Danny called.

I collected them at the counter, leaning in to smack a kiss to Danny's cheek.

"Thanks, babe."

"Anytime, handsome."

By the time I arrived at the resort, I was ten minutes late. I'd caught a ride with Fisher's dad—who was heading over to the fishing hole to join the Weekend Hookers now that he trusted my friend to run the store on his own—or I'd have been even later.

I hustled into the lobby, ignoring Brooks's scowl and shoving a cup into his hand. "All-Americano Alpha," I said. "You're welcome."

He looked down in surprise. "Oh. We have complimentary coffee."

"But it's not Danny's coffee."

He lifted the cup and took a sip and sighed. "You're not wrong."

I swept toward Skylar as he emerged from his office. "Sky, have I told you that you're the bestest, most gorgeous, sexiest boss ever?"

He chuckled, shooting a puzzled glance past me to Brooks. "Not lately, no..."

I held out a coffee cup. "Well, you are, and I'd totally be the cream in your coffee anytime you want."

"Cash," Brooks growled behind me, sounding exasperated.

I turned, blinking wide, innocent eyes. "Don't worry. You're invited too."

He grimaced. "Please don't put that picture in my head."

I laughed. "Too late. It's there, isn't it? In all its X-rated glory."

Skylar took a long drink of his Caramel Cockiato and smiled. "It's almost worth it for this coffee."

I opened my mouth, but Brooks beat me to the punch. "Don't encourage him."

I hefted the last coffee cup. "Is that how you want to treat the guy who got Grandma Kitty's favorite drink?"

Brooks visibly softened. "You didn't have to do that, man. Thanks."

"It was no problem," I said honestly.

I might not make enough money to help support my family *and* pay for my own place, but I could manage a few extra coffees now and then.

"Did I hear coffee?" Kitty's voice rang out across the lobby.

"You sure did," I called with a grin.

Grandma Kitty tried to hurry her step, and I met her halfway across the lobby so she wouldn't end up falling and breaking another hip. She'd recovered after her last fall, but it had taken a long, hard road that included a stay in an assisted-living facility.

She'd finally retired her cane and walked on her own, though she still had a hitch in her giddyup.

I extended the coffee. "One Spit-Roasted Blond for my favorite grandma."

"Oh, aren't you just the sweetest thing?"

She grabbed my shoulder and tugged, and I obliged by bending down so she could kiss my cheek.

"You keep this one around," she ordered Sky. "He's a good boy."

I smiled as I retreated to my spot behind the front desk, ready to take reservations, address guests' concerns, and greet new check-ins.

Grandma Kitty was probably the only person in my life who could call me a *good boy*, but I basked in her praise.

It wasn't like I was getting much of it at home—or in my nonexistent love life. A guy had to take what he could get.

CHAPTER TWO

Declan

"THIS IS JUST BEAUTIFUL COUNTRY AROUND HERE," MAI, a petite Vietnamese woman with a hulking—but blissfully quiet—husband, looked at me with bright eyes. "I can't wait to get out on the lake."

"Mm," I said, raising my cup to sip my coffee. Small talk wasn't my forte. I wasn't so good at regular talk, either. I forced myself to add a few words when she waited expectantly. "You have fun plans?"

That set her off on a spiel about boat tours and tubing and her poor pale husband, Jake, who needed to apply sunblock every hour to avoid frying to a crisp.

Mai wore a Weekend Hookers ballcap and a tank top that read, *I like it in the boat.* She'd clearly made a trip to Decked Out, a store full of kitschy lake apparel that she'd found hilarious. Jake was more circumspect in a simple blue tee and board shorts.

They'd booked the treehouse suite for the week, and by the

sounds of things—oh so *many* sounds as she chattered—Mai was having a blast.

An older couple, Agnes and Roger, chimed in with their quieter plans to do some shopping in town. The main house was fully booked, but the Myers had headed into town for breakfast and the Jensens had gone out early to go fishing, which left only my couple out in the Tree Hut. They were late sleepers, so I didn't expect to see them for a while.

Mai's enthusiasm for the day ahead carried the conversation through breakfast, and I stood to clear the plates away. I'd made a spinach quiche, bacon, and toast since it was a weekend. Quiche seemed fancy but was easy to make, thankfully, because I was no Paula Deen.

I tried to avoid eating with the guests when I could—as it just highlighted my anti-social nature—but Mai was too determined to *get to know me*. It would have been too rude to refuse, even for me.

"What about you, Declan?" Roger asked as I stood. "You puttering around the garden again?"

"I don't know. Maybe."

My roses could do with some pruning, and the battle against weeds was ongoing.

"Agnes and I might cross over to Swallow Beach after we're done here. Wanna come along and play tour guide?"

I loudly stacked plates. "Not really."

There was a stretch of awkward silence.

"It's, uh, not really my strong point," I added with a strained smile. Judging by the looks around the table, I hadn't pulled it off.

"All right," Roger grumbled. "I was just trying to be friendly."

Agnes rescued me. Her hair was a short white bob with a

purple streak through the bangs to indicate she was still *hip*. Her cat's-eye purple glasses coordinated nicely.

"I'm sure he gets offers all the time to tour the area, honey. He lives here and meets new people every day." She sighed wistfully. "What a lovely life. I'd love to run a B&B."

Everyone looked at me again. I cleared my throat and prepared to say something appropriately cheerful.

My phone rang.

Thank you, whoever you are.

I reached into my pocket to pull out my cell. "Sorry, all, I've got to take this booking. Please leave your dishes. I'll finish cleaning up."

"Thank you, Declan."

"Have a good day, Declan!"

"The quiche was delicious."

Chairs scraped back, silverware clattered against china, and feet shuffled. Jake, the quiet husband, patted my shoulder as he passed. Perhaps sympathizing with my inability to hold a simple conversation?

Then they were gone, and it was quiet again.

I answered the phone. "Nathan, you picked the perfect time to call."

"Every time I call is perfect," he said with a chuckle.

Nathan was the type of guy who had confidence for days, yet somehow it never came across as cocky. We'd worked together in the banking industry. I was a financial analyst, spending my days with data as my closest companion, while Nathan managed investment portfolios.

He'd left shortly after I did to go into hedge fund management. He loved playing the odds, taking risks for great reward—and sometimes great disappointments. I couldn't live so dangerously, but Nathan got a shot of adrenaline out of it.

"What did you need?" I asked.

Nathan and I were colleagues—he'd tried to take me rock-climbing exactly one time before he learned I was a better workplace acquaintance than actual *friend*—but he stopped in with coffee and dragged me away from my numbers to pick my brain about financial trends whenever he could.

"You see what's going on with Heske Tech?" he asked.

"Don't take that bait," I said. "It's artificially inflated now, but given the trends, it won't last."

"Aha! I knew you'd never abandon us completely, man. You should come back."

"What?" I startled. "No, I just..."

"Analyze financial data for shits and giggles?" he said with a snort.

"I wouldn't say *analyze*. I peruse. In fact, don't take my advice on Heske. I haven't done any deep dives into the data."

"I'd take your casual perusal over some other guy's in-depth study. Your talents are wasted out there."

"Maybe, but I can't run the B&B from Chicago, so..."

"I guess," he grumbled. "I could really use you. The analyst they've got here is cramping my style."

"Impossible," I said.

He chuckled. "So, you really like it out there?"

"Well..." I hedged. "It's different. Things are slower here. More relaxed. I have all the time I want to read and garden."

"Sounds like a retirement plan," he said skeptically.

I didn't disagree. Compared to the long hours I worked as an analyst, it *was* easier. And yet, having new people in my home every week, struggling to give them a warm welcome and connect the way they wanted, was more challenging than any financial report I'd ever read.

"Listen, Declan, I'm serious. If you ever want to come back, my door's open."

"I can't," I said. "I've got a B&B to run."

"Well, look, you own it, but you're not married to it. You could always—"

A harried-looking guest headed toward the front desk.

"Mr. Sullivan, sorry to interrupt, but we need you!"

"Sorry, Nate, I've got to go."

"But Dec—"

I hung up on Nathan. Not to be rude, but because the man didn't know the meaning of the word no. He could persuade a rock it was a shiny seashell. He was a good guy, but also the ultimate salesman, and I didn't have time for his pitch right now.

Not when Harrison Stroberg, the first guest to book my Tree Hut since I'd taken over the B&B, looked as if he'd just stepped out of a rainstorm on a bright sunny day.

"What happened?" I asked, already resigned to bad news.

"A pipe burst in the bathroom. It's spraying water everywhere."

"Did you turn off the water?"

"We tried, but it didn't work. Noah was turning the valve and—"

"Nevermind." I rounded the counter, running past him. "I'll take care of it."

I should have never opened the Tree Hut for bookings. It had sat vacant too long, and after a thorough cleaning and repainting, it was still giving me headaches.

When the Swallow's Nest Resort opened, I had actually been relieved. Maybe it would take away a few guests, and I could enjoy my weeks with fewer interruptions. I didn't need much to keep this place going since it was my house, too. Just a trickle of guests would suit me fine.

I'd mostly taken on the B&B for my aunt's memory, not out of a desire to actually house strangers day after day.

But instead of taking my bookings, the darn resort had somehow *increased* the flow of tourists. Their marketing had put

Swallow Cove front and center—even before they were open—and apparently a Treehouse B&B was just too charming to pass up.

So, as bookings filled, I opened up the Tree Hut for the first time. And now here we were, with a burst pipe, water damage, and damp, unhappy guests.

Harrison's boyfriend, Noah, opened the door when I arrived. He was six-foot-four and damn near wider than the door frame. He wrung his hands. "I tried to turn off the water to the toilet, but I made it worse."

"You better show me."

Noah turned, striding away, and I tried not to notice how very short his shorts were. It was tough with the way his hips swayed with every step.

Water pooled on the bathroom floor. It was tile, so that wasn't so bad. If the story ended there. Sadly, it did not.

Because it wasn't just water on my floor, but...sewage. The toilet must have been clogged. And the water turn-off valve that came out of the wall? It was broken clean off, with water spraying from the pipe, adding to the mess.

"Well, shit."

"Exactly," Noah said, looking guilty. "I tried to turn it off and the valve broke!"

Harrison spoke behind me. "We need to find the main shut-off."

"No kidding." I spun and darted past him, going out the sliding door onto the wraparound deck, then accessing the utility closet attached to the back of the hut. Inside, I found the turn-off and twisted it.

It resisted, and I threw my weight into it, grunting with exertion and praying to whatever evil entity reined over B&B owners that this pipe wouldn't break too.

I didn't have the strength of Noah, but the valve finally gave, inching its way toward off.

When it was done, I was breathing hard and pouring sweat. Was I really just telling Nathan about the relaxing life of owning a B&B?

That was karma for you. Always ready to be a bitch.

I returned to the hut, where Harrison and Noah waited for me.

"I'm so sorry," Noah said. "This is such a mess. I thought I could handle it, but I made it so much worse."

Harrison squeezed his shoulder. "It's not your fault, babe. The pipes were old and corroded." He tossed me an apologetic smile. "Part of its charm, I suppose."

"It's not very charming right now," I said sourly.

Harrison wrinkled his nose. "No, uh, and on that note... I know you've got to take care of all this, but we can't stay here."

"Of course not," I said with a sigh.

Then brightened as I found the silver lining. "How would you feel about a complimentary booking at the new Swallow's Nest Resort?"

"That new hotel just down the road?" Noah sounded excited. "I saw they have a pool bar."

"They do," I said with a chuckle. "Pack up your things and I'll call ahead. They're newly opened, so they should have some rooms available. I'll get you a reservation."

"That is so nice!" Noah flung his beefy arms around me, smelling like a disturbing mix of cologne, sweat, and shit.

Harrison tugged him back. "Easy, babe. Remember what we talked about. You need to ask before hugging."

Noah winced. "Sorry. I just really appreciate how gracious you all are here. What a nice place!"

"Well, it'd be nicer without the sewage on the floor," I said dryly, "but yes, Swallow Cove is a great place."

Even a guy like me— who couldn't be called social even on a good day—had managed to make a few friends. Hudson Nash, a transplant to town who ran Swallow Adventures boat tours, had latched onto a fellow outsider and adopted me as his best friend. And once he started dating Fisher, there was no avoiding the gaggle of *his* friends—not that I'd managed before that, when they took up so much space and energy and made so much *noise* when they gathered at The Rusty Hook, my favorite dinner spot.

It didn't help that Cash was among them. He'd taken an interest in me early on. When I hadn't returned it the first time, he'd seemed shocked. But instead of getting pissed, he'd grinned and told me I didn't know what I was missing.

I was pretty sure I knew exactly what I was missing. But... week after week, year after year, he flirted shamelessly with me. And I had to admit, it was flattering even when it went nowhere.

And then there was that kiss...that brief, sweet brush of lips that changed everything.

For me, anyway.

I couldn't see Cash without thinking of it. Not so much because the kiss was so amazing, but because I'd felt a flicker of attraction, a pull of connection, that was so rare for me.

But ever since my offer to let Cash stay at the B&B as needed—without a hookup for an excuse—he'd avoided the place.

I didn't know where he spent his nights. Probably the resort now with a whole new set of Amys and Rauls. He didn't need me or my B&B.

But that also meant he wasn't my problem anymore. Except for right now. He worked the front desk at the resort and I'd just promised Noah and Harrison I'd get them a room.

I left the mess on the bathroom floor and returned to the main house to retrieve my abandoned phone.

The phone rang twice, then connected. "Swallow's Nest Resort, this is Cash speaking. How may I help you?"

"Cash, it's Declan."

There was a long pause.

I cleared my throat. "Declan Sullivan, owner of—"

"I know who you are, Declan," he said, sounding exasperated. "I was just surprised. What can we help you with?"

"I've got a little situation over here at the B&B."

"Are you okay?" he asked, sounding concerned.

"Yes, but I booked the Tree Hut for the first time, and we have a bathroom crisis."

"That doesn't sound good."

"No. I was hoping I could book a room at the resort. For my guests Harrison and Noah."

"Let me see what we can do," Cash said, the tapping of keys audible in the background. "We can't have Harrison and Noah sleeping on the couch."

His voice was light, teasing even, but it took me straight back to the night I'd found him in my great room.

To the things that almost happened. That most likely *would* have happened if I was a different kind of man.

I cleared my throat again, shifting. "I'll pay the going rate, of course. If they could get a room with a view of the lake... I'd like to make up for ruining their treehouse experience."

"I'm sure you didn't ruin anything," Cash said. "But yes, we can do it. We're intentionally booking at only about forty percent capacity right now. Skylar wanted a soft opening to give us plenty of time to work out all the bugs as we take on guests. But I know he'll make an exception in this case. I've got them in the system. Just send them over."

"Thank you, Cash."

"Anything for you, Dec. Say the word, and I'm your man."

If only that were true. I'd offered him a place, and he'd rebuffed me. Possibly, he wanted more than a platonic place to lay his head. But that was the whole problem, wasn't it? If I gave him the truth—the whole truth—of who I was and how I lived my life, Cash would most decidedly *not* be my man.

CHAPTER THREE

Cash

I SLUMPED OVER THE FRONT DESK, CHIN SUPPORTED ON MY right hand, and checked the time on my computer screen. It read 6:50 p.m.

I sighed wistfully, like a princess trapped in a castle. If only some prince would come kiss me and set me free. Or was it that he needed to cut my hair? My hair was short enough already, and I liked this style, so maybe it was just as well—

"Brr! The air-conditioning is chilly when you're wet. My nips are getting all hard. Look, Harrison!"

Harrison attempted to shush his loud boyfriend as the two entered from the door that led out to the pool. While Harrison wore board shorts with a towel draped over his shoulders, Noah was clad in only tiny briefs that left little to the imagination and held the towel over one arm, doing little to shield his *nips* from the cold.

I grinned, happy for the distraction. Today had been relatively slow, aside from taking Declan's call and checking these two in earlier. We'd booked a large group reservation around 1 p.m., a request for room service at five, but largely it had been quiet on the home front.

If it weren't for Grandma Kitty's visits throughout the day to talk about everything from her favorite television shows to her little crush on old Chester—which Brooks was going to *love* when he found out—I'd probably have died of boredom by now.

No chance of that with Harrison and Noah heading toward me, half-naked and dripping wet.

"You two look like you're enjoying your stay."

"It's great," Noah said, giving an excited wiggle that drew my eyes to his very exposed body. And he had a *lot* of body to expose. He owned every bit of his beefy thighs, jiggly ass, and furry belly, though, and it was actually pretty damn sexy. "I had three daiquiris *in* the pool."

I chuckled. "I can tell."

Harrison grimaced. "For a big guy, he's kind of a light-weight. Sorry. We'll go to our room and put on some clothes. The hotel really is great. I'm glad Declan sent us this way."

Noah rubbed his nipples. "I could use some help warming up." He gave me a coy look. "When do you get off shift? You look downright *hot*."

I shot a look Harrison's way, but his gaze was more appraising than concerned.

"I'm off in a few, but I'm actually headed over to the B&B to see how Declan is doing with that mess at the Tree Hut."

The guys had told me all about the plumbing disaster when they'd checked in just before lunchtime.

"Oh, that's nice of you," Noah said. "I feel so bad about that. I tried to help, but I'm just a bull in a china shop!"

He flailed one big arm to demonstrate and knocked a display of brochures over. "See what I mean!"

I laughed as I came around the front desk to help gather them from the floor.

Harrison crouched beside me to help, but paused when Noah stage-whispered, "Harry, ask him!"

Harrison glanced sidelong at me then shook his head. "Not sure I should."

Noah grabbed his arm and pulled him up, whispering into his ear while shooting what he probably thought were covert looks at my ass. I finished gathering the brochures and replaced them on the front desk.

Noah was wiggling again, and there was something adorably puppy-like about him despite his size. Harrison dragged a hand over his face, then cut his eyes my way.

"I don't suppose...you're into men?"

I raised an eyebrow. "Into men or into the two of you?"

"You could be *into* me," Noah offered with a sloppy smile that I suspected was meant to be sultry. Maybe he would have pulled it off two daiquiris ago.

"Tempting, but I don't play where I work. Besides, I need to get over to the B&B..."

Noah pouted. "You could make an exception for us."

I chuckled. "I could, but I won't."

Noah huffed. "What's the good of all these hot men if they won't play with me?"

Uh-oh. I wondered if that meant Brooks had gotten an invitation as well. I could just imagine how that went over. Heaven help us all if they propositioned Skylar first. Brooks was possessive of his boyfriend.

"Don't sulk, baby, you've still got me."

Noah nuzzled into his side as Harrison ushered him away from the desk. "I love you best."

"I know you do," Harrison said, his voice fond. "Besides, I'm pretty sure Cash is more interested in Declan."

Noah craned his head to look back toward me. Damn, how transparent was I that Harrison could figure me out in just two conversations? No wonder my friends gave me hell about my fixation.

It was almost enough to make me second-guess my plan to swing by the B&B.

Almost.

The clock finally ticked over to 7 p.m., and I headed toward the staff entrance that led to the docks.

Sawyer was already in his personal boat, untying the lines as he readied to leave. He worked with Swallow Adventures, running boat tours for the resort, but this week he'd been lent out to help Ash Dixon—his former best friend and current enemy—with his new food boat, Master Bites.

This came *after* Ash kissed Sawyer out of the blue, so I suspected there was something cooking with these two, even though Sawyer had always dated women.

"Can I catch a ride home with you?" I asked.

He glanced over his shoulder. "Sure, hop aboard."

"How's it going on the food boat? You kill Ash yet?"

He gave me a steady look. "Correction. I'll give you a ride as long as you don't ask about Ash. It's been a long day, and I have no wish to relive it."

I pouted nearly as much as Noah. "You're no fun."

"That's been established." He sat in the captain's seat and started the engine. "You're too much fun."

"Not anymore," I grumbled.

He didn't argue, which meant he agreed because Sawyer was *always* happy to argue with me. He reversed the boat out of the dock, and the breeze tugged at my hair. It'd be even more of a tousled mess when we got to shore, but that was okay. It'd add to my rakish charm.

Not like Declan cared what I looked like, right?

We made the short trip in peace, but as Sawyer approached the dock at the RV park where he kept his camper, he piped up. "You want off here, or should I take you to the pub?"

"Here is fine," I said. "It's closer to home."

"Wanna hang out a while? I could fire up the grill."

I faked choking. "No. Please... I'm too young to die."

He flipped me the bird. "Fuck you, man. Just beer then. Stay and have a beer."

"Next time."

Sawyer's eyes narrowed in suspicion. "You're not going home, are you? You're heading over to the B&B to pester Declan."

Damn it. He knew me too well. I never headed home this early unless Kat needed me. I also never passed up a free beer.

"I don't *pester* Declan," I said with as much dignity as I could muster. "I haven't been over there in months."

"But you *are* headed over there tonight."

"Just to check in," I said. "He had a problem with the B&B. I'm being a good friend is all." At his look, I downplayed that. "A good neighbor. A good...colleague in the hospitality business."

Sawyer snorted. "Careful, Cash, you keep digging that hole and pretty soon you'll just be a good Peeping Tom."

"Shut up!" I said with a laugh as he eased into dock and cut the engine. "I don't really know how to classify it, okay?"

"How about you're hopelessly obsessed?"

"Harsh," I said. "Now I'm not giving you any advice about what to do about Ash."

"I don't need advice."

"Fuck him," I said. "It's the only way you'll figure out what you really want."

"Wow, Cash, so wise," he said. "And here I thought you'd stopped thinking with your dick."

"I'm not thinking with *my* dick," I said with a wink. "I'm thinking about your poor blue balls."

I dodged his shove and jumped onto the dock before he could toss me overboard.

Sawyer was conflicted. That had been obvious the first night he showed up to tell us that Ash had kissed him. I was just doing my part to make him consider that he might actually want the guy.

One day, he'd thank me for giving him shit.

Today was not that day.

He flipped me off. I waggled my fingers in a playful wave, then jogged off before he kicked my ass.

It took me only a few minutes to cut through the park and over to the B&B grounds. A series of old-fashioned lanterns lined a path to the entrance at the main house.

The B&B was actually a collection of three buildings. Along with the main house, there was a Tree Hut that was built on a platform actually in the trees, like an old-school treehouse for kids but way nicer; and a third cabin built on the rise of a small hill with a staircase and deck that extended up into the trees for some amazing views.

I rapped on the front door, hoping someone would be around to open it for me since I didn't have a convenient hookup with a key tonight.

A few knocks later, a cute woman in a Weekend Hookers hat answered the door. "Hey! Declan was fetching us some cards for a poker game. You want to join?"

Poker? Really?

She stepped back and headed for the dining area where Declan served breakfast. I knew because I'd gate-crashed a couple of times, to his immense displeasure.

I trailed behind her. "Is Declan playing with you?"

She wrinkled her nose. "Doubtful. He's more of a loner. Likes his crosswords and his gardens."

I smiled fondly. "That sounds about right. Actually, I'm just—"

"Cash?" Declan's voice cut through my explanation as he entered the room with a silver case. "What are you doing here?"

I widened my eyes. "Just checking to see if you have a gambling license, sir."

Declan set down the case, which the B&B guests flipped open to reveal rows of pristine poker chips. "This is just a friendly game." He sent his guests a stern look. "No money exchanging hands, right?"

An older woman with a streak of purple through her bangs giggled. "We're not breaking the law, I swear."

"Just a friendly game," a man with a bushy mustache said with a nod.

"Not even strip poker," the pretty woman who let me in said. "Unless you want to join?"

Her husband glowered. "Not cool, Mai. I'm right here."

She turned a grin on him. "Just keeping you on your toes!"

Declan took hold of my arm, his touch making my skin tingle, and pulled me toward the great room. "What are you doing here—and please don't say it's to hook up with someone. I don't have any single guests."

"That's not why I'm here," I gritted out. "There's more to me than just that, you know."

Declan reddened. "Sorry. No. I shouldn't have— Why are you here?"

I sighed, shoulders dropping. Why did I want this infuriating man so much? He'd rejected me flat-out the first time I hit on him, which pretty much never happened. It had intrigued me. And the more he brushed off my interest, the more interested I became.

Until, of course, I realized I was battering my head against a wall that wasn't ever going to give.

"I came by to see how you were doing with that mess in the Tree Hut?"

"Oh." He looked surprised. "I guess Harrison and Noah told you the ugly details?"

I nodded. "Did you get it sorted?"

He shuddered. "Well, I spent hours mopping up and disinfecting the floor. The water's turned off, so it's under control."

"And the plumbing repair? Did you get that made?"

"Not yet."

"Maybe I could take a look," I offered. "See if I can save you some money? I spent a few days apprenticing with Pipe Pirates."

"A few *days*?" he said, then paused. "Pipe Pirates, really?"

I snorted. "We clear the way for your booty. Argh!"

"Dear God."

"Are you really surprised after visiting Big Loads laundromat? This is Swallow Cove, home of the silly pun."

He shook his head, lips quirking up at the corners. My stomach fluttered, and I wanted more than a twitch of the lips. I wanted a full-blown smile.

"You've eaten at The Savory Swallow," I added. "And aren't you a regular visitor at The Dirty Hoe garden store?"

"Okay." He grinned. "Point made."

I basked in one of his rare smiles until he blinked and sighed. "I doubt you learned enough in a few days to handle my plumbing, though."

"Oh, trust me, I can handle your plumbing anytime you're ready." I fluttered my eyelashes at him.

He shook his head, not responding to my flirtation. Nothing new there.

"I'm just going to close the Tree Hut to bookings."

"Really? But it's so cool. If you got the cabin open too, you could accommodate a lot more guests."

Declan shuddered. "No, thanks."

"Sick of the tourists already?" I teased.

"Like you wouldn't believe," he admitted.

Oh, I believed. Declan had always struck me as an odd choice for a B&B owner. He didn't particularly like people.

"Well, if you change your mind about letting me handle your pipes—"

"Stop it," he said, but without heat. The man seemed immune to my flirting. "I won't change my mind."

"Well, my offer stands," I said. "Not just for pipes. For... anything you might need. I'm here to help."

"Why?" he asked, suspicion coloring his tone. I guess that was fair. I'd hit on him enough times that he probably thought I was hoping for some kind of quid pro quo.

"I don't know. I've stayed at your B&B a lot; it's the least I can do."

"That was a long time ago, and you were invited by guests," he said.

"Not the last time." My eyes met his and held for a long moment. The memory of that ghost of a kiss rose in my mind. I wondered if he ever thought about it? Probably not. But it haunted me.

Declan cleared his throat. "Uh, yes, well that was just... You don't owe me anything for that. You never did. Not that night. Not now."

I cocked my head. Something about the way he said that struck me as odd. But I couldn't quite figure it out, so I shrugged it off. "Okay, well, maybe I just want to be friends."

"Friends?" he said, forehead creasing.

"We got off on the wrong foot, and that's on me. I knew you

weren't comfortable with me coming here so often, and I did it anyway."

Declan looked confused. "Cash, you don't have to explain all that. I realized the last night you were here *why* you were doing it. It had nothing to do with me."

I chewed my bottom lip. That was partly true. I was avoiding going home a lot of those nights. But I got a sort of childish thrill out of cracking his composure, too. Declan was so closed off, so immune to my charms.

Something about him had always gotten under my skin.

But acting like a kid pulling pigtails was never the way to win a man like Declan. I knew that much.

Most of that was better left unsaid. It would only make Declan uncomfortable—and I was trying to do the opposite these days.

"Well, all I really wanted to say was that I hoped we could start over on better terms."

"It's not really necessary," he said. "But sure." To my surprise, he played along and held out his hand. "I'm Declan Sullivan, owner of this B&B. Nice to meet you."

I grasped his hand, reveling in his strong grip, rough with calluses. One I could too easily imagine on my cock, damn it.

My eyes met his, and I could *swear* there was a spark—and not just one way. I resisted the urge to flirt and ruin all the progress I'd just made.

"Hi, Declan. I'm Cash Hicks. I work at the nearby resort, and I'm a bit of a jack-of-all-trades. So if you need help with anything around here, just give me a ring."

Declan gazed at me searchingly for a long moment before releasing my hand and stepping back. "That's very neighborly of you, Cash. I'll be sure to do that. And if I can do anything for you—" He stopped abruptly. "Well, not *anything*."

I chuckled. "Don't worry, Declan, we're being neighborly.

No sex favors. Unless you've got more exciting neighbors than I do?"

He smiled ruefully. "No. Uh, I'd be glad to help you out sometime if you ever need a place to stay or...or...something else I can do."

"Actually, I'm staying in my own bed these days," I said, giving him a direct look that I hoped he'd interpret correctly, "but thanks for the offer."

CHAPTER FOUR

Declan

"When will my room be ready? I've been traveling all day. I'm tired."

I attempted a reassuring smile and missed by a mile. My newest guest had arrived a day before her check-in and *insisted* the mistake must be mine. She was all of five-foot-one, even in sandals with chunky heels, and wore a pink sundress.

Those pretty trappings were a decoy. Marigold Lawson was about as far from sweet as I was, though she knew how to put on a smile that initially lulled me into a false sense of security.

Now, on our third conversation, I knew better.

"Ma'am, as I said before, your booking was scheduled for tomorrow. You'll have to wait for my late check-out to leave before I can give you a room."

"How long will that be?"

I flicked my gaze to the antique cuckoo clock in the front hall. "Their check-out is in twenty minutes, so—"

She interrupted. "Twenty minutes is a long time to wait."

"Unfortunately, the room will still have to be cleaned, so you'll need to wait longer than that."

"How long does it take to change some bedding?" she said dismissively. "I'll expect to be in my room in twenty-five minutes or else I'll have to talk to your manager."

I bit down on a laugh. If only I had someone else to deal with this shit.

"I own the B&B."

"Oh. Well." She sniffed. "I'd hate to leave you a bad review." She glanced around. "This place is really...quaint."

"I'll get the room ready as quickly as possible," I said blandly. "Perhaps you'd like to go into town for lunch rather than wait here?"

She narrowed her eyes, then waggled a finger at me with a laugh. "Oh no, you're not tricking me into going out so you can take your sweet time. My husband will get here soon, and he won't stand for this nonsense." She raised her phone, eyes focused on the screen. "I *told* him we should book the new resort. I wish I was having a poolside margarita right now."

"Me too," I muttered.

She glanced up. "What was that?"

"The resort is quite nice," I said. "Maybe you can book it for your next stay."

"Hmm. Maybe I will."

She turned in a swirl of skirts and flounced over to the sofa where I'd found Cash sleeping all those nights ago. She sat with a huff and proceeded to glue her face to her phone.

The Jensens checked out ten minutes early—and I turned the room over in record time. When I returned to the great room to tell Marigold, she waved me off while tapping away at her phone, clearly in no hurry to claim the room I'd rushed to get ready for her.

Unbelievable. I set the key on the table at her knee and retreated to my quarters before I throttled the woman.

I opened a crossword app and lost myself in the clues.

3 Across. Wound up.

"Tense," I muttered as I filled it in. "Sounds about right."

The next couple were popular culture questions and beyond me. I skipped over them, looking for something else I could fill in.

5 Down. Calla lily's family. I perked up as I scribbled in *Arum.*

With each answer, I got a little hit of dopamine. Gradually, I began to relax. Enough that when the phone rang, I picked it up without dread.

"Treehouse B&B, how can I help you?"

"It's more about how I can help you. Great greeting, though. Very professional. I give you five stars."

I recognized Nathan's voice immediately. "Oh, hey, I didn't look at the Caller ID before I picked up."

"Obviously," he said with a chuckle. "I thought we should finish our conversation from last weekend. You rushed off to deal with something."

I sighed. "It's probably not the best time to talk to me. I just dealt with the rudest guest. She threatened to leave me a bad review if I didn't produce a room for her immediately, even though she showed up a day early, and frankly, I'm just over *people* right now."

I huffed with all the exasperation I couldn't show Marigold Lawson.

"Damn," Nathan said. "Did you get her a room?"

"Yes, not that it'll matter with someone like her," I grumbled. "She probably left one anyway."

"I can't imagine living to please other people," Nathan said.

Yeah, I wasn't loving it either—especially because I was so damn bad at it.

All this talk about reviews had made me curious. I tapped the Speaker button, then navigated my phone screen to the Google page for the Treehouse B&B.

My top review was nice enough. *Great town. Nice place.*

The next one made me suck in a sharp breath.

Owner could be friendlier. I really loved the view of the lake though!

"What's wrong?" Nathan asked.

"Nothing, just...made the mistake of reading the reviews."

"Uh-oh."

"Yeah." I zeroed in on the next critical comment. "Why did this guy open a B&B? He doesn't even like people! I swear this guy has the worst case of resting bitch face I've ever seen. He's more like a stern high school principal than a welcoming host."

The words hurt. Not just because it was a critical review. Because it was *true*. I was all wrong for this kind of job. I'd taken the B&B because I had fond memories of staying with my aunt when I was a lonely, bullied teenager in need of an oasis. But I wasn't my aunt. She was effortlessly warm and friendly. I was... rigid and withdrawn. Frigid even, if you asked some of my previous boyfriends.

"Ouch." Nathan paused. "This might be easier than I thought."

"What might be?"

"Talking you into coming to work with me."

I groaned. "I told you before—"

"Yeah, yeah. You own the B&B. I know. But what if you didn't have to own it?"

I blinked. "Uh...I'm not sure where you're going with that."

"I've got some connections through my work. One of my

clients is looking for lakefront property for a condo development. I think he'd love your spot in Swallow Cove."

"Oh, I don't know," I said. "We haven't had the best luck with big developers coming in."

"I can vouch for this guy," Nathan said. "He's got money to invest, and this would be a smart way to go about it. You told me yourself that Swallow Cove didn't have enough housing."

"Well, that's true," I said. "It has been a problem for a lot of the locals."

"Exactly," he said. "It's a win-win. You help the town and get out of the B&B business."

"And come work for you?" I said dryly.

He laughed. "Well, hey, I've never hidden my own motives."

"Fair point," I said.

"Think about it, will you? You don't sound happy there."

I glanced up at a framed photo of Aunt Millie beaming a huge smile down on me. I loved her. I loved what she'd built. But I wasn't her, and maybe it was time I accepted that.

My heart ached as I replied, "Yeah, I'll think about it."

The rest of the day went smoother, as did the next. Marigold's snootiness worked in my favor since she and her husband went out for breakfast every day.

But the guests just kept coming. The slower winter season when I could forget I lived in a B&B for whole weeks at a time was a thing of the past.

Every morning I provided some sort of breakfast, though during the week it was usually a selection of baked goods from the new Hot Buns Bakery that'd opened a few weeks ago or biscuits and chocolate gravy from Tastes Like Grandma.

Then I spent time checking folks out, flipping rooms, doing laundry—the freaking laundry never ended—checking *more* folks in, and digging up movies and games to entertain them in the evening while dodging their invitations to join in.

"Sorry, I'm headed out," I blurted when a clingy older woman invited me to join her for a movie—for the third time. "Plans with a friend. You know how it is. See you all later."

I snatched up my keys and wallet and darted out the door. I kept a small runabout boat docked behind the B&B, and I was already halfway down the shore toward The Rusty Hook when I realized I didn't have my phone with me.

Shoot. There went my plan to call Hudson to meet up for a beer.

I docked behind the pub and crossed the back deck strung with lights. I edged between tables filled with rowdy tourists, their drunken laughter grating on my nerves.

The atmosphere inside was quieter. I swept my gaze over the crowd as I made my way to an empty seat at the bar.

Two members of the Weekend Hookers fishing group—Chester and Ansel—were sitting at the far end, nursing cheap beer and steadily working their way through a plate of onion rings.

I took a barstool a few seats down so they wouldn't try to draw me into their latest complaint about fishing holes, tourism, or the price of gasoline.

Adriana Flores, the owner of The Grocery Spot, sat in a corner with Dustin Higgins, who was about fifteen years too young for her. That was sure to get some tongues wagging.

Mimsy and Pipsy, twins with matching white hair and dirt under their fingernails, waved to me and I shot them my first genuine smile of the day. They ran The Dirty Hoe, and garden talk was one language I could actually speak fluently.

And dead center in the room, around a round barrel table, sat Cash and his friends. Hudson's young boyfriend, Fisher, was tossing a fry at Cash's smirking face. There was no sign of Hudson, though, so he must be having dinner with his mother. Otherwise, those two tended to spend all their time together.

Ah well, that made me feel better about leaving my phone behind.

Cash glanced over, his eyes catching mine, and heat crawled over my neck and ears. I didn't want him to think I was looking for him. I wasn't. His friend group was right there in the middle of the room. How could I possibly miss them?

Still, I couldn't seem to drag my eyes from his.

"Can I get you a drink?" Felix asked from his spot behind the bar.

I jerked my head around so fast pain zinged through my neck and I fought a wince. "Yeah, do you still have that dark beer on tap?"

"Buffalo Sweat?"

"That's the one."

"You got it." Felix pulled the taps, efficient as he tilted the mug under the pour.

I drummed my fingers on the bar top, trying to ignore the urge to turn and see if Cash was still watching me.

He always was.

Right on cue, a presence warmed my side a split second before Cash said, "Felix, can we get a pitcher of the cheap stuff?"

"Yup," Felix said with an easy smile that I envied. "Give me two minutes."

"I'll do my best to entertain myself," Cash said, a playful lilt in his voice.

Felix grinned. "Don't watch me so hard your eyes cross. I know I'm fine, but we don't want you to hurt yourself."

Cash laughed. "I'll try to restrain myself."

Felix turned his attention to refilling Ansel's beer, and Cash still didn't look at me. I huffed an annoyed breath.

There was a time he'd have stood too close to me. He'd have

taken every opportunity to bat those pretty blue eyes my way and tease me about how much I liked it.

Good thing that's over.

Had been over since I'd refused his kiss.

Now, he wanted to be friends. Which was a *good* thing.

I lifted my glass and took a mouthful of the dark, malty beer to hide my scowl.

Cash wasn't punishing me for not indulging him. He was respecting boundaries I set. It was the mature thing to do. And yet, the new distance he kept nagged at me.

I turned to say something—anything—just as Felix set the pitcher on the bar. "Here you go."

"Thanks," Cash said with a smile that made me tense. "I'm good for a tip later."

"Just a tip?" Felix asked with a wink.

Cash laughed. "You're spicy tonight."

"Just kidding," Felix said. "You know I don't even swing that way."

"You'd be surprised how many people say that before they meet me," Cash said with a grin.

I couldn't hold back a snort. "So modest."

Cash's gaze landed on me. *Finally.* "That's me," he said. "Always a cocky bastard."

"With good reason," Felix said.

Cash picked up the pitcher and returned to his table. I finished my beer and ordered a second, valiantly trying to ignore the group of friends a few feet away.

I couldn't hear what they were saying, but even in the din of noise, I could pick out Cash's exact tone—and the moment it went silent.

There was a smattering of sudden applause and catcalls. Felix's eyes widened. "Oh, boy."

I spun in my seat and there they were—Sawyer and Cash.

Locked in a kiss in the middle of the damn pub.

A lump formed in my throat as I watched the way Sawyer's hands cupped Cash's face, the way they leaned in toward each other.

My heart tumbled into my stomach. Cash hadn't changed at all, had he? He'd gone from flirting with the bartender to making out with his friend.

And probably fucking someone else later. This is who he is. You know this.

I tossed a few bills on the bar and headed for the door. I couldn't stay and watch any more of this display.

CHAPTER FIVE

Cash

SAWYER WAS IN BIG-TIME DENIAL. OUR FRIEND GROUP HAD gathered at The Rusty Hook to find out how he was handling working with his nemesis. Turned out, he was *kissing* him and calling it anger management.

I called him on that shit because he needed to face the truth.

"You've kissed this guy more than once. You liked it or you wouldn't have kept doing it. Be real about what's happening here."

Sawyer chewed his bottom lip, looking conflicted. "Just because I like kissing him doesn't mean I *like* him."

"Maybe not, but it means you're not straight," I said. "Can you acknowledge that, at least?"

"Don't rush him," Brooks said. "Everyone has to define their own sexuality. You know that."

I huffed. "Maybe I'm tired of waiting on other people to figure their shit out. Maybe I just want to kiss a guy and have him know what the fuck he wants."

Okay, maybe I was projecting a little. Not two minutes ago,

I'd seen Declan watching me. Then when I went to the bar, he'd seemed annoyed I was there. It was always this push-and-pull with him. Like the night I tried to kiss him. He'd swayed right into that kiss only to stumble back out of it.

He obviously didn't know what the fuck he wanted. Just like Sawyer.

"Maybe I want to kiss a guy and know what the fuck I want too, man," Sawyer protested. "It's not that easy."

"Sure it is, Sawyer. If I kissed you right now, you'd know."

"No, I wouldn't."

"No?" I raised an eyebrow in challenge. "Then kiss me, bro. Kiss me and find out."

Our friends were chiming in, but I wasn't listening. I stared Sawyer down, daring him to admit the truth. He wanted to kiss Ash. He didn't want to kiss me.

Come on, Sawyer. Tell me you don't want to kiss me because you want him.

Sawyer grabbed my face and laid a hard kiss across my lips. My eyes widened in shock. He wasn't supposed to call my bluff!

The kiss was weird. Like a wall was pressing against my lips. Just pressure and force without the attraction that normally went with it.

He shoved me back, breathing hard. "Nothing. I feel nothing."

"Thanks, man," I said dryly. "But you weren't exactly inspiring me to write poetry, either."

There was the loud screech of a chair, then stomping footsteps heading for the exit. When I glanced that way, Declan was slipping out the door.

"Shit," I muttered, hopping up. "I'll be back in a minute."

My friends' teasing over my Declan obsession followed me to the door. No doubt they'd be scheduling a "friendervention" for me any day now. Unlike Sawyer, I wouldn't even fight it.

My stomach knotted up and my palms grew sweaty as I chased after a man who didn't want me. Or maybe just said he didn't? Either way, he was sure to be thinking all the wrong things about what he'd just seen.

"Declan, wait up a sec!" I called as I crossed the deck.

Declan jogged down the steps ahead of me, not slowing in the least. He headed for his boat at the dock, and I sped up to catch him before he could board.

I touched his arm. "Dec, please."

Declan jerked away from my touch, but his face was infuriatingly blank when he turned toward me. "I should get back to the B&B."

"About what you saw in there—"

"None of my business," he interrupted.

"It wasn't serious," I said, stepping closer to search his gaze.

I couldn't tell what was going through his head, but I doubted it was anything good.

He shrugged. "Okay."

"Okay? That's it? You stormed out like you..."

He tensed. "Like what?"

I raked a hand through my hair, tugging a little at the messy strands. "Nothing. Just... I didn't want you to get the wrong idea. That's all."

His smile was tight. "You don't take anything seriously, Cash. It's not exactly a surprise."

I flinched back. "That's not fair. I take a lot of things seriously. My life isn't all rainbows and puppies."

I'd told Declan more about my home situation than *anyone*. He'd shut down the kiss that night, but I still thought he'd *seen* the real me. The idea that he hadn't hurt worse than I expected.

Declan winced. "I'm sorry. I shouldn't have said that."

I swallowed hard. "You're honest, at least. I'll give you that."

"No, I was wrong to say that. I know your life is complicated, and I'm sorry about that. I just..." He turned toward the boat. "I need to go. Kiss whoever you like, Cash."

"Right." My chest tightened. "Well, unfortunately, I can't kiss whoever I like. I tried once, and he rejected me."

Declan kept his gaze on the water rather than me. A long silence stretched between us.

Well, I'd tried. But if Declan couldn't admit he wanted me—despite the obvious jealousy—there was nothing more I could do.

I turned away. "Goodnight, Declan. Sorry to have bothered you."

I made it two steps before his voice stopped me.

"It's not that easy for me," he said to my back.

"What do you mean?"

"The...kissing. Intimacy. It's not—"

I turned to face him, and he clammed up.

"Tell me," I ordered. Then quickly tacked on, "Please."

"You give out your affection so freely, Cash. To so many people. I don't do that. I can't be with someone who does that." He smiled wanly. "You'd get bored with me in about two minutes, anyway."

"What if you're wrong?"

"I'm not wrong." He reached for the ropes keeping his boat secured to the dock. "We'd only make each other miserable."

I could have kept pushing, but there was no point. Declan saw me as a fuckboy who couldn't get serious about life.

All these months flying solo, I'd proven to myself I was more than that. That I *wanted* more than that. I had thought that maybe Declan would see that, too.

But with all my concern over getting Declan to see me, I hadn't really stopped to think about whether I saw the real him.

I thought maybe I did now—and for the first time.

A man who was vulnerable, wanting, but afraid to reach for happiness.

I rejoined my friends inside. Sawyer had taken off, no doubt eager to dive back into denial. Fisher was gone too, back to the loving arms of his boyfriend.

I could go home, but I had an empty twin bed and a house full of alcoholism and despair waiting for me. Not exactly an appealing option. Mom was off work tonight, so at least I didn't have to worry about Katelyn.

Brooks lifted his eyebrows at me. "How'd that work out for you?"

"About as well as expected." I slumped into a chair, defeated. "I kissed another guy in front of him. He thinks I'm a man whore."

"He doesn't think that," Poppy said.

"He basically said as much. He used nicer words, of course, but that's what he thinks. I give my affection *freely* and he can't be with someone who does that."

Skylar leaned forward, looking intrigued. "Does that mean he'd want to be with you if..."

"If I wasn't a huge slut?" I smiled deprecatingly. "Maybe."

I could have sworn we had a connection. Despite the rejections, there was just something about the way he looked at me. Then again, maybe my ego just didn't know when to accept defeat.

Poppy tilted her head. "He said he couldn't be with someone like that. But is that because of you or him?"

"What do you mean?"

"Maybe it's not about you, Cash," Poppy said. "Think about it. If someone pursued me, I'd shut them down. It wouldn't be because of their faults. It would be because I don't...I *can't*...be with them that way."

"You're saying he's ace?"

"I don't know that he is," Poppy said patiently. "We don't have a secret club or anything. I'm just saying, it's possible that Declan isn't judging you or rejecting you. Maybe he's just doing what's right for him."

I pushed out my bottom lip. "That's even worse."

"Why is that worse?" Skylar asked.

"Because I can't even be upset with him for shooting me down for the hundredth time," I said.

"Aw, poor baby," Brooks crooned. "You're going to have to accept that not *every* person in the entire world wants you."

I smiled crookedly. "Well, I had to accept that when Skylar chose you, didn't I?"

"Eh, Brooks just got to me first," Skylar said. "You never had a chance."

Brooks jabbed him in the ribs, and Skylar jerked away with a laugh, then apologized profusely as Brooks tortured him with tickles. By the time Brooks had dragged him into an incredibly X-rated kiss, Poppy had already made her excuses and fled the scene.

I watched, waiting for some spark of arousal, but nope. There was nothing. Just standing near a man who didn't want me made my dick half hard, but watching Brooks and Skylar suck face?

Boring.

I tossed a few bucks on the table as a tip and pushed my chair back. "Well, I'm going home to jerk off over the man who ruined me with half a kiss."

Brooks and Skylar broke apart.

"Half a kiss?" Brooks asked.

I waved that off. "Long story."

"I bet," he murmured.

Skylar directed a sympathetic smile my way. "You don't

know that Poppy is right. Maybe he does just need to see how you've changed."

I lifted a shoulder. "Not much more I can do to display that. Though, obviously, kissing Sawyer in front of him didn't help. He says he wasn't jealous, but..."

"Maybe he was?" Skylar suggested.

"I guess it doesn't matter since he's decided I'm all wrong for him."

Brooks frowned. "I wish I had something more helpful to say. Sawyer hates Ash, and he's kissing him on the regular. Sometimes shit just doesn't make sense until it does. I mean, look at me. I never once thought I'd end up with a guy."

"But you were a goner for Sky almost right away," I said. "Declan's had all year to come around."

Brooks looked pained. "Everyone moves at their own pace?"

I chuckled. "In that case, maybe I'll get lucky in ten years." I pushed my chair in. "Goodnight, guys. See you at work next week."

CHAPTER SIX

Declan

I steered clear of Cash as much as I could over the next week.

I had more pressing matters to focus on than the strained conversation we'd had on the dock, even if my mind replayed it ten times a day.

I still had to decide what to tell Nate about that development offer. Could I really just sell the B&B and walk away?

Aunt Millie loved it, and I'd tried to love it too. I really had. But if the guests weren't even enjoying their stay—as their reviews suggested—then wasn't I doing a disservice to her memory?

On the other hand, she *knew* me and she'd chosen to leave me the B&B instead of my sister, Monroe. I had to believe that was because Monroe would have sold on Day One.

My thoughts circled round and round, never leaving me with a clear answer. I still didn't have one when Nathan called on a Monday morning. I had only one couple booked at the

B&B, and they'd gone into town, leaving me to enjoy my coffee over a crossword puzzle.

At least until my phone rang.

"Not trying to rush you, man, but it's been over a week," Nathan said after I'd answered. "This opportunity won't last forever."

"I know." I pinched the bridge of my nose. "I'll give you an answer soon, I promise."

"Do you know what that answer might be?" he said, tone cajoling. "Maybe give me a hint."

"Sorry, Nathan, if I knew that, I'd give you an answer now."

"Right, well—"

"I have to go. Talk later." I hung up before he could try to sell me. He was way too good at that, and I was too tired to fight his powers of persuasion.

I changed into some ratty cargo shorts and a gray T-shirt, then went out to my garden behind the house—the only place I could really find some peace. I made the rounds, watering my nearly ripened strawberries, my newly planted basil and cucumbers, the tomatoes just beginning to set fruit.

It was still early. A crisp breeze came off the water, gently fluttering through my hair. The smell of damp soil rose from the ground, setting me at ease. This was my oasis in Swallow Cove, the one place I belonged.

Here, I didn't disappoint anyone—except maybe the weeds.

I finished watering, then grabbed the pruning shears and went to work on the rosebushes and shrubs. By the time I'd moved on to ripping weeds out by their roots with a vicious satisfaction, the sun was high in the sky and I was pouring sweat.

I wrapped both hands around the base of the pesky broadleaf weed, tugging with all my strength.

"Don't test me, you bastard," I growled as I leaned back, straining to rip it from the ground.

"What a way to greet your best friend."

Hudson's voice startled me just as the roots gave up their grip on the soil and I fell back onto my ass with an exclamation.

"Fucking hell!" I tossed the weed aside. "Can't you warn a guy?"

Hudson chuckled and extended a hand down to help me up. I took off my gardening gloves, now covered in soil and bits of grass, then grasped his hand.

He tugged me to my feet with impressive ease. Hudson was brawny where I was wiry. I dusted the dirt from my knees and ass.

"You still up for grabbing an early lunch?" Hudson asked. "Or do you want to go back to wrestling weeds?"

"Shit, is it that time already?" I glanced down at my dirty, sweaty self with a grimace. "Sorry. I got carried away."

He grinned. "This look suits you."

I wrinkled my nose. "Dirty?"

"Earthy," he said with a chuckle. "Casual and comfortable."

"I guess that's one way to put it. Do I have time for a quick shower?"

"Sure. There's actually not much I need to do until my afternoon boat tour. Sawyer did a damn good job managing things for me."

Hudson had gone out of town for a week, so I hadn't had the chance to fill him in on my dilemma yet. I saw him briefly Saturday night—but he was at dinner with Cash and all his friends, so I hadn't stuck around long.

"Great, come on in."

Hudson followed me to my private quarters, and I left him on my sofa while I rinsed off in the shower. I dressed in casual slacks and a short-sleeved dress shirt, combed my hair, and applied cologne. I resisted the urge to shave, even though dark stubble colored my jaw.

I didn't want to keep Hudson waiting too long.

We decided on Catch of the Day, a casual cafe, for lunch. We placed our order at the front counter, then carried a number to our table so they could bring the food when it was ready.

While we waited, Hudson caught me up on his trip to Granville, Nebraska, where his boyfriend had family.

They'd gotten back only a couple of days ago with gifts for all their friends. Fisher had given his friends sex toys—I'd almost swallowed my tongue when I saw the monster dildo Cash accepted with glee in the middle of the dang pub—but thankfully, I'd received a box of treats instead.

"The doughnuts were delicious, by the way. Thank Fisher for me."

"They're amazing, right? How fast did you eat them?"

I chuckled ruefully. "They lasted one morning."

He nodded. "Glazed Holes knows what they're doing."

"That name though..."

He grinned. "I know."

Pam Willard, one of the owners, arrived with our plates. "Fried catfish for Hudson and seared trout for Declan. Enjoy, guys. Let me know if you need anything else."

I inhaled the scent of lemon pepper from my plate of fish and rice, my mouth watering.

"This looks great," Hudson said. "Thanks."

We both dug in. Hudson ate quickly, dipping his catfish in the sauce, getting his fingers greasy and not caring. I went slower, cutting each bite precisely and keeping an orderly plate: the fish lay on a bed of rice, which was fine, but the summer squash medley had to be kept separate. Otherwise, it'd taint the flavor of both items.

"So, did you miss this place while you were gone?" I asked before taking another bite.

"Mm." Hudson swallowed a bite and picked up his beer to chase it with a drink. "It was a nice break, but I'm glad to be back. Even though it's kind of strange to see how much I missed."

"What do you mean?"

"Well, when I left, Ash and Sawyer were at each other's throats. Then I come back, and they're a mushy couple. Funny how quickly things can change, you know?"

I nodded. I'd seen them together at the pub, holding hands and exchanging looks. Aside from approaching to say hello to Hudson and invite him to this lunch, I'd kept my distance.

The conversation with Cash after he'd kissed Sawyer still mortified me.

"I don't understand why Cash kissed Sawyer at the pub," I blurted. "If Sawyer and Ash are dating, then why—" I stopped short with an exasperated laugh. "Nevermind. I sound like a nosy old lady."

Hudson raised an eyebrow at me. "I wouldn't say that."

"Oh, well...that's good."

"But I can tell you why, if you're interested."

"I'm not interested," I protested automatically. "Just...confused."

He smiled, a touch of pity leaking into it that made me bristle.

"Just forget it," I said.

"The way Fisher tells it, Cash wanted Sawyer to see that kissing Ash meant something real. Sawyer was in denial about what was happening, and Cash knew he wouldn't enjoy kissing him, so..."

"It was an experiment?"

"I guess that's one way to put it," Hudson said with a shrug.

"They're all so young. They're still figuring things out, you know?" He groaned. "And god, can you believe I'm dating the youngest one of them all?"

I laughed. "And you better keep dating him since you dined and dashed on me just to get in his pants."

"I did not get in his pants that night!" Hudson protested. "He was drunk, and someone else was trying to take advantage. I was just..."

"Protective of his pants," I said. "Got it."

"Yes," he said. "Well..." He looked chagrinned. "I was the only one he really wanted."

I smiled, genuinely happy for him, but a tinge of sadness crept in. I didn't expect I'd ever have that kind of love. Not when I couldn't give a partner what they really needed.

Hudson picked up a napkin to wipe his fingers. "But enough about me," he said. "You mentioned wanting to talk about something?"

Nerves fluttered. I wasn't sure Hudson would understand my dilemma. He was so happy here, but me? I just never fit.

"I'm, uh, considering a business opportunity."

He braced his arms on the table and leaned forward. "Oh?"

I swallowed. "I have a friend over in Chicago. He wants me to come back and work with him."

Hudson's gaze sharpened. "Is that what you want?"

"Maybe. I was good at it. Better than I've ever been at running the B&B."

"And what about the B&B then? If you leave..."

I wet my lips. "Well, I've got an offer from some developers, but after what happened with the resort..." I cleared my throat. "I just want to be careful."

Hudson sighed. "Damn, man. You're really gonna leave me with all these kids? You were supposed to start dating Cash so I wouldn't feel like such an old man around them."

My heart wrenched, and the memory of Cash standing too close on the dock behind The Rusty Hook rose up in my mind. The soft, almost wounded tone of his voice as he said, "I can't kiss whoever I want. I tried once, and he rejected me."

Hudson painted a nice picture, but it wasn't realistic.

"I'm not the guy for Cash," I said firmly.

Even if deep down, I wished I could be.

"That's a shame," Hudson said quietly. "I've never seen that guy give anyone a second look but you."

I scoffed. "He gives everyone a second look."

"No, he gave them a thorough first look—"

"So much better," I grumbled.

"But that was a year ago or more. You know he's changed. You must have seen it."

I shrugged. "That really isn't my business. What to do about the B&B, about my future, can't be about someone else."

"No, of course not." Hudson sighed. "Your happiness is what's important. If your work gives you that, then you should pursue it. But if it's something else..."

"Like?"

"Friends. Family. Community." He cocked his head. "You're not alone here, you know? You have people who care."

My throat tightened. Hudson was a good friend, and sure, I enjoyed my gardening chats with Mimsy and Pipsy. Pearl and Ruth Marie at the Outdoor Market begged me for strawberries each year, and gave me jams and canned fruits in return.

I wasn't *alone* here, exactly, but I wasn't Hudson. I didn't have a loving boyfriend or a mother here in town.

Most of all, though, I wasn't an extrovert. I didn't enjoy meeting tourists. I didn't know *how* to deal with all the people who passed through the B&B, who intruded into my life, who made me feel uncomfortable and out of place in my home.

I didn't know if returning to Chicago would make me

happy. But it would be comfortable there. Easier to fade into the background, where my flaws weren't so damn noticeable.

"Swallow Cove is great, but...I think I have to explore this option, at least."

Hudson's brows drew together in a frown, but he nodded his understanding. Just one of the things that made him a good friend.

"I'd suggest giving Skylar a call. He bailed us out when those asshole developers tried to hoodwink Fisher. His dad moves in those circles, and he'll know more about that world. Maybe he can give you some advice."

"Yeah, that's a good idea." I smiled tightly. "Thanks."

Hudson startled me by placing a hand on my forearm. "But please, think on it long and hard. Once you sign an agreement, there's no going back."

"That's all I've been doing," I said. "I'm losing sleep over it, but...I can't shake the idea. It's taken hold." I took a breath. "I really think this is the right choice for me."

"Fair enough," he said. "But we'll miss you around here."

"Yeah, well, let's see what happens before you write me any farewell speeches. Maybe they'll lowball me and I'll tell them to take their offer and shove it."

He chuckled. "All right. Keep me updated, so I can be sappy at the appropriate time."

"I will."

CHAPTER SEVEN

Cash

Sawyer and Ash walked into the resort lobby with a woman who appeared to be in her late forties. I did a double take when I saw all the bags they carried.

"You guys moving in together or something?" I asked, mostly joking, although their relationship was moving at warp speed.

Or maybe it just seemed that way because my love life was going nowhere.

"Ash's mom needs a room," Sawyer said. "I called Sky to make sure there were openings."

"Oh. Sure." I smiled politely at Ash's mom. Deep furrows creased her brow, and she gnawed nervously at a fingernail.

"How many nights would you like to stay?"

"I'm not sure," she said hesitantly. "Can we start with a week and go from there?"

"Sure thing." I brought up the screen that would show me the open rooms. The phone rang while I navigated through screens. "Swallow's Ne—"

"Hey, it's me."

"Oh, hey, Skylar."

"Is Ash here with his mom?"

I flicked a glance toward them. Ash was rubbing his mom's back. Maybe she'd finally left that douche of a man Ash had called stepdad. "Mm-hmm."

"Make sure they get the family rate."

"Gotcha."

"And, Cash?" Skylar said hesitantly. "I, um, wouldn't normally repeat this, but I know how you feel about Declan, so I was just wondering if you'd heard that he's thinking about selling the B&B?"

"No, I didn't hear that." My heart quickened. "Seriously? That man." A sudden thought struck, making my throat tighten and my words go thin and wispy. "Do you think it's because of *me?*"

Sawyer shifted forward, his gaze locked on me. No doubt I'd get plenty of questions later.

Skylar's voice softened. "I wouldn't assume that. Declan said that he'd gotten some interest in the B&B, and he was considering returning to his former profession. I know he shot you down, but I really doubt he's running away from you."

"No, you're probably right. Okay. Thanks, Sky." I replaced the receiver and forced a smile as I refocused on Ash's mom. "Okay, I've got you a suite on the second floor with a balcony overlooking the lake. We've got an in-house dining room and bar, an outdoor pool bar, an upper-floor balcony bar." I winked playfully. "I guess people really like to drink around here."

She laughed, and Sawyer shot me a grateful smile. Good enough.

I finished checking her in, but my mind remained on that phone call with Skylar. I lasted exactly as long as my shift. As soon as I clocked out, I begged a ride from Hudson. He delivered me to the dock behind the Treehouse B&B, no questions asked.

I had questions, though. Plenty of them.

"You knew, didn't you?"

"About Declan selling?" Hudson said, proving he knew why I was charging over here. "Only that he was considering it. Is it a done deal?"

"It better not be," I said grimly.

He raised an eyebrow. "You do know he can make his own choices?"

"Well, it's a stupid choice," I exclaimed. "I don't understand this man."

Hudson smiled sympathetically. "Not sure he understands you, either. Maybe that's the problem?"

I clambered out of the boat ungracefully, nearly tripping when my toe hit a raised board. I stumbled a couple of steps forward, catching my balance before I could face-plant.

I turned toward Hudson, who was smirking at my performance. "Not a word."

"I wouldn't dream of it."

I whirled away. "Okay, I'm off to slay the stubborn dragon."

"Cash," Hudson called.

I paused, glancing back over my shoulder. "Yes?"

"Be careful. This is a delicate conversation to navigate. You understand?"

"Yep."

"I'd like him to stay, but if he's unhappy, we need to set him free."

"Your pep talk is shit."

Hudson grinned. "You needed to hear it. Good luck, man."

I strode toward the B&B, the scent of Declan's rose bushes perfuming the air. While I walked, I rehearsed what I could say that would change his mind. My track record for convincing the man of anything wasn't so great. But I could find the right words, the perfect argument to illustrate that he belonged here, right?

That his B&B could co-exist with the resort—and he could co-exist with *me*—if we all worked together.

As luck would have it, a guest was stepping out just as I arrived. I slid past them through the open door.

The front desk was empty. Most of the guests were out to dinner at this hour. I veered left and peeked into the kitchen and dining room, but he wasn't in either place.

Which meant he was probably in his private rooms. I walked down the short hall behind the dining area and rapped my knuckles on the blond wood door.

"Declan?" I called. "It's Cash."

Declan opened the door, dressed in his customary dress slacks and button-down shirt, the sleeves rolled to the forearms. It was a casual but sophisticated look that had always done it for me.

"What are you doing here?"

"I'm here to talk to you," I said, stepping forward.

Declan stood his ground, brow creased. "About what?"

"About this stupid plan to sell the B&B!"

I brushed past him into his living area without waiting for an invitation. Declan's eyes widened in surprise, but he didn't stop me.

"You heard about that, huh?"

"It's a small town."

He smiled wryly. "And I told your boss today."

I winced. "Don't blame Sky. He was just being a good friend to me."

Declan waved a hand. "It's not a secret, anyway. I just called Sky for some advice on how to deal with developers."

"Developers?" My brow creased. "You're not selling to someone who wants to run the B&B?"

"They want to put in condos. It'll be good for Swallow Cove to have more housing. Good for people like you, Cash. I know there aren't enough affordable places to live."

There were a lot of reasons I stayed at home. That seemed like the least significant one. He wasn't entirely wrong, but he also wasn't entirely right.

"You really think lakefront condos are going to be affordable?" I asked with a snort. "No. It'll just be one more place for wealthy summer residents to stay. The rest of us will be exactly where we are now."

Declan's face tightened. "You don't know that."

"Maybe not. But do you really know what you're getting into?"

He frowned. "Well, that's why I talked to Skylar. I'm not just going into this blindly, Cash. I'm in negotiations. I won't sign anything until I'm satisfied with the terms."

If he hadn't signed a deal, it wasn't too late to undo this.

"Don't sell," I blurted.

"Cash..."

"Please," I said quickly. "We can find a way for the B&B and the resort to both succeed. We'll funnel overflow bookings to you or maybe we can coordinate events. I don't know. We'll figure it out."

"That's not why I'm selling. The resort is bringing more people to Swallow Cove, not less. My business isn't suffering."

Oh, shit. It *was* because of me then.

I swallowed hard. "Okay. So I've been too flirty and forward. I'll back off and leave you alone, okay? I didn't mean to make you uncomfortable. I just... I like you. But I'll keep my distance, I promise. Just *stay*."

He drew in a sharp breath. "Oh, Cash, no. It's not because of you. You're one of the brightest spots in Swallow Cove."

I took a step closer, heart thundering. "Then why do you always push me away?"

"It's complicated."

I looked into his eyes, and there was nothing complicated there. I could see want and longing and so much loneliness.

"I want you to kiss me, then."

His eyes flew wide. "What? Why?"

"You want to. I can tell. What's stopping you?"

"So many things..."

I stepped forward into his space, careful not to touch him. Careful not to lean in and close the gap. But my eyes locked onto his, and there was a magnetic pull between us.

One I was certain he could feel, too.

I waved a hand between us. "Obviously, there is something here. Between you and me."

"There can't be."

"There already is."

He shook his head, but his eyes didn't leave mine.

"One kiss, Declan. What's the harm? You're leaving anyway, right? You're selling this place and leaving town, so why not?"

He huffed a laugh. "You're relentless, you know that?"

"I'm persistent," I said. "Within reason. I won't harass you. If you say no right now, then it's no. But—"

Declan leaned in suddenly, lips warm on mine.

It took me by surprise. I never expected him to give in. I grasped his shoulder, leaning into the kiss. Declan cupped my face, this thumb stroking along my cheekbone.

It was so fucking gentle I wanted to cry.

It's a goodbye kiss.

I tensed, heart tumbling, and Declan pulled back. "Was that okay?"

"Yeah," I rasped. "Better than okay."

He shook his head, a small smile playing on his lips. "Hardly better than okay."

"You want more?" I asked, leaning in. "You caught me by surprise, but I'm more than ready to blow your mind."

Declan put his hand to my chest with a small chuckle. "No. That was exactly what I wanted."

I paused, confused. "Okay."

"I don't want the same things you do," he said gently. "That kiss was...perfect."

"Then why did you say it wasn't better than okay?"

"For *you*," he stressed. "It was just okay for you."

"Wrong," I said. "The only thing I'd change about it is making it our first kiss instead of our last."

He tilted his head. "It wouldn't be enough, though. Not for long."

I nibbled my bottom lip, the suspicion that Poppy was right growing in my mind. "You're ace?"

"I haven't really labeled it," Declan said. "I suppose I might fall somewhere on that spectrum."

I nodded. "So kissing but no sex?"

"I, uh...didn't say that. It's not really that cut-and-dried."

"I can work with that."

"No, you can't," Declan said. "Trust me. I've tried it with other guys."

"Not with me."

He rolled his eyes. "You're so much worse."

Ouch. I took a step back. "Okay, then."

"Not as a person," Declan said quickly. "Just...you're more." He waved a hand to encompass all of me. "You get around a lot."

"Not lately," I muttered.

"You have needs, Cash, and I don't know that I could ever fulfill them. It's just a bad idea."

I bit down on the urge to argue with him. He might be right, after all. I'd fucked around a lot since losing my virginity. This past year was the first dry spell I'd ever had. I'd willingly forgone sex because I wanted a healthier relationship with it.

But could I be happy in a long-term relationship that limited how much sex I had? I wanted to say yes. Right now, after going without sex for months, I wanted to think I could handle it.

I just didn't know, though. I'd never know if Declan didn't give me a chance. But it wasn't fair to ask him for that. If I couldn't keep my word, I'd only hurt him, as other guys had clearly hurt him before.

"I think I understand," I said. "You could have told me sooner."

Declan shifted, averting his eyes. "It's not something that's comfortable to talk about for me."

"I'm sorry." I reached for his arm. "Can I, uh, give you a hug?"

He smiled dryly. "I'm fine."

"I'm not."

His eyes softened. "Okay. Then, yes, you may."

I wrapped my arms around his shoulders and pulled him to me. For once, I wasn't thinking about a man's body pressed to mine for sexual reasons. I was just taking comfort—hopefully giving it too—as my eyes slipped shut.

Declan stood still for a long minute, just tolerating the hug. But then he brought one arm around me, his hand landing on the nape of my neck and squeezing.

"Why are you really leaving?" I asked softly.

Declan drew away, leaving my arms too empty and my chest too cold.

"The B&B life has never been right for me," he said, sounding regretful. "I don't mesh well with people."

"That's it?"

He chuckled. "I'm not sure you understand just how bad I am at all this." He waved a hand around to encompass the B&B as a whole. "People leave reviews about my grumpy attitude and my resting bitch face."

"You're an adorable grump, and I like your bitchy face."

He rolled his eyes. "You're apparently the only one who does."

I bit down on a flirty comment. I'd just gotten Declan to open up about why he kept me at arm's length. I didn't want to give him more reason to shut me out.

Hudson's words came back to me.

If he's unhappy, we need to let him go.

Damn, but it sucked when someone acted wise and then they were *right*.

"I guess you've made up your mind, huh? You're not happy here."

"This B&B meant everything to my Aunt Millie. I have some very fond memories of summers spent here. I wanted it to be different, too. I've really tried, but..." He shook his head. "It's not the right fit."

"Okay, but why are you letting someone come in and tear it down? You could sell it to someone who'd keep it going. This place is so cool, Declan. It has so much potential."

"Potential," he said with a twist of his lips. "But it would take a lot of work to reach it. The buildings are deteriorating. The Roost is uninhabitable. The Tree Hut has the plumbing problem. Even this building is becoming a money pit. I had to close off the deck on the second floor for safety reasons. I've got two rooms I'm not booking because they've taken water damage from a leak in the roof."

"So it needs a few repairs," I said. "That's not impossible."

"A few." Declan chuckled, but it sounded sad. "My aunt had such dreams for this place. She drew up a renovation plan, but she died before she could ever implement it."

That was sad. If only there was a way—

I clasped Declan's arms as a thought hit. "This is your chance."

"What do you mean?"

"You can fix this place up. Honor your Aunt Millie's memory by turning it into the B&B she envisioned."

"But..." He shook his head. "Even if I did that, nothing would change, Cash. This place isn't right for me."

My chest ached, but I knew Hudson was right. If I cared about Declan's happiness, I couldn't persuade him to stay for *my* sake. Especially since I couldn't offer him any assurances that I would be the man who'd love him for who he was, no strings. Even if I could, I doubt he'd believe me.

I had only one card left to play that would be right for everyone involved. That would give me at least a little more time to figure out what Declan and I could or couldn't have— and which would give us both closure to move on if he left as planned.

"Fix up the B&B and sell it to someone who will treat it right," I said. "You can leave knowing your aunt's home is in good hands."

He looked torn. "That's a big job."

"I know, but you don't need one. I'll help you. I've done a ton of odd jobs. I'm pretty handy."

"I'm well aware," he said dryly.

That surprised a laugh out of me. "I said handy, not handsy." I wiggled my brows. "Though I can certainly be both."

Declan's brows drew together. "But why would you want to

do that, Cash? You've already got a job, and even if I can find a buyer—"

"You *will* find one," I said, enthused. "It's a beautiful B&B on lakefront property."

He pursed his lips. "You have an answer for everything, don't you?"

"I try." I raised an eyebrow. "What do you say, Declan? You can give this place, your aunt's pride and joy, a fighting chance to go on."

"Damn it," he muttered. "I was all set to run for the hills and then *you* show up."

I resisted the urge to fist pump. "Is that a yes?"

He sighed. "You know it is."

I bit my lip, hit by the simultaneous urges to cheer and kiss the stuffing out of Declan.

I couldn't fight a shit-eating grin. "You won't regret this."

"Oh, I'm sure I will," he said, but his lips quirked toward a semblance of a smile. "But I'd regret not trying more."

CHAPTER EIGHT

Declan

"Morning, Declan! We've got an assortment of cinnamon rolls, lemon-raspberry scones, and blackberry tarts ready to go."

Jasmine Price set a big box emblazoned with the Hot Buns Bakery logo on the glass counter for me.

"Perfect." I set the box I'd brought in beside it, this one brimming with freshly picked strawberries from the garden. "And I've got a little gift for you, as promised."

I'd spent my early morning hours in the garden, carefully plucking strawberries from their stems. This was only the first batch I'd had time to harvest. I'd pick more for Pearl and Ruth Marie at the Outdoor Market. Pearl made jams while Ruth Marie sold brandied fruits—both of which I supplied in some of my B&B breakfasts, mainly because they'd harass me endlessly if I didn't. The two were extremely competitive, so I'd have to be careful to give them precisely the same amount of fruit.

"Ooh, those look fabulous!" Jasmine turned toward the door that led into the kitchen. "Abe!"

A giant of a man came through the swinging door, brow furrowed. Jasmine pointed toward the strawberries. Without a single word, he picked them up and returned to the kitchen.

"Sorry, he's focused on baking right now," Jasmine said.

"Don't apologize," I said, thinking of my own less than stellar people skills. "He should apply his talent where it's best suited."

The same way I will by going back to the finance sector.

By leaving Swallow Cove.

Leaving Cash.

The memory of kissing him resurfaced. I couldn't stop thinking about it. Not so much the kiss itself. It wasn't the warmth of his lips, his small gasp of surprise, or the firmness of the body leaning into mine that played on a loop through my mind.

It was the sweet ache in my chest that bloomed and spread into warmth. It was the look in his eyes when we parted, a look that said I was the most important person in the room. Cash had always looked at me that way, tempting me to try again, to trust that this time it would be different.

But it was never different. Three failed relationships was evidence enough of that.

And now I'd gone and agreed to this foolish plan that would mean spending even more time around him.

My stomach fluttered, and I huffed in annoyance. I was *not* going to develop some kind of schoolboy crush now. Not after deflecting Cash's interest for the better part of two years. Not after making the choice to finally leave town.

I said goodbye to Jasmine and carried my pastries to my boat, waving distractedly when Fisher called out a greeting from the dock in front of the Bait & Swallow fueling station near the marina as I passed.

I let myself in through the back entrance of the B&B after I docked, going straight to the kitchen to transfer the pastries from the box to the serving platter. I arranged the cinnamon rolls around the outer edge, then the larger tarts formed the next circle, with the scones piled in the center. In the space remaining, I placed fresh strawberries.

"Looks almost as delicious as you do," a low voice murmured behind me.

I jumped, tilting the platter and sending my carefully arranged pastries tumbling over one another.

Cash must have come in the front entrance. I shot him a glare over my shoulder. "Really?"

He smiled sheepishly. "Sorry, didn't mean to startle you." He held out a large coffee cup. "Picked you up the *Cinnamon Do-Me Latte* from Just The Sip. Don't worry. I know you won't actually *do me*." He winked. "A guy can dream, though."

Cash was a flirt. With everyone. It was something I'd learned to let roll over me. But today—after giving in to the urge to kiss him—it didn't blow right by me, but danced along my skin, making heat rise in my cheeks.

"You know my coffee order?" I asked, seizing on the only part of our exchange that wasn't a landmine.

"Of course I do."

"Most people assume I take my coffee black," I mused.

"Most people haven't seen how much chocolate gravy you pour over your biscuits," he said. "Or how much syrup you drench French toast in when you make it. Or how much sugar you add to—"

I picked up a scone and shoved it into his mouth.

"Mmph." Cash raised his hand to take the scone from his mouth, but only after taking a bite and chewing with a hum of pleasure.

I'd forgotten how many breakfasts he'd spent at the B&B.

After rolling out of bed with one of my guests. I took a drink of my coffee to hide my scowl.

Of course, he knew my breakfast preferences. I knew his, too. That's why I'd subconsciously requested the lemon-raspberry scones, wasn't it? I'd known for two days that Cash would come by this morning to tour the property and come up with a plan of attack for renovations.

The cinnamon dolce was delicious as usual, the sweetness and spice of cinnamon and sugar blending with the bold espresso flavor. I gulped half of the cup before I could stop myself.

Cash finished the scone, chasing it with a few swallows of his own coffee from Just The Sip. I nodded toward it.

"You like the DP, right?"

"That's a rather personal question," he teased, even though he knew perfectly well I meant his coffee drink, the double-praline.

"Not when you advertise it all over town," I said waspishly.

"Ohhh!" He laughed. "I forgot how spunky you get in the morning." He picked up the coffee carafe. "Just be careful. It gets me all hot."

"Cash, have you forgotten our talk from Saturday night?"

His eyes met mine. "I haven't forgotten a single second of that evening."

Why did I get the feeling the kiss had been playing through his mind as much as it had mine? That was silly, though. A kiss like that would mean nothing to Cash. He'd shared one with Sawyer only two weeks ago, after all.

For all I knew, he'd gone straight out and found the nearest warm body to lose himself in after he left Saturday.

A bitter taste flooded my mouth. I couldn't be with Cash, but that didn't mean I liked the idea of someone else enjoying him, either. It was...a confusing contradiction.

Cash's flirty smile dropped away. "I'm just teasing you, Declan. A good laugh eases the tension, you know? But if you want me to stop making flirty comments, I will." He paused. "Well, I'll try my best. It's kind of engrained into my DNA, so you may have to correct me a time or two."

To my surprise, I didn't like that idea. He wouldn't be Cash if he wasn't flirting.

"No, don't censor yourself," I said. "Don't treat me with kid gloves. If you want to flirt, flirt. Just be prepared to be shot down hard."

He pretended to shiver. "Making rejection sexy. Only you can do that."

I shoved his shoulder. "Go pour coffee. My guests will have to put up with the poor substitute I brew here. I have to fix my platter."

After Cash left the room, I took a deep breath, only aware now of how much oxygen he'd taken up. I wasn't sure which had gotten to me more—his flirting or his offer to respect my boundaries.

When people found out I was some flavor of asexual, they usually either asked awkward questions about my sexual history or they tiptoed around me on eggshells, assuming that even the vaguest reference to sex would send me running.

Cash had swaggered into my kitchen and acted as if nothing had changed. As if I was the same guy he'd lusted over for two years. And as much as I'd tried to shut down that lusting, a part of me was relieved that the truth hadn't changed how he saw me.

I appreciated his offer to respect my boundaries. It reassured me he wouldn't be pushing for something that couldn't happen. But ultimately, I wanted Cash to be himself, even if occasionally it meant losing my breath in his presence.

I rearranged the platter, moving the pastries back into their concentric formation, then entered the dining room.

Cash stood at the head of the table, coffee carafe sitting in front of him forgotten as he spread his arms. "And then he said, *Tell these tourists to keep their rods out of my hole!*"

Janice, a middle-aged divorcee who'd come to Swallow Cove to visit her sister, gave a throaty laugh. "He did not say it that way."

"He did. I swear he did." Cash flashed me a grin. "Declan can tell you."

I froze as all eyes turned to me expectantly. My eye twitched.

"I was just telling them about the Weekend Hookers," Cash said. "Tom bought one of their hats, and I thought he should know who he was representing."

Tom, who'd booked a room with his quiet wife, Ellen, chuckled. "I didn't know I was buying a piece of local notoriety. Figured it was just a funny play on words."

"Oh, it's that too," Cash said. "We have a lot of both here in Swallow Cove."

"Well, now, I almost wish I'd booked at that new resort so I could see this Chester fella in action," Tom said.

Cash flashed me an apologetic smile. "Oh, you don't need to go to the resort to find him. He's at The Rusty Hook pub most nights. He'll be the guy loudly complaining about strangers messing around in his hole."

That set them into another round of giggles. I set the platter of pastries into the center of the table.

"Sorry for the delay this morning. I'll get Cash out of your hair so you can eat in peace."

"These pastries look delicious," Ellen said with a smile as she reached out to take a tart.

"Everything from Hot Buns Bakery is amazing," Cash said. "Declan is spoiling you all."

Janice laughed. "You never told us these pastries came from a place called Hot Buns, you naughty man!"

"Oh, ah, well...it didn't come up."

"Right." Tom looked back to Cash. "So, where else should we go in town while we're here?"

Cash launched into a recitation of some of the best spots in Swallow Cove. He brought up Little Clay Pot, which his friend Poppy ran with her dad; Just The Sip, sending the group into more stitches over Danny's naming conventions; and a few less touristy spots like The Dirty Hoe garden store and the Red Hot Cod Pieces food cart.

I hadn't planned to share breakfast with the guests, but with Cash playing host, it was easier to join them. I'd forgotten the way he drew all attention to himself. All those mornings he'd joined a guest at the table I'd been too annoyed to think about the fact that I didn't have to fumble through small talk.

Cash charmed everyone he met.

I took a tart from the platter and bit into its flaky crust, eyes slipping closed as the sweetness of the fruit coated my tongue. Abe had really outdone himself with these.

There was a brief lull in the conversation. I opened my eyes to see Cash watching me. I dabbed at my mouth with a napkin, concerned I'd smeared the fruit filling over my lips. A quick glance at the napkin showed nothing but a few crumbs.

"Where is your favorite place to take a date, Cash?" Tom asked. "Ellen and I are celebrating twenty-eight years tonight."

Cash blinked, seeming to come back to himself. "Wow, twenty-eight years. Congratulations. That's impressive."

Janice added her congratulations, and after a pause, I did the same. "Right, yes. A big milestone."

"It is," Ellen said, smiling at Tom with blazing hearts in her eyes, and he enfolded her hand in his with a sappy smile.

The display made my chest hurt.

"So, a good place for a date?" Tom asked again, looking to Cash. Because I obviously wasn't the guy offering helpful tidbits of information. I certainly knew the town well enough, but I didn't know how to inject irreverent stories into my recommendations.

I was like a prickly bush blending into the background of the garden, while Cash was the brilliant splash of flower petals.

"Cash doesn't go on dates," I said, the words slipping free without my permission. "He just *hooks up.*"

"Appropriate for a fishing town," Janice joked.

Cash flashed her a smile that didn't reach his eyes. "Now you're getting the hang of the lake town puns." He shot me a pointed look. "Declan's right. I haven't dated since high school. Not that I *wouldn't* go on a date for the right person."

My face heated. "Sorry, I didn't mean that to sound…"

Judgmental? Jealous? Petty? Maybe all three.

"It's fine," Cash said, though it really wasn't. "Luckily, I have some very sappy friends. So, most people will tell you to go to The Savory Swallow. It's our high-end fine dining option, but it's run by a real snob. If you want a real life at the lake experience, you should book a sunset dinner cruise."

Ellen brightened. "That sounds lovely."

"Is it too late to get a cruise for tonight, though?" Tom asked.

"You know, I might be able to pull a few strings for you. Let me make a call."

Cash pulled out his cellphone, stepping out of the room to call in his favors.

Janice turned to me as soon as he was gone. "Where on earth did you find such a charming man?"

"He really is lovely," Ellen chimed in.

"Hey now," Tom said with a chuckle. "Don't leave me on our anniversary."

Ellen giggled, cheeks flooding with color. "Oh, you!"

Everyone looked at me, waiting for an answer. I shifted uncomfortably. "Oh, Cash is a friend. He's here to help me with a project at the B&B."

Cash leaned back into the room. "Tom, you're set. Just go down to Swallow Adventures over at the resort near dusk. They'll take care of you."

"Thank you so much."

He turned. "Declan, you ready to get to work yet?"

"I've been ready," I grumbled as I pushed back my chair and crossed the room toward him. "You were too busy charming everyone to notice, I guess."

Cash grinned, gaze panning to the guests. "Don't mind him. He likes to pretend to be grouchy, but he really loves me."

Janice chuckled. "How could he not?"

"I know, right? I'm awesome." Cash grasped my arm and tugged me from the room. "Hope you don't mind me cutting your breakfast short?"

"Please, I wanted out of there before breakfast started."

We re-entered the kitchen, heading for the back door. There was a path that led through the gardens and over to the outbuildings. That was where the majority of work needed to be done.

"Maybe you should be running a B&B," I said as we walked. "You play host pretty well."

"I guess I've picked up a thing or two working at the resort."

No one picked up social skills like that. Cash was a natural people person, just like my Aunt Millie—except flirtier. That reminded me of how I'd put my foot in my mouth at breakfast.

"I'm sorry about that crack about dating," I said. "It was a stupid thing to say."

"Especially since you won't date me," Cash said, arching a dark eyebrow.

I winced. "I don't remember you ever asking me on a *date*."

"Would you say yes if I did?"

"No."

"Well, there you go." He swept his gaze over the landscape, which included the cabin, the Tree Hut, a garden shed, and an overgrown gazebo that had seen better days. "Show me what we're working with."

"All right," I said grimly. "Don't forget that you asked for this."

He grinned. "I never turn down a challenge."

Somehow, I got the sense he was talking about more than renovations.

CHAPTER NINE

Cash

THE ROOST WAS AN OCTAGON-SHAPED CABIN BUILT ON TOP of a hill—amongst a thick cluster of trees—with steps set into the earth at two-foot intervals leading up to it. Wild grass and weeds had overtaken the path. Declan's regular gardening around the main house clearly didn't extend this far.

We picked our way to the door and Declan pulled out a keyring. "I keep it locked, but sometimes teens find their way in and trash it. This won't be pretty."

He was right. The empty beer bottles, broken glass, and trash didn't concern me as much as the rotting floor boards under a boarded-over window. Judging by the bubbled paint on the windowsill and the discoloration of the wall, water had gotten in.

Not much of a loss, considering the walls were cheap paneling. We'd need to hang sheetrock and paint. Patch the floor and refinish it or lay carpet, if Declan wanted to take the easier route.

That was all cosmetic and easily dealt with.

I spun in a circle, taking in the angled walls that formed the octagon shape of the building. A large window set into each gave absolutely stunning views. Even though The Roost was farther inland than the main house and the Tree Hut, it was also on an incline and had a perfect view across Declan's property to the lake.

"Wow, this place is just going to waste," I said with a shake of my head. "Why haven't you opened it up?"

"I'll show you." Declan led me to a wooden swinging door. We stepped through into an absolutely gutted kitchen. The floor was torn up. Only a rough frame for the cabinets remained. No sink. No countertops. No appliances.

"Remodel gone wrong?"

"Abandoned, more like," Declan said. "My aunt had big plans for this building. She started the remodel, but she ran out of funds. When I inherited this place, it was in debt up to its neck. The landscaping was a mess, and the main house had its own issues. There were just so many other priorities..."

"But this is great, because now we can put in a bomb-ass kitchen!" I spun toward the wall separating it from the living area. "In fact, we could knock down this wall and open it up to be an open-floor plan. Really modernize this whole place."

Declan's eyes widened. "That's, uh, a lot to take on. I just wanted to get it functional."

"Why stop there, though? Your aunt wanted more for this place, didn't she?"

"Well, yeah."

"So, let's do it, then. We'll make it so gorgeous you'll never want to leave."

"Cash..."

Oops. That was not the goal.

"Just kidding! It'll be so gorgeous that anyone would be

thrilled to take over the B&B and preserve what you and your aunt have built here."

He shifted uncomfortably. "I haven't built anything."

"But you will be." I met his eyes dead-on. "That's what we're doing here, right? We're building—or at least remodeling—your aunt's dream."

"That's a nice way of looking at it." He sighed. "We shouldn't get ahead of ourselves, though. This isn't the only project we'd have to tackle. There's still the second-floor deck at the main house and the plumbing at the Tree Hut—"

"And updating your ancient furniture," I interjected.

Declan paused. "What? You don't like the furniture?"

"Dec, I mean this in the nicest way possible, but it looks like a Barbie Dream House mated with an antique store and had mismatched babies."

Declan shuddered. "That imagery is..."

"Accurate?"

He winced. "Maybe a little."

"This place is on the lake. I think a beach house vibe would be amazing and more appealing to the guests, don't you?"

He pursed his lips. "Well, I was trying to adhere to Millie's vision, but..." He cringed. "I *have* always hated the interior design."

I laughed. "Why do you punish yourself like this?"

Declan gave me a considering look. "Old habit. Hard to break, I guess."

There was something deep and pained in his eyes that made me swallow the tease poised on my tongue. "Well, I guess this is an opportunity in more than one way, then."

Declan swallowed. "I guess it is. But that means it'll be an even bigger job than I envisioned."

"I'll try to keep the budget as lean as I can. I'll do the labor for free, but—"

"Absolutely not," he said sternly. "I'll pay you for your work. The land holds more value than the buildings. I'll recoup the expense and then some when I sell it."

"I'm not doing this to make a payday," I protested.

"I know," Declan said. "And if it's too much for you, I'll understand. I could still take that investor's offer."

"No way," I insisted. "Let them tear down this amazing place?"

His face tightened. "I don't really want that."

"Then we'll figure it out," I said. "This looks like a lot, but it's really just cosmetic. I can handle it, and I know a guy who can help, if that's okay?"

"Yes, of course."

"Does all the electrical work?"

"Yeah, I have it inspected yearly," he said. "I don't want to risk it burning down or something."

"Smart," I said. "And the plumbing?"

He nodded. "As far as I know."

"Perfect." I crossed into the hall and peeked into each bedroom. They could use some sprucing up, but there were no major concerns. The bathroom, too, could use a revamp, but it wasn't gutted like the kitchen. "We can do this, Declan. I'm sure of it."

His tiny hint of a smile bloomed into the sexiest grin I'd ever seen. Declan Sullivan was a truly gorgeous man. His dark hair and eyes gave him an intensity that drew me in, but the smile transformed all that surliness into a roguish charm that was almost unrecognizable on him.

"Let's go to my quarters."

"Whoa, Declan, I'm not that kind of boy!"

He chuckled. "You absolutely *are* that kind of boy."

I widened my eyes. "Did you just make a joke?" I pulled out my phone. "Time of joke, 10:43 a.m. Wednesday, July—"

"Stop it." His scowl returned, but there was no real ire behind it. "I want to show you Aunt Millie's plans. Now that you've convinced me you can do this, there were some other ideas she had."

"Oh, great!"

What had I gotten myself into now?

I escaped—er, left Declan's home office—just before lunchtime. Once I'd convinced him I could handle renovating the B&B, he'd gotten a lot more excited about fulfilling Millie's vision.

Oh, that Millie. She had *quite* the vision. Sunroom additions and a greenhouse and an attic conversion for additional booking space. It was no wonder Declan hadn't tackled most of this. Other than the greenhouse, he'd only be inviting in more guests and it was pretty obvious he didn't love the number he had now.

But I could see it. See everything the Treehouse B&B *could* be. It was something pretty incredible.

And I'd possibly bitten off a lot more than I could chew. But I'd figure it out, right? Probably while flailing around like a person in the dark—but with style—like I did everything else in my life.

Mom's car was in the driveway, which meant she'd gotten off her early-morning shift. She worked for a commercial company that loaned their cleaners out for housekeeping jobs, as well as office buildings, hospitals, and other industrial needs. Mom was technically a subcontractor and could take the jobs she wanted.

Because she needed the money, she took whatever she could get. Which meant an unpredictable schedule. She'd posted this week's work rotation on the refrigerator. I checked it and sighed.

Yep. She was working another split, and would be going back to work at 6 this evening when the bank she'd be cleaning would be closed to the public.

Looked like I'd be spending my night off at home so Katelyn wouldn't be on her own with Dad.

The television was playing in the living room, and I could tell he was awake because he was cussing at the NASCAR race he was watching.

I opened the refrigerator to grab something for lunch. "You want something to eat, Dad?" I called.

"What?"

"Do you want—"

"Bring me a beer!"

I groaned inwardly just as Katelyn stepped into the doorway.

"There's nothing to eat anyway," she said.

I surveyed the contents of the fridge, and she wasn't wrong. There was half a six-pack of beer, a few slices of cheese, and some sketchy-looking leftovers in the back that had been in the fridge too long already. I pulled out a container of cottage cheese and lifted the lid, jerking back with a cringe. Yep, that was expired.

"All right, I guess a shopping trip is in order. Where's Mom? We can make a list."

"She's sleep—"

"Where's my fucking beer?" Dad bellowed, cutting through Katelyn's soft words.

I was tempted to pour his precious beer right down the fucking drain. Katelyn grabbed a can from the fridge and took it to the living room.

"About time," Dad grumbled.

I guess that's what went for thanks in his world. I scowled.

Katelyn shook her head. "Don't start anything. Mom's trying to sleep."

I closed the refrigerator and grabbed the keys off the hook by the door. "I don't want to start anything," I muttered. "I really want to finish it."

Katelyn looked stressed enough that I relented. "You coming with me? You remember what foods everyone likes better than I do."

She seized on the opportunity to escape. "Yeah, you'd be hopeless without me." She detoured to the junk drawer under the microwave and pulled out a thick envelope. "Coupons Mom has clipped. Bet you would have shopped without them."

"You'd win that bet."

Dad bellowed at the television, making us both cringe. Mom shuffled into the kitchen bleary-eyed a minute later.

"What's going on?" she asked, glancing at Katelyn as she sorted coupons. "Oh, shoot. I meant to hit the store before I got home."

"No worries. We've got it covered. Right, Kit-Kat?"

My sister huffed. "Not a little kid, Cash. My name is Katelyn."

"So formal," I teased, tousling her hair just to annoy her. She squealed and danced away from me.

"Be quiet, will ya!" Dad called. "I'm watching TV."

If my eyes rolled any harder, I'd probably have a brain aneurism. The man had woken Mom with his bellowing, but *we* needed to quiet down.

"Do you need money?" Mom asked. "I'll get my purse."

"Nah, I got it."

She hesitated, but I didn't miss the look of pure relief crossing her face. "Are you sure? I can pick up an extra weekend shift."

"The resort gig is good and regular, Mom. What else am I going to spend my money on?"

She frowned. "Not *this*. You should be spending it on dates, or fun days out on the lake, or, or—"

"I'm not dating right now, and Sawyer's my hookup for fun on the lake. No money required. Besides, I just landed a second job unexpectedly, so...I'm good. Seriously."

Her brow furrowed. "A *second* job?"

"Yeah, so maybe you could give yourself a day or two off." I nodded my head toward Katelyn. "This job will be flexible. I'll work it around our existing schedules."

She smiled wanly. "You're too good to me."

"Nah. We're a team, right?"

She blinked misty eyes and nodded. "We are. The whole family," she said, shooting a smile to Katelyn. "That's how it's supposed to be."

There was one *team member* conspicuously absent from the kitchen. One that Mom was careful not to mention. We'd argued over Dad enough times that I knew she wouldn't change her mind.

He'd been the love of her life before he got hurt in a commercial boating job. He'd slipped on the deck while helping move cargo and ended up with a broken back and chronic pain.

He was a drag on this family and the reason my mother worked too many hours for a shitty company that paid her too little. Even with me contributing to expenses, we barely got by.

Dad won a worker compensation claim that covered most of his medical debt, along with a small amount of disability for the first year, but he refused the physical therapy required to continue receiving benefits.

He *could* get better, but he chose not to.

Mom thought it was her job to take care of him. I sure didn't see it that way, but unless I let my mom and sister go down with him, I was just as stuck as they were.

Dredging up old arguments wouldn't change that.

"Come on, Kit-Kat. Let's go get some food."

"Finally," she said. "I'm starving."

I paused in the doorway. "Anything special you want, Mom?"

She checked the refrigerator as I had done. "Better get your dad a case of beer. He won't last the rest of the day."

"Seriously?"

She turned toward me. "What? You know how he gets when he runs out."

And we just kept enabling it...but when you were living with an alcoholic who didn't want to change, what else could you do? It would get very ugly very fast if we tried to dry him out against his will.

We needed help. Outside intervention or a rehab stay for Dad, maybe. But with our limited resources, I wasn't sure how to even begin that process. Or if it was even possible without Dad's cooperation.

But I said none of that.

"I'll get the beer. But what about you?" I pressed. "Don't you want something?"

"Oh, honey, just get whatever you two want me to make for dinner this week. You know I'm not picky."

That was the truth. If she were pickier, maybe she'd leave Dad's ass and force him to face the truth.

His drinking was about avoiding reality rather than facing a life that didn't turn out how he'd hoped. It was about dulling his pain instead of doing the hard work to actually recover from his injury.

Most of all, it was about the addiction that had its claws in him.

And if we weren't careful, he'd eventually drag us all down, too.

CHAPTER TEN

Declan

"No Cash today?"

I poured a coffee refill for Janice. "Afraid not."

"That's too bad," Tom said as he cut into a biscuit covered in molasses. I'd brought in breakfast from Tastes Like Grandma today. "I wanted to tell him how wonderful his suggestion was for that sunset cruise. Ellen and I had an amazing night."

Ellen giggled, her pink cheeks telling us *exactly* how amazing their night had been. Of course, I'd heard in more detail than I'd like exactly how their anniversary had ended. An impressive feat, considering how thick the walls in this old house were.

Not even Cash had kept me awake so late with one of his conquests. Although, there was one night—

No. I squashed the thought. Living through it once was quite enough.

"I'll pass your thanks on to Cash when I see him," I said.

Tom and Ellen were checking out later this morning, thankfully, so I could get some rest tonight.

"It's too bad he's not here," Janice mused. "I was going to tell him about these *cocks* I saw for sale in town. *Cocks!* Like roosters. Get it?"

She cackled loudly, continuing to regale the other guests with the wackier things she'd found at the Outdoor Market.

Some were sexual innuendos like the "cocks." Others were just Ozarks backwoods humor, like the toilet-turned-planter. There was actually an event in this region for racing outhouses, so nothing surprised me anymore. When she got to the needle-point with naughty sayings like, "Kindly Fuck Off" I decided it was a good time for me to do the same.

"I've got to make a call. Enjoy your breakfast, and just leave your plates. I'll clear them when I'm free."

"Tell Cash thanks again!" Tom called.

"Will do."

"You're the best!"

No, Cash is the best.

The thought didn't rankle nearly as much as it should. Maybe because I'd be leaving all this behind soon enough. I was done trying to force my bitch-face personality into a smiley-face shape.

The flutters in my gut when I heard Cash's name had nothing to do with it.

I wasn't lying about the phone call I had to make. I retreated to my quarters and opened my laptop. On the screen, a Zoom page labeled *Amelia's 8th Birthday!* waited for me.

I clicked the button to join the video chat.

Noise immediately assailed me.

A child's squeal. A jumble of voices. The squeaking over and over of a toy, followed by a bark.

That would be Bowser, wanting in on the action.

I smiled as I watched the chaos play out on screen for a solid two minutes before my family noticed I'd joined.

My younger sister Monroe leaned in, her face filling most of the screen. "There you are, Declan. I'm glad you could make it. Melia's been so excited."

Amelia squeezed in next to her mom and held up the SpongeBob Lego set—complete with a pineapple house. "I got your present! It's so cool because I like to build stuff *and* I like SpongeBob!"

"That *is* cool," I said with a chuckle.

Monroe grinned. "Yeah, it's almost like Uncle Declan planned it or something."

"I know!" Amelia said, completely missing the sarcasm. Ah, to have the innocence of youth and take everything at face value.

"How's your birthday going?" I asked.

"Amazing! Except Jasper keeps trying to tell me how to play with my toys." She huffed. "They're *my* toys."

Monroe tsked. "Brothers are the worst."

"Hey now, some of us are great," I protested.

Monroe's husband ducked down, filling the screen with a bushy beard. My sister went for the bear type, but Will's heart was big and generous. He'd always treated my sister and his kids like precious gems, which was good enough for me.

"Hi, Declan. Good to see you."

"You too."

He turned to Monroe. "We're going to do bubbles in the backyard. Do you want to stay here and catch up with Declan?"

Monroe gave a relieved sigh. "Bless you, you wonderful man. I would *love* to stay here and rest—er, I mean, *catch up* with Declan."

Will laughed and pressed a sweet kiss to her cheek. "Take your time." He scooped up Amelia with one arm. "Come on, birthday girl. Let's go play!"

Amelia squealed in delight. "Bye, Uncle Dec!"

"Happy birthday!" I called. "Have fun!"

Monroe slumped with a groan when the room quieted, the clamoring voices and squeals trailing away as the kids all went outside.

"If you ever have kids, don't have the party at your house. Pay the exorbitant fees to hold it at an arcade or a bowling alley. It'll be worth every penny."

I smirked. "I take it the party is going well, then..."

"My house looks like a tornado just hit it."

"No jokes like that allowed when you live in Tornado Alley. You're tempting fate."

She pulled a face. "Sorry. My house looks like a hurricane hit it."

Little chance of a hurricane hitting Missouri. I nodded in satisfaction. "Better."

She picked up a Diet Coke and took a swig. "We're supposed to be catching up. Tell me something new I can tell Will later."

"Well..." I hesitated.

She straightened, perking up like a hound who'd just caught a scent. "Oh, this must be big. What is it?"

I huffed, annoyed. How did big sisters always know?

"I've decided to sell the B&B."

"I see."

I couldn't read her expression. Where was the shock or the horror?

"It wasn't an easy decision to make," I said irritably.

"I don't imagine it would be," she said. "You've spent years there, trying to prove you can be worthy of Aunt Millie's gift."

I tensed. "You know she wasn't playing favorites, right? You had your flower shop already, and the kids love seeing Mom and Dad every weekend. You wouldn't have wanted to move to the Ozarks."

"Plus, I never lived there for a whole school year," she pointed out.

Guilt niggled at me. "Was she playing favorites, then? Did you want to—"

"No." She cut me off with a laugh. "I hated it there when we visited. I couldn't tolerate more than a week or two."

I swallowed. "Right. That's what I thought, but..."

"You've always felt a little guilty she left you the B&B," Monroe said, because of course she'd noticed. "But there's no need for that, Dec. I wasn't upset. That place saved you when you needed to get away from the homophobia and bullying here."

"Not like the Ozarks were much better," I muttered. "But no one knew me here. I could disappear."

She smiled sadly. "You learned to blend into the background because you had to, and sometimes I think Aunt Millie just wanted you to bloom like one of her flowers, you know? I think she thought the B&B could do that for you."

I scoffed. "Well, I think it's safe to say that experiment failed. I'm not good with people, Mon."

"I know," she said. "So, do you have a buyer lined up already?"

I thought of the investor offer I still hadn't formally declined. "I have one possibility, but I'm still exploring my options. A, uh, friend of mine convinced me to fix the place up. Try to find a buyer who'd run the B&B the way Aunt Millie would have wanted. I found this plan she drew up for the place. Remodels, additions, expansions. It's a little idealistic, but I thought maybe we could bring some of her dream to life..."

Monroe's gaze softened. "That's really sweet, Declan. Aunt Millie would understand if the B&B life wasn't for you. She wanted you to have it, but she never stipulated in the will what you did with it."

"I can split the proceeds with you."

"After running that place on your own for years? Putting in all that money and time? No. The Treehouse is yours."

There was a rap on my door, then it edged open and Cash peeked inside. "Am I interrupting?"

I checked the time on the bottom display of my screen. Sure enough, I was supposed to meet Cash for a shopping trip to get our first round of supplies. We'd decided to start with basic repairs before moving on to more ambitious remodeling projects.

"Sorry," I said. "Just chatting with my sister."

"Ooh, another Sullivan." Cash let himself in and crossed the room, crouching beside my chair to grin at Monroe. "Does Declan glower at you all the time, too?"

Monroe laughed. "Oh, I've got a whole childhood of glowers from this one."

I sighed. "The abuse is unending."

"I love his glowering," Cash said, glancing sidelong at me. "It gives him so much character. Anyone can walk around smiling like an idiot." He pointed to his own grin. "Just look at me."

"Oh, I'm looking," Monroe said archly. "My brother's even looking, and that *never* happens."

My face flamed. "Monroe."

"What? It's true."

"*Really?*" Cash only grinned wider. "I can work with that."

I shook my head. "You're undoing all my progress, Mon. I should say goodbye before you put any more ideas in his head."

"The ideas are already there, Declan," he said in a low voice.

He placed a hand on the back of my neck, squeezing gently, and tension bled away as if he'd injected me with a drug. What sort of magic was this?

Cash and Monroe kept up a running stream of chitchat, but I lost the ability to focus as Cash gently massaged my neck, casually touching me as if it wasn't blowing all my circuits.

It wasn't a sexual thing, but this gentle touch was undoing me all the same.

Just like when he'd hugged me last week, my walls dropped. I leaned in for more, craving the comfort and care and connection.

All things I told myself I didn't need because they always came with strings. But Cash wasn't asking for anything. He wasn't trying to make a move on me.

The noise picked up on the video as the kids streamed back inside. Amelia and her older brother bounced into view.

"Hey, who's that guy?" the boy asked.

Cash answered before I could. "I'm Declan's friend, Cash. Who are *you?*"

"I'm Jasper, his nephew!"

"And I'm Melia!"

Cash grinned. "Melia, the giver of the SpongeBob pajamas, am I right?"

She giggled. "How did you know?"

Cash glanced at the stuffed Sandy squirrel from the cartoon tucked under her arm. "Wild guess."

"Wow, you're good at guessing!"

Cash charmed my family as easily as he did the guests—and all the while, he smiled at me, touched me, made me feel like the center of his attention even as he talked to everyone but me.

When he withdrew to give me some privacy to say my good-byes, I instantly missed his warmth.

It was the middle of an Ozarks summer. His warmth should have been stifling, and yet...

Monroe eyed me through the screen after shooing the kids off. "You didn't tell me you had a boyfriend."

"A boyfr— No, absolutely not," I said. "He's just a friend. A casual acquaintance, really. He's going to work on the B&B with me, that's all. He's a contract worker. I'm going to pay him. Not to date me."

"You're going to pay him not to date you?" she teased. "Well, that's one way to keep a man at arm's length."

I glared. "That's not how I meant it."

"Declan," she said, voice soft. "You just gave me a whole lot of words to explain away Cash's importance."

I winced. "Well, I didn't mean he wasn't important."

"Because he obviously is," Monroe said. "The way he looks at you..."

"I know." I pressed my lips together, hope and fear warring inside me. "You know I don't have any luck with that stuff."

"That stuff being love?"

I shrugged a shoulder.

"Well," she said thoughtfully. "We don't always expect love when it finds us. I certainly wasn't looking for Will. The man was buying flowers for his ex-girlfriend to woo her back, remember? When he came back to ask me out, I thought I was his second choice. I refused him for weeks."

I smiled, remembering just how dramatic my sister had been at the time. How *sure* she'd been that Will thought she was that easy. She'd made him work for it.

And he had.

"Will's a great guy, and your situation is different from mine."

"Yes, but you're still human. There's nothing wrong with wanting companionship."

The phantom feeling of Cash's hand on my neck returned. The warmth of his smiles, his voice. The *looks* he cast my way, a message in them that seemed to say that I was the center of his world.

I wanted that. I wanted it so much.

But could I ever have it without the other side of the coin? Without disappointing him or leaving him so unsatisfied that he'd seek out other partners?

And a guy like Cash? Anyone would snap him up in a heartbeat.

Anyone but me, that was.

Because deep down, I knew I couldn't keep him. No matter how fondly he looked at me or how much I liked the small fragments of affection he cast my way.

CHAPTER ELEVEN

Cash

AFTER DECLAN FINISHED HIS VIDEO CHAT WITH HIS family, I followed him to the attached garage, where he kept his aunt's 1962 Ford F150 pickup truck.

I ran a hand over the faded pale blue body, admiring the curves of the antique beauty. The cab was smaller than modern trucks, more rounded in design. Chrome ran across the front of the grill, surrounding each pair of headlights. It was pretty damn sweet.

An antique truck like this would most likely never survive daily driving, but in a town like Swallow Cove, you didn't need to put all that many miles on a vehicle.

"Hop in," Declan said, reaching for his door handle.

The door stuck, and he had to try a second time, grunting as he tugged it open. I reached for my door, ready for a battle, but it swung open easily.

"Don't say a word," Declan said as I slid onto the bench seat beside him. "It's old and finnicky, but it gets the job done."

"Hey, I think it's cool," I said. "I'm a little surprised you haven't bought something newer, though."

I'd always seen Declan as a little uptight. The kind of guy who'd take his car in for oil changes like clockwork. Who'd spend days researching the gas mileage and features before choosing a car to buy.

"I don't drive all that much," Declan said. "When I do, it's usually because I need to haul something. The truck is handy." He paused. "Besides, I learned to drive on this truck."

"No kidding?"

Declan turned the key, and the engine rumbled to life. "Yep. I lived here for a year as a teenager."

"How did I not know this?"

Declan worked the shifter, putting us into reverse.

"It was a long time ago." He sent me a pointed look. "High school isn't a recent memory for me."

"It feels like a lifetime for me."

"It sure does," he agreed.

Declan hit the clutch with his left foot and seamlessly shifted into first, taking us down the bumpy path to the main road. From there, it was a few miles of curvy blacktop inland.

The store's big red sign was visible as we rounded a corner and came up on the far side of The Grocery Spot—aka The G-Spot, as we had coined it. *Dyck's Hard*, it read. The "ware" had faded away sometime ago, and the owner, Ray Dyck, said everyone found it so entertaining he decided to leave it. So now, we shopped at Dyck's Hard when we needed tools or appliances.

Or wood.

Hard wood, that is.

I snickered as we entered through the sliding doors. Declan sighed. "You're such a child."

"Guilty." I nudged him. "But it's funny. Admit it."

"Maybe the first time I saw it."

"And the second and the third," I teased.

"But not the twentieth," he said firmly.

His lips twitched.

"Aha! I saw that."

"Saw what?" he asked, pretending ignorance as he grabbed one of the utility carts with a big platform on the bottom and a small tray on top.

I poked the corner of his mouth. "Your lips twitched up. You were totally smiling."

"That's not a smile."

"For you, it is." I traced his lips with the tip of my finger. "It's small and it's almost hidden, but I see it."

Our eyes met and held. Declan swallowed hard and stepped back. My hand fell away from his mouth.

"Sorry," I said. "I was just—"

"Being you," he said. "Come on, let's go find what we need. You have the list?"

"Yep." I pulled my phone out of my pocket and opened the list we'd made for our first shopping trip. "We can check out the appliances first, since you'll probably need to order what you want?"

Declan nodded. "Lead the way."

Dyck's didn't have the large supply that a big-city store would, but he had several reasonable models of refrigerators, stoves, and dishwashers. Declan proved my theory about him right when he spent nearly an hour going over the pros and cons of every feature each model had.

I was gonna throttle him if I hung around to watch, so I slipped away to complete some other parts of the shopping trip. I wanted to get some wood cut to replace the rotten boards in The Roost's floor. I'd need a hand sander and sandpaper, as well.

I'd wait on the sheetrock until I could talk to Gray, one of the new boaters at the resort. He'd helped with a few house remodels before taking the job with Swallow Adventures, and I was hoping to pick his brain—and hopefully get his help with a few of these projects.

I got what I needed and was on to the painting supplies aisle when I spotted Danny Wray on his tiptoes, stretching to reach the paint pans on a higher shelf. I left the cart at the end of the aisle and sidled up alongside him.

"Hey, shorty. Need some help?"

Danny sent me a glare that surprised me. "No."

I started to raise my arm. "I can—"

Danny pushed my arm down, hissing, "You're ruining my plan. Just move along unless you want to be my consolation prize."

Consolation prize?

I followed Danny's far-from-subtle head nod toward the end of the aisle. A large, hulking man was studying packets of hardware a few feet away. His skin was smooth and dark, standing out in our whitewashed Ozarks community. But *hot damn*, he was gorgeous.

"Who is that?" I whispered.

"My dream man," Danny said. "He works at the new Hot Buns Bakery."

"Ahhh." I'd only seen the woman who ran the front of the shop. "And Jasmine is..."

"His sister, obviously," Danny said. "Now get out of here!"

Danny gave me a little push, then swatted my ass when I took too long to get moving.

"Okay, I'm going!" I whirled toward the end of the aisle with a laugh, right into a glowering Declan, who was standing by our cart, watching me with narrowed eyes.

"Hey, Dec. Figure out what you want yet?"

"What is that supposed to mean?" he said sharply.

"The appliances..." I winced. "Sorry for ditching you. I just couldn't take all the analysis. I'm more the type of guy who sees what he wants and just goes for it."

"Clearly," he muttered, gaze shifting over my shoulder. "Are you and Danny..."

He trailed off.

I blinked at him, lost. His gaze focused on something behind me. I looked back to see the hot baker pulling down a paint pan for Danny, who was fluttering his lashes and making the big guy blush. Surely, Declan didn't think...

"Me and Danny *together?*" I barked a laugh as I turned back to Declan. "No, of course not."

"I don't mean a relationship. I know you don't do those."

"I don't?"

"I just meant, you know...hooking up?"

I tilted my head, trying to understand this baffling man. He said he didn't want to date me because he couldn't have the intimate relationship I would want. But he also seemed upset anytime he thought I was involved with someone else.

"No, Declan. Contrary to popular belief, I don't hook up with people everywhere I go."

"I didn't mean—"

I grasped his jaw, and strangely, he leaned into the touch, as if he craved more. I stroked my thumb along his cheek, dragging it over prickly stubble. "There's only one man I'm interested in."

He wet his lips. "I'm leaving though. And I can't..."

"I know." I dropped my hand. "Doesn't mean I can magically move on as if my feelings for you never existed."

"Feelings? It's more than attraction?"

I rolled my eyes. "Of course it is, Declan. You're totally infuriating!"

He huffed a laugh. "I'm aware." He looked a little embarrassed. "And it's really none of my business who you sleep with. You're free to hook up with anyone you want."

"Did it ever occur to you, Declan, that I might want more than sex?"

He blinked. "Uh, well..."

"I know you're ace, and maybe it *seems* like the rest of us are just sex-crazed fools looking to get off. But I want a relationship too. I want love and connection. Laughter and hugs and cuddles on the couch. All that good stuff, you know?"

"I'm sorry," he said. "You're absolutely right. I assumed—maybe unfairly—that sex was the most important thing to you. I mean, you've had a *lot* of it."

I started pushing the cart toward check-out, and he fell into step beside me.

"*Had* being the operative word, Dec. I haven't been having much of it at all for months now."

"No?"

"Nope. Just me and my hand."

"Oh." He cleared his throat. "Uh, well, maybe I misjudged you. I admit it."

"That's okay. I sort of asked for it after all those visits to the B&B last year. I was...going through something, but I'm sorry it took me so long to understand why it bothered you."

"Why do you think it bothered me?"

I sent him a smile. "Because, Declan, you're totally into me."

He started to sputter out a denial, and I laughed and left him behind as I rolled the cart into the line. Declan's reaction today had told me something important. He might be planning to leave, and he might be unsure that I was relationship material, but Declan Sullivan liked me.

Hell, maybe he even more than liked me.

What exactly that meant to a guy on the ace spectrum? I wasn't quite sure. But I intended to find out.

CHAPTER TWELVE

Declan

A few days later, I parked in front of The Dirty Hoe. Cash would start work on The Roost in two days—the first opening in his schedule—and I wanted to clear that overgrown path of brush and weeds, plus ensure it stayed cleared once I had.

The Dirty Hoe looked like an overstuffed garden shed attached to a greenhouse—a mix of the quirky and functional just like its owners. A wheelbarrow planted with a brightly flowering hibiscus sat just outside the door. Three sets of wind chimes dangled from an awning: silver metal fish, glass butterflies, and little brass birds with bells.

I ducked as I reached for the door, having walked straight into them enough times to have learned my lesson. As if the wind chimes weren't enough, more bells jangled to announce my entry.

"Be right there," Mimsy called from the vicinity of the greenhouse. I recognized her voice because she was the sweet one.

"Oh. It's you again."

And that would be the other owner, Mimsy's twin, Pipsy. She scowled at me, her crinkled face scrunching up. "Weren't you just here the other day? What do you take us for, some sort of enabler?"

I bit down on a smile. Pipsy was obviously my favorite, but I couldn't let her know that.

"I've got a legitimate reason today."

"What's the reason now? You've already practically bought me out of fertilizer this year."

I chuckled. "So sorry to keep your store running on a profit."

She scoffed. "As if we do this for money. We'd have closed ages ago."

I didn't doubt she was right. This was the kind of passion business that folks ran as a side gig when they retired. Something they enjoyed that made them feel useful after their hard-working years were behind them.

I wanted to be like Mimsy and Pipsy when I grew up. For now, I was stuck running a B&B.

But soon you'll be running numbers instead...

The idea wasn't exciting, but it was comforting. I knew how to deal with data much better than guests who demanded my interest and attention whenever they wanted it.

I was a little like Pipsy that way.

"Well?" she said, sounding impatient. "What is it you're shopping for today? I've got my show on in the back, and I was busy doing actual work before you showed your grumpy face."

"Ha, you're one to talk."

"My face is lovely and cheerful," she deadpanned, her lips upturned in a saccharine-sweet smile.

Mimsy swept in then, all genuine warmth and grace, completely her twin's opposite—aside from the fact they shared identical DNA. "Declan, dearie! So good to see you again."

Her short silvery braids sported bright pink ribbons to match her lipstick, and she wore a bright floral muumuu in place of Pipsy's country-style overalls. But just like her sister, her fingers were gritty with potting soil. The sign of any good gardener.

"What can we help you with?" Mimsy asked. "You don't need more mulch, surely?"

Okay, maybe I'd overdone it with the gardening supply runs this year, but I had a very large property to maintain.

And maybe I'd expanded my vegetable garden just a smidge and moved some hydrangea bushes to an area where they got more shade, plus I'd planted some new azaleas to better frame the entryway...

And maybe you really are addicted to gardening.

It had started as a way to get out of the house more and—yes —avoid my B&B guests when I needed a breather. The landscaping had been a mess when I first inherited the place, left to grow unchecked for several years while Millie wasn't in the best of health.

But what started out as a chore had blossomed into love. There was just something about working outdoors, smelling the fresh scent of soil and new growth, that made me feel more alive, too.

"I'm clearing an overgrown walkway," I told Mimsy. "I need a weed barrier, maybe some landscape fabric to put down along the edges and cover with decorative rocks?"

"Oh, I've got just the thing," Mimsy said. "Follow me."

I could have found what I needed on my own, but Mimsy loved to be helpful. I let her explain the types of weed barriers, along with half a dozen suggestions about how to shore up my path if it was going to have regular use.

She made a good point about putting down gravel or pavers to stand up to regular use. I'd add it to the list of improvements I was making with Cash. Mimsy was so excited about the path, I decided not to mention the greenhouse plans. She might expire on the spot, and then Pipsy *really* wouldn't like me.

Twenty minutes later, I escaped Mimsy's clutches with my purchases and made a quick stop by the grocery store.

My phone rang on the drive back to the B&B, but I didn't have my Bluetooth on, so I let it go to voicemail. When I got inside, I put away the groceries and changed into some work clothes to head over to The Roost. The place was a mess, and I didn't want Cash to waste his time with cleanup.

It was nearing six, but this time of year it stayed light until around nine o' clock, so I had plenty of light. I grabbed cleaning supplies, along with a broom and dustpan, and headed across the yard.

My phone rang just as I got started. Shoot, I'd forgotten about that missed call. My sister's name flashed up on the Caller ID. I rolled my eyes. Of course she was calling again.

She'd texted me almost immediately after the birthday party chat to say, ***Please tell me you're going to rob that cradle!***

There'd been a string of suggestive emojis.

I'd pretended I didn't know what she meant. I had enough hangups about Cash without thinking about our age difference. Honestly, that had barely registered with me. Maybe because Cash was far more experienced than me with romantic entanglements.

Or at least, sexual ones.

I was tempted to ignore Monroe's call, but then she'd really give me hell. I propped the phone on the counter and hit the Speaker button. "Hey, I'm busy."

"Busy doing that gorgeous man all but drooling over you?"

I sighed. Well, I'd walked right into that one. "No, I'm

cleaning out The Roost. Cash"—she drew her breath in, expecting news she would not get—"is starting repairs out here in a couple days."

"Because he's good with his hands?" she asked hopefully.

"Monroe," I growled. "Grow up."

She snickered. "Never!"

At my unimpressed silence, she relented. "Okay, so he's helping you with repairs at the B&B. Tell me more about how that happened?"

My stomach fluttered as the memory of that night flooded back. Cash stepping close, eyes pleading. *Kiss me.*

He'd been so warm and solid when he hugged me. That was the most difficult part of pushing Cash away. The affection that poured off him was like rays of sunlight, and I was a plant left in the shade too long.

But even if Cash could accept what I could offer—prickly thorns and all—I was leaving Swallow Cove soon. There was no reason to start anything now.

I pushed the broom across the floor, sweeping the trash into piles, while I filled Monroe in on the more detailed plans Cash and I had made for the B&B.

"A greenhouse," she said when I'd paused for breath. "Wow. That's..."

"Ambitious?" I said with a chuckle. "Aunt Millie always wanted one."

She hummed. "I bet you'd love one too."

"Well, yes, but it's not for me."

"Right." Her tone was airy.

"I'm selling the B&B."

"I know."

I paused, brow furrowing. "Then why don't you sound like you believe me?"

"I believe that's your plan," she said. "As for what will actually happen? I guess we'll see."

Well, that wasn't infuriatingly cryptic or anything.

My phone beeped. "I've got a call. I should go."

"Yeah, maybe it's Cash," she teased. "Ready to be *handy*."

"Stop it," I said sternly.

"Never. I live to rile you up."

I leaned the broom against the wall and clicked the call over to the other line—only to discover it was Nathan. Shit. He'd texted me twice this week already about the development deal I'd unofficially agreed to before Cash convinced me to try another plan.

I wasn't ready to cut off this avenue of possibility—not until I was sure that Cash and I could actually pull off all the repairs this place needed—so I needed to stall.

"Hey, Nate, it's late to be calling, isn't it?"

"Is it?" he said lightly. "You know I go on all cylinders until nearly midnight."

"Right. Yeah. I guess I'd forgotten about that."

He chuckled. "You'll remember soon enough when you're back in the city. That backwoods place has you acting like a senior citizen."

I winced. First my sister pointing out my age gap with Cash, and now Nathan calling me old. I was really winning today.

"I'm actually busy with something," I said, shaking out a trash bag noisily.

"What are you doing, making a kill room?" He laughed. "Maybe I should call you Dexter."

"Yeah, obviously that's the most common use for plastic and not trash bags," I said dryly.

"Well, this will only take a minute. I just wanted to see if you got that paperwork I faxed over."

"Uh, yeah, I think so."

"You haven't looked at it?"

"Well..."

"Declan! These guys won't wait forever. It's great you gave us a yes, but we need to get all the t's crossed and i's dotted. This is a big project."

"Right, I know," I said, stomach squirming with guilt. "I just want to be sure before I sign anything."

"What do you mean?" His voice sharpened. "I thought you *were* sure."

"It's a big decision. I said yes to considering a deal, but there's no taking it back once I sign."

"I know. There's also no moving forward until you do." His voice took on an edge. "I vouched for you. I went out on a limb. Don't screw me, man."

His vehemence had unsettled me.

"I never asked for that."

"I know," he said, "but we're friends."

"I don't want to yank you around, but this is too important to rush. If you can't wait—"

"I didn't say that," he said hurriedly. "Of course we can wait a reasonable amount of time. A few days?"

I exhaled. "Maybe this was a bad idea. I don't want to hold up a project, and it sounds like these guys are in a hurry."

"A couple weeks then," Nate said. "I'll explain you're having a lawyer examine the paperwork. It's smart to be thorough."

I hadn't said I was doing that, but it was a good explanation. Still, I didn't want Nathan to pay for my indecision. "If the developer needs to move on and consider other locations, I'll understand."

"Nah, I'll smooth it over. No worries."

"But, Nate, I can't give you a guarantee. You understand that, right?"

"You're a smart guy, Declan. You're my numbers guy for a reason. You do all the analysis you want. In the end, you're going to see this is the right move. That, I can *guarantee*."

CHAPTER THIRTEEN

Cash

GRAY'S PICKUP JOLTED OVER THE BUMPY PATH THAT wound through the Treehouse B&B grounds. I bounced on my seat, which was torn and patched with duct tape, while a motorcycle-shaped air-freshener dangled from the rear-view mirror.

"Just park here," I said as The Roost came into view atop its small hill. There was a graveled parking area off to one side.

The truck gave one last jolt as it hit a dip in the ground and stopped.

"You need some new shocks, dude."

Gray chuckled. "Would cost more than the whole truck. Just be glad I'm hauling your ass around."

"Hey, no shade on your baby." I patted the dash as Gray parked. "I'm damn glad you're here, and with a monster toolbox and a skill set I don't have. Thank you, man, seriously."

Gray raised one eyebrow. "I am getting paid, right?"

"Yeah, of course." I'd pass along my pay from Declan if need be. Gray was going to make this job ten times easier to pull off.

"Then thank *you*," he said. "I've been saving up for another motorcycle. Had to sell my last baby."

That explained the motorcycle-shaped air-freshener. Gray looked like a guy who knew his way around a bike. I wasn't one to stereotype, but he rocked the bad boy look with shaggy hair and tats.

We got out of the truck and went around to the back. Gray lowered the tailgate, and I jumped up to unhook the ratchet straps keeping his big-ass metal toolbox on wheels in place.

"This thing couldn't have been cheap."

"Nope." Gray pulled out a ramp, then joined me to help wheel it down. "Cost about as much as the whole truck."

"How'd you swing that?"

"Eh, tried to make a full-time go of the remodel gig. I was picking up a lot of jobs over the winter. Folks wanted their vacation houses or rentals repaired before the tourist season."

I nodded. "Makes sense. So, why did you apply at Swallow Adventures, then?"

Gray worked for the boat tour company that Hudson owned —and Sawyer planned to buy into.

"It's good regular work. These jobs come when they come, and really, I can work around my boat tours most of the time."

"Well, I'm glad—"

I broke off with a grunt as we shoved the toolbox over the gravel and onto the dirt path. It wasn't the smoothest trip, with bits of rock and grass in the mix.

We didn't talk much as we hauled it up the steps built into the path. Thankfully, it wasn't too steep of an incline and a hell of a lot less overgrown than the last time I'd seen it.

Declan must have cleared the way.

Gray let out a low whistle. "Who is *that?*"

I damn near lost my grip on the toolbox. A few feet ahead of us, Declan wielded a machete, hacking away tall weeds and grass. Though it was still early in the day, he was shirtless—tanned muscles rippling through a surprisingly strong back.

All that gardening has done nice things for his body...

"Cash?" Gray asked with a laugh. "You okay over there?"

No. No, I really wasn't. I think I swallowed my tongue.

Declan turned, pulling out an ear bud. "I didn't hear you come up. Sorry. Am I in the way?" He stepped to the side, making room for us to pass, and tossed the machete into the grass. "I hoped to be done before you got here, but these weeds were..."

"A bitch?" Gray supplied with a smirk, his gaze skimming over Declan's glistening chest.

Declan smiled. He fucking smiled for Gray. "Yeah, you could say that."

"Come on." I gave the toolbox a shove, forcing Gray to stop ogling my— Well, my *friend*, I guess.

Declan didn't seem to mind Gray looking, which was odd. He'd told me he wasn't into dating or relationships, but—

I squashed the stupid jealous thoughts trying to surface. Declan was just being nice to a guy who was going to help remodel his property. I needed to be nice, too.

We rolled the toolbox past Declan and through the front door of the house. As soon as we made it inside, Gray busted out laughing.

"Damn, your face, man," he said. "You'd think I was swooping in to steal your man."

"Shut up," I grumbled. "Did you have to stare? Some people don't like to be ogled like a sex object, you know."

This only made Gray laugh harder. "I was not ogling him. Jesus. You've got it bad."

I flipped him the bird, but just then Declan stepped inside. He'd put on his shirt but left it unbuttoned, giving tantalizing glimpses of his chest and stomach. Somehow, that was worse.

"I'm going to serve breakfast to the guests in about half an hour. Do you two want me to bring you something?"

"That would be real nice," Gray said, stepping forward to extend a hand to shake. "Hi, Declan. I'm Gray. I think Cash is too flustered to make introductions."

Declan glanced my way, brow slightly furrowed. "Flustered?"

"Ignore him," I said. "You know I never get flustered."

Declan chuckled. "That's true. You're the most unflappable person I know."

"Really?" Gray murmured. "*Interesting.*"

I shot him a warning glare, and he raised his hands with a shit-eating grin. "I believe I'll have a look around and give you two a minute."

Once he was out of sight, Declan said, "What was that about?"

"Nothing," I said quickly. "Gray has experience with remodeling work. He knows what he's doing so you won't have to worry I'm going to screw this up."

Declan frowned. "I wasn't worried about that. I trust you, Cash."

My heart squeezed. "Really? Because you once said I didn't take anything seriously, and I just wanted you to know that I take *this*—I take *you*—very seriously."

Declan stepped close enough I could smell the grass and sweat clinging to him. "I never should have said that to you. It was wrong."

"I know why you would think—"

"I was wrong," he cut in, his eyes holding mine captive. They were more compelling even than his naked chest had been. Because in them, I could see so much emotion. "I'm sorry."

My breath hitched. Jesus. What was wrong with me? It

wasn't *that* big of a deal. Yes, I wanted Declan to believe in me. To trust me. But I was used to people underestimating me. Used to being seen as the one-dimensional party boy, the flirt, the fuckboy around town.

Declan hesitantly cupped my shoulders. "I want to hug you, but I'm all sweaty and—"

I pushed into his arms, hooking my arms around his back. "I don't care about that."

"Okay," he said softly, one hand stroking down my back. "Thanks for doing this for me, even though I didn't always treat you right."

"You treat me fine," I mumbled into his shoulder. "Better than fine."

The hug lingered. As my emotions settled, I became more aware of his body against mine. I wanted to slip my hands under his shirt and stroke over that sweaty skin. Maybe kiss his neck, then along his jaw...

I pulled away. "We should get started."

Declan's arms dropped to his side, and I could have sworn a look of regret passed over his face. "Yeah, of course."

My gaze dipped to his chest then away. I bit my bottom lip hard to hold in the flirty comments that would love to escape.

"Do you really find me that attractive?" Declan asked, sounding baffled.

My gaze jerked to his. I wasn't shy in the least, but knowing that Declan didn't return the attraction made it more exposing than usual for me. I swallowed hard.

"You already know I do, but I'm sorry if it makes you uncomfortable. I'm trying to tone it down."

"I'm not uncomfortable." He sounded surprised. "I know you'll respect my wishes. It's just... You could have any man you want. I don't know why you'd pick me out of all of them."

"Maybe those men are too easy."

Declan chuckled. "Well, that's one thing I'll never be."

"I know," I said. "I'm okay with that. We're really not so different."

He looked incredulous. "How do you figure that?"

"Well, people don't see me for all that I am, and I'm guessing it's the same for you. But I see you, Declan, and I still like you. And maybe...you like me too."

Declan was the one flustered this time. He reddened with an adorable blush and pulled his shirt closed. "You don't know what you're getting into. You'd be better off focusing on someone like your friend Gray."

"Gray?" I snorted. "No. Not happening."

"Real nice," Gray said, emerging from the hallway. I didn't want to think about how much he'd overheard. "I'm considered a fairly attractive guy, I'll have you know."

That was modest, considering he had the facial structure of a leading man in Hollywood, even with his rough edges.

"Meh," I said. "Been there, done that."

At Declan's horrified look, I clarified, "Not with Gray specifically. Just guys like him."

Shit. That wasn't much better judging by Declan's expression.

"Uh, right. I should..." Declan waved a hand toward the door and beat a swift retreat.

"Smooth," Gray said as he rejoined me in the living room.

"Yeah, you don't have to say it. I always become an idiot around him."

"That's cute. You think you're not an idiot the rest of the time."

"Rude!" I slugged him in the arm, and the fucker barely flinched.

He chuckled. "Seriously, man, you two should go for it already. You're both putting off some very needy vibes."

"It's complicated," I said.

He rolled his eyes. "So make it simple."

Oh, if only I could. If only I could press Declan to a wall and kiss him and make him believe I'd accept whatever he wanted to give me. But then, was that true? I wasn't doing the greatest job of accepting only friendship, not when I only wanted to get closer to him every time we were together.

Still, Declan hadn't denied that he liked me. His eyes seemed to plead for me to give him something he didn't know how to express. I wasn't ready to give up on the idea that maybe we *could* have something.

And so what if it looked different from other relationships? I'd never seriously dated anyone before. Being with Declan always would have been different for me. Something deeper and meaningful.

As long as I had a hand and toys, I could get the sexual release I needed. I'd been doing it for months, hadn't I?

But it was all a moot point if Declan left Swallow Cove.

With a sigh, I turned to Gray. "Where do you think we should start?"

"Well, we're still waiting on cabinets for the kitchen, so I think we should start in the living room. Get the floor patched up. Get up on the roof and track down the leak, so it doesn't just keep damaging the walls."

Declan had cleared the place of trash and broken glass, but now the damage to some of the flooring was even more evident.

I nodded. "And all this paneling?"

Unfortunately, it wasn't the rustic wood planks of a cabin, but the 1960s imitation paneling that covered the walls.

He wrinkled his nose. "Yeah, that's pretty outdated. The best bet is to pry it off the sheetrock. It's glued, essentially. If we're careful, we can preserve the sheetrock, sand it down, and then paint it." He gazed around with a considering look. "It would be kind of awesome to give this the cabin vibe though, considering the original wood floors. We could do some wainscoting over the bottom third, give it a more updated panel there? Maybe a lighter wood to keep the room brighter since the flooring is darker?"

I nodded. "I'll have to talk it over with Declan first, but I think that sounds good."

Gray's lips twitched, but thankfully he refrained from teasing me about my Declan obsession. Good thing too, because I needed his expertise and he might quit if I kicked his ass.

"We've got plenty to keep us busy until we reach that point," he said. "Do you know where Declan keeps the ladders around here?"

"He's got a garden shed. We can try there."

He nodded. "All right, let's get to work."

CHAPTER FOURTEEN

Declan

THE NEXT FEW DAYS, I WATCHED A SLOW TRANSFORMATION at The Roost that was equally exciting and disconcerting.

"It'll get worse before it gets better," Cash had assured me when I'd gaped at the holes in my floor after I'd brought the guys a couple of sandwiches the first afternoon.

"It's just growing pains," Gray had added.

I'd nodded dutifully, reminding myself that I'd promised Cash just that morning that I trusted him. And I did. More than I ever would have expected.

Cash wouldn't let me down.

He was here, working during his off time when he didn't have to—and hard enough that his shirt stuck to him with sweat, clinging to muscles I didn't even know the man had, though it explained how easily he drew the eyes of other men and women.

Still, when I'd swung by a couple of days later to see paneling ripped off the walls, I couldn't hold in my gasp of horror. Cash had talked over their remodeling plan with me, and

I'd agreed, but seeing sheetrock mottled with glue and remnants of paneling that had gotten stuck to the walls was different than envisioning the final product.

Cash laid down his tools and came to take the bottles of water from my hands. "Breathe, Dec. It's gonna be great. You have my word."

"I know. It's just..." I waved a hand at the wall. "It looks like a lot of work. I should be helping."

Cash tossed a bottle of water to Gray, then lifted his own to his lips and took a long drink, his throat working as he swallowed.

"You are helping. We appreciate you clearing the path outside."

"And the food and drinks," Gray added, saluting me with his bottle of water.

It wasn't enough. Cash was working around his hours at the resort—and Gray was working around boat tours. I could work around the B&B needs, too. I had to get a couple of rooms ready for guests arriving that afternoon, but I could go over once the check-ins were done for the evening.

Unfortunately, the last guest arrived later than expected—so it was seven-thirty before I was free of front-desk duties.

I went to the kitchen to whip up an easy dinner for the guys, my heart sinking when I saw the taillights of Gray's truck bounce along the path outside the window.

I picked up my phone and texted Cash.

Declan:

Sorry I didn't make it over tonight. Had a late check-in.

His reply took a few minutes to come in.

Cash:

No problem, man. You've got a full-time job over here.

Declan:

You've got a job at the resort too. You're doing too much for me.

Cash:

I'm doing exactly what I want to do. Listen, I'm kinda busy. Want to come over and just talk to me face-to-face?

I blinked at my phone dumbly.

Declan:

Wait. You're still over there? I saw Gray's truck leave.

Cash:

Yeah, he had a booze cruise to cover, but Mom's home tonight, so I thought I'd get some hours in while I could.

Jesus, this man. He was *still* working.

I sent a quick text to let him know I'd be right over, then finished sauteing the ground beef in the skillet and made quick work of assembling a few tacos in soft flour shells.

I packed them up, along with a couple of beers, and headed over to The Roost. My heart was beating a little quicker than usual, but I chalked it up to the surprise that Cash was still here and I could contribute to the project after all.

Of course, then I opened the door and saw him.

Cash stood on a stepstool, his back to me, as he sanded sheetrock. His arm flexed, his whole body tensing and relaxing with his movements, and there was just something so familiar and welcome about the sight of him.

My chest warmed, my gut fluttered, and I froze where I was, just staring at the amazing man who'd volunteered so much of his time and energy to me.

I never would have pegged Cash as a hard worker, based on his playful nature, but he was dedicated to helping me.

Even though I'd done nothing but push him away.

A breath shuddered out of me, and he half turned, glancing over his shoulder. A smile lit up his face. "Hey, you."

"Hey." My voice came out a little hoarse. I cleared my throat and lifted the platter in my hands. "I brought tacos."

"Oh, I'm starving. Thanks, man."

I didn't love Cash calling me *man*. Like I was just one of his friends.

I frowned down at the tacos, as if they held the answers to my conflicted emotions. Cash hopped to the floor and reached for the plate, his hands brushing over mine.

"Let me take that. What's wrong?"

I shook my head. "There's no table. I should have brought one for you."

"That's all right," Cash said, his voice teasing. "I like it rough."

I glanced up in surprise. It was the first time he'd thrown a sexual innuendo my way in a while, and for some silly reason, it reassured me.

Cash took the plate from me and sat down in a folding chair he and Gray had set up in a corner. He patted the one next to him. "Sit down. Have you eaten yet?"

"There's six tacos on that plate. What do you think?"

"You're right." He grinned. "Obviously, they're all for me."

I chuckled as he lifted a taco and bit into it with relish. He took big ravenous bites, cheek bulging. His poor manners should have been appalling, but he resembled an adorable chipmunk. I smiled as I watched him start on the second taco approximately ten seconds after he started the first.

"Wha?" he mumbled around a bite.

"You really were hungry," I said, lips twitching.

He straightened up, lifting his arm to wipe at his chin. He winced and rolled his shoulder.

"Sorry. I worked up an appetite."

He rolled his shoulder again, grimacing, before he tore into the tacos again. I reached over and snagged one, because at this rate, he really might eat all six. I took a small bite and glanced around the room. The walls were still torn up, but several panels of sheetrock had been sanded smooth. There was white dust all over the floor—and Cash.

On impulse, I leaned over and plucked a piece of sheetrock from his dark hair.

His eyes shot to mine in surprise.

I showed him the white papery substance between my fingers. "You're a mess."

"No lie there. I feel filthy." He wrinkled his nose. "Sorry if I stink. I've probably sweat out a gallon of water today."

I ran my fingers through his hair again, brushing dust out of it, but really just absorbing the silky feel of his strands under the pads of my fingers. It was nice.

He tilted his head into my touch, eyes closing as he sighed. I continued finger-combing his hair, gradually trailing my fingers down the back of his head and kneading his neck.

"You're not working too hard, are you? I'm going to come over and help more. You shouldn't be taking so much on."

The corners of his lips hooked up. "You worried about me? That's sweet."

I pressed my lips together to hold in the truth. Yes, I was worried about him. I cared about his well-being. Probably too much.

I dropped my hand away and took another taco. "Let's finish eating and get you home for some rest."

Cash grabbed a third taco and ate it—a little slower now that he'd gotten two in his belly. He interspersed his bites with gulps of beer. "How was B&B life today?"

I hummed. "Well, it was a busy day for check-outs. I had to

remake a lot of beds. You'd think I'd be a pro by now, but I still have to wrestle the damn queen in the Apple Tree Room every time."

Cash chuckled. "Why don't you hire a housekeeping service? My mom works for a service that could help you out."

"It wouldn't be worth it to have them out for one or two rooms every few days."

"I suppose not."

"Maybe something like the resort…"

Cash nodded. "Yeah, Skylar has contracted them. Mom cleans there at least a couple times a week."

"You must enjoy working there," I said. "You're a natural with my guests."

"Do I sense a hint of annoyance in your tone?" Cash asked with a grin.

I huffed. "Well, it's tough enough to get them to like me without you showing up like the damn guest whisperer and making me look bad."

Cash lowered his beer bottle. "Shit, I was never trying to do that. I'm sorr—"

"No, no." I chuckled. "I made that sound like a complaint, but it wasn't."

"I'm not sure I follow."

"I envy your ease with people, Cash. I admire it."

"Oh."

"And when you're at breakfast, conversation is so effortless. I didn't realize until you joined us the other morning. It was true, even when you were here with another guest. I'd forgotten, because—" I hesitated, but Cash's gaze was fixed on me, so intent and interested in what I had to say, that I couldn't hold back. "Because I didn't like you being there for that reason."

He grimaced. "I'm sorry."

I squeezed his knee. "No, don't apologize. You were free to sleep where you wanted."

"But it's your B&B. If you didn't want me around, you should have said."

"That's not it, Cash," I said, frustration leaking into my tone. "I always want you around, and that scares the shit out of me."

Cash leaned toward me. "What? Declan, I'm—"

He froze, face twisting as he let out a hiss.

"You're in pain," I said, setting aside my plate.

"Just a little sore," he gritted out, raising his hand to hold his shoulder.

I rose and circled behind him, setting my hands on his shoulders. "May I touch you?"

"Yeah." I gently squeezed his shoulders, and he groaned. "For future reference, you never have to ask."

I pressed my thumb into a knot above his shoulder blade and he hissed again.

"Even when I hurt you?"

"Especially then," he rasped.

My gut tightened at the tone. I recognized the sensation, though it had been a long time since I'd experienced it with anyone.

It made me nervous, and I turned my focus to working the knots out of his shoulders. His shirt bunched up, getting in the way. I reached down to tug at the hem.

"Is it okay if we take this off?"

"Now you're undressing me too?" Cash murmured. "Naughty."

I withdrew my hands. "Sorry. No. I—"

Cash caught my hand as I retreated. "Kidding, Declan. Always. I respect your boundaries, and I always will, okay?"

I exhaled. "Yeah, of course. You're such a flirt."

He smiled sheepishly. "Guilty. Sorry about that."

"No, I...I like it," I admitted in surprise. "Don't stop flirting. You wouldn't be you if you did."

He smiled faintly. "Okay. Then take off my shirt, baby. I'm ready."

He added a ridiculous wink that reassured me he was just playing.

I grabbed the hem, tugging it up and over his head. Cash lifted his arms, and I could tell he was still hurting by the slow way he moved. I draped his shirt over the empty chair beside him, then started on his shoulders again.

His skin was a nice toasty tan this far into the summer and hot as a summer day under my hands. I kneaded his shoulders, waiting for him to relax before I dug into the problem areas. Cash exhaled and sank back against my hands, slowly melting as I worked at him.

I traced my thumbs along his shoulder blades, pressing in, then used my other fingers to rub and knead his upper back and neck. Slowly, I worked out each knot.

His body was firm but malleable, and it was the first time in a long time I'd touched a man this way, skin to skin.

Cash's breath grew a little uneven, and I glanced down to check he was okay. My gaze slipped over his chest and abs, moving with each breath, to the very obvious hard-on in his pants.

I froze.

"Sorry," he muttered, pressing the heel of his hand to his erection. "It's just my damn body liking this massage. I know nothing's going to happen."

Those words, more than anything else, made me relax. "You must want some relief."

"Later," he said. "I'd suffer a hundred hard-ons to spend a little more time with you."

My heart stuttered. Was that romantic? It *felt* pretty romantic. "Do you mean that? You'd really..."

"Yeah," he said. "But if you want it to go away, maybe let me put my shirt back on."

He started to move, but I brought my hands back to his shoulders, keeping him in place. "Wait."

"Okay..."

"If you wanted to, uh, touch yourself while I do this—"

Cash whipped his head to look at me, and I gently guided him to face forward again.

"I don't want to do anything that would make you uncomfortable. I'm fine."

"I know," I said. "That's why I want you to do it."

"You..." His breath caught and his hand went to his crotch, hovering uncertainly. "You actually *want* me to?"

"I want to see you feel good," I murmured in his ear. "Touch yourself for me?"

"Fuck." He sucked in a sharp breath. "Okay. Damn. Anything you want."

"Then open your pants."

CHAPTER FIFTEEN

Cash

DECLAN'S HOT BREATH CARESSED MY NECK AS HE SPOKE into my ear, and the last of my blood rushed south so fast my head spun.

I tried to keep my wits about me, but once Declan said he *wanted* this too, my brain shut off. My body vibrated with need, and sitting here shirtless while he put those work-callused hands all over me had been a torturous test of my self-restraint.

I fumbled with the button and zipper on my shorts, my hands *shaking* I was so worked up. This was *Declan* standing behind me. Declan, whose hands still stroked over my shoulders. Declan, who was always off-limits...

My pants opened, and I slipped a hand inside, grasping my cock with a low groan of relief. I hesitated a moment, enough sense restored to wonder if he *really* wanted to see me desperate and horny.

"Show me," he said into my ear, making me shudder.

I felt his gaze burning down my exposed chest, over my twitching abs, to where my cock begged for release.

I tugged it out of my briefs, hissing as cold air met the moist tip. "What should I..."

"Just do whatever you'd do if you were alone. I want to see what you like."

I licked my dry lips. "This may not last long."

"There's no timer running," Declan said, sounding amused. "No one's scoring you, Cash. Just do what you like. That's what I want."

Well, that was easy enough. I stroked my cock from root to head a couple of times, lifting my free hand to tweak my right nipple.

A small sound escaped me as pleasure ping-ponged between my dick and my nipple.

"You like that, huh?" Declan said. "Do it again, harder."

"Fuck," I whispered, obeying instantly as my blood burned hotter.

Declan's hands moved into my hair, combing through it, tugging a little, adding fuel to my fire. He wasn't touching me the way a typical lover might, but he was here with me. He wanted this too.

My pleasure was building too quickly. I eased off my stroking, dipping my hand down to roll my balls and tug at the sac.

"Are you still watching?" I asked, needing to know we were in this together.

"Yes, Cash. I see you."

I glanced over my shoulder—needing to see him watching me. Our eyes met and held.

My hand sped up on my cock again as I bit my lower lip with a muffled groan.

Declan used his thumb to tug my lip free of my teeth, then caressed my mouth. "Let me hear you."

The salt of his skin touched my tongue, and my climax

slammed into me. I arched, giving a strangled cry, as my cock erupted in my hand.

Declan brought his mouth down on mine, kissing my trembling lips, his taste and scent adding to the overwhelming pleasure crashing over me.

It took me a few minutes for my brain to start firing on all cylinders. Declan ended the kiss but continued to run his fingers through my hair, soothing me as I came down from my orgasm high.

"Do you..." I half turned toward him. "I could do something for you, too."

"You already have," he said, fingers dipping down to stroke along my jaw. "This is exactly what I wanted."

He touched me so gently, tracing his fingers over my eyebrows, down the bridge of my nose, and finally over my lips again. Somehow, those soft touches were more intimate than the kiss we'd shared while I was coming.

I kissed his fingertips, reveling in the closeness between us. His gaze met mine, full of a warmth I thought I'd never see there. Declan felt our connection, too.

"Let's go over to the house," he said, his voice husky. "You can clean up before you go home."

I glanced toward the wall I'd been sanding. I tried to muster up the energy to go back to work, but my limbs were heavy and slow to respond.

"You've done enough work for tonight," he said. "I'll be here to help more tomorrow, too. I don't want you killing yourself to get this done."

I grabbed my T-shirt and wiped my hand clean. "I made a promise, Dec. I plan to keep it."

He rounded the chair, giving me a hand up. "I know you'll keep it. You don't have anything to prove."

Declan picked up our discarded dinner plates. I grabbed our

beer bottles—mine nearly empty, and Declan's nearly full—and followed him to the door.

We turned out the lights and locked the door, and I followed him to the main house in a daze. I wasn't that shocked I'd put on a show for Declan—or that I'd come so hard I could hardly think straight. But the fact Declan had suggested it? That was surprising.

And encouraging.

Maybe there was a way for this to work between us. Maybe a relationship with him didn't have to look like Brooks' or Sawyer's relationships to still be everything I wanted.

"Declan, about what happened—"

"It was good, Cash. Let's just leave it at that, okay? It doesn't change anything. I'm still me."

I caught his hand and raised it to kiss his palm. "And I like you as you are."

He cast me a sidelong glance. "That's possibly the orgasm talking."

"No." I shook my head. "I can give myself orgasms too, you know."

His steps faltered. "I'm aware of that."

"I'm just saying, it's not the destination that matters to me. It's the journey. And my traveling companion, of course." I winked.

"Hmm." He cast me a small smile. "Well, I, uh, like you too, but I really can't promise more journeys like that."

"I know."

"Yeah?"

"I've been reading up on asexuality."

"Really? What have you learned?"

"That you may experience little to no sexual desire for someone," I recited from memory as we passed by the garden shed. "Or you may only experience it sporadically or in certain situations."

"That's about right. It's not even something I understand, so I can't imagine anyone else would."

"They could try though." I paused. "*I* could try."

"Cash, you've been around the block...around two hundred blocks of the sexual variety."

I cringed. "I wasn't that bad, was I?"

Declan raised an eyebrow, and my shoulders slumped.

"Okay, maybe I was, but that's in my past. I sowed my wild oats. Now I want something more."

"Well, it's a moot point," Declan said as we reached the back door to the B&B, and he opened it for me. "I'm selling the B&B and leaving town anyway, so..."

I stepped into the kitchen, heading toward his quarters and hoping none of the guests were around to see me shirtless and smelling of cum.

I waited until we were safely closed into Declan's private quarters before I said the words that were on my tongue.

"You don't have to leave."

"Cash..."

"You don't," I insisted. "Even if you sell the B&B, why can't you stay in town and do something else? Go work at the library, or...I don't know, become a groundskeeper since you love gardening."

Declan chuckled, and I scowled. "Why is that funny?"

He cupped my face. "You're just sweet, the way you're such a dreamer."

"Maybe you should try dreaming a little more."

"Maybe I should," he murmured before drawing away. "You can use my shower."

I bit down on the urge to invite him to join me. That wasn't going to happen. Declan had made it clear tonight was good, but a repeat was unlikely.

"Thanks," I said, taking the towel he held out. "I'll be quick."

"Take your time. You can use my shampoo and body wash."

He retreated, closing the door. Apparently, he'd gotten his fill of watching me. The memory of his gaze so intent on me while I jerked off for him was damn near enough to get me hard again.

I rinsed quickly, taking the time to wash with Declan's shampoo and body wash, which smelled like eucalyptus and rain. When I got out, I dried and pulled on my briefs and shorts. I couldn't bring myself to put on my filthy shirt, so I left the bathroom topless.

Declan sat aside the crossword puzzle book he was working on and got a shirt from his closet for me. It was white with blue words that read, *Shore Daddy*.

"Really?" I asked, smirking at the shirt.

"My sister thinks she's hilarious," Declan said. "You can keep it."

I snorted. "Yeah, I bet. I'll tell everyone my daddy Declan gave it to me."

"On second thought..."

He tried to grab it back, but I danced out of his reach and tugged it over my head. "Nope, it's mine now."

He sighed and rolled his eyes heavenward as if I tested his patience. That was legit. I tested a *lot* of people's patience.

Declan gestured to the couch. "Want to sit? I, uh, can get you another beer unless you need to get home?"

I'd planned to work late anyway, so I wasn't in a rush. "I can have one more."

He nodded and left to get it from the kitchen. I wasn't sure what we were doing, but I was curious to see where Declan led me.

I sank back on the couch, spreading one arm out along the back of it. When he returned, he sat beside me, rather than in his armchair. In front of my arm.

Which basically demanded I put my arm around him, right?

Declan grabbed the remote and clicked it on. A show about baking came on, with the contestants engaged in some sort of creative cake challenge that involved making things like house cats and fairytale castles out of sponge cake and moldable chocolate.

It was all beyond my skills, though I was sure Ash would love to give it a go.

Declan sat back, and I lowered my arm slowly, giving him time to move away. When he didn't, I rested it over his shoulders.

"Want to cuddle?" I asked, half expecting him to run.

Instead, he sighed and curled in against me, resting his head on my shoulder. My heart damn near burst with happiness.

This was what Declan needed, I realized. My body might crave the endorphin rush of orgasm, but he craved closeness and affection—and damn if I didn't love that too.

I wrapped my arm tighter around him and held him closer, dropping a kiss on his head. "This is nice."

"Yeah," he said, sounding drowsy. "Just one episode to relax, then you can go."

"Mm-hmm. Whatever you want."

We cuddled for two more episodes, until my arm was going numb from being in the same position for too long, but damn if I'd have moved for anything.

Eventually, Declan dragged himself upright. "Do you want to sleep here? I mean, on the couch."

"Your couch is comfortable, but no, I should go."

"Do you want to take my pickup?"

I blinked. "You'd let me do that?"

"You're coming back tomorrow anyway, right?"

"Yes. My shift at the resort starts at eleven, so I'll be here around six in the morning."

"Then take it." He went to a hook by the door and grabbed a keyring. It included keys to the B&B property. He didn't bother to remove any of them. "I don't want you walking home late at night."

"That's sweet, but Swallow Cove isn't exactly dangerous."

He gave me a flat look. "I didn't say it was dangerous. I just think you need to get some rest."

I grinned. "Like I said, *sweet.*"

He rolled his eyes and pushed me toward the door. "Okay, enough. Get going."

"Do I get a kiss goodnight?"

He hesitated.

I tapped my cheek, and he blushed adorably as he leaned in and pressed his lips to my jaw. "Goodnight, Cash," he murmured. "Don't get used to it."

I grinned. "Oh, I would never presume you were a Shore Thing, Daddy."

He shoved me out the door and slammed it in my face, but I heard his laugh on the other side. I smiled to myself as I let myself out of the B&B and headed to the garage where he kept his aunt's antique pickup.

I didn't know what I was doing with Declan, where we were going, or how we'd even get there. But I resolved to enjoy the journey—wherever it might take us.

CHAPTER SIXTEEN

Declan

I woke early the next morning with a strange fluttering in my gut. Memories of the night before slowly surfaced as I blinked away the sleep fog.

Cash, working so hard for me that he was in pain. So earnest and dedicated to making this project happen.

Me, deciding to massage his shoulders and—admittedly—indulge in some platonic touching. Of course, it hadn't stayed platonic, and ironically, that was all on me. Cash had told me to ignore his reaction, that nothing had to happen. But for once, I'd *wanted*...something. Maybe not everything Cash would have been up for, but I'd craved intimacy and closeness.

Which was a terrible fucking idea because I'd been down this road before—and I was leaving, anyway.

I shifted in the bed, and my morning wood brushed against the sheets, sending a rush of need through me. I was used to waking up hard. It was biology. But this morning, it was pulling at my focus more than usual.

I threw back the blankets and headed for the shower. I'd

take care of this little problem quickly, then dress in some old, ratty clothes to meet Cash over at The Roost to work.

The fluttering started in my stomach again.

Stop it. You can't have him. It would be a disaster and you know it.

With that uplifting thought, I turned on the shower and stripped off my silk pajamas. I climbed into the lukewarm water, too impatient to wait for it to heat fully, and started washing.

My stubborn dick remained hard, waving in front of me. With a sigh of annoyance, I squirted some body wash into my palm and started stroking.

I jerked off as much as any other man, but most of the time it was a means to give my body relief and move on. I started the same way, stroking my dick on autopilot while my mind fuzzed out and played a reel of abstract sexual images that didn't mean much to me.

No faces, no real people, just...sensations. The act of sex was good in the moment. I just didn't crave it often.

Pleasure built as I worked my dick, but suddenly Cash snuck into my mind. Not surprising, with the way he was getting under my skin against my better judgment.

The memory of last night blazed to life: Cash arching, face twisted, lips parted in pleasure—and his gaze seeking mine, connecting with me in the most intimate way possible.

I gasped as my orgasm crashed into me, stunned by the realization that Cash Hicks had just made me come.

I rinsed away the mess and got out, drying and dressing in faded blue jeans with grass stains on the knees and an old T-shirt with a Voyager Corp. logo from the bank chain that used to employ me.

It occurred to me halfway through my shave that I should have left the shower until *after* the sweaty work at The Roost.

I regularly got up and gardened before I showered, so I shouldn't have automatically showered first. Unless...

I subconsciously wanted to look good for Cash. But that was ridiculous. I wanted *less* attention from men, not more. I didn't put effort into my appearance for anyone.

I wiped away the last of the shaving cream—grimacing at my clean-shaven, groomed appearance. This nonsense had to stop.

By the time I made a pot of coffee, Aunt Millie's pickup was passing by the window. I poured two mugs and headed out the back door and across the yard.

Cash beat me there, parking and waiting by the path where I'd spent two days weeding, graveling, and putting down landscape barriers and rocks to keep it clear.

His eyes lit up as I extended a cup to him. "Coffee from a gorgeous man in the morning. Does it get any better than that?"

I scoffed. "I'm wearing grass-stained jeans."

"Mm, and it's sexy." Cash leaned in to murmur, "You must spend a lot of time on your knees."

"It's from gardening," I said stiffly.

"Those lucky weeds," Cash teased.

I didn't know how to respond to that. I knew he was just teasing, but unlike in the shower when Cash was just in my head—now he was too real.

I lifted my cup for a quick gulp and started up the path. Cash dropped into step beside me.

"It's just more sanding this morning. I can only stay for a couple of hours, but Gray will be out this afternoon."

I nodded. "I've got to serve breakfast at nine anyway." I glanced sidelong at him. "You want to join us?"

"I don't know. Will I make you look bad by entertaining your guests?"

"Without a doubt, but you'll also make the whole ordeal easier to handle."

Cash chuckled. "You really aren't suited to hospitality, are you?"

"I'm really not."

We got to the door, and I reached for my pocket, only to realize I didn't have my keys. Cash produced the keyring. "Looking for these?"

"Ah. Yes."

"You're very trusting. I could have come in and watched you sleep like a creeper."

I took the keys and unlocked the door. "You, uh, didn't though. Right?"

He grinned. "Wouldn't you like to know?"

I shook my head. "I think I'll choose to be blissfully ignorant in this case."

Cash followed me inside, and the vision of the torn-up walls assaulted me all over again.

"I started with a gutted kitchen, and now there's a gutted living room too. I'm not sure this is better."

Cash slung his arm over my shoulders and tugged me in against his side. "We've been over this, grumpy bear."

I tried not to show how much I liked snuggling in against his side. Cash smelled awfully good for someone about to engage in hours of work. Had he done that for my benefit?

I breathed in the spicy scent of his aftershave and decided I didn't care.

"It's like surgery," Cash continued. "We have to cut open the patient before we can fix them and sew them up again."

"That's a *terrible* analogy."

He dropped his arm and stepped away to put his coffee on the windowsill and start gathering the sanding tools. "Is it? I thought it was good."

I shuddered at the thought of Cash doing surgery. "I just hope you're better at fixing walls than you would be at operating on actual human beings."

He snorted. "Well, luckily, my patients can't die." He paused. "I don't think, anyway. Maybe if I took a sledgehammer to them—"

"Okay," I cut in quickly. "This is bad enough. Let's not test the theory and start *fixing* things."

He grinned and gave me a hand sander. "You got it, honey bear. Get your butt on the step stool and start sanding."

"Why am I suddenly all varieties of bear this morning?"

"Because your snarl is just so cute I can hardly stand it."

My heart skipped because obviously I was a fool. I couldn't be developing a crush on the most sexually active man I'd ever known. That would be idiotic. Not to mention, I was *leaving town.*

I attacked the wall, working out some frustration, but I didn't get far before Cash stopped me.

"Whoa there. We're not trying to bore a hole through the wall. Smooth strokes, Declan. Just like you watched me do last night."

I huffed in exasperation. "Will you stop flirting?"

"Who says I'm flirting?" Cash gave a shit-stirring grin. "You saw me sanding the wall, right? What else could you possibly think I mean?" His eyes widened comically. "Oh, Dec, you weren't thinking of"—his voice lowered to a dramatic whisper—"*something dirty*, were you?"

I brandished the sandpaper in his direction. "Keep it up and I'm gonna sand your grin right off your face."

He laughed. "I had no idea you were so violent."

"Me either," I muttered, "but clearly you inspire me."

I hadn't meant that as a compliment, but Cash smiled like

I'd said something sweet. Hell, maybe I had. He had me all muddled up lately.

Thankfully, he let the matter drop and got to work beside me, each of us sanding away bits of glue and particles of paneling left behind.

We moved along the walls, inching our way across the room. Soon, my arm was burning from the repetitive motions of sanding, and I tried switching to my left arm for a while. I was less coordinated though, and I was soon back to the right.

Twenty minutes later, the dull ache was more of a throb and I stopped to rub my shoulder.

"Am I going to have to give you a massage this time?" Cash asked, eyes on me.

"You wish," I mumbled.

"I really do."

With one last rub, I went back to sanding. The room was silent except for the scritch-scritch-scritch of the sandpaper against sheetrock.

"It wouldn't have to end the same way," Cash said.

I paused. "What?"

"A massage," he said. "It could end any way you liked."

The teasing tone was gone. I glanced over to see a pensive look on his face.

"I like to flirt, but I just want you to know—"

"I do," I said.

It was true. Cash already understood me better than any of my past boyfriends had—partly because he'd made the attempt to learn.

It didn't change his needs, though. Didn't change the fact he was a man in his prime who deserved everything he wanted, everything I couldn't give.

My phone alarm went off, ending the conversation before it drifted into dangerous waters.

"I need to run to the bakery and pick up breakfast."

Cash nodded. "I'll keep at this and meet you over there in twenty minutes?"

"Sounds good."

I made the drive to Hot Buns to pick up an assortment of baked goods. When I arrived, Danny from Just The Sip was there.

And he was fluttering his lashes at the big, brooding baker, Abe, while Jasmine looked on with a smirk.

"I'd love to carry some of your goods in my shop," Danny was saying, "but I need someone to bring them over for me."

"I could do that," Abe said.

"Yeah? I'd give you free coffee. Free anything you want, actually."

"I don't need anything."

Danny pouted. It should have looked ridiculous on a thirty-something man, but Danny was so small—five-foot-six—next to the hulking Abe that it somehow worked for him.

"What if I want to give it to you, though?" Danny said.

I cleared my throat. "Uh, I hate to interrupt, but I need my breakfast order."

"Of course," Jasmine said. "Let me grab it."

But Abe was already turning away to head back into the kitchen for it. Danny turned a dirty look on me. "I was *this* close to getting that man to smile."

"Sorry," I said. "I'm just on the clock."

"Me too. I'm not getting any younger."

"And I am?"

"Well, you've got Cash wrapped around your little finger."

"I don't have anyone," I said quickly, heart lurching—with fear, unease, excitement? I didn't even know.

"Oh, yeah?" Danny grinned. "Maybe I'll ask out Cash, then."

"Go ahead," I gritted out. My teeth had clenched involuntarily.

"I just might," Danny said with a sigh. "Abe sure isn't giving me the time of day."

"He's just shy," Jasmine said. "Give him time to warm up to you."

Danny raised his eyebrows at me. "What do you think?"

"Why are you asking me? I don't know anything."

"Clearly. If you were smart, you'd snatch up Cash before someone else does."

"I'm not— We're not..."

Danny smiled at Jasmine. "I'll be back later to work out the details on the business arrangement. Unless Abe wants to stop by." He winked. "You all know where to find me."

He sauntered out the front door, leaving me confused.

"What just happened?" I asked as Abe returned with the carry-out box of pastries.

"That's what I'd like to know," he rumbled quietly.

It was the most words I'd heard him speak.

His sister snorted. "I think you're both hopeless."

Well, I couldn't fault her logic. I paid for the order, wished them both a good morning, and headed back to the B&B.

The whole way there, Danny's words haunted me.

If you were smart, you'd snatch up Cash before someone else does.

But how could I snatch up a man that I couldn't please for long—one that I was planning to leave in a matter of weeks?

Answer: I couldn't.

But the idea of his smiles and his sweetness and his warmth —even his silly flirtations—being directed at someone else sat in my stomach like a heavy rock.

CHAPTER SEVENTEEN

Cash

"I hate you!" Kat shrieked.

A door slammed down the hall, followed by my dad's nasty chuckle.

"Why do you wind her up like that?" Mom said in exasperation, her voice drifting back from the living room. "She's a teenage girl."

Great, Dad was picking at Kat again. Lately, it seemed like his favorite pastime.

"Exactly," Dad muttered as I stepped out of my bedroom. "She needs to know what to expect from guys. Look at Cash. He just fucks around all the time. No respect for anyone, even himself."

I reached the living room, my mouth running before my brain could think better of it.

"Because you'd know a lot about self-respect. Don't worry, Dad, if you want to warn Kat off guys, all she has to do is look at you."

Mom winced, and Dad's glazed eyes narrowed on me. "You watch your mouth. I put a roof over your head."

"No, actually, that's Mom and me. I may be a fuckup, but I pay more bills than you do."

"Get the fuck out of here," he snarled.

"Gladly." I stormed down the hall and pushed open Katelyn's door. "I'm going out. Come with me. It's going to be one of those nights."

My sister didn't need to ask what I meant by that. She grabbed her phone and her purse and followed me out of the house.

"Where are we going?" she asked.

"Cookout at Sawyer's."

She pulled a face. "Haven't I been punished enough for one night?"

"Very funny. Don't worry, his boyfriend does the grilling now."

Her eyes lit up. "The food boat guy? Benny and I stopped there last week, and he made the best tacos."

I smirked. "You should tell Ash that when we get there."

Ash hated that people seemed to appreciate his tacos more than some of his more creative inventions, and I was a shit-stirrer, so I couldn't wait to see his reaction. They were damn good tacos, though.

"He's really cute too," Kat said.

I chuckled. "And you should tell *Sawyer* that."

There was nothing I enjoyed more than getting under Sawyer's skin. We'd always been like that. We were oil and water, usually on opposing sides of most arguments, but somehow our friendship worked. For a while, Fisher was convinced I wanted to date Sawyer, but that stupid kiss had put that question to bed. We had *zero* chemistry.

Besides, he only wanted Ash, and I only wanted...a man I

couldn't have. Yeah, I was screwed. I knew Declan wouldn't necessarily invite me to jerk off for him every day just because he had once. But I'd hoped for, I don't know, maybe more kisses? An acknowledgment that we could turn this connection between us into something more before it was too late.

But maybe it was already too late. The man was leaving town. It didn't get much more hopeless than that.

Sawyer's place wasn't a long walk. We cut through the Swallow Cove Park and came in behind the oddball collection of campers and RVs at the LandShark Retreat. If I were to move out of our house, I'd most likely end up in a place like this.

Swallow Cove had mansions in the hills, moderate houses and rentals farther inland—in short supply and all occupied by long-term residents—and campers aplenty. A lot of tourists bought them, thinking they wanted the lake life, only to decide they'd made a mistake and sell them to locals for a steal.

A steal was still beyond me when I was helping my mom maintain a mortgage, cover utilities, groceries, and other needs. Not to mention, Kat needed me at home as a buffer.

"What's going on with Benny, anyway?" I asked Katelyn as we wound between trailers. "Why was Dad giving you grief?"

She huffed. "Why does he ever? He's mean when he's drunk, which is like all the time."

I slung an arm over her shoulder and tugged her close. "So nothing happened with your guy?"

She leaned into me. "He's texting with some girl he says is just a friend. I shouldn't have told Dad. It was stupid."

"Need me to kick Benny's ass?"

She giggled. "As if you could. He's a linebacker."

"Yeah, yeah, but I was a pitcher for the baseball team."

"Which means what?"

"I can bean him in the head with a baseball."

She laughed some more, which was the goal, and by the

time we entered the clearing in front of Sawyer's teardrop camper, we were both more relaxed. It wasn't easy living in a toxic environment, and Katelyn got to escape it a lot less than me.

"Hey, it's both the Hicks sibs!" Fisher called.

"Hey, everyone," Katelyn said, waving. "Sorry to crash the party."

"No, this is great," Poppy said, smiling from her spot at the picnic table. "I'm always outnumbered by the guys."

Katelyn and I joined Poppy at the table, across from Fisher, Brooks, and Skylar. Ash was working the grill, sending a delicious barbecue scent drifting across the yard.

"Hudson's not here?" I asked.

"He's hanging out with Declan tonight," Fisher said. "Which I guess explains why you're here and not at the B&B like every other night."

I shrugged. "Gray's got a booze cruise, and we're not really in a place to start the next project without him. Declan told me to take the night off."

I would have gladly spent my night off with Declan, cuddled up together on his couch—where we'd landed three out of the last five nights I'd worked at the B&B—but he'd told me he had plans.

The camper door opened and Sawyer came out with a cooler full of drinks. His neighbor kid Shua followed with a bowl of potato salad, which they put in the center of the table.

Tonight, Shua was wearing a ballcap paired with overalls and a frilly pink shirt. I couldn't have assigned a gender to that outfit even if I wanted to, and given that Shua was nonbinary, that was as it should be.

"Hey!" Shua's gaze landed on Katelyn. My sister was a few years older than them, but still much closer in age than the rest of us. "Wanna see my turtle?"

"Uh." Kate glanced sidelong at me.

"It's an actual turtle," I said with a laugh. "Shua adopted it."

She shrugged. "Okay, sure."

She stood up, and as she and Shua passed by Ash, I heard her say, "I love your tacos at the food boat!"

Ash's pained smile made me laugh. Sawyer shook his head. "He's going to love that."

I grinned. "I know."

"You're nothing but trouble," Sawyer said, obviously clueing in that I'd put her up to it.

"She also thinks Ash is cute."

He rolled his eyes and took a seat. "I'm not taking your bait tonight. My man is *very* happy with me."

"Good," I said, "because I never want you to kiss me again."

Fisher choked on his beer, spluttering. Poppy hid her smile, while Brooks and Sky laughed.

Sawyer glared. "The feeling is mutual, asshole."

Brooks took a drink of his beer, then asked, "So, what's going on with you and Declan? You're spending a lot of time over there."

"It's a big project," I said. "I only have so much time around my resort hours and when I need to be at home for Kat."

He nodded. "Sure. But is that the only reason?"

All my friends were staring at me now. I cursed under my breath. "This isn't one of those frienderventions, is it? Because I'm fine."

Sawyer snorted. "Exactly what I said when you all cornered me."

"And me," Fisher added.

"Hey, how come Brooks never got a friendervention?" I asked, hoping to deflect the attention away from me.

Brooks grinned. "Because I didn't go through denial like the rest of you idiots. I wasn't about to hide from my feelings for Skylar."

"Aw." I pantomimed gagging. "So cute."

"You're just jealous," Brooks said.

"Damn right. Skylar is hot."

Skylar blushed, which had been the goal. Brooks's eyes narrowed on me as he wrapped an arm around Skylar's shoulders. He was reliably a possessive boyfriend, even if Skylar held all the cards in that relationship. Brooks was hopelessly smitten and would do anything Skylar asked at the drop of a hat—and they both loved it.

"I know what you're doing," Brooks said. "It won't work. I was asking about you and Declan."

Damn. I'd been so close to sidetracking him.

"Declan's great," I said. "I'm finally getting him to warm up to me."

Brooks's eyebrows shot up, and I pointed a finger at him. "Not like *that.*"

Well, a little like that, if you counted him whispering in my ear while I jerked off in front of him. But that might never happen again.

I'd meant the talking, the small smiles, the casual brushes of his hand against my back, or the way he leaned into me when I slung my arm over his shoulders. And when we were alone on the sofa, with no one watching? He curled into me like a love-starved cat.

Declan wanted love. I was convinced of that. He just didn't know how to accept it. But that was all too private to share with Brooks.

"We've become friends," I said instead.

"Just friends?" Fisher asked, sounding skeptical. "You've been obsessed with him for two years."

"Obsessed is a strong word," I muttered.

"But accurate," Poppy said.

Well, hell, if Poppy was saying it, it must be true. She wasn't a shit-stirrer like the rest of us.

"Fine, maybe I have been. But he's selling the B&B and leaving town. I can't exactly ask him for more." I shrugged. "But if he falls madly in love with me and stays, I won't be sad about it."

Skylar looked concerned. "Do you really think that's likely? He sounded pretty determined to leave when I talked to him."

"I don't know," I said honestly. "But I can't just turn off my feelings for him, so..."

"This isn't healthy," Brooks said. "If a guy doesn't want to be caught, you stop chasing him."

"That's what you all told me too," Fisher pointed out. "But Hudson *did* want me. He just needed a little incentive to figure that out. Maybe it's the same with Declan."

I lifted the bottle, taking a long cool drink of the beer Sawyer had brought to the table.

"Declan is different from most guys," I said. "I'm not chasing him. He doesn't like that. I'm just...letting him come to me on his terms."

"And if he doesn't?" Brooks asked.

"It'll suck," I said bluntly. "But this is my only chance. I convinced him to let me help him renovate the B&B. At the end of it, he'll either decide to stay or..."

"He'll go," Skylar said softly.

"Yeah." I swallowed. "Either way, I'll have my answer."

"You might be setting yourself up to crash and burn," Sawyer said. "You know that, right?"

"I do." I sent him a grin. "But when have you known me to do anything halfway?"

Brooks chuckled ruefully. "Just try not to obliterate yourself in the process, okay? We're here to pick up the pieces, but there's only so much we can do."

Skylar reached out and squeezed my arm. "You're worth loving, Cash. I hope he sees that. If he doesn't, it will be because of him, not you."

My throat grew tight, and I took another gulp of beer to loosen it up. "Thanks, guys." I gave them a suspicious look. "*Was* this a friendervention?"

Ash came over to the table with a platter full of barbecue chicken that instantly made my mouth water. "Did you guys friendervent without me? Not cool."

"It wasn't a friendervention," Fisher said. "There would have been more yelling."

"More denial too," Brooks added. "You're way too self-aware to need one. For better or worse, you know what you're doing."

I gave a sharp nod. "Yeah, I do."

Maybe I was on a foolhardy mission that would only end in heartbreak, but damn it, I was going to see it through.

CHAPTER EIGHTEEN

Declan

"What do you think?"

Cash stood back from the wall we'd just finished painting, stretching one arm over his head, triceps bulging as it flexed. His T-shirt—the Shore Daddy one, which he kept wearing to tease me—came up a few inches, revealing a dark fuzzy trail over a flat stomach.

"Is your shoulder sore again?" I asked.

He lowered his arm and shot me a flirty grin. "That depends. Will it get me another massage with a happy ending?"

I rolled my eyes. "I guess you're fine."

"I am *fine*," Cash agreed. "And so are you."

I turned to the wall, taking in the textured cream paint and knotty pine wainscoting. After sanding down the salvageable sheetrock and replacing two panels, we'd spent the week painting, and it looked pretty great. Along with the pine paneling on the bottom third of the wall, pine window frames and solid beams running across the ceiling, the room was the perfect mix of modern and rustic. The floor still needed work, and the kitchen remained gutted, but I could *see* so much potential.

"It's beautiful." I smiled as I did a turn, taking it all in. "Aunt Millie would have loved it."

"Well, I love that smile you're rocking, Mr. Sullivan."

I *was* smiling, wasn't I? I couldn't stop. After getting this glimpse of what The Roost could be with a little TLC, there was no way I could ever let someone tear it down to manufacture condos.

"Thank you, Cash. For pushing me to do this."

He drew closer, smiling too. That wasn't unusual for Cash. He always brought so much joy to everything he did.

Impulsively, I grabbed his waist and tugged him closer. His eyes widened, but he came into my arms. "You're something special," I murmured into his ear.

"You too, sugar bear."

I drew back, bemused. "Sugar? No one's ever accused me of being sweet."

"Well, then they don't know you very well, do they?"

I didn't have a response to that. I gazed into his eyes and let myself imagine, for the first time, that I could have a partner like Cash, someone who liked to make me smile and called me *sugar bear*.

"Cash." I wet my lips. "Do you think—"

A sharp ring cut through my words.

"Hold that thought," Cash said as he reached into his pocket to pull out his phone. He checked the screen. "It's my sister."

"Go ahead and take it. We're done here, right?"

"With the painting, sure. With us? Maybe not."

Heat rose to my face as he turned and answered the phone. The same old worries tried to surface: What if I was creating expectations I couldn't fulfill? What if I was leading him on?

But then Cash's words began to register and I forgot all about my silly internal angst.

"Why the fuck are you in Swallow Beach?" he exclaimed. "Shit. I'll come for you. Just try to figure out exactly where you are. Get an address from someone and text me, okay?"

His whole body went rigid a beat later. I moved close enough to hear the blast of music and words coming from his cellphone.

"Don't worry, my man, I'll take *real* good care of your girl while she's here."

There was laughter, and a girl's voice shouting in the background.

"Listen, asshole, you lay one finger on her—"

The guy laughed, and there was something nasty about the tone of it.

I snatched the phone from Cash, speaking into it.

"That girl is fifteen years old, so I suggest you give her the phone and keep yourself out of jail, all right? We will be there in fifteen minutes, and if Katelyn isn't perfectly happy when we arrive, the cops will be right behind us."

"Shit, all right, we were just having a little fun."

"Go have fun with someone over eighteen."

"Yes, sir. We don't want any trouble."

The phone was handed off, and Katelyn's voice came back on the line. "Cash?"

"No, this is Declan Sullivan, over at the Treehouse B&B. Hang tight. Your brother and I will come for you right now."

She sniffed. "Oh my god, this is so embarrassing. I'm sorry."

"That's all right, Katelyn. Just be safe. Don't drink anything, all right? Don't go anywhere with anyone. Text Cash the address, and wait for us."

"I will. Thanks."

I handed the phone back to Cash. "Sorry for taking your phone like that."

He surged forward, diverting at the last second to press a firm kiss to my cheek. "Thank you for backing me up."

I cupped his face. "Did you want to kiss me for real?"

"God, yes. Always."

"Then kiss me. You don't have to ask anymore."

Cash's mouth was on mine instantly, his tongue teasing along the seam of my lips. I opened tentatively, half afraid he'd try to maul me, but I should have known that Cash would seduce, not bulldoze. He tugged my bottom lip with his teeth, then gently flicked his tongue along mine. He kissed like some people danced, starting slow and building a tempo, graceful and sensuous.

My hands tightened in his hair, tugging, and he groaned against my mouth. "Fuck, you kiss so good."

"I think that's all you," I murmured against his lips.

"Maybe it's both of us," he said, eyes flicking up to meet mine. "We're good together."

My heart lurched. Now was not the time to consider whether he could be right. Maybe we'd work out, or maybe once the kissing escalated and Cash wanted more than me, we'd implode like all my relationships. Right now, we had more important matters to worry about.

"Come on. We'll take my boat."

By the time we'd untied and boarded the boat, Cash had received the text from his sister. He relayed the address to me, and I tapped it into the GPS. It took us ten minutes to cross the lake. The Lake of the Ozarks was long, but it was relatively skinny, which meant we got to Swallow Beach in good time, but then we had to cruise northeast for a while.

"There!" Cash pointed toward a private dock cluttered with

expensive boats. Light and music poured from the open doors of a huge house. As we approached, I could see a crowd of people on the deck, along with a few smaller clusters on or near the boats.

Two girls on the deck of a mini yacht flashed Cash, lifting their tops and squealing with laughter as we passed. I cut my gaze toward him, but he was too busy scanning the party scene before us to notice the breasts on display.

The relief that hit me was ridiculous. Like Cash hadn't seen all the breasts he could handle already. Like he couldn't *still* get a taste of that anytime he damn well pleased.

I slowed to a crawl and edged past boats worth ten times the amount of mine, squeezing into a space in front of the yacht and a sporty speedboat that cost upwards of half a million dollars.

Cash vibrated with impatience, and I half expected him to leap onto the dock and leave me behind. He was obviously worried about his sister, alternating between checking his phone and scanning the partiers for a sign of her.

"Where is she?" he muttered. "C'mon, c'mon... There. I see her."

"Go," I said.

He hesitated. "Are you sure?"

"Yes, go! It'll be easier if I don't have to tie up."

Cash stepped up onto the edge of the boat and jumped down to the dock, landing with an ease that reminded me he was a hell of a lot younger than me. He skirted past the vapers and broke into a run.

I kept an eye on him, following his path through the crowd. If he ran into any trouble, I'd have to tie up the boat and join him, but I was hoping that wouldn't be the case. Cash reached his sister and turned to talk to a couple waiting with her. I held my breath until he shook the guy's hand and then started back toward the boat with Katelyn in tow.

"Hey, sexy Daddy!" a voice called out.

I glanced up on reflex, and there were the topless girls. One of them was waving her pink bikini top. At me? I glanced around as if there would be some other *sexy Daddy* for them to call out to.

"You here to party?" the other called, her voice flirty.

"Uh...no. Sorry."

"Awww," the first crooned, tossing her bikini top toward me, the white straps fluttering in the breeze before it landed at my feet. "Are you sure we can't change your mind?"

Before I could assure her that there was *nothing* she could offer that would interest me, Cash's voice cut through the night.

"Get your own sexy Daddy," he called. "This one is mine."

The girls—well, young women, as I sincerely hoped they were well over eighteen—squealed with delight. "Ohmigosh, that's so hot!"

Cash ignored them as he helped his sister aboard. I decided to follow his example. "Everyone ready to go?"

"Yep. Unless you want to flirt with those sorority chicks some more?"

I scoffed. "Don't be ridiculous."

He grinned. "They're not wrong. You *are* a sexy Daddy."

"Ew." Katelyn scrunched up her nose. "Can you guys stop flirting? It's weird."

"Kat," Cash scolded. "Declan is doing us a favor by being here. How about you not act like a brat?"

She ducked her head, looking sheepish. "Sorry. I appreciate the ride. It was stupid to come over here."

"Hell yes, it was," Cash said emphatically. "Why would you do something like that?"

Katelyn glanced uneasily in my direction, so I turned my attention to getting us out of dock and out to open water. The

DJ JAMISON

engine noise and wind snatched away a lot of their words, but I heard enough to follow along well enough.

"...broke up with me," Katelynn said. "And Dad said ... what I deserved."

"What the fuck?" Cash exclaimed loud enough I didn't miss a single one of his words. "That asshole. Jesus."

"He's just so..."

I could fill in those blanks easily enough, even though I missed her soft words.

"He sure as fuck is," Cash said, fuming. "When we get back, I'll talk to him, okay? He can't say shit like that. I don't care if he's drunk or hurting, it's not fucking right."

"No, don't," Katelyn said. "You'll just make it worse."

"But—"

"Please, Cash! Just... I don't want to deal with him. I—I don't want to go home. That's why I went to the party. I just needed to get away. I'm sorry."

"Don't apologize," Cash said.

There was a sob and a sniffle, and I glanced back over my shoulder to see him holding her. He caught my eye and grimaced. I turned forward to give them some privacy, pushing the throttle and speeding up as we left the party behind.

My heart ached for them. Cash was in his twenties. He should be out at parties like this having fun, not working his ass off to pay the bills and comforting his sister because their father broke her heart.

I thought back to that night a year ago when I'd found him sleeping on the couch in my B&B. Who comforted Cash? Who fought for him?

The siblings talked in hushed voices I could no longer make out. A few minutes later, Cash dropped into the seat beside me.

"Everything okay?" I asked.

He swiveled the seat toward me, his knees brushing my

thigh. The small contact was reassuring. "Yeah. I really appreciate you helping us out tonight."

"No problem," I said, glancing toward him. "It's the least I can do after all the help you've given me at the B&B."

"That's not the only reason, is it?"

"No, of course not," I said softly. "I wanted to be there for you."

"Good." He smiled. "Katelyn doesn't want to go home, so—"

"Stay at the B&B."

He blinked. "I was going to text Brooks and Skylar about getting a room at the resort."

"Oh. Well, of course, if that's what you want. You're coming back to the B&B in the morning anyway, though, aren't you?"

Cash nodded. "Yeah, I am. Are you sure..."

"I'd be happy for you both to stay," I said. "I've got one room open. Your sister can have it."

"Okay. I guess that means I'm stuck on the couch in your quarters again?"

I hesitated. If he went to the resort, he'd surely get a comfortable bed. I should offer him the same, shouldn't I? It had nothing to do with the fact that I couldn't bear the thought of Cash sleeping on a sofa feet from my bed. Or that I wanted him close all the time.

"Declan?" he asked with a chuckle when I didn't reply. "You okay? If you want me to sleep somewhere else—"

"My bed," I blurted. "You can sleep with me."

His eyes met mine. There was a long beat as I questioned my sanity. Was I really inviting a man into my bed again? Hadn't I learned my lesson yet?

"Okay," Cash said.

"Okay?" I repeated.

"Yeah." He smiled slow and sweet. "I thought you'd never ask." I flushed, but before I could say anything else, he leaned across the aisle and brushed a quick kiss over my lips. "Just sleep. No shenanigans. I promise."

For once, it was a promise I didn't need.

Cash wouldn't push for anything I didn't want to give, and tonight? I wanted to give more than I had in a long damn time.

CHAPTER NINETEEN

Cash

"So, why hasn't Mom called me looking for you?"

Katelyn dropped onto the corner of a full-size bed covered in a white comforter accented with red blossoms. Declan had given her the Dogwood Room for the night before retreating to let us talk alone.

"This bed is nice," Katelyn said, then wrinkled her nose. "The decor is a little weird."

"It's the Dogwood Room." I waved toward the red blossoms on the bed, then the dog-shaped throw pillows. "Get it. Dog...wood?"

She snorted. "You really like him, don't you?"

Okay, so the decor *was* a reach. Aunt Millie had obviously had an odd sense of humor. Declan had told me this room rarely booked up. Along with its odd decor, it was tucked onto the bottom floor with a view of only...yep, you guessed it, a dogwood tree.

"He didn't decorate the room. It was—" I stopped and

waved my hands. "You know what? Don't change the subject. Why isn't Mom looking for you right now?"

Katelyn dropped to her back with a gust of breath. "I told her I was going to Jenna's."

I crossed my arms and towered over her, like an intimidating asshole, but in this case, it was my job as her big brother. "Why didn't you go to Jenna's? The parties in Swallow Beach are no joke."

"I know."

Not good enough. "If you know that, then why are you putting yourself in danger, huh?"

"Benny dumped me, and Dad said I had it coming, and Jenna's been telling me to give up on him, and I didn't want to hear one more person tell me I deserved what I got, okay?"

Tears sprang to her eyes, and I dropped down onto the bed beside her. The time for towering intimidation was over. "Hey, I'm not ever going to say that to you."

She sniffed. "I know, but I just hate life right now. I wanted to escape."

I knew that feeling. A little too well.

"I get it, Kat, but I've been down that road. It doesn't take you anywhere good."

"I'm not anywhere good now," she muttered.

"Then we need to change that."

She looked dubious. "I don't see how we can."

"Well, for starters, I should always be your first call. If you need an escape, I'll get you a safe one, okay?"

"Even if you're working?"

"You know you can always come to the resort. Skylar is cool. And if I'm here, come over and help. We could use some cheap labor."

She giggled. "Declan won't mind?"

"I'll check with him, but no, I don't think he will. He's a good guy."

"So, what's going on? Is he your boyfriend?"

I stood up. "And I believe the sibling pep talk is complete. I'll see you in the morning, okay?"

She smirked. "Right after you wake up in Declan's bed, right?"

"Shut it. That's none of my baby sister's business."

I crossed the living area and dining room to reach the entrance to Declan's living quarters. I hesitated, wondering if I should knock, but he knew I was coming.

I opened the door and entered, but I didn't see him. The faint sound of a shower came from the bathroom.

I went over and tapped the door. "Declan? Just wanted to let you know I'm back so you don't come out of there naked." I paused. "Unless you want to." I winced. My flirty tongue always got me in trouble. "Kidding! I'm just kidding."

"Cash? Come in. I can't hear you."

He wanted me to come in? Okay, no big deal. It didn't mean anything sexual would happen. I needed to play this cool and show him I wasn't always a horn dog.

I eased the door open. "Hey, man, I just wanted to tell you I was back, and..." I trailed off as my brain processed what I was seeing. Declan had tugged back the shower curtain and damn, the view was distracting.

He'd slicked his dark hair back from his face, making his cheekbones and the cut of his jaw look sharper. Water trickled over his shoulders and down to his chest, where a light covering of dark hair trailed between his pecs and down to—

I jerked my gaze back up before I got busted for staring at the man's cock. That was an invite-only kind of show.

"Do you want to shower with me?" Declan asked.

My heart skipped. "Really?"

"It's been a long day. I don't want to make you wait."

Well, that was true. Exhaustion and achiness tugged at me after hours of painting. I'd been burning the candle at both ends, getting up early and working late—and often cuddling later—with Declan.

"Okay, sure." I stepped into the bathroom and closed the door behind me. Declan let the shower curtain fall shut, and I stripped down. My cock was already trying to thicken. I glared down at it and mentally ordered it to behave.

When I pulled aside the curtain to step in behind Declan, I got a view of his shoulders and back flexing as he ran his hands through his hair, rinsing it of shampoo. The suds ran down the small of his back and onto a perfect peach-shaped ass.

I bit my lip and closed my eyes, willing the rush of lust away.

"Here, step under the spray. I'll wash your back for you."

Well, okay then. Apparently, this was going to be a full-service type of shower. I opened my eyes enough to shuffle past Declan, our wet skin gliding and sending sparks of want crackling through my body.

He gently guided me to face the front, then used the removable shower head to wet my hair thoroughly before applying shampoo. His fingers worked through my hair, scrubbing but also massaging, and I sighed as some of the day's tension washed away.

"There you go," he murmured softly. "Go ahead and lean back against me. I got you."

I sagged, his firm chest supporting me, and closed my eyes, luxuriating in the pampering.

"I don't know what I did to deserve this, but it's really nice."

Declan worked a sponge over my shoulders and chest,

scrubbing me clean. It should have seemed perfunctory, but his hands were on my body, and my body really liked that.

He stepped back to rinse me down, sliding his hands over my skin until he reached my ass.

I sucked in a breath and almost choked on shower water, suddenly aware my cock had *not* behaved and was rigid and waving like a flag trying to get Declan's attention.

"Maybe don't touch me there."

Declan removed his hands. "What's wrong?"

"Nothing. I just..." I waved at my dick. "My body gets its own ideas, and if you keep touching my ass like that—" I cut myself short. "It doesn't mean anything, okay?"

"Cash, it's all right if it means something," Declan said. "I'd be a little insulted if it didn't."

I glanced back over my shoulder, meeting his eyes. "I don't understand..."

Declan kissed me, his lips wet and slippery. I moaned as all the lust I'd been trying to fight back swamped me.

He guided my hand to my dick, and I wrapped my fingers around the shaft, stroking. "Keep doing that," he said. "I need to finish washing you."

I flushed with heat, a mix of lust and shame at the thought of jerking off for Declan while he seemed unaffected. But then he shifted behind me, and I felt his hard dick brush the back of my thigh.

"Are you...?"

"Yes," he murmured. "I'm with you."

"I want to touch you."

"Not yet." Declan turned me and began the torturous process of washing my chest and stomach. When he went to his knees to wash my legs, I about expired from the sight of him in front of me.

"Declan." My voice was full of pleading, and I winced. I was supposed to be going at his speed, not mine.

"I've got you, sweetheart."

He pushed my hand away and wrapped his long fingers around my shaft. His hand was soapy, making for a natural lube as he stroked me. My head fell back as I lost the fight with my body and began rocking my hips, thrusting harder into his hand.

When Declan pulled away to rinse me of soap, I almost cried. I was on the precipice of orgasm, and the freaking man was edging me. Of all the things I'd expected of a relationship with someone who was ace, it wasn't that he'd turn me into a quivering, needy mess begging for relief.

"Please, please please. Declan, oh my god, I need to come."

He chuckled. "You're not the only one."

My eyes flew open, and I glanced down at his hard dick between his legs. My hole fluttered suddenly as the idea hit me that maybe he'd want to fuck me. "Let me touch you, then. Do you want my mouth? My ass? You can have anything you want."

He looked at me steadily. "And what do you want, Cash?"

"I just want to please you."

His eyes softened. "You do, sweetheart. All the time."

I trembled, my body craving orgasm while the rest of my being wanted this moment to last forever. "I want to make you come."

Declan rose to his feet. "All right, then, how do you want to do it?"

My mouth watered. "Can I, uh, suck you?"

He pressed my shoulder, and I'd never been so happy to drop to my knees. His cock was thick enough I could imagine the burn of him sliding into me. Could that ever happen? Maybe. I sure as hell never expected to be here with him. I would have gladly taken only kisses and cuddles if that's all Declan wanted.

I looked up the length of his body. "Do you want this? Because I only ever want to give you what you want, Dec."

He smoothed back the hair from my forehead. "I believe you, sweetheart. And yes, right now, right here? I want this as badly as you do."

That's what I needed to hear. I lunged forward, taking Declan's cock into my mouth and drank in the sound of his choked groan above me. I used my lips and tongue and fingers to make it the best damn blow job I'd ever given.

I was beginning to understand that Declan wasn't celibate. He'd want sex sometimes. This wasn't my *only* chance to please him. But if we weren't going to have quantity, then I wanted to give him quality. So much damn quality that no one else would ever compare.

"Jesus, Cash," Declan murmured above me. "You're too..."

I drew back. "Too greedy?"

"No." He chuckled. "Too good. Don't stop."

He put a hand on my head and pushed my face toward his dick, and that was so damn hot I just about came hands-free. I sucked him back in, taking him deeper, working him over until he uttered a warning and pushed on my shoulder. I eased back enough to see him shoot onto my chest, his cum streaking across my skin and then sluicing away with the hot water.

Declan grabbed my arm and helped me stand on shaky legs. "Your turn."

He grasped my dick, reminding me I was still hard and wanting. I'd gotten so lost in pleasuring him that I'd damn near forgotten how desperate I was, but the need came rushing back now.

I whimpered, lightheaded as my cock throbbed in his hand.

Declan leaned in, kissing me, and with nothing more than a hard press of lips and a single stroke to my dick, I came so hard I nearly passed out.

We got out of the shower, and Declan dried me off with a fuzzy terrycloth towel. Somewhere in my hazy mind I registered that this was different. I didn't normally float away because of an orgasm or let my partner take care of me the way Declan had tonight.

But everything was different with him, so why not this too?

He led me to the bed, and I climbed between the sheets. He joined me, warm, bare skin pressing up against my back as he wrapped his arms around me.

"Is your sister okay?" he asked.

"I have a sister?"

He chuckled, his breath tickling my neck. "You know damn well you do."

I smiled into my pillow. "You blew my mind tonight. The brain is not firing on all cylinders. But yeah, Kat's okay."

He squeezed me. "It was really good for me, too."

"Just good?"

"Amazing," he said. "Truthfully, probably the best experience I've ever had."

I glanced back over my shoulder. "Really?"

He pressed his lips to my shoulder. "Yeah. You don't push for sex. You wait for me to show interest. That makes all the difference. With my exes..." He trailed off.

I rolled over to face him. "Tell me?"

He sighed. "Well, they just got impatient. They had needs, and I don't fault them for that. I couldn't meet them." He shrugged a shoulder. "I hated feeling like I couldn't satisfy them, so I'd try to go through the motions..."

"I don't ever want you to do that." I cupped his face. "If I were lucky enough to be your boyfriend, I wouldn't care about how often we had sex. As long as we both want it when it happens."

"You have needs too though. Just like they did."

"And sex is just one expression of that need," I said. "This? Talking to you in the dark, that's intimacy too. Cuddling on the couch, holding you, hell, just getting one of those rare smiles? They're all expressions of"—I caught myself about to say the *L* word and diverted to an acceptable synonym—"affection."

Declan closed the gap between us, kissing me softly. "I love the way you think. I don't know if you'll feel the same when you've got blue balls, but I appreciate the sentiment."

"Well, I already went without sex for eight months while I was waiting for you to come around, so..."

Declan's eyes widened. "You did what?"

"I mean, that was before I knew you were leaving."

"Oh."

My whole body heated with what I was pretty sure was a blush. No one had made me blush since I was about fifteen years old, but here I was, burning up over this obsessive crush I'd been unable to shake.

I looked down, unable to meet his eyes. "Not that I regret it," I said softly. "Even if this is all I get, it was worth it."

"Ah, Cash..." He put a finger under my chin and lifted it so he could meet my eyes. "I have a lot to figure out. I can't make any promises."

"I know." I smiled sadly. "I went into this with my eyes wide open."

"But my eyes were closed," he said. "Or maybe my mind was. I didn't expect this. Any of it."

I brushed a kiss over his lips. "I'm stealthy like that."

He chuckled. "Trust me, nothing about you is stealthy." His eyes sparkled. "But I wouldn't want you any other way."

My chest warmed. "Ditto, sugar."

He rolled his eyes. "Again with the sugar."

"Again with the sweetness," I teased back.

He smiled at me, one of those special smiles that I'd told him were just as good as sex—and it must be true, because damn, it hit me right in the solar plexus.

He closed his eyes, tugging me closer and curling us into a comfortable position. "Sleep," he murmured softly.

And like all the other orders Declan had murmured into my ear, I obeyed.

CHAPTER TWENTY

Declan

THE FIRST THING I NOTICED WHEN I WOKE WAS THE warmth along my front. Then the tickle of hair against my nose.

A sigh...that wasn't mine.

My heart stuttered. A *man* was in my bed.

That hadn't happened in six years.

I opened my eyes to confirm what I already knew. Yep. There Cash was, his back to me, his body curled up, and my body spooned right around his, my arms holding him tight, as if I didn't want to allow even an inch of space between us.

I buried my nose in the hair at the nape of his neck and breathed in, my eyes stinging. I'd picked the worst possible time to invite a man into my bed, but here we were. I wouldn't take it back. But I also didn't know how to make our timing any better.

Cash stirred in my arms. "Time to get up?"

I pressed a kiss behind his ear. "Not yet."

He turned in my arms and nuzzled into my neck. He stroked a hand down my side to cup my ass. "So, what are your plans for the day?"

There was an unasked question in his body language, one that said he'd be up for more sex, but I wasn't in the right head-space. I kissed the tip of his nose. "I've got to head out to the garden, then pick up some breakfast for the guests."

"Okay."

"But Cash, last night..."

"I hope you don't regret it."

"No. I could never do that." I cupped his face and brushed a soft kiss to his lips, keeping it brief. "I'm glad you're here this morning. I haven't woken like this...in a long time."

"I haven't either."

I raised an eyebrow, skeptical, but he shrugged a shoulder. "It's all relative, right? Even when I was sleeping around more, I was waking up with a stranger. This isn't the same, Declan. You know that, right?"

"Yeah, I know." I ran a hand through his hair, reveling in the touch that I'd been missing for so long. Even with my last partners, I'd started avoiding too much affection in case it led to sexual overtures. But Cash never pushed, always waited for me to lead the way.

Maybe things really could be different with him. But only if I found a way to stay.

"Sleep some more if you want. It's still early."

"Maybe," he murmured, his eyes already slipping closed.

I watched him for a moment, still reeling to have a man in my bed. I shouldn't want him there, all tousled and naked in my personal space, and yet, I did.

I went out to the garden to harvest some strawberries, then stopped in to grab my keys to head to town. Cash was awake and dressed in his work clothes from the night before.

"Hey, I'm going to grab Kat and get out of your hair. Thanks for letting us stay last night."

"Anytime," I said, and meant it.

He came to the doorway, his feet bare, and kissed me. "Good," he murmured. "Because I hope to stay over again some-time, if you...want that?"

I should tell him no. I didn't yet know what my future held, and the more we did this, the more danger there was that I'd hurt him.

"Anytime," I said again—and meant it.

Damn, I was in too deep already, wasn't I? The way his eyes lit up, I suspected he was too. We were in this together, good or bad.

Pearl was eagerly waiting for me when I got to her table at the Outdoor Market.

"Well, it's about time you brought me some of those famous strawberries!" she exclaimed, making grabby hands as she watched me approach with a box of the freshly harvested fruit.

"I think you mean *us*," Ruth Marie said, crossing the path to join us at the table covered in Pearl Pantry jams. Peach, black-berry, traffic jam—a mix of multiple flavors—and her Ozark specialty, tomato jam, were on display.

Meanwhile, Ruth Marie's table held jars of brandied peaches, pears, cherries, and other fruit mixes. The two were notoriously competitive vendors.

"You don't even need strawberries," Pearl said dismissively.

Ruth Marie squawked, "And what do you think folks use for their strawberry shortcake?"

"Store-bought topping, most likely."

Ruth Marie drew in a sharp breath, and I cut in before this turned into a repeat of the food fight incident at the last Dock Hop food festival.

"There's enough for you both." I chuckled. "I've got more strawberries I can harvest if you think you'll use them."

Pearl instantly turned her attention to me. "Aren't you just

187

the sweetest man? People say you're a grouch, but they don't see how you put your love into the ground."

"Er, thanks?"

"Are you growing more tomatoes this year? They were so delicious! Really made my tomato jam shine."

"Ah, well, I don't know," I hedged.

Once I sold the B&B, I'd be working as a financial analyst again. I didn't know if I'd have space to garden, much less time to do it. And, of course, I'd be nowhere near Swallow Cove.

My stomach turned over uncomfortably.

"Your fruits and veggies are always such a treat," Ruth Marie said. "I imagine you could sell them here at the market if you wanted."

"I wouldn't want to take business from Burt."

Pearl waved a hand. "Oh, he can hardly get the produce out here anymore. He sells at a road stand closer to the farm."

"Oh, well..." I trailed off. "I hardly grow enough for all that."

"I guess not," Ruth Marie said. "You'd need a greenhouse and a lot of time. I don't blame you for not wanting to take that on alongside the B&B."

"Right," I said, guilt prickling at me.

I hadn't told the ladies I was selling the B&B and leaving town—and for some reason, I didn't want to say the words.

Hudson strolled up, a cardboard box bearing the Hot Buns logo of the new bakery.

"Hey, grabbing some breakfast?" I asked.

"Picked up some goodies for Fisher," he said. "We were in a rush this morning. Didn't get a chance to eat anything."

Pearl chuckled. "You two have been rushed a lot of mornings lately, Hudson Nash. I wonder *what* could be keeping you so very busy?"

"Pearl, don't be rude!" Ruth Marie chastised. "You're embarrassing the man!"

Hudson was turning red, but it wasn't until Pearl said, "I'm not criticizing. Love is love!" that I realized what she'd been teasing him about.

He and Fisher weren't just running late. They were running late because of morning sex.

You could have been late this morning too, if you were wired that way...

An uncomfortable sense of *other* hit me, that feeling that I wasn't made right. Cash had been in my bed, warm and affectionate, and I'd just gotten up and left.

My stomach tightened, but my memory kept going.

Right to the moment he murmured in a low, sweet voice that he wanted to spend the night with me again, if I wanted it too.

Some of my tension released. I hadn't disappointed Cash. He wanted to spend more time with me. And, really, I had bigger fish to fry than whether I'd ever let Cash make me late with morning sex.

I had to figure out what the hell I was going to do with the B&B, Nathan's development deal, the job offer in Chicago, and my desire to explore this thing with Cash.

"You okay?" Hudson asked.

Everyone's eyes were on me. I cleared my throat. "Yeah, fine. I should get going. I've got to pick up breakfast and get it back to the B&B."

"I'll walk with you," Hudson said.

"Okay." I patted the box of strawberries. "I trust you two can divide this up without any brawls?"

Pearl tittered. "As if we'd ever do that."

Hudson smirked at the lie, but it was good enough for me. I turned from the table, hurrying my step. "Quick, before they start arguing and we have to intervene."

Hudson chuckled but lengthened his stride to match mine. "So, what's going on with you today?"

"Nothing."

"Didn't seem like nothing. You were pretty distracted back there. Something bothering you?"

I hesitated. "Um. I, sort of..."

I mumbled the rest quickly, my words barely intelligible.

"You what? Talk slower and enunciate."

I heaved a sigh. "I slept with Cash."

A grin spread across his face. "Well, hot damn, this is great news."

"Is it?" I grimaced. "I don't do this kind of thing, Hud, and especially not when I'm supposed to be leaving town."

His smile faded. "Ah, well, the timing is tricky."

"The timing is *horrible*."

He studied me for a minute. "Do you think that's why you did it?"

My brows drew together. "Why would..."

"Maybe it enabled you to let down that iron-clad guard of yours. Obviously, you like Cash." He hesitated. "Right?"

"Of course I do!" I lowered my voice as we passed Margie Owens. She'd shamelessly tell half the town my business if she heard a peep of this. "I more than like him, Hudson. He's really great. I kind of feel stupid for pushing him away for so long, but I haven't had the best luck in that department."

"I can relate." His smile went sappy. "It took me too long to pull my head out of my ass with Fisher. Don't be like me."

I snorted. "You were hopeless even in denial."

"Thanks." He motioned to me. "Pot." Then to himself. "Kettle."

I pulled a face. "Okay, but my situation is complicated. With relationships, I mean. I'm...well, I'm kind of ace, I guess."

Hudson nodded. "I thought so."

I drew back in surprise. "Why?"

"Eh, little things. You didn't always pick up on flirtation.

You didn't seem to know Cash was crashing your B&B to get *your* attention."

"No. What?" I thought back to those days over a year ago when he'd regularly hooked up. "No, that's ridiculous."

"I don't think he even understood what he was doing, but yeah. The friends talk, and Fisher tells me Cash has crushed on you for ages. I don't think you're just a casual interest for him, Declan. He cares about you."

That tracked with what Cash had told me last night about giving up hookups while he waited for me to see the possibility between us.

I raked a hand through my hair. "Why couldn't I have figured that out before I was leaving town?"

Hudson paused at the end of the Outdoor Market. He would need to turn left to go to the bait shop where Fisher worked, and I'd need to head right to pick up my order at Hot Buns. "Maybe you don't have to leave?"

I shook my head. "The B&B isn't for me."

"So sell it. You can find other work here."

"The financial analyst industry is just booming in Swallow Cove," I said dryly.

"Are you really telling me you couldn't work remotely? Maybe fly in for the occasional meeting?"

"Well..."

"If you really care about Cash, you can figure something out."

"We're not even dating properly yet. Is it smart to plan my future around a possibility?"

"I think you should plan your future around your happiness, Declan. What will make you happier? A job in the city or a life here with a chance at love?"

Well, when he put it that way, it didn't seem like a difficult choice.

But I still had to deal with Nathan's reaction. I'd be pulling the plug on the development deal he found me *and* asking to change the terms of the job offer, too.

He'd gone out on a limb for me, and I hated to disappoint him. He was my only friend from the city. But the friendship I had with Cash—the *more* than friendship we were developing—was worth seeing through.

CHAPTER TWENTY-ONE

Cash

I knocked on the door of the Dogwood Room until I heard a muffled, "Go away!"

I let myself in and perched on the side of my sister's bed, ruffling her hair and making her duck farther under the blankets.

"Come on, sleepyhead. We should get home so we can talk to Mom about your adventure."

She peeked out of the covers. "Do we have to tell her?"

I nodded. "We do."

"She'll be mad I lied."

"Maybe, but she'll understand. You don't want to lie and keep secrets, okay? That'll only make everything worse."

"Can it even get worse?" she grumbled.

"Pretty sure it can." I yanked back the covers, making her squeal a protest. "Come on. Gray is letting me borrow his pickup. I'll bribe you with a hot chocolate if you hurry."

Katelyn grimaced. "You're not gonna ditch me alone with Dad, are you?"

"Nah. You can come to work with me at the resort later. Hit the pool."

She brightened a little. "Okay."

"But you have to be straight with Mom and deal with the consequences."

She groaned and flounced back on the bed.

"Ten minutes," I said as I slipped out to wait for her.

Fifteen minutes later, she dragged her butt out of the room and we walked over to The Roost to climb into Gray's rusted-out truck. He'd gotten started installing the kitchen cabinetry without me. I'd told him he could wait, but he'd waved off the offer and told me to deal with my business.

If only it were that easy...

The engine sputtered and coughed when I started the truck, and the route out was as bumpy as the one in the other day. Katelynn grabbed the oh-shit bar above the window and glared at me. "Do you have to drive like an idiot?"

"Would you rather walk?" I asked sweetly.

She wisely kept her trap shut.

I found a parking space in front of Just The Sip and left her sulking in the truck to go order our drinks.

I was surprised to see Danny slumped over the front counter, chin in his hand, looking more glum than I'd ever seen him.

"Hey, I need a DP Cream and a hot chocolate for my little sis."

"Okay."

Danny didn't make a single flirty comment about my drink order—or call me out for avoiding the menu name *Hot Cock-a-Lot* when ordering for my sister.

The drink names were fun and all, but I had to draw the line somewhere.

"Anything else?" Danny asked as he turned to start making the first drink.

"Yeah. I'd like to know what alien race you are."

He blinked. "Huh?"

"Obviously, you body snatched my barista, Danny. He's cute and flirty. Always has a smile and a wink for his customers."

He pumped syrup into the cardboard coffee cup. "Sorry, guess I'm not myself today."

I hesitated. "You okay?"

He smiled wanly. "Yeah, just a bruised ego. I'll recover."

"Good, because not to make this all about me or anything, but I've got a tough conversation coming up at home, and I came here because you're cute and flirty and always have a smile for me."

Danny huffed a small laugh, which was the goal. "As long as it's not all about you."

"I'm selfless like that," I said with a grin.

"Well, anytime you want to help me make Abe jealous, say the word," he said as he moved through the motions of making my drinks on autopilot. "Maybe we can work a little magic on Declan at the same time."

"Oh. Uh..."

Danny's eyes widened, and he paused in the act of spraying whipped cream on top of the hot chocolate. "Shut up. You and Declan?"

"Shh, no. I didn't say that."

"You didn't have to." Danny waggled his brows, getting a bit of his spunk back. "Guess I'll have to pine away on my own."

He finished the second drink and set it on the counter. I gave him my card to swipe. He ran the tab and handed it back. "Receipt?"

"Nope."

"Tip?"

"Yeah." I tapped in fifteen percent, then he finished the transaction.

"Always just the tip for the sad little barista," he joked, though it was missing a bit of his usual pizzazz.

I hesitated. "Maybe I don't need to make Declan jealous, but if you need help winning over Abe, let me know if I can do anything."

His eyes brightened. "Really?"

I was almost sure I was going to regret offering by the spark in his eye. "Yeah. But nothing illegal and no sex."

He lifted his hands. "I would never do Declan that way."

I rolled my eyes. "And keep your big mouth shut about that, too."

"Oh honey, you love my big mouth, but don't you worry, I know how to swallow a secret."

Reassured that Danny was his usual ridiculous self, I took my drinks and headed out to the truck.

I handed Katelyn hers. "Here, this counts as your birthday present."

She scowled. "Please, it's a bribe to get me home and you know it."

"You're wise beyond your years."

I put the truck in Drive and headed inland, curving around the backside of the park and pulling up to our little house on a block of modest two-bedroom bungalows.

Katelyn drank down her bribe, slurping the last dregs of it by the time I got to our empty driveway.

Shit. Mom's car wasn't there.

I checked the time. There was a half hour until she should have left for work. Unless...her schedule changed again and I didn't know it because I hadn't been home to check for updates.

Great. She was usually our buffer when Dad was in one of his moods. We'd have to hope he was still sleeping.

"Come on, let's go change and get cleaned up before my shift at the resort. Looks like you won't have to tell Mom just yet."

We climbed out of the truck, and I opened the door quietly, hoping we could sneak in and do what we needed without waking Dad.

"And just where the fuck have you two been?"

I froze in the doorway while Dad glowered from the recliner, a beer in his hand.

He was up, which meant it was one of his better days. That also meant it'd be one of our *worse* ones.

On Dad's bad days, he lay on the sofa and slept a lot. But on his good days? He sat in the recliner and he spouted every toxic feeling inside him onto us.

"We're fine, thanks for asking," I said.

His eyes narrowed. Dad never had liked my backtalk. Admittedly, I was a little punk when I was younger.

"Don't be a smartass and answer the question."

"I spent the night with Jenna," Kat said. "I told Mom."

"Jenna called over here," Dad said. "So you're just a fucking liar, aren't you? Just because you're crying over some goddamn boy doesn't mean you get to run out and act like a little whore."

"Hey!" I cut in. "Don't call her that."

"You shut up," he bellowed. "It was bad enough when you ran crazy, but at least you weren't gonna come home pregnant."

"I'm sorry," Katelyn said in a tiny voice, sounding on the verge of tears. "I was just upset about Benny and—"

"I don't want to hear your excuses," he growled.

"I kept Kat safe, okay? Nothing bad happened, so let's all just stay calm."

"Oh, you're giving me parenting advice now?" Dad said derisively.

"Seems like you need it."

"Watch your mouth," Dad snarled. "I'm the goddamned man of the house here."

My mouth was really on a roll because a jagged laugh spilled out. "You're a man? Please. You don't even know the meaning of the word."

"What did you say to me?"

"A *man* wouldn't make his daughter feel like crap about her breakup," He started blustering, and I steamrolled on. "A man would take care of his family, not make them all miserable. A *man* would stop being a goddamn drunk and—"

"Get the fuck out of my house," he bellowed. "You think you can stand under my roof and talk shit to me? Go do it on the streets. Go find some whore and spend the night with her. Isn't that what you usually do?"

"Stop it!" Katelyn cried. "Please—"

"You're a sorry excuse for a man," I said. "And I like men too. I've told you a hundred times! I'm bi."

"Who cares where you stick your dick?" he shouted. "You're setting a terrible example for your sister!"

"Maybe I'm not the best example." A sense of surreal calmness came over me. "But it doesn't take much to do a better job than you, does it?"

Dad lurched forward as if to reach for me, then stopped short, face reddening, then twisting with pain.

Katelyn choked on a sob. "I hate it here!"

She ran from the room. Shit. I probably owed her an apology for escalating the situation. I was never very good at putting up with Dad's shit, which was exactly why I'd spent so many nights out with random hookups.

"Goddamn fucking ungrateful bitch of a whore kids," Dad muttered as he fell back into his chair with a pained groan.

"Real nice, Dad," I said caustically.

I left him swearing and followed Kat to her room, where she was screaming into a pillow. She tossed it down when she saw me.

"I'm sorry, Kat. I didn't handle that well."

"I can't stand this anymore, Cash! I'd rather *die* than live like this one more day."

She was fifteen. She was dramatic. I knew she wasn't really suicidal, but the pain in her eyes? That was real. I knew because it was my pain, too. Dad had only gotten worse in the past couple of years. There was no light at the end of this tunnel.

I had an escape route anytime I wanted it. I'd chosen to stay for Mom and Kat. But my sister was trapped for at least three more years, and it wasn't fair. And maybe I couldn't fix that for her, but I could do something right now.

"Pack a bag," I said. "We're getting out of here."

Her eyes widened. "And going *where*?"

"I'll figure something out."

I pulled out my phone and texted Declan, Skylar, and Sawyer. One of them would have a place for us. I hated to ask them, but I knew they'd come through.

I went to my room and threw shorts and tees into a duffel, then added my shampoo, body wash, razor, and shaving cream. By the time I finished packing, I had three replies.

Skylar:

We can book you rooms if you need them. Just let me know what you want to do.

Sawyer:

Ash just moved out of the houseboat, but I'm sure Hudson would let you stay there, man. I'm

sorry things are so shitty at home right now. Hang in there.

Declan:

Come back to the B&B. Both of you. Stay as long as you want.

I paused over the messages, but I already knew which offer I wanted to take. I clicked into Declan's text stream.

Cash:

Does this mean I'm sleeping in your bed again?

Declan:

As long as it's where you want to be, you're welcome. There's another room opening up if you'd rather have your own space.

I'd never typed so quickly.

Cash:

Your bed is the only place I want to be, but I've got other offers.

Declan:

Don't you dare take them. Come back to me.

Despite everything, I smiled. I didn't know where this thing with Declan was going—or where it even *could* go. But he wanted me with him, and that made this situation just a little easier to take.

I returned to Katelyn's room to find her working on her third bag. "Come on. That's enough. We're not moving out forever."

"I wish we were," she muttered, but she zipped her bag closed, and I picked up two of them to carry along with mine. Katelyn shouldered the remaining bag, staggering under its weight.

"What did you pack in there? Barbells?"

"Books," she said.

I rolled my eyes, but my sister was a total bookworm, so I

knew better than to talk her out of lugging half her library along with her. We headed down the hall.

"Just don't engage if he tries to talk to us," I said. "Just go out the door."

She cast an anxious glance at me. "Is this going to make everything worse?"

"Can it even get much worse?" I asked, echoing her words from this morning.

"I don't know."

I nudged her with my shoulder. "We'll talk to Mom. We'll figure out a way to make things better. But right now, we just need to leave and let everyone cool down a little. Get some space so you're not feeling so trapped. Okay?"

"Yeah." She swallowed hard. "I know this is my fault. I'm the one who lied about where I was going last night. Dad was mad at me, not you, and—"

"Kat." I shook my head. "Dad is always mad. At you or me or Mom. Doesn't really matter what we do or don't do. He's angry at the world. He's bitter and miserable, and you can't take the blame for that, okay?"

She sniffed and dashed away a tear that leaked from the corner of her eye. "Yeah, you're right."

"Then let's go."

I led the way into the living room. Dad did a double take when he saw us. "Just where the fuck do you think you're going?"

"Just keep walking," I muttered to Kat.

We continued toward the door.

"Hey! Stop. I'm talking to you. You fucking bastards—"

I slammed the door on his tirade, silencing his toxic words and leaving them behind.

At least for a few days.

"So, what now?" Kat asked. "Where are we going?"

"Back to the B&B. Declan said we can stay for a while."

"What about Mom?" she asked hesitantly.

"I'll let her know what's happening. We'll talk to her soon, okay?"

"Okay."

We threw our bags into the back of the truck and I climbed behind the steering wheel. I took a minute to look at our house.

Then I flipped it the bird and peeled out.

Katelyn burst into surprised laughter, and I relaxed for the first time since we'd arrived.

Finally, we could both breathe easy—if only for a few days.

CHAPTER TWENTY-TWO

Declan

"It's looking pretty good, don't you think?"

I stood in The Roost, taking in the cabin's transformation. Gray had been hard at work in the kitchen, and it now had knotty pine cabinets and a gorgeous white quartz countertop with bronze swirls that tied all the colors together in a blend of rustic and modern design.

The biggest renovation project was coming together nicely. Better than I could have imagined.

I had Cash to thank for that. Without him, I wouldn't have even tried.

But instead of focusing on the newest improvements, all I could do was stare at my phone and the texts I'd just exchanged with Cash.

Cash:

Your bed is the only place I want to be, but I've got other offers.

Declan:

Don't you dare take them. Come back to me.

My stomach somersaulted. I was glad I could be there when Cash needed a soft place to land. Damn glad. But I couldn't stop wondering...

If I left Swallow Cove, who would Cash go to when he needed support? Would he crash with a friend or find someone to comfort him another way? A more...intimate one.

I hated the thoughts running through my head. Jealous, possessive thoughts.

He belongs with me.

He's mine to comfort.

No one else should have him.

I barely recognized myself, but there was no doubting that I'd grown attached to Cash right when I should have been cutting ties with my life here.

"Declan?" Gray prompted. "Everything okay?"

I lowered my phone, refocusing on the kitchen taking shape before my eyes. "It's looking really great."

Gray grinned. "This place has so much potential. I'm glad Cash called me in on this. It's been really fun to be part of its transformation."

He glanced around, almost as if he was seeing it again for the first time. "It reminds me of my home growing up. The old man always had some sort of maintenance project going." He chuckled. "And he was always dragging me into it."

"I guess we have him to thank for your skills then?"

"Yeah." His smile faded. "I guess that's one thing he did for me."

There seemed to be a story there, but I didn't know Gray well enough to push. But if Cash was anything to go by, family dynamics could be complicated. I was lucky to have had a stable upbringing with parents who'd loved me enough to let me live with my aunt when the bullying at my high school had gotten tough.

They'd only ever wanted what was best for me, and I still saw them every holiday. My sister saw them even more often. They'd moved to St. Louis a couple of years ago to be closer to their grandkids.

Returning to Chicago would not only take me from Swallow Cove, but farther from my family as well. Why hadn't I considered that before?

Gray cleared his throat. "We should be ready to move on to tile tomorrow, then refinishing the floors a couple of days after that."

He continued talking through the rest of the plans for The Roost. I nodded along, but my mind was a thousand miles away.

Well, closer to four hundred miles away, give or take. It was past time I talked to Nathan and officially pulled the plug on the development deal he'd helped broker.

"...and once we reinforce the stairs to the deck—"

"Sorry, Gray," I cut in, wincing at my own rudeness. "It all sounds great. Really. I trust you. I've just got a phone call I need to make."

Best to do it now before I lost my nerve. Nathan was bound to be annoyed by my wishy-washiness on this whole deal. I couldn't really blame him, either. I'd dragged my feet, and now I was backing out.

But looking at the gorgeous remodel under way, I couldn't regret my choice. Aunt Millie had a beautiful vision, and thanks to Cash's optimism—and Gray's know-how—I would get to bring it to life for someone who could fully appreciate it.

Thankfully, Gray wasn't put off by my interruption. "Go ahead. I've got plenty to do until my afternoon boat tour."

I hurried down the hill, eyeing the edging as I did. I might be stressed, but no weeds were getting in on my watch.

While I crossed the garden, I pulled up Nathan's contact.

He answered on the first ring, which wasn't surprising. The man lived with a Bluetooth headset on.

"Declan, about time you got back to me."

I winced. I'd dodged a couple of calls, but I was done stalling.

"Hey, Nate, sorry," I puffed out between heavy breaths. I guess I'd walked a little too quickly across the stretch of land separating The Roost and the B&B.

"Are you okay?"

"Yeah, yeah. Just walking while I talk." I pulled open the back door and stepped into my kitchen. "I've been really busy with some renovations at the B&B."

"Renovations? But why would— Oh, no." Nathan was a quick guy. He put it together instantly. "No, man. Tell me you're not backing out of this deal!"

"I'm sorry," I repeated.

"Declan! I went out on a limb for you with this. These guys are pros, and they don't dick around. They're going to be fucking pissed."

"I didn't ask you to do that," I said tightly. "It was your idea in the first place."

"Which you agreed to," Nathan said, voice gaining an edge. "You said yes."

"But I didn't sign anything—"

"Goddamn it, Declan. I'm trying to be a good friend here, but you're making it really hard. I thought you wanted to leave that B&B crap behind and come work for me."

"Just a minute." I filled a glass with water and took a long gulp. It cooled me down a little and calmed my nerves. "I do still want to work for you. That hasn't changed."

He exhaled. "Okay, then, what's the hangup? Is it the terms of the deal? We can negotiate."

"No, I, uh...I'm going to sell to someone who will run the B&B. I want to keep my Aunt Millie's memory alive."

The view from the window over the sink was stunning. Lush green grass, crimson rambler roses, purple petunias, and cheery little hibiscus blossoms dotted the gardens, leading into the strawberry patch, the herb and vegetable garden, and the wild blackberries that had cropped up.

It was all too easy to picture the greenhouse Aunt Millie had wanted on the grounds between the main house and The Roost, with the waters of the lake sparkling under a bright sun just beyond.

A sense of peace descended. Keeping this place alive—realizing its full potential—was the right choice.

"I can't believe you," Nathan said, voice dripping with disgust. "This is primo lakefront property. How do you know anyone you sell to won't do the same as these guys? At least they're being upfront with you."

That was a good question. One I'd have to sort out.

"I'll find the right buyer. It'll have to be someone I know and trust. Someone with real ties to Swallow Cove."

"Right," he said testily. "And you're going to manage that from Chicago?"

"Actually, I was hoping to work remotely from Swallow Cove."

"Jesus fucking Christ."

"In our industry, there's no reason—"

"No way. No deal. You want to pussy out on this deal? I can't stop you. I can tell you that you're making a huge fucking mistake and you'll regret it—"

"Nathan," I said sharply.

"—but I won't reward you with a fucking remote job you can work in la-la land. What the hell happened? I thought we were on the same page."

"I met someone."

There was a long silence. Then Nathan started laughing. "Tell me you're joking. You met someone. You fucking *met* someone? Jesus, Declan. Come up here, and I'll help you meet half a dozen someones who'll blow your mind."

"This is someone special," I said. "It's serious."

"You're going to throw everything away for a fucking woman?"

"No. For a man."

There was a beat of silence. "Ah, well, whatever floats your boat. Just think about this, Declan. Think hard. Relationships come and go. Sex is great in the beginning and then it fizzles. And when it's over, you're going to be sitting in some podunk Ozark town with nothing but burned bridges, and when you try to sell that property—because you're not finding some idiot to buy it for even a fraction of what we offered, I can tell you that, the whole value is in the land, not some B&B—you'll be shit out of luck."

"Nathan, we're friends. I'm sorry I misled you. That was never my intention. It all happened a little too fast, and I wasn't ready to make a decision. But I don't want this to come between us."

"We *were* friends. I thought we were. But you just yanked me around, and I don't appreciate it."

"I can do the job from here. I know I can."

He snorted. "Maybe, but you won't be doing shit for me."

"But—"

"No fucking way. Don't ask me for any fucking favors. Not after this shit. Not now. Not ever again."

"Okay, if you really feel that way..."

"No, I take that back," he said, making hope flicker to life.

"Really?"

"Yeah. You get one favor. You can change your fucking mind. You have two days."

Click.

He'd hung up on me.

I set the phone on the counter and released a shaky breath. I hadn't expected Nathan to take the news well, but I hadn't expected *that*.

It had been his idea to contact those developers. His idea for me to sell and return to the financial industry.

I hadn't even considered it until he planted the seed in my mind.

I'd assumed Nathan was merely a contact for this deal. His reaction made me wonder if he was more involved than it first seemed? If so, did he ever have my best interests at heart?

Nathan was a wheeler and a dealer. I always knew that about him. But I'd thought he'd genuinely respected me, too. Now, I couldn't help wondering if he was only looking to close a good deal.

And if I wasn't so hopeless at understanding people, maybe I'd have seen it way before now.

If I was so wrong about Nathan, could I be wrong about Cash, too? Did he *really* feel everything I did? Last night, when we were tucked into bed together, Cash had seemed so sincere, so vulnerable.

But my judgment had failed me spectacularly before. Not just with Nathan, but with every ex-boyfriend who'd promised he loved me only to cut me loose when I wasn't everything he wanted in bed.

Cash wasn't like that. I *knew* he wasn't. Every interaction between us, every sweet touch that wasn't demanding, every kiss that was on my terms, every cuddle that fed my soul told me that.

I needed to talk to him, to lay everything on the table once and for all.

But now wasn't the time. Not when he was at odds with his father and worried about his sister. I needed to support him, not make demands of him.

I'd just blown up my only job lead and I still didn't want to run the B&B. But if he cared for me the way I *thought* he did, I wanted to stay.

I wanted to stay for him, for this thing that was growing between us, for the sense of potential that had taken root here in this little lake town.

Happiness. Friendship. Love. Family.

I was so close to everything I wanted. Closer than ever before.

I just hoped I wasn't deluding myself, as I so clearly had been with my only so-called friend in Chicago.

CHAPTER TWENTY-THREE

Cash

SKYLAR HOVERED NEXT TO THE FRONT DESK WHEN Katelyn and I entered the resort lobby. A part-timer, Leo, was covering the phones, so I knew Skylar was there to meet me.

Brooks emerged from the direction of the bar with his adorable grandma. The deep grooves in his forehead gave away his concern.

"Either Grandma Kitty told Brooks she's dating Chester or he's worried I'm about to steal you away," I joked. "He looks like he's about to pop a blood vessel."

Skylar didn't laugh. "We're worried about you. Are you okay?"

"Yeah, we're fine." I nudged my quiet sister. "Right, Kit-Kat?"

She nodded, smiling faintly, and lifted the shimmery turquoise two-piece bathing suit in her hands. "Cash said I could use the pool. If that's all right?"

"Anytime," Skylar said as Brooks and Grandma Kitty reached us. "We've got a couple of rooms too, if you need—"

"We're all set," I said quickly. Katelyn might want to take him up on it, but I wasn't turning down Declan's direct invitation to continue sleeping in his bed. "We're going to stay at the B&B."

Brooks arched an eyebrow. "Really? There's plenty of space here, and you wouldn't be an imposition."

Grandma Kitty clucked. "He means to say we'd *love* to have you." She held open her arms. "Give Grandma a hug."

I leaned in, letting her squeeze me. Comfort washed through me, the kind I hadn't found anywhere other than Declan's arms. I wished I could go cling to him for a few hours and forget that my family was falling apart, but that would hardly reassure Katelyn that everything was okay.

I pulled out of Grandma's arms, forcing a smile. "Thanks, Grandma Kitty. You give the best hugs."

Grandma Kitty smiled. "You come get one anytime you need." She turned to my sister. "You get over here. Grandma's not done."

My sister rushed into her arms so quickly I worried she'd knock poor Kitty right off her feet. Kitty was sturdier than she looked, thankfully. She wrapped Kat in a tight hug, rocking from side to side.

"We've got plenty of rooms," Skylar said tentatively.

I shook my head. "I'm working over at the B&B every day, anyway. It makes sense to stay there."

Katelyn pulled out of Grandma Kitty's arms and smirked. "Yeah, *that's* why we're staying there. It has nothing to do with you sleeping in Declan's bed."

I elbowed her in the side. "Shut your piehole."

She stumbled a couple of steps to the side, giggling. "Declan and Cash sitting in a tree, k-i-s-s—"

"Okay, I should get to work," I said loudly, speaking over her song. I patted the duffel bag over my shoulder. "I've got a change of clothes in my bag. I'll just hit the bathroom and get clocked in. Sorry I'm a little late today."

"Don't worry about that," Skylar said. "If you need to take the day off, we can work something out."

I shook my head. "I'm good. Kat's going to hit the pool for a while. Declan is bringing Gray over for work this afternoon, so he'll take her back to the B&B if she's ready to go home before my shift ends."

"All right, if you're sure," Skylar said.

"I am."

Grandma Kitty wrapped an arm around Katelyn. "You can get changed in my room. Maybe I'll even join you out by the pool, if you don't mind an old lady cramping your style?"

Katelyn looked pleased. "I don't mind."

"Good."

I smiled as Kitty led my sister down the hall. "You're so lucky, Brooks. I wish I had a grandma like that."

"You do," Brooks said. "Anytime you need a grandma, she's right here, and she loves you."

My heart twisted in my chest. "Yeah," I said around the lump in my throat. "That's really... I appreciate you sharing."

He clapped my shoulder. "Anytime. And don't think we're not talking about this whole *sleeping with Declan* business. That's a big deal."

My instinct was to deny it. I didn't know what Declan would want me to say to anyone about our relationship, such as it was. But these were my closest friends, and I needed someone to talk with, so I nodded agreement.

"I guess it is a big deal. I just don't know yet how big of a deal. Not with his plans to sell the B&B."

"Let's grab a dinner on your break later," Skylar suggested. "We can all talk. I know everyone's worried. We'll get the whole gang here."

"So another friendervention, huh?"

"Nah, more of a friend love fest."

"Well, I do enjoy a good love fest," I said lightly, doing my best to ignore the burn behind my eyes.

My home life might be in the shitter right now, but I had a group of friends who rallied around me, ready to support me through any storm. They were the family I could always count on.

I got clocked in before Skylar and Brooks could make me cry —just *barely*—and spent the next few hours trying not to think about anything but room bookings, guest questions, and fielding complaints about housekeeping.

"No one brought towels, and I specifically requested more. The room hasn't even been picked up once since we arrived," a woman in Room 203 told me over the phone.

She was understandably frustrated. I was just puzzled. Skylar subcontracted with the housekeeping company where my mom worked. There was no reason for the room to be neglected.

I assured her I'd have towels sent up, then called Skylar in his office to explain the situation.

"What on earth..." Skylar huffed. "This isn't the first complaint I've gotten. I'll put in a call to Cove Cleaners. It might be time for a change."

"My mom works for them. I could try to ask her..."

"I don't want to put you in that position right now," Skylar said. "You've got bigger fish to fry. Besides, she's not in charge of the company. I don't doubt she does great work."

"Yeah," I said quietly. "She works hard."

"I know. I've chatted with her a few times. She's always friendly, but quick to get back to her work."

"You think you'll fire the company?"

"Maybe," Skylar said. "Will that hurt your mother?"

I hesitated. She subcontracted through them, and it wasn't like the resort was her only job, but she needed every job she could get. I settled on the only answer I could give. "I don't know, but you can't make your decision based on that."

"No, that's true," Skylar said. "Well, for now, it's just a conversation. We'll go from there."

"Okay. I'll get towels up to the room. I can take out their trash and tidy a little while they're out, too."

"Thanks, Cash. I know that's not in your job description."

"No worries. My mom taught me a thing or two about maid service."

Skylar chuckled. "I bet she did. Thanks."

I grabbed a keycard and went up to Room 203. I set a stack of fresh towels on the back of the toilet, picked up the discarded towels on the floor, emptied their trash, and made the bed.

I didn't have a vacuum, so I couldn't do a full cleaning service, but the room looked tidier, at least. By the time I got back downstairs, it was time for my break, and the troops had assembled.

Poppy and Fisher stood in the lobby, chatting while they waited.

"Don't you two have work to do?" I challenged as I came out of the elevators.

Poppy shrugged. "I'm an artist. I make my own hours."

"My Dad was bored, anyway," Fisher said. "He'll enjoy running the store for an afternoon without me bossing him around."

I laughed. "So you're the boss now, huh?"

"Pretty much," he said, though there was no arrogance to it. "Dad has finally embraced the idea of transitioning toward retirement. It's a good thing for us all."

"That's great, man."

"But we're not here to talk about us," Poppy said.

I grimaced. "Might be more fun."

"Nope." She hooked an arm through mine and urged me toward the restaurant and bar. "No dodging. You've been avoiding this topic with us for years."

"Time to let us help," Fisher added.

"There's nothing you can do."

"We can listen," she said.

I sagged a little, chest aching. I'd held in so much about my dad's alcoholism, how intolerable it was at home, the lengths I'd gone to avoid it until I realized I was only hurting myself and Katelyn.

But as I sat down with all my friends, every set of eyes filled with worry for me, I knew the time for keeping secrets was over.

"Things are really fucked up," I admitted. "I told Kat we were going to take off for a few days until things cool down."

"That seems smart," Skylar said.

Brooks had poured drinks for us all, and I picked up my beer and took a fortifying gulp. "Yeah, the thing is...I don't know if I can make myself go back there. But I also can't just send Kat back. And my mom, she needs us. She can't carry that burden alone."

I gave them the rundown on my father's condition, the attempts we'd made to get him help before, the resistance he showed to change.

"For a long time, I avoided being home whenever Kat didn't need me there. That's why..."

Poppy was the first to catch on. "That's why you hooked up with so many people? To stay out for the night?"

I nodded. "It wasn't healthy. Declan made me see that."

"What's going on with Declan, anyway?" Sawyer asked. "You're staying with him?"

"Yeah. We're getting close."

"Close enough to share a bed," Brooks added. "You ready to talk about that?"

I spread my hands helplessly. "I'm not sure what he'd want me to say about it."

"We're your friends," Poppy said. "Anything you tell us stays here."

"Well," I said. "He's ace, and he's possibly leaving, so basically I'm just floundering around hoping I don't screw up everything. But we've, uh...we've been intimate. On occasion." I hurried to add, "Only when he wants it."

"Well, of course," Poppy said. "So he's not sex-repulsed."

"No. I guess he's more...gray ace? Like, sometimes he's good to go and sometimes not. I just try to follow his lead."

"Doesn't that get confusing?" Fisher asked. "Like, what if you read him wrong?"

I shrugged. "He gives me lots of cues, I guess. Sometimes I just ask to be sure."

"Communication is never a bad thing," Sawyer said.

"I think it's great," Skylar added. "You'll never cross a boundary if you ask first."

Brooks slanted a glance toward Skylar, then cleared his throat. "You know, when Skylar and I got together, it wasn't simple either."

"You mean because you were a dumb straight boy?" I teased.

He laughed. "Uh, not exactly."

Skylar leaned forward, keeping his voice low. "I was a bit fragile after my last relationship. You all heard a little about that, right?"

I nodded. Skylar's ex had been a toxic, controlling asshole who'd shown up in town after Skylar left him. Brooks had stayed out at Skylar's house to make sure the guy wouldn't try anything.

"Well, as a result, I was nervous about relationships or even, um, being intimate. But knowing Brooks would always respect my boundaries? That was everything."

My heart stuttered as I thought of the many times I'd hit on him.

"Shit, I hope my flirting didn't make you uncomfortable." I winced. "I was just trying to rile up Brooks. I wasn't thinking..."

Skylar smirked. "Cash, your flirting is borderline ridiculous. It made me laugh. Don't worry about it."

I rubbed my chest. "Ouch. Kick a guy while he's down, why don't you?"

Brooks chuckled. "Your ego will survive. Especially if you managed to finally get Declan's attention after all this time."

"Which he obviously has," Sawyer said, nodding toward the doorway. "Because there he is."

I twisted in my seat. Declan was just entering the bar, looking hesitant.

I met him halfway across the room. "Hey."

"Hey. I just brought Gray over," he said.

"Thank you. And, uh, thanks for offering me a place to stay tonight. And giving Kat a ride back." I laughed a little. "I guess I owe you a lot of thanks."

"You don't owe me anything." He cupped my jaw with one gentle hand. "How are you doing? Are you okay?"

I'd been fine all day. I'd been wrestling emotions too close to the surface, sure. I was stressed and worried about my family. I was navigating a delicate relationship, often out of my depth. I was burning the candle at both ends, working two jobs.

And with Declan's soft words, I couldn't fake it anymore.

"N-not really," I croaked.

Then I fell into his arms, and he hugged me as tight as Grandma Kitty had. Her hug had been comforting and sweet.

This one, though, was different. Grandma Kitty kept me from falling apart. Declan? He held me together when I shattered.

He kissed my temple. "Shh. It's okay. I've got you."

"It's stupid to be upset," I mumbled against his chest. "Nothing has really changed."

"Well, maybe it's time it did," he said. "Maybe it's past time, even."

I took a deep breath, his words resonating with me. Yeah. Maybe it *was* time. I'd been treading water, struggling not to drown with my family, for years. Maybe it was time to reach for a lifeline.

I looked up at Declan, wondering if he could be that for me. My anchor. And for how long?

He swiped his thumbs under my eyes, clearing my tears away. "It's going to be okay. I'm here for you."

"Tha—" I started to say, but he silenced me with a soft kiss.

Right there in public. It shocked my thoughts away. He glanced over my head, seeming to notice our rapt audience. I turned, and Fisher gave a cheeky little wave. Damn. It was a good thing most of my friends were more tactful than me. I'd have been whistling or catcalling for maximum embarrassment.

I grinned. "You're going to start all sorts of rumors about us, Mr. Sullivan. Naughty, naughty."

Declan reddened a little but said gamely, "Are they rumors if they're true?"

"In that case, kiss me again. I want everyone talking about us, especially if it makes you blush like that," I teased.

To my surprise, he indulged me with one more kiss. "I'll see you tonight, okay? Call me if you need me. For anything."

My heart skipped a few beats, and I practically floated back to my chair. My friends all looked at me with varying degrees of amusement.

"About time," Fisher said.

"I still can't believe it," Sawyer added. "I never thought he'd get anywhere with Declan."

"Me either," Brooks said.

"It's not that surprising," Poppy said. "Declan just needed to see that Cash was serious. He plays so much that people can't always tell."

"She's right," Skylar said. "Cash puts on a good front."

"Cash is right here," I mumbled, a little disconcerted by how well Poppy had read the situation.

"You're not the player everyone thinks you are," Poppy said. "Maybe for a while you played the part, but I think that's all it was, right? It's not what you really want. Not anymore."

"No," I said. "Maybe not ever. I don't know. This thing with Declan, it's..."

"Serious," Skylar said.

"Yeah."

"And what about when he leaves?" Brooks asked, forehead creased again. "What then? Maybe you should put a stop to this now."

I shrugged helplessly. "I can't just let this moment pass me by. I'm seizing the fucking day."

"But—" Brooks started, but Skylar laid his hand on his arm, quieting him.

"Can't you see, Brooks? Cash is in love with Declan. It's already too late for him to do anything else."

My stomach flip-flopped to hear it stated so plainly out loud, but I'd already known, hadn't I? I'd been falling hard since the moment Declan stopped pushing me away.

Consequences be damned.

CHAPTER TWENTY-FOUR

Declan

I woke the next morning to find Cash bundled in my arms again. I was holding him so tightly I wondered how he could breathe. He squirmed a little, and I drew back.

Cash caught my arm before I could move to my slice of the too-small bed. "Stay," he rasped. "Just needed to move a little."

He pulled my arm around him and pressed my hand flat over his heart. It seemed to beat for me, thumping steadily under my palm. I nuzzled closer, breathing in the scent of his forest mint shampoo. It smelled fresh, sort of like a Christmas tree, but it worked for him.

"How are you doing?" I asked, before pressing my lips to the back of his neck.

"Mm. Always good when I'm with you."

I coasted my hand up and down his chest and stomach. I wasn't looking for anything sexual. I just loved touching him, absorbing the smooth skin and curves of bone and muscle under my fingertips. It made the moment more real. Cash in my bed, in my arms, in my heart.

When my hand accidentally bumped his cockhead, I peeked over his shoulder to see he was hard.

"Sorry." He flashed me a sheepish grin. "Body is greedy after all that touching."

He turned his head, grazing his lips over my arm. "I like it. Just ignore my dick."

I chuckled and stroked my hand back up toward his heart, where I was more focused today. "How did your talk go with your mom yesterday?"

Cash tensed, but I peppered kisses across his shoulders until he relaxed back into the mattress.

The night before, I'd picked him up from the resort and brought him back to join his sister for dinner. We'd all eaten in my small quarters in front of a baking show on the TV. Katelyn sat between us, preventing us from touching, and I'd been hyperaware of Cash's distance all evening. So much so, I'd wondered if I was becoming addicted to touching him.

When she'd gotten up to take the plates to the kitchen, we'd reached for each other at the same instant. Cash slipped an arm around my shoulders, and I leaned in, settling a hand on his thigh and squeezing.

Katelyn had taken one look at us upon her return and declared she was going to read in her room. I'd soaked up the affection he gave me so easily—without the expectation of more that my last ex had always placed upon any touch—until his phone rang with a call from his mother.

He'd taken it outside, and afterward he hadn't wanted to talk much. This morning, he seemed more relaxed, though.

"Mom's not thrilled about this arrangement," Cash said as we cuddled in bed, "but she agreed to give us some space. So if you don't mind us staying a few days..."

"Of course. Stay as long as you like."

He turned his head a little, his dark stubble scraping along my upper arm and making me shiver. "Promise you'll tell me if you need Kat's room. There's always space at the resort."

I tightened my arm around him instinctively, as if he might try to leave me.

"I want you here," I said. "I want us to—"

My phone alarm cut through the room, and I groaned with annoyance.

"Wow, you actually need an alarm?" Cash teased. "With your early morning gardening, I figured you rose with the sun."

I rolled over to silence my phone. "It's not an alarm to wake up. It's to start cooking breakfast. It's the weekend."

"Ahhhh, you can't just phone it in today, huh?"

"Nope." I rolled out of bed and opened a dresser drawer to pull out a pair of navy blue shorts and a white button-down with short sleeves. "Feel free to take your time. I'll be in the kitchen."

"Aw." Cash threw back the blankets and got to his feet, stark naked. Early morning sunlight cut through the blinds, bright stripes of light and shadow playing across Cash's taut skin.

My gaze skimmed over him, because I might be ace but I appreciated his beauty. Wasn't sure anyone would be totally immune to *that*. Cash caught me looking and raised an eyebrow.

"You're gorgeous," I said simply.

His lips quirked in a bemused smile. "I didn't know if you'd notice that sort of thing."

"Of course I do. I just don't want to jump on your dick because of it."

He grinned, taking a loose hold of the hard dick making itself known and stroking it. "Too bad. My dick would like that."

I moved closer. "Well, tell your dick that I'd love to jump on it some other time. But not because you're gorgeous."

"No?"

"No. It's because you're so sweet."

I pressed one last kiss to his scruffy cheek, squeezed his fingers around his dick, making him gasp, and gave him a grin of my own. "Enjoy that shower."

"You're evil," he accused as I backed toward the door.

I could tell my teasing didn't actually bother him. If anything, he liked it. Judging by the stranglehold he had on his dick, he'd be coming in my shower while moaning my name.

I headed for the kitchen, my heart light. I'd never played with a partner this way before. Never teased him about his desire, because I was always so dang afraid of leading him on. Cash made it easy to be honest, though. He didn't take my rejections to heart, but knew they were temporary, just waiting for the right moment for my desire to awaken, too.

I put on an apron, got some bacon in the skillet, and whipped up pancake batter. Katelyn joined me in the kitchen, offering to help with the scrambled eggs. She seemed to have the basics down, which was about all I could offer, so I let her go to work.

Cash came in later, flushed from the heat of the shower—and perhaps sexual release—and smiled at the two of us. "Well, isn't this domestic?" he teased. "Shall I make the coffee?"

"Get to work, slacker," Katelyn said as she took the eggs off the stove.

We got everything on platters and out to the table by the time the first guests wandered in. And with Cash and Katelyn both there to carry the conversation, I didn't have to put in nearly as much effort.

I sipped my coffee and enjoyed the salty crispness of the bacon while my newest guests, Rob and Deidre from Oklahoma, asked about a hundred questions about Swallow Cove, the Ozarks, and even our renovation project on The Roost.

"It's nearly done," Cash said. "Although we have to start on the greenhouse next."

"A greenhouse?" Deidre's eyes lit up. "How lovely. Which of you is the gardener?"

"Declan is a great gardener," Cash said, a note of pride in his voice. "Kat and I are just guests, really."

"Oh, I thought..." She trailed off uncertainly.

Another guest across the table, a younger guy who'd been more interested in his phone than the conversation until now, snorted.

"You don't have to hide that you're boyfriends. We're cool." He glanced at Rob and Deidre, and said in a firm voice that dared them to argue, "*Right?*"

"Yes, of course," Deidre said, wincing. "You're not...worried about that, are you? I know we're in conservative country, but we're not homophobic."

My gaze shot to Cash, who—for the first time ever—didn't seem to know what to say.

Katelyn giggled, saving us both. "It's just new with them. They don't know what they're doing yet, but they're *totally* boyfriends, and it's gagworthy." She scrunched up her nose. "Cash is my brother, and I do *not* need to see him drooling over Declan."

Everyone at the table laughed, the tension easing. The conversation had reminded me, though, of a talk Cash and I needed to have.

We finished breakfast and cleared the dishes.

"I'll give you a ride to the resort," I said. "We should talk."

"Okay," he said hesitantly. "Nothing bad, I hope?"

"No." I cupped his cheek, a glutton for touching him. "All good. I promise."

He turned his head to kiss my palm. "Okay, I'll grab my stuff."

We went out to my boat and worked together to untie it and start the engine. I sat down in the captain's seat, steering us toward the resort.

"What did you want to talk about?" Cash called over the wind.

"Us," I said. "The future, I mean. After we sell the B&B."

"Oh." He looked away, expression pensive. "We can—"

My phone rang, cutting him short. I pulled it out to check the caller ID, heart thumping when I saw it was the Mallory Investment Group. I'd put out a few feelers for other job opportunities after Nathan freaked out on me.

"I need to take this," I said. "Do you mind taking over for me?"

Cash and I switched places, and I answered the call. "Hello, this is Declan."

"Declan, this is Leland Marsden. I heard you're in the market for some investment work."

"Yeah, as an analyst," I said. "I've got a resume I can send. You're based in Chicago, but have offices in New York and LA as well, right?"

"That's right."

That boded well. With a business not anchored to one spot, he might be more open to an employee who wasn't in the same building.

"But where are you?" Leland asked. "Do I hear a boat?"

"Yeah." I laughed. "Sorry. I live in a lake town, but we're nearly to dock."

Cash throttled down the boat, as if on cue. His attention was focused on the docks ahead, so I couldn't tell if he'd followed any of my conversation over the boat and wind noise.

"Well, now I'm jealous," Leland said. "That must be a nice life. I don't know why you'd want to leave it."

"I don't," I said.

"Ah. Remote work?"

"If it's an option."

"I'll have to think about that. Things move quickly. We need someone available when decisions need to be made."

"I understand, and I can be available when you need me."

Cash cut the motor. "We're here."

Leland was talking in my ear about projects they had in the works, upcoming deadlines, and how soon they'd need to make a hiring decision. I managed to get him to pause long enough to say to Cash, "Can we have dinner tonight? I want us to talk."

He cast a wary glance at the phone, then gave me a tight smile. "Sure."

Leland was back to talking, and I interjected cursory listening sounds while we docked the boat.

I got up to help Cash, but he waved me back into my seat, tying up the boat on his own. By the time Leland gave me an opening to end the call, Cash was gone.

His wallet, though, was lying on the floor in front of the co-captain's seat. It must have fallen out of his pocket when we switched places.

I grabbed it and headed for the staff entrance closest to the dock. A long hallway ran past the kitchen and eventually exited into the lobby.

Cash was there, texting on his phone. Brooks was beside him, making Cash laugh about something and shake his head.

As I approached, I opened my mouth to call a greeting, but their words reached me before I could.

"...surprised you haven't gone on a date with Danny before now."

Cash chuckled. "I know, right?"

"When are you going?" Brooks asked.

"Well—" Cash looked up from his phone and his gaze landed on me. "Declan?"

I held up his wallet. "You forgot this."

"Oh." He reached out. "Thanks."

I slapped it into his hand with a little too much force. "I'll let you get back to talking about that date with Danny."

His eyes widened. "Oh, no, Dec. It's not what you think."

"It's okay," I said, though it definitely wasn't okay. My throat was closing up and my insides had turned ice-cold. "This always happens. I'm used to it."

"No, no, no," he said as I turned away.

He caught my hand, tugging me back around, and raised his hands to cup my face. "It's not a real date, Declan. It's just a favor."

"A favor? I don't..."

"He wants to make Abe jealous. You know, Abe, at Hot Buns? That's who Danny wants. He just needed a friend to play along. It's only a fake date."

"But maybe it should be real," Brooks broke in. "Since you're leaving Swallow Cove and Cash, anyway. There's no real reason for you to be jealous, is there?"

"Brooks," Cash said sharply. "I'd never go on a real date with someone else." His eyes met mine. "For as long as you're here, Declan, I am, too. I know you got that call about a job and you're probably leaving soon, but until that happens, I'm with *you*. I want every moment I can have with you, okay?"

It took me a minute to process everything. Cash wasn't seeking out another man to date. He wouldn't do that to me. He said so. But Brooks was right. I'd not given him any reason yet to think I was staying. In fact, that call from Leland had given him the wrong idea entirely. If Cash *had* been making a real date, I'd have no room to be upset.

"Declan?" Cash prompted. "Do you hear me?"

I sucked in a breath. "Yes, but I'm not going to leave."

"What?"

"That's what I wanted to talk about at dinner. I'm going to stay in Swallow Cove. With you. If you're sure you really want to tie yourself to me and not date other men? I know I'm not the easiest—"

He threw his arms around me, cutting off the rest of my words. "Of course I want to be with you! Are you *kidding* me? I'm batshit crazy for you."

I laughed. "I'm a little crazy for you, too."

He drew back, eyes bright as they met mine. "Just a little, huh?"

"A lot," I confessed. "I can't leave you. Not now."

"But you don't want the B&B."

"No, I don't."

"And that call this morning—"

"I'm looking for remote work," I said. "I'm hoping I can do it from my home office here in Swallow Cove."

"Took you long enough," Brooks grumbled.

Cash shot him an annoyed look. "Can you stop?"

"No, he's right. I should have talked to you sooner, but you had all that stuff going on with your dad, and I didn't want to put more on your plate. I just wanted to be there for you, not make demands for me."

"You're the sweetest," Cash murmured. "Now, kiss me already, and tell me that you're my boyfriend."

"I'm your boyfriend," I said, my head spinning. I hadn't ever thought I'd have that label again.

He drew me down into a chaste kiss. I traced my tongue along his lips, prompting him to open with a soft sound of need. Brooks made himself scarce, and I relaxed into the kiss.

When we broke apart, Cash's grin was mischievous. "So, you were really jealous, huh? Of Danny."

"Of course I was."

"Because I'm yours."

"Well, that's kind of a caveman attitude."

He smirked. "Say it, Declan."

"You're mine."

"With feeling."

I leaned in, growling into his ear. "You're mine."

He sagged against me. "Fuck, that's hot. I can't wait until you let me get on my knees for you again."

"Maybe I'll get on my knees for you."

He groaned. "So evil."

I laughed. "Have a good day at work, Cash. I'll pick you up for that dinner date."

He drew back. "You still want to do that, even though we talked already?"

"I can't let Danny be the first one to take you on a date."

Cash grinned. "Pretty sure the plan with Danny is off. Once I go out with you, Abe won't ever buy his ruse."

I hesitated. "Do you want to wait?"

"No way. Declan Sullivan is asking me on a date after I've been flirting with him for two years. I'm not saying no to that."

"Two years? It hasn't been that long."

Cash patted my cheek. "Ah, my sweet summer child. It's probably been *longer*. It just took you a while to notice me."

"I see you now."

His eyes met mine. "I see you too."

"Tonight then." I pressed one more kiss to his lips before pulling away, though it was hard. I wanted to hold him all day. I wanted to touch him for a week, a month, a year. I wanted to possess him—every smile, every brush of the hand, every hug and kiss—until everyone knew that Cash had chosen *me* above all others.

And he could have so many others if he wanted.

My old insecurities tried to rise, but I silently told them to shove it. I had found a man who was patient, sensitive, affectionate, and sexy without asking for anything in return.

Cash Hicks was the holy grail of boyfriends, and he was *mine*.

CHAPTER TWENTY-FIVE

Cash

Brooks opened the walk-in closet in the custom suite Skylar had designed as part of the resort remodel. Their permanent residence might be in a hotel, but it was as spacious as an apartment. "Skylar has tons of clothes, so help yourself."

"Wow." My gaze traveled over suits in black, gray, blue, lavender, and cream. Dress shirts in every shade of the rainbow —and just about every texture too, from starchy formalwear to clingy silks and breezy cottons. There were shelves to the right and left. One side held shoes and belts, but I was *much* more interested in the other one.

I picked up a red lacy scrap of something and held it up. "Skylar, you naughty little minx."

Brooks snatched the lingerie from my hand. It looked to be a top of some kind, but transparent and lacy and sexy as fuck. "Boundaries, man. He said you could borrow a shirt, not grope his lingerie."

"Touchy touchy," I teased. "I knew you two were kinky, but—"

"Shut it," Brooks said. "It's not about kink. Skylar wears it for him, not me."

"Okay, fair. And you don't like it at all, right?"

Brooks neatly folded the lacy top and replaced it on the shelf. "I didn't say that. He's gorgeous in it. Not that it's any of your business." He shot me a glare. "Don't be picturing it, either."

I chuckled. "Relax. I'm here to get ready for my own date, remember?"

Brooks smirked. "Does Declan wear lingerie for you?"

I laughed, thinking of his silk pajamas. "Not in a million years, but I'm okay with that."

After giving the contents of the closet another scan—there wasn't enough time to go through every item—I tugged a white Hawaiian shirt patterned with artsy blue leaves and flowers in different shapes and sizes—off the hanger. "This looks good."

It wasn't as loud—or as tightly fitted—as the clothes in my closet back at my parents' place, but it was more my style than the too-nice dress shirts or pastel solids Skylar favored.

It would match well enough with the khakis I wore to work, but I snagged a belt to dress up a bit.

"You look almost respectable," Brooks said after I'd exchanged shirts and buckled the slim belt at my hips.

I flipped him the bird. "Don't insult me."

He chuckled. "Sorry, my mistake. You look trashy as ever."

"Much better."

I raked my fingers through my hair, fluffing and smoothing, until Brooks grabbed my elbow and steered me away from the mirror on the closet door. "Seriously, Cash, you look great. Just get out there or you'll keep him waiting."

"Right." I took a breath to calm my suddenly racing heart. I'd slept in Declan's bed last night, yet *now* I was nervous. "What if I mess it up?"

Brooks shook his head. "Man, if you haven't scared him off by now, you never will." He gave me a little push toward the door. "He looked like he wanted to die when he thought you were going out with Danny. He's all yours."

Everything Brooks said was true, but tonight was nerve-wracking. I'd hooked up a lot, but dated? That wasn't something I had much experience with. And dating Declan was something I'd wanted for so long but never actually believed I'd achieve.

Half of me expected the lobby to be empty when I got there. As if the universe didn't work unless Declan was unattainable.

But as I emerged from the hallway, he was the first person I saw. The *only* one I could see.

He didn't look much different from usual. Declan was always a nice dresser when he ventured out of the garden. He wore white slacks and a pale blue button-down, open at the neck to reveal just a hint of dark chest hair. His jaw was smooth of the dark stubble that encroached by afternoon, and as I drifted closer, the spicy scent of his aftershave teased at my nose.

"You look amazing," he said. "I was going to take you home to get ready, but..."

Home. He said it so casually, as if the B&B was more than a place for me to stay for a day or two. I wished it were true. The more space I had from my father's toxic presence, the less I could imagine willingly going back to it.

"Skylar let me borrow something," I said with a sheepish smile. "I don't have anything suitable for a date in my duffel bag, and even if I did, it'd be wrinkled as hell."

Declan drew closer and brushed a kiss to my cheek. "Well, you look gorgeous."

I smiled. There was a time I'd have never imagined that type of compliment from Declan. But I'd learned a lot about him these past few weeks. He felt attraction—even if it wasn't sexual. The warmth in his eyes was all for me, and I drank it up like a desert flower.

"Thanks. You look really good too, but then you always do."

He smiled ruefully. "I'm predictable."

"Not today. I didn't expect you to say you'd stay."

"How could I not?" he asked, eyes boring into mine. "You kept breaking down all my barriers."

"Oops?" I said.

He chuckled. "You're not sorry."

"No, I'm not."

Declan had the boat waiting out at the dock. I had no idea where he'd take me for a date, but I was a little surprised when he pulled up outside The Drunken Worm.

"Is this okay?" he asked. "The Savory Swallow seemed too snooty for your tastes, but I didn't want to take you to the pub where you hang out with friends or ask you to spend even more time at the resort, where you work. We could go over to Swallow Beach if—"

I leaned in and kissed him. Declan's rambling put me at ease. I wasn't the only one here who was nervous.

"This is great, Dec. Anywhere we go together is great."

He drew in a breath. "Sorry. Just a little nervous. This is a big deal for me."

I stroked his cheek. "It's a big deal for me, too. I'm not used to dating. Hooking up casually, maybe, but this is different."

"It better be."

"You know it is."

His expression shifted, softening a fraction. "I do. I know. Sorry."

"It's okay. We're both a little nervous. That's good, right? Shows we care. But I'm all for the portion of the evening where we drink margaritas and eat burritos."

"All right, let's go."

The restaurant was as bright and loud as usual, and Declan's expression gave away that this choice was very much for me.

I'd been here many times before. Sometimes with friends, sometimes to grab a drink and hook up with a stranger. Maybe that should have been weird, but it wasn't like Declan could take me anywhere in town that I hadn't been before.

Instead, it felt significant.

The Drunken Worm was the same, but I had changed.

Instead of cruising at the bar, I sat down at a cozy little booth with my boyfriend on our first official date. The first of many, I hoped.

We spent the first few minutes studying the menus. The Drunken Worm had an extensive margarita selection, but I knew what I liked. When our server Reba stopped by to take our orders, I asked for a mango margarita, and Declan asked for a Dos Equis amber beer.

Finally, we were alone, and I had questions.

"I thought that call today was a job offer in Chicago," I admitted. "I thought you wanted to have dinner to break the news."

Declan reached for my hand and squeezed my fingers. "I'm sorry I gave you that impression. I've been trying to figure out what I should do. If I stay here, I have to find remote work. I originally thought I'd be able to work for my friend Nate, but he didn't take it too well when I backed out of the development plan."

I winced. "I didn't know that plan was with a friend."

"It wasn't his development plan or anything. He was just helping me out with his connections. He works with a lot of investors. But he got really angry. So angry I'm not sure we're even friends anymore. Either way, the job with him is off the table."

"I'm so sorry."

"It's not your fault." His eyes met mine. "I guess I didn't know him as well as thought I did, but I don't regret the choice I made. I've got other job options I can explore."

"Like the call this morning," I said, and he nodded. "Think that will work out?"

"I don't know yet."

Reba returned with our drinks and we each placed a dinner order. Declan got a taco salad and I ordered the chipotle steak burrito.

Once she'd gone, he smiled ruefully. "This is terrible date conversation, isn't it? Let's talk about other things."

"Hey, you're staying in Swallow Cove. That's the best conversation I could imagine."

"I am," he said softly. "I want to build a life with you." He swallowed. "Is that...too much too fast?"

"Nothing about this has been fast. Not to me. I want that too."

Even if we'd only today said we were dating, we'd been in some kind of undefinable relationship for weeks, and I'd seriously wanted him for years.

"So, we're on the same page? We want a future together."

"Yes, one hundred percent."

"Okay, good." He hesitated. "So, we've talked about my future, but what about yours? Do you want to stay with the resort?"

I thought about that. I'd never been career-driven. I'd always worked for the paychecks I needed. But my time at the resort had been the best fit I'd ever found.

"I like working in hospitality," I said. "I'm good with people."

"Too good sometimes," he grumbled.

I smirked. "Is that your jealousy trying to peek out again?"

He stabbed a lettuce leaf and shoved it in his mouth, opting not to answer.

I chuckled. "I probably will stay at the resort unless some other opportunity arises. I never want to go back to plumbing." I shuddered with disgust. "Those are three days scarred into my psyche forever."

Declan laughed, and his smile punched the air right from my lungs. Damn, but I loved that I could bring out this side of him. That he could relax with me and let down those barriers he'd mentioned.

I wanted to make him laugh again and again.

"Too bad you didn't inherit a B&B," he said. "You'd probably love it."

"I probably would." I hesitated. "But I understand that it's not for you. I'm just glad you're trying to stay."

"Not trying," Declan clarified. "I *am* staying. I'll find something to do. If I have to...I don't know...start a greenhouse and sell produce at the Outdoor Market, then I will."

I grinned. "You say that like it's a last resort, but it sounds like something you'd love."

He tilted his head thoughtfully. "You know, you're right. Pearl and Ruth Marie put the thought in my mind and it keeps rattling around, even though it's unrealistic."

"Why is it unrealistic?"

"I'm a financial analyst, and that's a big undertaking I couldn't manage alongside a job." He shook his head. "It's just a pipe dream."

"It's only a pipe dream until you find a way to make it happen."

His lips quirked. "I guess that's true. I'm usually a little too practical to chase dreams."

"Well, you're in the unique position of doing whatever you want going forward. Maybe it's time to be a little more fanciful."

He smiled. "I don't know if it's in my DNA, but then again, I never saw you coming."

"Because you were blind," I teased.

He laughed. "I guess I was."

CHAPTER TWENTY-SIX

Declan

AFTER TWO MARGARITAS, CASH JOINED ME ON MY SIDE OF the booth, leaning in close enough for our shoulders to touch, one hand dropping to squeeze my thigh.

Hudson's mother, Judy Nash, sat a few tables away with her boyfriend, Ansel. She smiled and leaned forward to say something that made him look our way, bushy eyebrows rising in surprise. Well, that meant the whole town would know about our date in no time. Ansel was the loudest mouth in Swallow Cove, aside from his buddy Chester, who was doing his darnedest to court Brooks's grandmother.

Cash snickered. "We're going to be the talk of town, Dec. You okay with that?"

"I didn't bring you on a date to keep you a secret."

"No? I've got a reputation in this town..."

I glanced down, surprised to see Cash looking at me with wide, worried eyes. "I know, love, but they don't know you like I do."

He smiled and nuzzled in close. "Say that again."

"I know you."

He chuckled. "No, call me love again."

"Love," I murmured in a soft voice.

He bit his bottom lip. "Damn, that's so sexy." He hurriedly tacked on, "And sweet."

"You're pretty sexy right now too," I teased. "And sweet."

I surprised a laugh out of him. "Yeah? You want to get out of here, so we can be sweet and sexy without an audience?"

"That sounds like a great idea."

It was a beautiful night, dusk painting the sky in lavender hues as we left the restaurant. Water sloshed against the sides of the boat as we boarded it. Cash leaned over to shove off from the pylon on the dock. As soon as we had the space, I started the motor and headed for open water.

We were a couple of minutes from the B&B. When we got there, things could go one of two ways. We could sit on the couch, cuddle close, and soak up our affection for each other, which I always loved.

Or...

My heart skipped.

It wasn't often I thought about that other option. Tonight was different. There was a thrum in my veins and a warmth in my chest that had begun to travel to other regions.

It unnerved me a little, this rush of heat. It wasn't something I experienced every day—or hell, even every month. Cash's easy acceptance of me, of *loving* me for exactly who I was and not just who he wanted me to be, made it easier to figure out what I actually wanted for myself.

Not what my boyfriend demanded. Not what society might dictate. But what I really *desired*.

Not sex for the sake of lust. But intimacy. Closeness. A bond that only we could share. I wanted those things with him.

"Shit," he exclaimed.

I startled out of my thoughts. "What's wrong?"

"I meant to order something for Kat." He winced. "I haven't thought about her all night."

I got the impression that was unusual for him. "A family checked in today. There's a teen her age. They were going to stay in with a pizza and watch a movie. They invited Kat to join."

"Girl or boy?"

"What?"

"The teen her age? Are they a girl or a boy?" He paused. "Or something else?"

"A boy, I think. We didn't exchange pronouns."

Cash swore again, only more creatively this time with a string of fucks. "Drive faster."

"Cash, his parents are there, too."

"Don't care. I know what guys his age are like. Drive *faster*."

Bemused, I pushed the throttle forward. As soon as we arrived, he hopped out of the boat to rush inside. I hurried to follow. It wouldn't do for Cash to get charged with an assault on one of my guests.

The Jackson family was in the living room. Katelyn curled up in an armchair, and Marcus—the sixteen-year-old whose presence worried Cash—sat on the couch with his parents.

He was watching Katelyn more than the movie, so maybe Cash hadn't been totally off-base, but to my relief, there would be no need for bloodshed.

"Hey," Katelyn said when she noticed Cash. "I didn't think you'd be back this soon? What kind of date night is that?"

"The best kind," Mr. Jackson murmured.

His wife elbowed him, and he grunted.

Cash bent down to say something to Katelyn, and she turned beet red and slapped his arm. Then he turned a look on

Marcus. "I'm Kat's brother," he said. "I'm very protective of her, and I'm right here in the same house. Understand?"

"Yeah, man."

"Good. Hope you enjoy the rest of the movie."

"We will," Mrs. Jackson said. "And don't worry. We're keeping an eye on the kids."

We left the Jacksons to watch the movie—and Marcus to apparently worry about what Cash might do if he stepped out of line—and went to my quarters.

As soon as I closed the door, I apologized.

"I didn't realize you'd be concerned about Kat spending time with a boy. My sister's older, and she's been married for years..."

"That's okay." Cash wrapped his arms around my waist, bringing our chests together. "I probably overreacted. I just remember how I was at that age."

"Dare I ask?"

"Let's just say that I wouldn't wish me on anyone's little sister—or brother. I'm too fucking good at getting people into bed."

"And yet we're just standing here talking."

"Well, that's—" He stopped short, one dark eyebrow rising. "Is that an invitation?"

"Maybe it is."

His gaze sharpened on me. "For cuddling, or..."

I swallowed hard. Pushed the words past the nervous tightening of my throat. I wanted to know all of Cash. Wanted to experience the passion he shared when he wasn't holding back.

"I'd like to see that side of you," I said.

"I need you to be really clear here," he said, body tight and coiled. "I don't want to misunderstand."

He was so cautious about my boundaries, and it had allowed

us to get here. But I didn't want him tiptoeing around on eggshells for the rest of our lives. I wanted to know when he wanted more intimacy.

If I said no, he'd listen. But other times, times like now, I could say yes.

I cupped his face and looked into his eyes. "I want you to take what you want tonight."

He wet his lips, still hesitating. "You want it too?"

"*Yes.*"

The second the word left my lips, he was on me, fingers spearing into my hair, mouth latching onto mine. My back hit the wall next to the door with a thud, and I gasped as Cash's dick—so hard already—ground against my hip.

This wasn't like the other times we'd had sex, where Cash had let me lead and followed my cues. He'd been almost submissive in those moments, accepting whatever I gave him.

Now he was *taking*.

The force of his passion was impressive. Consuming. Just shy of being too overwhelming. But it was exactly the right amount tonight, because it shut down my brain.

I sank into the sensations.

His teeth nibbling gently at my bottom lip. His tongue following with teasing kitten licks. I opened up, inviting him in with a groan, and he thrust his tongue in, bold now that I'd given him what he wanted.

He broke the deepest, filthiest kiss I'd ever had to gasp out, "Still good?"

Was I? I felt stripped bare even though I still wore my clothes. A little shaky, but in a good way. Asking me for words now was asking too much, but I managed a nod of assent.

His lips curled up, eyes hot on me as he murmured, "This is going to be fun."

I shivered at the dark, sensual tone to his voice. Damn. Cash unleashed was something to behold.

He moved his lips to my throat as he worked the buttons on my shirt. "I want to fuck you tonight. Is that—"

"Yes," I gasped, body clenching at the thought of someone inside me after so much time.

"Fucking hell," he growled, yanking my shirt open with enough force to send a few buttons pinging to the floor. "I want you so much."

"Take me, Cash," I managed. "I'm yours."

Everything moved fast then. He shoved my shirt over my shoulders, and I reached for his. Cash danced away from my fumbling hands. "This is Skylar's shirt. Brooks will kill me if we yank all the buttons off this one, too."

I laughed, reaching for my belt instead. Together, we undid buttons, pushed aside fabric, and finally came back together, naked. I was surprised at how comfortable I was. Too often, sex stressed me out. I ended up in my head the whole time, worrying about my partner's expectations of me, worrying I wasn't giving him the responses he wanted, worrying he'd get fed up and move on.

Everything with Cash was different.

I knew instinctively I could stop us in our tracks, and he wouldn't get angry or resentful. That knowledge allowed me to relax and enjoy our closeness.

I didn't fool myself. Cash hadn't magically changed my sexuality. I would always be some flavor of ace. But he'd given me the space to enjoy our intimacy when it happened.

He kissed me, his hands coasting along my flanks, slipping down to squeeze my ass. "Want to take this to the bed?"

My stomach flip-flopped at the thought of what was to come. "Yeah, just...go slow. It's been a while."

Cash met my gaze, his smile slow and sweet. "Anything you want."

He meant it. I kissed the sweet words from his lips, took them into my heart, and reveled in how damn lucky I was that Cash had kept trying even when I pushed him away.

We made our way to the bed, and when we were finally beside it, I shoved him down on the mattress. He bounced once, long legs hanging over the edge, cock swaying with the motion. His body was pale, his hair a contrast where it lightly fuzzed his chest and formed a trail down his abs to the thatch at the base of his cock.

But it was his playful grin that captured my attention.

"Who's taking who here?"

I flushed. "Sorry."

He smirked, spreading his legs in invitation. "No worries. I'm vers." He paused. "Although, I did eat a rather large burrito."

"Well, let's not tempt fate, then."

I opened my side table drawer to retrieve lube. Ace or not, I jerked off as much as the next guy and I had the supplies to make it more comfortable. I even used toys sometimes, though nothing like that gargantuan dildo Fisher had given Cash.

That thought made me pause.

"So, you're vers, but do you have a preference?"

"Not really. I like it every which way, as long as I make my partner happy."

"Good." I tossed the lube onto the mattress and straddled his waist. "Because I want you inside me."

He sucked in a breath. "Hell yeah, I want that too."

"And all I had to eat was a salad," I added.

He laughed. "I've never been so thankful for fresh greens."

I hesitated. "Do we need a condom? I've been with no one but you since I tested two years ago, but…"

"A year for me," he said. "I think we're good, if you're comfortable with that?"

"I trust you."

"Good." An evil grin spread across his face. "Now, back to the plan. I believe you wanted to see my take-charge side."

He grabbed my waist and rolled. My back hit the mattress, pinned beneath him. He bent down to nuzzle my nose, then bypassed my lips to press an open-mouthed kiss to the pulse point in my throat.

I drew a breath as his teeth scraped. At the same time, his hands explored, slipping down to tug at my nipples. I arched with a gasp.

"That's it," he murmured. "I'm going to touch you everywhere for as long as you let me."

He worked his way down my body, teasing out sensitive spots with his fingers, lips, and tongue. My head spun, overtaken by the sparks he set off in nerve endings unused to the attention. I felt like a live wire, full of electricity and ready to blow a circuit.

Cash sank his mouth over my cock, making me groan. He took me deep, his mouth so wet and eager. There was no hesitance, no inhibition in this man.

He seemed like such an odd match for me, and yet...his boldness complemented my reserved nature. Lick by lick, suck by suck, he broke down my barriers until I was gripping his hair and ordering him to finger my ass.

Cash grabbed the lube, happy to give me what I wanted. More than happy.

A slick fingertip circled my rim, teasing, prodding, gently flicking until I couldn't take it and shoved my hips down with a growl.

He sank his finger inside me, tearing a needy groan from me.

"Fuck yes," he murmured. "You've got a gorgeous ass."

I gave a ragged laugh. "I doubt that view is gorgeous."

"You'd be wrong," he said. "I've been admiring this ass for years, and seeing your hole wrapped around my finger only makes me want to bury my cock so fucking deep in you."

Heat blazed through my whole body. "Jesus, Cash."

"Too much?"

"Less talk, more action."

He laughed, not offended by the demand. He added a second finger, then a third, getting me nice and stretched. By the time he lined up his cock, I was trembling with need.

"Please, Cash, hurry."

"I got you, sweetheart."

He grasped my thighs, folding them back, and surged forward. My thoroughly prepped body only put up token resistance to the intrusion.

I stretched, reforming to *his* shape as his thick cock filled me inch by inch. Cash's moan was so decadent that it lit up my body as if his enjoyment was my own. Hell, maybe it was. I sought out his gaze, latching on, needing that emotional connection.

Cash's eyes were glazed with lust when they met mine, but there was so much more in their depths. Emotions swirled, flickers of warmth and wonder and so much fucking love.

He sank deeper, nudging up against my prostate, and I gasped.

"That good?" he rasped.

"So good," I confessed.

He withdrew slowly, torturously, then rocked back in, angling for maximum pleasure. I cried out, hiking my legs around his hips and rocking up to meet his next thrust.

Cash hadn't just had a lot of sex in his life. He was really *good* at it.

I wasn't sure how he did it, but he read my needs expertly. When I craved more emotional connection, he instinctively slowed, holding me and whispering such sweet words of praise that I wanted to cry.

"You're so amazing," he murmured into my ear. "Every moment with you is a gift, do you know that?"

"God, Cash," I gritted out, arms tightening around him. "You're the gift."

When I grew restless, wanting more, he held my hips in a bruising grip and thrust hard into me, angling to hit the bundle of nerves that lit me up with every stroke. Tension wound in me, tighter and tighter, until I thought I'd break apart.

He grasped my cock, giving it a couple of rough strokes between our bodies.

I shattered with a rough shout, all that tension snapping and releasing a tsunami of pleasure. My cock shot, my ass tightened around his dick, and he groaned out his own release, coming in pulses inside me.

I melted into the mattress like a pile of goo. It had been a very long time since I'd had an orgasm that intense. Most of the time, I was more than satisfied by jerking off, but damn if my body didn't appreciate the mind-blowing release.

Cash slumped on top of me with a shuddery breath. "Fuck. That was so good."

I smiled and wrapped my arms around him, holding him tight while our ragged breathing calmed.

He tensed, lifting his head. "It was good, right? For you?"

"Of course. You were inside me. You should have felt how very good it was."

He smirked. "Well, yeah, physically, your body liked it. But that's not always the issue, is it?" He tapped my temple. "Was it good, here?" He tapped my chest. "And here?"

I raised my hands to cup his face. "Yeah, Cash. It was good on all levels."

He exhaled with a shaky smile. "Good. That's what I hoped."

"You don't have to worry about that, okay? I'll stop you if something doesn't feel right."

Cash nodded. "This was just a lot more intense and I know I can get carried away in the heat of the moment. I don't want to hurt you, or pressure you to keep—"

I pressed my hand over his mouth. "Stop it."

His eyes widened in surprise.

"First of all, you checked in with me several times. Remember that?"

He nodded wordlessly.

"Secondly, I'm fully capable of speaking up for myself. I'm a big boy and strong enough to toss you right out of bed if I don't want you there."

He chuckled, his hot breath gusting against my palm right before he licked me. I pulled my hand away with a yelp and he swooped in to kiss me.

"I just don't want to mess this up."

"You won't." I smoothed his hair back from his face. Emotion swelled, threatening to burst out of my chest. "You said you were crazy about me, right?"

"I am."

"Well, I'm crazy for you. I...I love you, Cash."

His eyes warmed. "I love you too."

He *loved* me. Fuck, I wanted to rejoice in that. Wanted to laugh and cry and hold him so tightly he'd never leave.

But first, I had to make sure we understood each other.

"We won't have nights like this all the time. Not every day, probably not even every week. But when we do, I don't want you to spend them trying to guess how I feel. I will *tell* you how I feel. What I want or don't want. Okay?"

"Okay."

"Never be afraid to kiss me or touch me, okay? I can't promise to always be on the same page, but I can promise that I love you even if I'd rather cuddle on the couch."

"Hey, those couch cuddles are awesome," Cash said. "I'll never turn them down."

I smiled up at him. "That's what makes you such an amazing boyfriend."

"Wow, I'm rocking this dating thing," he said. "One day in and I'm already amazing."

I gave a strained laugh, his weight pressing on my chest. "Yeah, but if you were really amazing, you'd move so I can breathe."

"Oh, shit! Sorry."

He scrambled off so quickly he nearly fell out of the bed.

I laughed as I caught his arm and tugged him back to safety. "Easy, I'm not on the verge of dying."

"Are you sure?" he teased. "You're pretty old."

I shoved him out of the bed. He hit the ground with a gratifying thump. "Ouch. Guess I deserved that."

"Damn right," I said, leaning over to make sure he was okay.

He surged up to catch me in a kiss. When we parted, his eyes were full of renewed lust. "Want to go again?"

I chuckled. "Love the enthusiasm, but raincheck, okay?"

Even if I'd wanted to go again—and I really didn't, not so soon—my body couldn't have rebounded that quickly.

"Okay, I'll just jerk off in the shower," he said with a grin.

That, more than anything, reassured me this relationship could work. Cash was as horny as the next allosexual guy, but he was okay with taking matters into his own hands when necessary.

He reached down to squeeze his cock.

"I'll be thinking of you."

"Mm-hmm. Don't be afraid to take that giant dildo from Fisher if you want," I teased.

He laughed, eyes bright. "I think I'll save that for a night when I haven't indulged in a burrito."

I snorted. "Probably a good idea."

CHAPTER TWENTY-SEVEN

Cash

I WOKE WITH A CONTENTED STRETCH, ALL MY MUSCLES languid and body warm and heavy. My dick was hard, but that was just morning wood. I recognized the morning-after glow instantly.

I'd had a *very* good fuck last night.

Declan's arm tightened on my waist, and he huffed a breath against the back of my neck. Correction: I'd had a *very* good fuck with my *boyfriend* last night.

Reels of the night before played through my head, making my dick harder. I chanced a glance over my shoulder, but Declan was still out cold. Usually, he woke before me. I must have dicked him down really fucking good.

I grinned into the pillow. It was tempting to wake him and ask for more, but he was unlikely to want it again so soon. He'd told me not to worry about asking, but I didn't want the guy to feel under siege just because I was a horny bastard.

The images from last night were more than enough to get

me off. I lowered my hand and stroked my dick nice and slow, breath hitching as my flicker of arousal ignited into a blaze.

Declan was solid against my back, his chest hair tickling my skin, and teasing breaths drifted across the nape of my neck and shoulders.

I shivered, working my dick harder, biting my bottom lip to keep in the sounds of pleasure. Tension built to the breaking point, and just as I was on the verge of coming, Declan stirred.

"Cash, what are..."

I shuddered with orgasm, coming into my hand with a small whimper I couldn't suppress.

"Didn't mean to wake you," I rasped as Declan levered up to look at the mess I'd made of myself. "I'm ridiculously horny for you right now."

He pressed a kiss to my shoulder, lips lingering just enough to send another jolt through me. "Seeing your pleasure is not a bad way to wake up." He stroked a hand down my arm, then back up, and nuzzled in against me. "This is my morning delight right here."

I chuckled. "I like this part too."

"Good."

He continued to caress me, bringing his fingers up to comb through my hair and massage my scalp. I sighed and relaxed back against him, practically purring. With all this attention, my jerk-off session didn't feel like a solo act anymore.

I turned my face, seeking a kiss, and Declan delivered, though he kept it brief. "Need to brush my teeth."

"Me too. Kiss me anyway."

He kissed me again, indulging my neediness with sweet, clinging lips. I was straining my damn neck, but I didn't care. I'd twist myself up for this man anytime.

My phone rang, the sound startling us apart. I turned toward the table on my side of the bed, where I'd plugged in my phone last night after my shower. I reached out with my right hand, saw it was still a mess of cum and switched to my left.

Gray's name was on the screen or I might not have answered at all. He was due to start work on The Roost early. We were refinishing the floors today, the final step in the remodel Declan had approved. I still wanted to knock out a wall between the kitchen and living space—but Gray had said that wasn't really necessary to bring the building up to amazing rental standards, and besides, we had more projects to do.

Declan had lined up plumbers to take care of the problem in the Tree Hut, but there were still roofing issues on the main house, water damage in two rooms, and of course—our biggest undertaking, building a greenhouse on the grounds.

"Hey, Gray. I overslept but—"

"We've got a problem," he cut across me. "I need you at The Roost ASAP."

My stomach flipped. "What kind of problem?"

"Someone broke in. It's a mess, but well...It's probably best if you see for yourself." He hesitated. "I'll let you decide how to break the news to Declan."

"Too late," I said wryly as Declan leaned over me, brow furrowed in concern. "He just heard you."

There was a pause, then a gruff, "Damn, man. Sorry to disrupt your morning."

"That's all right," Declan said from behind me. "We'll be right over."

We rolled out of bed, and I took the quickest shower ever—a rinse and dash to get rid of the cum. I dried and dressed so quickly my clothes stuck to me.

Declan wore navy blue shorts and a white polo, looking put together even when we rushed. By comparison, I was a slob in a wrinkled and stained T-shirt out of a duffel full of wrinkled shirts. My hair probably stuck up every which way, but fuck it.

We cut through the B&B. It was early for breakfast, still, though Declan had an automatic coffee pot that was doing the good work. Mr. Jackson sat at the table, nursing a mugful.

"Morning."

"Morning," I said as Declan passed by, face tense. "Got a problem at another building. We'll be back."

Mr. Jackson rubbed a hand over his dark beard. "That's a shame. Hope it works out."

I had to jog to catch up with Declan. He might not be the most social guy, but he didn't usually ignore his guests, so I knew how worried he must be. "Don't panic. Whatever it is, we'll fix it."

His shoulders lowered a fraction. "You can't promise that."

"I sure as hell can," I said, slinging an arm around his shoulders and slowing him from his fast walk. "We've transformed that place into a gorgeous lake cabin, haven't we?"

His lips tipped up in the tiniest hint of a smile. "You've done amazing work."

"Okay, then. We've got your back."

And it was a good thing too, because as we crested the hill to the front of The Roost, the first thing I saw was the massive front window. Broken. Shards of glass littered the ground beneath it.

Declan swore. "Those are custom windows. Goddamn it!"

I winced. I'd talked a good game on the way over here, and I was sure Gray and I could replace that window. But paying for it? That was Declan's problem. "You have insurance, right?"

"Some, but..." He cringed. "I dropped to the minimum coverage on the outbuildings because I wasn't actively using them. I don't know if it'll cover vandalism."

"Shit."

Gray opened the front door, which had taken its own beating, the wood splintered and ragged near the lock. Must have been kicked in. On these older properties, charm came before security, so it wasn't reinforced. Breaking it hadn't been necessary, considering the shattered window, so I assumed the vandals did it for pleasure rather than access.

"Hey, guys," Gray said, lips pressed into a tight line. "There's more inside. The assholes made a mess, but it could be worse."

"If it was worse, I'd probably keel over from a damn heart attack," Declan said. "I'm supposed to be *improving* the B&B for when I sell it, not passing it on in even worse condition."

"Well, hey," I said, desperate to find a silver lining for him, "unless they gutted the kitchen, you're still in better shape than you started."

Declan gave me a flat look. "You're a glass-half-full kind of guy, aren't you?"

I smiled gamely. "You already knew that about me, didn't you?"

He shook his head, but again, a small smile tugged at his lips, and his tension eased a notch. *Win.*

Gray led us inside, and it sure as shit wasn't pretty.

Cream-colored paint streaked across the wooden floor, paint cans tipped on their sides. We hadn't yet refinished the floors, so I wasn't sure if that could be sanded away or we'd have to find another solution.

The bastards had spray-painted a big X on two of the walls and damaged the sheetrock on a third. There was half an X painted on the kitchen wall as well—the one I'd originally wanted to knock out between the two rooms.

Declan was mourning the broken light fixtures over the counter, but I was stuck on that half an X.

"Why only half an X?" I mused. "There's room for the whole X here."

Gray nodded. "Yeah, my guess is something scared them off. Maybe someone came in late last night?"

"We were back relatively early," I said. "The Jacksons were already in for the night."

Declan snapped his fingers. "I've got a couple in their twenties. They hit the party scene over in Swallow Beach. They probably came home between two and three in the morning."

"Maybe the vandals saw their headlights and cut out then," I said. "If they came by boat, they'd have an easy getaway with the docks behind the property."

"It's usually just bored kids," Declan said. "They could have taken off on foot."

"Wait, didn't you say you put up a camera to discourage them?"

"Obviously didn't deter them," he grumbled.

"No, but—"

"Where's the camera?" Gray asked.

We all rushed back to the front entrance, where Declan had kept the little Google camera set up. We found the smashed remains of it a few feet away.

"There goes that idea," Gray said.

"Doesn't it stream somewhere, though?" I asked. "Would you have footage in the cloud?"

Declan shook his head. "I get alerts to my phone and none came in. The battery must have died, or else they managed to turn it off or trash it without setting off an alert."

"Damn. That doesn't give you much to go on with the sheriff," I said.

"No," Declan agreed. "There's really nothing they can do. I'll make a report, but if the insurance won't cover it, I'll have to eat the costs."

"I'll call in at the resort so I can help Gray clean up. I'll get

Kat over here too. She's got too much time on her hands with that boy hanging around."

Declan shook his head. "I can't ask you to miss work. This is my problem."

"*Our* problem," I said, moving over to kiss his cheek. "And right now, you've got a B&B to run. Breakfast won't make itself."

Declan groaned. "I can't believe I forgot."

"Go deal with breakfast, call the police, call your insurance," I said. "We'll get photos of everything and send them to you, okay? Everything is going to be okay. I promise."

"Thank you, love. You're really the best."

I smiled teasingly. "Even when I insist on seeing the glass half full?"

His lips quirked. "I suppose I can tolerate it."

"That's the spirit!"

Declan headed back toward the main house. Behind me, Gray swore and kicked a rock. The rock was thick and solid, mired in the ground, so it didn't move. Gray swore louder, hopping on his other foot, and grabbing for his injured toe.

I shot him a look. "Really, man?"

"Shut up," he grumbled as he limped toward the porch and sat down hard. "It's been a shitty day."

I aimed my phone at the broken window and clicked my camera app open. "Vandalism isn't a fun wake-up call."

Kissing Declan while he pet me like a cat? That had been much, much better.

"It's not just that," Gray said, surprising me.

I took the photo, then joined him on the porch. "What's up?"

He shook his head. "Just...family shit."

I raised an eyebrow. "I know something about that. Hit me with it."

He sighed and raked a hand through his hair. "You don't need to hear this today. We've got enough to deal with."

"It's bothering you, and honestly, today is gonna be shitty enough without this storm cloud over your head. So spit it out."

Gray tugged a folded piece of paper from his back pocket. "Got this letter from my foster brother."

"Foster?" I said in surprise.

"Yeah, my parents died when I was a kid. I bounced from one place to another, but I was lucky to land in a house when I was eight and pretty much stay put."

"So you had a brother there."

"Three brothers, actually," he said with a rueful smile. "We were a real handful, but my foster mom was great." His smile faded. "She died when I was seventeen. Everything kinda fell apart without her there as the glue, you know?"

"I'm so sorry."

He shook his head. "Anyway, turns out the old man finally croaked too."

I could tell by his tone he didn't have the same fondness for his foster dad.

"Holden is trying to save the business Dad ran into the ground. Wants me to come back."

"Do you want to go back?"

A series of emotions too complex for me to read crossed Gray's face. "That's the million-dollar question," he said quietly. "Part of me never wants to see Riverton again. The other part?" He shrugged. "Feels like I have unfinished business, you know? My brothers—" His voice cracked, and he had to clear his throat before continuing. "My brothers never knew why I left. I didn't want to drag them into the conflict with our dad."

"Why did you leave?"

He shot me a tight smile. "I liked dick too much for his liking."

"Ah. Damn."

"He found out, pitched a fit, said I couldn't be *that way* under his roof, so I took my gay ass and found another roof."

"I'm sorry, man."

"Water under the bridge." He returned the letter to his pocket, but not before I saw it'd been folded and refolded about a dozen times. He was going to wear a hole through that paper soon.

"Not entirely. You wouldn't be angsting over that letter if it was all behind you."

"Guess not." He pushed to his feet with a groan. "But moping about it won't fix this cabin."

"True that." I nudged him. "But maybe deciding to visit home would take a load off you, huh? You don't have to stay forever. Just put your ghosts to rest."

"Maybe." He reached for the door. "Come on, let's get started. This mess won't clean itself."

"No, it won't." I lifted my phone and took a photo of the battered door, then followed him inside to capture the rest. My heart was heavy as I documented the damage.

Declan had only pursued this renovation because I'd convinced him to do it. He'd wanted to sell clean and simple to those developers. Now, he'd sunk money into supplies and labor expenses to Gray and me. We were saving him by not hiring a formal contractor, but all this mess would add to the tab.

At what point was I causing him more trouble than it was worth?

CHAPTER TWENTY-EIGHT

Declan

I STEPPED INTO THE ROOST TO SEE KATELYN ON A stepladder, touching up the last of the trim near the ceiling while Cash did touchups along the edge of the wainscoting.

You could hardly tell vandals had touched the cabin, but the cleanup had set us back three days. And it would have been a lot worse if I'd had to do it on my own.

Between making calls to the police and insurance—three times for the latter— I barely had time to run the B&B, much less board up the broken window, install a new door, replace damaged sheetrock, and repaint.

I bought a new camera and got it installed the first night, though. I checked the video stream so often that Cash asked whether he should feel jealous of the attention I gave it, but if those kids came back, I wanted to know it.

"You got paint on you," Cash said.

Katelyn craned her neck to look down at her body. "I don't see any."

"You don't?" Cash swiped his paint roller over the back of her knee. "It's right there."

"Cash!" she shrieked with a laugh.

Katelyn swung out with her paintbrush, just missing him as he danced away. "I'm going to get you back!"

She scrambled down the ladder and chased him across the room, the two of them laughing like loons.

Good thing the floor was already covered in paint.

I smiled and shook my head. "Seems like this is a good time to call it a day."

They both froze like a couple of naughty children caught in the act. Cash smiled sheepishly. "Sorry. We were just..."

"Taking a break from working really hard." I crossed the floor to kiss his cheek, carefully steering clear of the dripping paint roller in his hand. "Thank you." I looked at Katelyn. "Both of you."

Cash's sister looked surprised. "You don't need to thank me. You let me stay here all week."

"And it was a pleasure having you," I said. "You don't have to paint my walls for that. As long as I own this B&B, you're welcome here."

She glanced at Cash uncertainly. "Really?"

I wasn't sure if she was asking me or him. Cash answered before I could figure out what to say.

"Yeah, Kat. He means it." Cash smiled at me. "He always means it when he says things like that. He's pretty great that way."

She let out a little watery laugh. "I wish I could stay longer."

"Yeah, it's a miracle Mom let it go this long," Cash said with a grimace. "I've got three missed calls from her. We'll have to go home soon."

Kat wrapped her arms around her stomach, her expression more queasy than awed now. "Yeah. Guess so."

My heart wrenched—and not just for them. I selfishly couldn't imagine sleeping in my bed without Cash warming my side. I loved the quiet, intimate talks we shared in the dark. Loved the innocent expression on his face when he was sleeping —one that was definitely never there in the light of day. Loved stroking and caressing his skin, soaking up closeness and cuddles.

Cash's phone rang. He dragged it out of his pocket.

"Is it her?" Katelyn asked, sounding anxious.

Cash shook his head as he raised the phone to his ear. "Hey, Sawyer. What's up?" He paused, nodding. "Yeah, we're packing it in for the day. We're almost done with the work out at The Roost. We'll be starting the greenhouse soon, but..."

While he caught Sawyer up on our progress, I drew Katelyn toward the doorway a few feet away. "Are you okay going home? You seem worried."

She looked surprised by the question. "It doesn't really matter what I think."

"I disagree," I said. "What you want matters. You and Cash both."

Her expression turned knowing. "Cash doesn't have to come back with me. He's an adult. He can move out and be with you."

"That's not what this is about."

She patted my arm. "Thanks for letting me stay as long as you have. I know I'm not your problem."

I wanted to argue, but Cash joined us then. "Hey, my friends are having a cookout. How about we go celebrate finishing up this paint job? Ash is grilling, so the food will be good."

Katelyn brightened. "That sounds fun. Maybe Shua will be there again."

"They probably will," Cash agreed. "They hang around Sawyer's place all the time."

"Cool. I'll go change!"

Katelyn took off down the hill toward the main house, weaving right to avoid the stacks of supplies that had been delivered for the greenhouse we'd be building over the next couple of weeks. My stomach fluttered. That was one project I never thought I'd see.

It would probably be smarter to finish all the maintenance on the property first. Hell, it would probably be smarter not to build it at all. It was part of Aunt Millie's dream vision, yes, but hardly necessary to sell the B&B. The new owners might not even want to use it, but...

Once I'd imagined it, I just couldn't seem to let the idea go. There was plenty of space and it couldn't *hurt* property value any, so why not just get it up? It would be fun to stage it for sellers. I could build raised beds, bring in soil, figure out a hydroponics system and which varieties of vegetables I could plant—er, which ones the *new owners* could plant—for the best results.

"I haven't seen Kat that happy in a while," Cash said.

"Yeah. She's less happy about going home."

He grimaced. "The feeling is mutual."

"You don't have to go. Either of you."

Cash shook his head. "Declan—"

I held up a hand. "And before you jump to the conclusion Kat did, no, I'm not just saying that because I'll miss you here. I'm saying, you're an adult, and if you take responsibility for Kat, maybe you could both have a better situation."

Many of those little chats in the dark had filled me in on just how toxic their home life had gotten. Cash knew it was bad, but I wondered if he realized just *how* bad. After all, sometimes when you were just getting through each day, you didn't see the bigger picture.

"But you *will* miss me, won't you?" Cash teased.

"That's not the point."

He tapped my nose playfully. "Say it."

I sighed, exasperated. "Yes, of course I'll miss you once you're gone. Hell, I'll miss you tonight while you're out at that cookout too, but you deserve to go have some fun after all this work."

He squinted. "Why would you miss me? You're coming too."

"What? But—"

"Declan," he said with a laugh. "You're my boyfriend, right?"

"Yes..."

"So, any invitation to a cookout at Sawyer's includes you too. Besides, I haven't really gotten to show you off to my friends yet. I need to rub it in their faces because I took a *lot* of crap for the silly crush I had on you."

I snorted. "So I'm going as arm candy?"

"Basically." He slapped my ass. "So let's go get ready."

We arrived at the LandShark Retreat RV park twenty minutes later, mainly because Kat had taken that long to do her hair and makeup. Apparently, sitting around a bunch of trailers at a campground required full glamor.

When I mentioned it to Cash, he laughed. "I can tell you've never been with a woman."

I scowled. "And you've been with so many?" He opened his mouth, and I raised a hand. "Don't answer that!"

"I haven't been with that many," Cash said. "My preference has always been tall, dark, and grumpy."

He kissed me playfully while Katelyn pretended to gag behind us—and in full view of Cash's friends, which included Hudson. At least I had one ally in the bunch.

It reminded me of what he'd said to me only a few weeks

ago. That I was supposed to date Cash and make Hudson feel less like an old man among them.

It had seemed so impossible when he said it, and yet here we all were.

"The lovebirds are here!" Fisher called from where he sat cozied up on Hudson's lap in an Adirondack chair.

"You're one to talk!" Sawyer called from his spot by the grill.

He followed up his words by eating a bite of shrimp from his boyfriend's fingers with an indecent moan of delight.

"Neither are you," Poppy said, sticking out her tongue. "I'm all alone on The Love Boat and you're all making me seasick!"

The woman seated beside her at the picnic table nudged her. "What am I? Chopped liver over here? I don't have anyone slobbering over me either."

As we rounded the table to take the empty seats next to Brooks and Skylar, I was surprised to see Poppy's friend was the baker from Hot Buns.

"Slobbering sounds so romantic though," Cash teased. "How can you resist?"

Jasmine snorted. "Been there, done that. Now I just want someone who'll listen to me bitch and moan about my crap day, you know? My brother has no patience for me, and Poppy here has been a great listener and all, but I worry I'll drive her up the wall."

Brooks chuckled. "You can't be any worse than the rest of us. Poppy is kind of our relationship glue."

"Ironic, huh?" Poppy joked. "I'm the aro ace, and yet I keep these guys in line when they're being stupid about love."

Poppy's ease with speaking about her ace identity surprised me. For too long, I'd treated my asexuality like a dirty secret, a source of guilt and shame that I couldn't fit in the same as everyone else.

Before Cash, I'd given up on relationships. I hadn't just given up on love, I'd given up on even *trying*.

I reached for his hand, lacing our fingers under the table. So much had changed. I didn't think I'd ever be able to express to him how happy he made me.

Hudson grabbed a couple of beers from the cooler and handed them out. He clinked the neck of his beer bottle against mine. "How are the repairs coming along at the B&B? It's a shame about the vandalism. I could come by and help on my next day off."

"We're nearly done with those repairs," I said, nudging Cash's shoulder. "This guy is the hardest worker I've ever met."

Sawyer pretended to be shocked. "Cash? Hard-working? I don't understand..."

The friends laughed and trash-talked each other, but there was no meanness to it. Skylar jumped in, singing Cash's praises at the resort. It didn't surprise me. Cash was dedicated when he cared about something, and despite initial appearances, he cared deeply for his friends.

And for me.

Ash brought over a platter with skewers of shrimp, steak, chicken, and slices of bell pepper, onion, and thick mushrooms. He set a sauce dish beside it.

"Kababs with a homemade teriyaki sauce," he said. "I hope you enjoy."

Sawyer went inside and came back with a bowl of salad. "And here's some rabbit food, which is all I'm allowed to prepare these days."

"Thank all that's holy," Cash cried.

Sawyer smacked the back of his head before dragging another Adirondack chair over close to the table and plopping down into it. He patted his thigh. "C'mon, Ash, sit down and feed me some more."

"I shouldn't have to watch this," Poppy said.

"I'd pay to watch it," Cash joked.

Katelyn smacked his head as she returned with the neighbor kid, Shua.

"Ow. Why is everyone hitting me?" Cash complained.

"Hello? Your boyfriend is right there. Don't be that guy."

"I'm joking!" Cash said, leaning in against my side. "I've kissed Sawyer once. I don't want to kiss him ever again."

"You better not," I grumbled, wrapping my arm around his shoulders for good measure.

Hudson laughed. "Wow. Never thought I'd see this moment."

"That makes two of us," Cash said, glancing up at me with eyes full of love. "But I'm really glad we finally got there."

"Me too," I said softly, dropping a kiss to his forehead.

"Aw, so sweet," Jasmine murmured. "I hope Abe's night is going as well as yours is."

"Where's Abe?" Skylar asked.

"Out with a very persistent barista."

Brooks barked a laugh. "I guess Danny didn't need to pretend to date you after all, Cash."

"I'm hurt," Cash said. "What am I, chopped liver over here?"

Jasmine grinned. "I doubt your man would say that."

"I certainly would not," I said firmly.

Cash was good at making jokes. Everyone laughed and had a good time. But I knew that sometimes, underlying those jokes were true insecurities. I didn't want him to ever question how I felt.

"He's the best thing to ever happen to me," I said.

Skylar sighed and pressed a hand to his heart. "Damn. I wish my boyfriend was that sweet."

Brooks huffed. "I say sweet shit all the time."

"Sawyer is *never* that sweet," Ash chimed in.

"If you wanted sweet, you'd have never chosen me."

Ash laughed. "That's true."

"I don't know why everyone is calling me sweet," I complained. "I'm just being honest."

"Well, I think it's great," Hudson said. "This will be good for you both."

"And entertaining for the rest of us," Fisher put in with a snicker.

"Cash deserves it," Poppy said. "He's waited long enough." She paused, giving me a considering look. "I'm guessing you deserve it too, and have probably waited even longer."

"You're not wrong," I said quietly.

She smiled. "I'm always here if you need someone to listen."

"And *this* is why I want to date you," Jasmine burst out. At Poppy's horrified look, she added, "As friends, I mean. No romance! No sex! Just...awesomeness."

Poppy tilted her head. "Huh. That actually sounds kind of cool."

It seemed as if even an aro ace could find a special someone —even if it was just a really close friend. Somehow, I found that reassuring. My relationship with Cash wasn't a fluke or a wild stroke of luck.

It was just two people coming together and knowing they were better together than apart.

CHAPTER TWENTY-NINE

Cash

I RAISED THE CARAFE OF COFFEE THE NEXT MORNING, where Declan's latest round of guests sat at the breakfast table. "Who wants a refill?"

Gray had called with questions about the greenhouse project, and Declan had looked so excited to go talk shop that I'd offered to cover breakfast service.

A broad-shouldered guy in a plaid shirt named Chuck raised his cup. "Hit me. I'm used to coffee darker than oil. This fancy stuff isn't cutting it."

I smiled gamely and refilled his cup. His wife, a sturdy sort of woman with curly red hair and tons of freckles shook her head when I offered her the same.

"Well, I love the coffee," Jade, a blonde in a flowery tank top said. "It's just right for us lightweights."

Her boyfriend, Drew, lifted his cup, saluting me. "And for those of us with a hangover. Fill 'er up."

"Did you all hit Shallow Beach again?" I asked as I poured the dark brew. Jade and Drew were the couple who were out late the night of the vandalism. Unfortunately, they'd told Declan they hadn't seen anyone when they got in that night.

Chuck snorted. "That's an appropriate nickname. I've never seen so many bikinis in my life."

He must not get out much. I was fairly certain Ft. Lauderdale would have us beat by a mile. But the partying got pretty rampant across the lake.

"It's wild over there," Katelyn said from her spot at the table. "I've only been to a party there once, and I thought Cash would kill me when he caught up."

"Nah, I'd have to hurt any guy trying to lay hands on you though. You're only fifteen."

"Aw, you're a protective big brother," Jade said. "That's sweet."

Drew slung an arm over her shoulder. "Now, don't go getting any ideas, Jade. You'll break my heart."

She laughed and slapped his arm. "Stop it! You know Declan is his boyfriend."

Drew grinned. "Eh, some guys go both ways."

"He's not wrong," I said, tapping my chest. "Bi guy. But I'm also loyal, which means no cheating with pretty guests."

"That's good news for me," Drew muttered.

Jade laughed and blushed a little. "Don't be silly."

Katelyn sighed. "So gross. Why do people think you're so hot?"

"It's the burden I have to bear," I said with a put-upon sigh as the guests all laughed. The conversation moved on to their plans for the day, and Chuck got into a lively debate with Jade about the best kind of vacation. He insisted there was nothing better than fishing in a quiet spot at the lake, enjoying nature, while she liked to get out and experience the local culture.

I could see the appeal to both, but I had no desire to wade

into that mess. I mentally checked out while I finished my breakfast plate.

My phone rang shortly before the end of breakfast service. I pulled it out to check the screen.

Mom.

"I've got to take this," I told the guests. "Take your time. We'll clean up later."

Katelyn looked at me with questions in her eyes. I nodded to confirm that the call was from our mother. When I headed toward the private quarters I shared with Declan, my sister followed.

I answered the phone as I stepped through the door. "Hey, Mom."

"Cash, I'm glad you answered. It's time to come home."

I sighed. I knew as soon as I took her call that would be her take. It's why I'd avoided talking to her the past few days. I hadn't been ready for the reprieve to end.

"Will things be different?" I asked.

"Your father has cooled down. I explained to him why Kat was upset. We just want things to get back to normal."

Normal was a shit baseline though, wasn't it? I couldn't forget what Declan had said to me the day before. That I didn't have to go back. That maybe Kat didn't either.

I'd continued living at home far past the point I wanted to leave because I didn't want to abandon my sister. But maybe there was an alternative. Declan would let us stay here, and when he sold, I could work out some sort of arrangement with Skylar.

I wouldn't be able to help Mom with as many bills, but maybe that would encourage her to see Dad for the albatross he was.

"Cash?" Mom prompted. "I want to see Kat there when I get off work at 11, okay?"

"You're calling from work?"

"I'm on a break." Her voice faltered. "I really can't go another day without seeing her. She doesn't pick up when I call."

Damn. It hadn't occurred to me that Mom would call Katelyn too, but of course she would. What did it mean that Kat was avoiding her as much as I was?

Probably that we were both at our limit for family drama.

"Okay, we'll come home today to talk. I can't promise we'll stay."

"Cash—"

"We'll see you in fifteen minutes."

Katelyn whirled away and stormed out the door. I hung up the phone and followed, finding her shoving things haphazardly into her duffel while dashing away tears leaking from her eyes.

"Kat, we're just going to talk to them."

She grabbed up an armful of clothes, sniffling. "We both know they're going to make me stay."

"Then I'll stay with you."

She shook her head hard. "You've got a good thing here. Why would you come back? Why did you stay so long in the first place? I'd leave now if I could."

"For you, Kat. I stay for you."

She dropped the wrinkled mess of clothes into the duffel bag and turned to me with wide eyes. "No, you don't."

"Of course I do."

She scrubbed at her teary face. "But I..." Her voice gave out and she tried again. "I wouldn't stay for you. If it was the other way around, I mean."

"I know." I smiled, not hurt in the slightest. She was fifteen. At that age, I wouldn't make the same choices either. Plus, she was my *baby sister*. It was my job to protect her, not the other way around. "But we both know I'm the better Hicks sibling."

I startled a laugh out of her, and she slapped my arm. "You wish."

We finished packing her bags in a few minutes. By the time we left, she looked more resigned than heartbroken. But I wasn't so sure of the outcome just yet. Declan had planted some thoughts that were taking root.

Why had I thought staying was the only way to look out for Kat? Why hadn't I considered that helping my mom with bills only enabled my dad's behavior?

We arrived at the house a few minutes early and headed for the door. It was like a replay of the last time I'd brought Katelyn home after the night of that party. She'd been ready to apologize and accept consequences for going—but Dad had laid into her instantly, saying inappropriate, disgusting things. In another situation, I might have said that Kat deserved a good lecturing after lying and putting herself in a dangerous situation. But Dad had been the one to provoke her into that rash action by insulting her, cutting her down, always drunk and ready to spread his misery.

It was a toxic environment she shouldn't have to live in.

I eased the door open. Dad lay on the sofa, eyes only half open. "'Bout time," he slurred. "One of you get me a beer."

Katelyn turned for the kitchen, but I stopped her. "We're not feeding your addiction anymore."

My sister turned wide eyes on me. "Cash, you know how he gets."

I shook my head. "Things have to change if we're coming back here. Dad has to get help."

"Help." He barked a sharp laugh. "There's no help. You two are fucking useless."

"Where's Mom?" Katelyn asked in a small voice.

"Working. Always fucking working," Dad mumbled. "Dunno why she keeps going back to those assholes."

I secretly agreed with that sentiment. Mom deserved better hours, better pay, better respect. But Dad was the hugest hypocrite, lying on that couch, doing nothing to help.

"You're not paying the bills," I said.

"Neither are you," he snarled. "Fucking loser."

Katelyn made a wounded sound and whirled toward the front door. "I can't do this anymore!"

She fled outside.

"Goddamned drama queen," Dad snarled.

I decided Kat had the right idea. I went outside, closing the door hard behind me. Mom was just coming up the driveway in her old Chevy beater. She opened the driver's door.

"Good. You're here."

"And we're leaving," I said flatly.

Katelyn was already climbing into the truck and slamming the door behind her. Mom looked from me to the pickup. Then she sagged. "What happened?"

I shook my head. "Dad's a bastard. What do you think?"

"Don't talk about him like that," she said sharply.

"I'll respect him when he earns it," I shot back. "But we both know he never will."

Her eyes welled with tears. I looked away, unable to face the pain in her face. This had always been my weakness. Mom loved, and she loved hard, but I couldn't keep living by her choices.

Declan was right. I was an adult now. That meant taking control of my life.

"I'll talk to him," Mom said after a tense pause. "I'll get him to work on it."

"He won't change. He's an addict, Mom."

"He's in pain. He's suffering—"

"So are we!"

She flinched back against the car, and I took a deep breath

and forced my voice to soften. "So are we, Mom. We can't go on like this. You might choose this life, but I can't do it with you anymore."

"You're an adult. I can't stop you if you want to leave. But Kat is a teenager. She needs her mom."

"She needs a home life that doesn't make her want to die, Mom."

Mom sucked in a shocked gasp, tears spilling. "Wh-what... Did she say—"

"The first time we left, yeah. I think she was being dramatic, but today." I shook my head. "If you'd seen her face when she ran out of there. She can't take it anymore. Dad targets her. She's a teenager, and she's going to cry over boys and make bad choices, and having someone eviscerate her for it is going to permanently damage her self-esteem. Her self-worth. If it hasn't already."

"I don't know what else to do," Mom said.

"You could leave Dad."

She shook her head. "But he...he's injured and in pain. It's not his fault he's like this. Do you know what it's like to live with that pain every day?"

"I don't know," I said. "I hope I never do. But, Mom...he refused the therapy that could have helped him manage the pain."

"You don't know that it would have worked."

"You don't know that it wouldn't have."

She cast a bleak look toward the pickup truck, where Katelyn was slumped down. It looked as if she were trying to hide in the hopes Mom would forget she was there. No such luck.

"So this is an ultimatum? Leave your father or lose my kids?"

"It's not an ultimatum, Mom, but we can't live like this

anymore. You can make whatever choice you need to make. But I have to make choices, too."

"I can't stop you from going, but Kat is a minor. I can send the authorities to bring her home."

"I know." I swallowed. "I hope you won't make that choice, though. If you want to stand by Dad, let me stand by Kat. Please. I'll take care of her."

"It's not that easy to raise a teenager, Cash. You're in your twenties. This is all too much for you."

"I've been taking care of her my whole life." I shrugged. "Why stop now?"

Mom surged forward from the car and threw her arms around me, hugging me tight. "I need to think about all this. Give me a little time. Please?"

"Yeah," I said. "I'll take Kat back to the B&B for now. She's happy there."

"I miss you both so much. I wish..."

"We'll make a coffee date, okay? Swallow Cove is a small place. We're not cutting you out of our lives, Mom. I'll see you at the resort whenever you come to clean."

She huffed a breath. "The resort is ending its contract with my company. Apparently, there's been some issues with work not getting done."

I nodded. "Yeah, I saw it firsthand one day."

She drew back, pressing her lips tight. "We have a lot of turnover."

Probably because of the shitty hours and pay. I decided not to rub salt in the wound, though. "Maybe without us to worry about, you could look for a better job," I suggested. "Let the house go and rent a smaller place?"

She looked gobsmacked by the idea. "Oh, I don't know." She glanced toward the house. "We have some happy memories here. Before...you know?"

"Yeah, I remember."

My father hadn't always been a miserable drunk. He'd worked a lot, but when he'd come home, he'd tossed the baseball with me in the backyard, grilled burgers out on the deck, and fixed leaky taps in the bathroom. He'd been a little gruff, a little impatient, but nothing like he was now. He gave great hugs. I remembered that so clearly my chest ached.

But good memories didn't change the past decade. It didn't change that Katelyn barely remembered that man at all. He was gone. Maybe someday, Mom would realize it too.

Until then, I'd made my choice.

So had Kat.

Mom went inside and packed a couple more bags for us. When she brought them out, her face was tear-stained, her shoulders slumped in defeat.

"I'm sorry," she said quietly as she passed the bags over.

"Me too."

We stared at each other a beat, but there was really nothing else to say.

I joined Katelyn in the truck, and we drove away. Neither of us looked back.

CHAPTER THIRTY

Declan

The B&B phone rang just as I was coming in from the garden, my knees still dusted with dirt. I'd spent an hour weeding and watering, then gone over to check out the progress on the greenhouse.

Gray had brought in a couple of extra guys to help build it while Cash and I worked on some of the easier repairs at the main house. They hadn't yet started installing glass, but the wood framing had gone up, giving it a tangible shape.

My stomach flipped with excitement. Aunt Millie would be so thrilled to see her vision becoming reality. And it was all thanks to Cash pushing me to dream a little.

Just like he had a week ago, when we'd gone on our date at The Drunken Worm and he'd told me I didn't have to get a financial analyst job. That I could pursue anything I wanted now.

It was such a big, nebulous idea, but as I circled the greenhouse...maybe I could see it a little more. A life working in the garden instead of a stuffy office, growing and selling produce instead of analyzing data. I was good with numbers, but I didn't *love* them.

Once I sold the B&B, I'd get a payout. But would it be enough to walk away from a more practical job for good?

By the time I got to the host's desk at the edge of the great room, Cash had already picked up the phone.

"Treehouse B&B. This is Cash, your booking extraordinaire. How can I help you?"

While he spoke, he tapped at the laptop keys, navigating to the booking software. He'd picked up so many calls and entertained so many guests over breakfast in the past few weeks that he could run this place without breaking a sweat.

I could just see it now...Cash charming every guest that booked in, the reviews on the B&B shifting from "owner is unfriendly and grumpy" to "owner is wonderful and sweet and hot!" The Treehouse would probably become one of the best spots to stay in Swallow Cove—not because it was the only option, as it had been for so long, but because guests would finally get the friendly, intimate experience I could never provide.

"Third week of September, let me check..." Cash covered the mouthpiece on the phone. "Should I book that far out?"

"Go ahead. We don't know how long it'll be on the market. We'll get the buyer to honor existing bookings."

He nodded and resumed the call. "Okay, you're in luck. I've got you down for our Cottonwood Room. It's got a gorgeous view of the lush gardens and trees, but also the lake, which let's be honest, that's why you're visiting, right? Can't miss that." He chuckled as they replied, keeping up the friendly banter as he finished the booking.

But his smile didn't quite reach his eyes.

In the three days since Cash walked away from his parents,

we'd settled into a routine that fit as comfortably as my favorite cardigan on cold winter days.

In the mornings, he helped me with breakfast service before heading off to a coffee date with Poppy, then to work at the resort. On his off days, he continued to help with repairs, mostly focusing on the smaller updates needed at the main house while Gray oversaw the greenhouse construction.

In the evenings, we made dinner—or occasionally picked something up—along with Katelyn. She seemed relieved to be back here. When I'd told her to stay as long as she wanted, she'd hugged me tight and told me I was the best. Cash, though? He'd smiled tightly and promised to look for a place of their own.

I didn't *want* him in a place of his own.

I headed for my quarters to shower off the dirt and sweat while Cash wrapped up the phone call. I trusted that he'd get the coffee started while I did. When I returned, I'd make breakfast, and we'd both fall into the routine of another day.

Cash took off soon after, giving me a quick kiss on the cheek before he did. The B&B kept me fairly busy. I had two rooms to turn over, with hours of laundry, vacuuming, and dusting. When I wasn't working on those, I was paying bills, which were steadily stacking up with all the extra renovations.

It was late that night before we were alone and could really talk.

I cuddled up to him in bed, my chest tight. Because I was so dang happy, but he was obviously hurting, and I didn't know how to help. "What can I do?" I murmured. "How can I make you happy?"

"Well, there's one thing that *always* makes me happy." He wiggled his eyebrows at me.

I didn't take it seriously. It was Cash's way to mask his pain. To brush away concern, to widen his smile, and up his antics.

"Fine," I said to call his bluff. "If a blow job will make you feel better..."

I tugged the blankets down, but he grabbed my wrist. "Wait. No. I didn't mean that."

I raised an eyebrow. "Want to try actually talking to me, then?"

He closed his eyes, face tightening with emotion. "I think I fucked up."

"What do you mean?"

His throat worked. "I was so quick to walk away, but... I've been looking through rental listings, and there's not much I can afford. And now I've got to get a place big enough for Kat, too. I could maybe buy a trailer like Sawyer did, but I've got no savings. Not after helping my mom pay the bills every month. Hell, I don't even have a boat or a car I could sell. I've got *nothing*."

"Hey, that's not true." I put a hand on his arm. "You've got me."

He opened eyes glassy with unshed tears. "We can't go on like this forever, though."

My heart stuttered. "What do you mean? We're together. I don't want that to end." I pulled away. "Do you?"

"No." He sat up quickly, grasping my hand and squeezing. "That's not what I mean. The B&B is going on the market. You're gonna sell. I don't know where you plan to live after, or if there will be space for me and Kat, and—"

"Of course there will be. Wherever I end up, I want you with me. You and Kat. You're a package deal, and I'm perfectly happy with that."

His brow furrowed. "Declan, it's asking too much of you. I'm the one who took responsibility for Kat, not you. I'm the one who has to take care of her."

"Can't we all just take care of each other?"

283

He blinked. "But you're dating me, not my sister."

"I love you," I said. "And you love Kat. Which means I love Kat too. It's simple, Cash. I thought you were the one who understood relationships."

He gave a startled chuckle. "Uh, maybe I mostly understood sex. The relationship part is new for me too."

"What do you think of it?"

He smiled at me, and this smile *did* reach his eyes. It jolted my heart and started flutters in my gut. "Right now, it's looking pretty good."

He cupped my face, and I leaned in to kiss him, warmth flooding me. "I love you too, by the way," he murmured against my lips.

"Good." I slid my fingers through his silky hair while I kissed him once more. "Because I don't want you to go anywhere."

Cash drew back. "I'll help pay expenses. And if I don't have enough to cover it, I'll get more work. I won't take advantage. I promise."

"Sweetheart, you already practically run this place for me. Do you really think I'm worried about it?"

"I don't do that much," he said. "I just help pick up the slack here and there."

"Well, it may not seem like a lot, but it makes my life a lot easier and I appreciate it."

He ducked his head, looking almost shy. "Glad I can help."

I put a finger under his chin, tilting his face up so I could look him in the eye. "So we're clear on this, right? I'm asking you to live with me."

He wet his lips. "Would you ask if my living situation wasn't so unstable?"

"Yes," I said without hesitation. "I might have waited longer. I wouldn't have wanted to rush you. But I got used to having you in my bed. Got used to sharing dinner and waking up with you beside me. I don't think I can go back to living separately, Cash. I don't want to." I paused, heart pounding. "What about you? Would you agree to live with me if things were better at home?"

"Oh, hell yeah." He grinned. "As long as Kat was safe and happy, you couldn't pry me out of your bed."

I laughed, relief sweeping in. "Okay, then. We're on the same page."

"I guess we are." Cash faltered, and I could tell there was still something bothering him. "But I'm leaving my mom high and dry."

My heart ached for him. "It's not easy to cut ties."

"I help her with the house payments, and now she's just on her own? Like oops, sorry, guess you'll just lose your house." He scrubbed his hands down his face. "I'm a terrible son."

"No, you're not," I said sharply. "You're protecting yourself and your sister."

"Why do I feel so shitty then?"

I wrapped my arms around him, hugging him tight. "Because you love her. It's not an easy thing you're doing, but easy isn't always *right*."

"My mom shouldn't have to pay the price for my dad's behavior."

"Maybe not," I said. "But she made a choice. And now you're making one too. And in the end, maybe your choice will help her figure out she needs a change, too."

Cash slumped against me, tension leaking away. But I wasn't so sure he was relaxed as much as exhausted. Emotional turmoil took a toll.

"I wish it wasn't so damn hard," he mumbled. "I wish I wasn't the one making these choices."

"I know, love." I pressed a kiss to his temple. "It'll get easier.

You just have to get through it. There's a light on the other side. I promise."

He settled back onto the pillow, and I held him and whispered reassuring words, unsure of how much they helped. But as long as I kept saying them, kept holding him close, at least I was doing *something* to ease his pain.

"I couldn't do this without you," he murmured sleepily, patting my arm, which was still wrapped around his middle. "I'm so happy to be here."

Cash could have done it without me. He had a whole group of friends who were supportive as hell. But I was glad he didn't have to. I wanted to be the man he counted on, the one who comforted and reassured him.

I squeezed him, heart full. "Don't ever leave."

"Okay," he whispered.

Just as I was about to drift off, my phone chirped. I checked it, fearing it might be the camera alert at The Roost, though there'd been no more signs of trespassers.

I rolled over and picked up my phone while Cash's soft snores drifted across the room. It wasn't the camera alert. Just a text.

Nate:

Hey, man, sorry for over-reacting the other day. Let me know if you change your mind. Ball's in your court, however long it takes.

A second text followed the first.

We can talk about the remote job, too. If you're still interested in working with me.

Huh. It wasn't like Nate to apologize. He'd definitely gone too far when we spoke last. He'd seriously made me doubt our friendship. Maybe he'd just been in bulldog mode, though. Nate was a closer, and he closed *hard*. It probably hurt his ego that he couldn't bring this deal home.

Still, there was something about his one-eighty that rubbed me wrong. Maybe it was just that I had more people in my life now, people I trusted, people I *loved*. I couldn't imagine Cash— or hell, even Hudson or Skylar—pressuring me the way Nate had.

Taking the job offer with him would solve a lot of problems, though. I'd just told Cash he could count on me. Could I really afford to go chasing dandelion dreams instead of a reliable paycheck?

I hesitated a moment, then answered.

I appreciate the apology. I'll think about the job. But the development deal is still a no-go.

Nate responded instantly.

For now. But you'll change your mind. I'm sure of it.

CHAPTER THIRTY-ONE

Cash

DANNY WAS WHISTLING A JAUNTY LITTLE TUNE WHEN I joined Poppy at Just The Sip. I envied his good mood a little.

Declan had reassured me a lot last night. I loved that he wanted me with him—wherever he ended up living. And it meant a lot that he was willing to include Katelyn in our future together. But I hated that it was happening in the middle of all my dysfunctional family drama.

Declan was right, though. I couldn't blame myself for the choices my mom made. If she insisted on drowning alongside Dad, if she refused to grab a lifeline or swim for shore, I couldn't save her.

Danny pointed at me with me a grin, practically beaming waves of happiness my way. "Don't tell me. You want the DP."

I smiled back, my mood lightening. "You know me so well."

"It'll be ready in two minutes." He grabbed a large travel cup and whirled away to make the drink.

I turned to Poppy. "Do I look okay?"

"Uh, yes?"

"I don't smell bad or something?"

Her forehead furrowed. "No..."

"Then why is Danny, the biggest flirt in town, not so much as winking at me over ordering The DP?"

Poppy laughed. "I think maybe he's got another guy on his mind."

"Is that right, Danny? Have I been thrown over by a big man who's good at kneading your mounds of dough?"

Danny cast a look over his shoulder. "You're one to talk. I hear you've shacked up with Grumpy Bear."

Poppy snorted a laugh.

"Yep," I said proudly. "I'm living with my boyfriend. I'm that guy, and I don't care who knows it."

Danny finished my drink and set it on the glass counter between us. "Good for you. I'm glad it worked out."

"Same to you. Sorry I had to bail on Operation Fake Date."

Danny waved it off. "That's all right. It was a stupid idea, anyway. Abe isn't really the kind of guy who responds to games."

I nodded. "I know what you mean. How did we end up with such mature men?"

"It's a mystery!"

He whipped up Poppy's drink next, then ran my credit card to cover the order. We took turns paying, and I was sure I owed her by now.

"I guess I don't need to ask how the house hunt is going," she said as we took a seat.

"Nope." I sipped my double-praline cream, sighing at the sugary goodness. "I was pretty stressed about trying to find a place. I didn't want Declan to feel obligated, you know?"

She nodded. "I'm guessing he changed your mind?"

I smiled. "Yeah. He isn't just offering me a place to stay. He wants to live together, you know? That makes it different somehow. It probably doesn't make much sense outside of my muddled head."

"Sure, it does. You're not a burden. You're his partner who he wants with him."

"That's it, exactly." I sighed. "He loves Kat, too. He's totally happy for her to stay with us. I...still have mixed feelings about that. He didn't sign up for raising a teenager, you know?"

She scoffed. "Please. He knows your situation at home. What do you think single parents do when they meet someone? You're building a future and a family, Cash. If he can't handle that, he's not in it for the long haul."

"I hadn't thought of it that way." I chuckled. "How did I get so damn lucky?"

"Maybe it's karma," Poppy said.

I raised an eyebrow. "You think I deserve good karma after fucking around for so long?"

"No." She kicked my ankle. "I think you deserve good karma for being a good person, Cash. For looking out for your sister. For trying so hard with your family, trying for longer than a lot of people would have. You deserve this happiness. You've waited a long time for it, so try to enjoy it, okay?"

I nodded, my throat too tight to answer right away. I took a few gulps of my decadent coffee. "Thanks, Pops. You're a great friend."

"I know I am."

"If it weren't for you explaining the ace spectrum to me like I was a kindergartner, I might have screwed up this thing with Declan. I owe you so much."

"Well, you just bought me a hot chocolate," she said, lifting her drink. "Let's call it even."

It wasn't close to even, but Poppy didn't like it when people made a fuss. "I'm buying the next round, too," I said.

"Deal."

Poppy, proving she was the best friend ever, gave me a lift over to the resort so I wouldn't have to grab a water taxi at the marina. I clocked in and greeted Grandma Kitty with a tight hug that made her squeal and slap my arm.

"You look happy today, Cash."

I rounded the front counter in the lobby, taking up my station and logging into the booking system. "I guess I haven't been the best company over the past few days."

"Oh, no, I wouldn't put it that way," Kitty said. "But you've obviously been worried."

I nodded. "I'm seeing everything I have to be grateful for today," said. "Like the best Work Grandma ever."

She chortled. "You just keep buttering me up, mister, and I might bring you a cupcake later."

"Ooh, you're the sweetest grandma, too. Anytime you want to throw Brooks over and adopt me, I'm ready."

She laughed. "Grandma's heart has plenty of room for everyone."

A few hours passed while I did the mundane tasks of my job. I took a room service order, answered a question about our cable service for another guest, and gave a young couple directions to the Outdoor Market.

I wondered if Declan and I were doing the same thing right now—and how much he hated it. It was a shame that the B&B life wasn't for him, because I loved it over there. Even when I was taking a booking call or chatting up a guest, it was so much more relaxed that it never really felt like work.

The phone rang, and I picked it up on autopilot. "Treehous—er..." I cleared my throat, aware that Skylar had just approached the desk. "Swallow's Nest Resort. This is Cash speaking. How may I help you?"

"I've got an important question," a blustery voice said. "Why the *hell* can't your resort keep tourists out of my hole?"

291

I recognized Chester's voice and rolled my eyes. "Hold that thought."

"But—"

I stabbed the Hold button and looked at Skylar. "It's the daily vent session from the Weekend Hookers. Did you need something?"

Skylar grimaced. "Do you want me to take it?"

"Nah, that's why you pay me, right? Don't go punishing yourself for no reason."

He laughed. "Okay. Just come by my office when you're done. We need to chat."

"Okay." My stomach swooped. "Nothing bad, right? I know I flubbed the greeting on the phone. That won't happen again. I've just been answering phones over there a lot too..."

"I'm sure your head must be spinning from working both places."

Uh-oh. Was Skylar annoyed I was devoting so much time to a competitor? It wasn't really his style, but...

"It's nothing bad," Skylar assured me. "Wrap up the call and then we'll talk."

Reluctantly, I took Chester off Hold. "Okay, what's wrong now?" I said. "Too many men poking their rods in your hole?"

Chester missed the innuendo. "Exactly that! Skylar *promised* us we'd get to keep our fishing spot. It has our name on it!"

"The resort allows guests there during restricted hours. That's all Skylar promised. You don't own the lake, Chester."

He harrumphed. "I tried to take Miss Kitty on a lovely picnic and show her my favorite bait, and the place was overrun!"

"Mm-hmm. Just what kind of bait were you intending to *show* Brooks's grandmother? You better be careful."

"What do you mean?"

"You know Brooks is living with Skylar. You piss him off, and there might be no hookers in that hole."

"Are you threatening me, young man?" he said so indignantly I almost laughed.

Grandma Kitty liked Chester for some bizarre reason, but he was so damn easy to wind up.

"Just a friendly warning," I assured him. "Be a gentleman with Miss Kitty."

"I always am."

"Good, keep it that way and I think we'll all be happy."

"Okay..."

"Thanks for calling. Have a great day!"

"Oh, but what about—"

I hung up quick before he could launch into his original complaint. What would be the use of sidetracking him so nicely if I had to stand there and listen to his whining about the fishing hole? The Weekend Hookers had been a tough sell on the resort, and Skylar had done what he could to give them some ownership of their favorite fishing spot while still making it accessible to tourists on weekends.

Of course, with a guy like Chester, if you gave him a fishing hole, he'd just want the whole lake. He was never satisfied.

I turned toward the other clerk working the desk. "I've got to step away. If Chester calls back, tell him to stop being so uptight and share his hole."

"Uh...okay."

I headed to Skylar's office. The door was open, but I rapped on the door frame to alert him I was there.

"Hey, come in," he said.

"What's up? I hope my working over at the B&B isn't a problem. I know I've kinda been helping your competitor."

He waved me to a chair. "You know I don't care about that. Declan's important to you."

"Yeah." I dropped into the seat. "So, you called me in to thank me for handling Chester every day? I *do* deserve a raise. You're correct."

He chuckled, perfectly aware I was kidding. I got paid a good wage for my position, and I was grateful for it.

"I do appreciate skipping that headache," he said. "But actually, I wanted to talk to you about housekeeping."

"Uh-oh. More problems?"

"I've decided to transition to an in-house housekeeping staff, which means I'm looking for a head of department. I've been taking applications for someone to manage scheduling, supervise staff, and ensure it all runs more smoothly so it's not my problem."

I wasn't sure why he was telling me all this, but I nodded along. "Sure, makes sense."

He hesitated. "Your mother has applied."

My stomach flipped. "Oh."

"But I know your relationship is strained right now, and I don't want to make things uncomfortable for you if I decide to hire her."

A wave of relief hit me. "No, that would be great. I've wanted her to leave that agency for a long time. The hours are terrible, and the pay—" I stopped short. "She'd get better hours and pay here, right?"

"She'd manage the department, yes. I'm offering 50k a year to start, along with health insurance, vacation and sick benefits, and the opportunity to earn bonuses during our busiest booking weeks."

"That's amazing."

With that kind of pay, Mom could manage the house payment. If she insisted on staying with Dad, at least I wouldn't have to worry about them becoming homeless.

"She'd primarily work Monday through Friday, the daytime

shift, though she might have to make up staffing shortages at times. She'd be compensated, though. I don't believe that salary equals unlimited hours of servitude. I've seen how corporations operate, and I'm trying to build something different here."

"I know, Sky. My mom couldn't ask for a better job. I hope you offer it to her." I paused. "But please only do it if she really is the best candidate. I don't want those kinds of favors."

"I figured you'd say that, but she's more than qualified. She's my top candidate, but I didn't want to move ahead without talking to you first."

"Well, if that's the case...it'd be great to see her get the job. Thanks for the heads-up."

"No problem."

With the increased salary, Mom might be less likely to leave my father out of desperation. But I didn't want her to leave for that reason. I wanted her to make a change because she wanted a better life.

With this job, maybe she'd finally see that she *could* have more than the bare minimum.

CHAPTER THIRTY-TWO

Declan

When Cash and I arrived at The Rusty Hook, only two other boats bobbed at the dock and one lone group sat around a table on the deck, a cloud of smoke drifting from their cigarettes.

I laced our fingers together, holding Cash's hand as we went up the steps. He shot me a smile. "This is pretty different from the last time we were here, huh?"

The last time...

Oh. The night Sawyer kissed Cash, and I'd stormed out like a jealous fool.

I winced. "I tried to pretend I wasn't upset over that kiss."

Cash's lips quirked. "I remember. Good thing you have a bad poker face, huh? I knew you cared more than you wanted me to know."

"Yeah," I agreed. "Real good thing."

Cash paused to kiss me before we went through the door. "Just for the record, I prefer kissing you to anyone else."

"Good, because I'm the last man you're ever going to kiss."

Shit. That sounded bad.

Cash just laughed. "I'm going to take that in a fairytale-ending way instead of the creeper serial killer vibes you just gave off."

"Sorry." I chuckled. "That sounded better in my head."

He grinned. "I like that you're not holding everything inside anymore. And, uh..." He leaned in close. "I kinda dig the threatening vibe. Don't hurt me, Daddy. I'll be a good boy."

I shoved him through the door while he laughed. Freaking brat.

The pub was relatively quiet on a Wednesday night, so we had our pick of tables. I chose one by the bay window with a great view of the sun setting over the lake.

Orange and pink streaked across a lavender sky, its reflection bouncing across rippling water, creating a mirror effect.

"Sometimes I forget how beautiful it is here." I shook my head. "I can't believe I actually considered leaving that view."

"Not to mention this one." Cash pointed to his face and fluttered his lashes.

I grinned. "Well, of course. That's my *favorite* view."

"Good answer." He nudged my foot with his playfully. "Because you're going to be stuck with it forever, apparently."

He was teasing me about that *last man you'll ever kiss* crack, and probably would do so for the rest of our lives.

I just smiled. "Lucky me."

We picked up the menus, and when the server came by, we placed our orders. Cash asked for a burger with loaded fries, eating like someone who didn't yet understand the toll shitty food would take on his body. I ordered the skillet trout and summer veggies because sadly, I wasn't in my twenties anymore.

We both got the beer on draft, since it was on special.

"Kat could have come with us, you know," I said, apropos of nothing. "I don't want her to think she's a third wheel."

"That's sweet, but I don't usually invite her on dates."

"You know what I mean. We're more than dating. We're all living together as a..." I hesitated, not wanting to cross a line.

"What?"

"Well, we're kind of like a family now, right?" I wet my lips nervously. "I mean, I know it hasn't been very long, and I'm not saying I could ever replace her parents. I just...want her to feel welcome."

Cash reached for my hand. "Declan, that is sweetest thing I've ever heard. You're lucky we're in public."

"I am?"

He lowered his voice. "I seriously want to throw you over the table and rip your clothes off."

"Oh, uh...yeah. Probably not the best time for it."

He smiled, a sexy tilt to his lips. "You just let me know when the time is right."

"I will," I promised, nudging his foot this time.

"But don't worry about Kat. She's out with her friend Jenna for the first time in weeks. She's really happy that we left home." He chewed his bottom lip. "It looks like I made the right choice."

"Of course you did. I know you've been worried about your mom."

He nodded. "Yeah."

"But Skylar is a great employer. She's going to be okay."

He smiled, some of the tension leaving his body. "She is, isn't she? This job is a great opportunity for her."

"It's very good timing," I agreed.

Almost too good. I wondered if I should send Skylar a thank-you card. I doubted he'd hire Mrs. Hicks if she wasn't qualified, but the fact she was Cash's mom certainly hadn't hurt her chances, either. Skylar looked out for his friends.

And Cash seemed more relaxed than I'd seen him since he'd walked away from his parents.

Darlene returned with our drinks, and we chatted about our workdays, passing the time companionably enough.

"I'm anxious to see the greenhouse come together," I said. "Gray has had too many boat tours to do much more than frame it out."

"It's their busy season."

I nodded. "I know. I'm not complaining. Gray has been amazing. I'm so grateful."

Cash gave me a mock glare. "Don't appreciate him *too* much. You've already got a boyfriend."

"A very wise boyfriend who got me some qualified help."

"That's right. I should get all the credit for Gray's work."

I raised an eyebrow as I raised my beer for a drink.

Cash smirked. "What? Too much?"

"Just a little."

Cash's eyes widened. "Oh shit, look who it is."

I turned toward the door, expecting to see Cash's gaggle of friends crashing our dinner. Always a risk when at The Rusty Hook, where they hung out often. But I was okay with that because the goal tonight was to make Cash happy. If that meant hanging out with friends, that was just fine.

But it wasn't any of the usual crowd we'd seen at the cookout.

Danny and Abe had just stepped inside together, looking like the coziest, most mismatched couple ever.

Danny leaned in close, his head barely reaching Abe's shoulder. Abe had one giant hand pressed against Danny's back, guiding him through the doorway.

Danny's gaze landed on us, and he grinned and waved, heading in our direction.

"Do you mind if they join us?" Cash asked. "I can tell him we want to be alone."

"No, it's fine," I said. "After all, you still owe him a date."

Cash swatted my arm with a snort. "That was just a scheme to get Abe."

"So you say," I muttered, though I couldn't entirely hide my smile.

Cash rolled his eyes. "Abe is looking at Danny like he's the best thing since freshly baked bread. I don't think you need to worry."

"Oh, I'm not worried," I said. "If I worried about every guy interested in you, I'd probably stroke out."

Cash's eyes widened as he laughed. "What?"

I nodded toward the side of the room, where a young guy—clearly a tourist judging by his brand-new Swallow Cove T-shirt—was checking out my boyfriend.

Cash winced. "I was hoping you didn't notice that."

So, Cash had *seen* him watching. I shouldn't be surprised. He'd worked pubs like this for hookups for years.

Cash half stood, leaning over the table. He cupped my face and leaned in, so close I could see the striations of color in his blue eyes, little flecks of green encircling dark pupils. Pupils that were dilating.

"I only want you," he said, right before he kissed the hell out of me in front of the whole pub.

His kiss was aggressive, pressing in and demanding I open for him. I hadn't been kissed this way since the night I'd invited him to take me without holding back.

He was *claiming* me, I realized. Showing me that no one else mattered. Showing *them*, too.

I raised a hand to his face, brushing my thumb over his

scruff, so damn grateful that I had a man who would make me feel like the center of his world.

"Whew! Are we interrupting something?"

Cash drew back, eyes still on mine. "I don't know," he said. "Are they?"

I shook my head, struck mute by the emotions clogging my throat. Cash dropped back into his seat with a satisfied smile. It was a little smug, probably one I'd have taken as arrogant when we first met. Now, I knew it was more of a promise than a brag. He wanted me to know he'd kiss me again that way anytime I wanted.

I shifted in my chair, surprised to find that I did want it quite a bit just now. I wasn't an exhibitionist, but Cash's devotion to me was damn inspiring.

"Good," Danny said, dropping into one of the open seats at the table. "Because now I *really* want to join." He wiggled his brows and reached for Abe's hand, tugging him down into the chair beside him. "Right, babe?"

Abe blushed as prettily as any schoolkid with a crush, but he didn't argue.

"Isn't he the cutest?" Danny continued, as if we were in the middle of a conversation. "He's so shy."

Abe sighed, but when Danny leaned in, he slung his arm over his shoulders with a tiny smile.

"So," Cash said, "did Danny tell you the lengths he was willing to go to for your attention, Abe?"

Danny gasped dramatically. "How can you do me dirty like that, Cash? I thought we were friends!"

"I mean, I'm just making sure Abe understands what he's getting into," Cash teased. "You're a handful."

"Oh trust me, Abe knows *exactly* how many handfuls I am." He winked.

"Dear god," Abe muttered.

I chuckled, taking pity on the guy. "So, how are you liking Swallow Cove now that you've had time to settle in?"

He cast a warm look at his spitfire boyfriend. He was continuing to speak in so much innuendo with Cash it was like the two of them had another language.

"It's been...surprising."

I smiled to myself. "Life can be that way."

Abe glanced at Cash with a wry tilt to his lips. "We didn't stand a chance, did we?"

I chuckled. "No, I don't think we did."

"Lucky us," he said, fondness coating his words.

I couldn't disagree.

By the time we left, it was fully dark, with bright stars sparkling in a velvet sky. Cash sat beside me, head tilted back as he drank in the sight. "Tonight was really great. Thanks for taking me out."

"I'll take you out anytime you want," I said. "Just because I'm a homebody doesn't mean you have to be."

He rolled his head toward the left, smile soft and sweet. "I like being at home with you, too, you know? My job gives me plenty of social outlet with all the people I meet."

"No kidding," I said. "I don't know how you do it, but you charm every guest."

With Cash's charisma, I could probably happily run the B&B for years to come. But of course, I'd never have that. Although, I did have Cash by my side now...

That changed things, didn't it?

We tied up the boat behind the B&B and disembarked, a gentle breeze fluttering our hair as we stepped onto the dock.

It was a sweet, balmy night. I was relaxed and happy.

In love.

"Hey, Cash," I said.

He turned toward me. "Yeah?"

"Remember when you said to tell you when it was the right time to rip my clothes off?"

His lips were on mine in a heartbeat, warm and inviting. He wasn't forceful yet, still testing the waters with a tentative brush of tongue.

I kissed him back, opening for him, and giving back too, the want building gradually, rising from a simmer to a boil.

Cash trailed kisses along my jaw to my throat.

"It's such a nice night," I murmured.

He paused. "Does that mean I should stop?"

"No." I threaded my fingers in his hair and tugged him back enough to look into his eyes. "I want you out here."

He shuddered. "Fuck, really?"

"Is that too exposed for you?" I asked. "I don't think anyone's outside, but—"

"Hell no." He ripped his T-shirt off and shoved his shorts and underwear down. In three quick moves, he was entirely naked in front of me.

I sank to my knees, and he sucked in a sharp breath as I leaned in to brush my lips along his hard shaft. I raised my eyes to his. "It was really moving the way you claimed me tonight, kissing me in front of everyone."

He swallowed. "Yeah? I'm glad that didn't embarrass you."

"No. We're so different. Sometimes I need reassurance."

Cash waved to his dick. "This is only for you now, Declan. I'm yours."

The affirmation sent a wave of affection through me. I leaned in and took him into my mouth, sucking him slow and sweet, savoring the sounds he made as I edged him toward his end.

Cash tangled his fingers in my hair, holding tight. His eyes clenched and his jaw tightened. "Gonna—"

He came in a wash of cum over my tongue. I did my best to

swallow, sputtering a little. Cash dropped to his knees and kissed me hard, sweeping his tongue in and tasting himself on me.

He dropped his hand to the bulge in my shorts, caressing my length. "My turn."

He pushed me down onto my back and attacked the button on my shorts. I stared up at the sparkling sky, need dancing through my body as Cash swallowed me down.

Heat, pressure, then sweet, sweet friction.

I came in a rush, my cry echoing and my pleasure pouring out to the whole sky.

We cleaned up in the lake and started toward the house, both of us exchanging goofy smiles. I'd surprised him tonight—surprised myself a little too—but I loved the freedom to express my love in whatever way felt right to me in the moment.

Sex. Kisses. Cuddles. Hugs.

Cash took whatever form of love I had to give, and he treasured it equally.

"Tonight was—" I stopped short as the sound of an engine cut through the night. "What was that? No one should be out right now."

Cash's eyes widened, and he took off running for The Roost. Shit, had the vandals returned? I pulled out my phone, but the security cameras showed no notifications.

Cash met me at the base of the hill, shaking his head. "Everything looks fine. Maybe one of your guests was out late?"

"No, not tonight. Do you really think I'd have done all that if I thought someone could watch?" I swallowed as bile rose in my throat. "God, you don't think—"

"No," Cash said. "Of course not. The motor sounded more distant. They were probably nowhere near us."

He was probably saying that to make me feel better, but I was relieved anyway.

"I think we should take a look around," Cash said. "Be sure nothing else was disturbed. Maybe a tourist got lost and used your property to turn around."

It wasn't the worst theory. And I liked it a hell of a lot more than vandalism. We did a more thorough check of The Roost, checked out the Tree Hut, then headed toward the greenhouse.

I could just make out its shadowy shape in the moonlight.

"Shit," Cash said.

"What?" I turned on my phone flashlight, shining it around, looking for what had made Cash react that way. It wasn't what he was seeing, though, but what he *wasn't* seeing. "Goddamn it."

The piles of polycarbonate sheeting for the walls were missing. The industrial toolbox Gray had kept out here was gone, too. Every hammer, every nail, every extra plank of wood.

All gone.

Someone had stolen all our supplies. And now, under the glow of my flashlight, I saw they'd graffitied the shit out of the framing with red spray paint.

Not just Xes this time. A warning, too.

LEAVE.

"I have to call the sheriff," I said numbly.

"I'm so sorry," Cash said. "You're probably wishing you'd just sold to those developers and avoided all this trouble, huh?"

"What? No." I waved a hand toward the greenhouse, anger flashing through me. "If I'd sold, I wouldn't have seen my aunt's dream fulfilled and realized it's *my* dream too. I won't be chased off by whoever the hell is pulling these stunts. This is *my* B&B, and no one gets to tell me to leave."

Cash watched me, a furrow in his brow illuminated in the glow of our phone flashlights. "I thought you wanted to sell the B&B, anyway?"

DJ JAMISON

I looked from the obvious confusion on his face to the green-house that I'd begun to daydream about every day.

"Right, I...uh...just meant no one gets to tell me what to do."

"Is that what you meant though?"

My stomach clenched and my mouth went dry. "I don't know. I just...I loved the idea of this greenhouse so much. I was already envisioning what I could grow in there. Pearl and Ruth Marie thought I could sell produce at the Outdoor Market, but..." I shook my head with a nervous chuckle. "Those are just silly daydreams."

Cash stepped in close, grasping my face. "Declan, sweet-heart, if you don't want to leave the B&B, it's okay."

"But...that was the plan. We remodel and we find someone who wants to run it, because I can't keep doing that."

He nodded. "I know. But if you're happy here, maybe there's another solution. You could hire a manager to run the B&B and—"

"But that's stupid."

Cash stopped short, looking wounded.

"Okay. Never mind."

I realized how badly that must have sounded. I grasped his arm, tugging him closer. "No, no, I just mean why would I hire a manager when you're perfect for the job?"

He blinked. "You mean..."

"If you wanted to do it, yes, it'd be the perfect solution. I don't want to be the face of the B&B. I don't want the pressure of entertaining guests. But you're so good at it, Cash, and you're my partner now, right? If I stay, you'll stay too. But—" I winced. "You probably want to work at the resort with your friends."

"Well, now, that's stupid," he teased me with a smile. "Of course I'd choose running your B&B over just about anything else in the world."

The fact either of us could smile right now, standing next to the scene of a crime with a call to the authorities imminent, had to mean something.

"Our B&B," I said as a sense of rightness welled inside me. "It would be ours if we did this."

He took a breath. "Okay, then, I guess we better get the sheriff out here so we can nail these bastards who are targeting *our* B&B."

CHAPTER THIRTY-THREE

Cash

DECLAN'S PHONE ALARM CUT THROUGH THE ROOM THE following morning.

"Ah, god, already?" he grumbled, his voice muffled by his pillow.

He was normally an early riser, but he'd been up late making a report to the sheriff's deputy, then compiling a list of all the supplies taken, property damaged, and locating receipts for the value of everything to submit to the sheriff's department.

Some of that could have waited for morning, but I suspected he was too wired to sleep.

Eventually, I'd crashed out while waiting for him to come to bed.

I rolled over and nuzzled the back of his neck. "Late night, huh? What are the chances the authorities can catch this asshole?"

He sighed. "Not very good, and insurance won't cover my lost supplies."

I squeezed the back of his neck, massaging gently. "I'm sorry. I wish I could do something more."

"You're here with me." He rolled to face me. "That makes it easier."

"Good." I dipped down to kiss him and he turned his head so my lips grazed his jaw instead.

"I feel like something died in my mouth. Do not kiss me right now."

I laughed. "Okay."

His eyes fluttered shut, and he looked flat-out exhausted.

"Tell you what, how about I cover breakfast this morning?"

His eyes flew open. "Shit, what time is it?"

"Time for you to sleep in." I patted his chest. "I'll handle it."

His brow furrowed. "I can't ask you to do that."

"Last night, you said you wanted to keep the B&B and let me manage it. Did you mean that?" I asked.

"Of course I did."

"Then I might as well get started, right?" I said lightly. "I'll have to give the resort a couple of weeks' notice before I can take over entirely, but I can do this for you today. Rest up."

I showered and dressed, then whipped up some simple pancakes and bacon for the guests since it was the weekend. It wasn't anything fancy, and I made a mental note to text Ash later and ask for some kick-ass breakfast recipes.

If I was going to manage this B&B for Declan, I wanted to do a damn good job. He was putting a lot of faith in me, and I never wanted him to regret that choice.

Katelyn dragged her ass out of bed in time to help me serve coffee. "Where's Declan?" she asked, still sleepy-eyed.

"Sleeping in," I said. "He had a late night."

Kat wrinkled her nose. "I don't need to hear about your sex life."

Last night, we *did* have some pretty incredible sex. I was

tempted to overshare the details just for that smart-ass remark. But I had a feeling Declan would never agree to an outdoor blow job again if I did that.

"No, brat. There was a theft on the property last night."

Stacy Gillespie, a cute thirty-something blonde who looked more like twelve with her hair hanging in two braids, looked up from her phone. "A theft here?"

Rina, her roommate—and probably girlfriend, though they hadn't explicitly said—frowned at me. "Should we be worried?"

"It wasn't here at the house. It was tools and supplies by the greenhouse."

The women visibly relaxed, but another guest—Jed Hartnett—walked in just then. "What's going on?"

I winced. Apparently, on my first day managing the B&B, I was going to be telling the guests about crime on the property. Not the best PR. But it was only smart to alert them in case they had seen something last night.

Unfortunately, no one had noticed any strange trucks. Or rather, they'd seen so many they didn't pay any attention to them. With Gray and his couple of guys working on the renovations, it was normal to see vehicles coming and going.

Maybe not so normal at night, but by that point, most of the guests were in for the day. Unlike the first instance of vandalism, we didn't have any partiers returning late last night.

After breakfast, I went outside and found Declan already up and talking to Gray. He must have slipped out the kitchen door while I was busy in the dining room.

"I'm going to buy out Dyck's supply of cameras," Declan was saying. "If you could help get them installed every damn where a vandal or thief might strike, I'd appreciate it."

"Of course. I can't believe this shit happened again," Gray said. "I wanna kick this motherfucker's ass."

"You and me both," I said, stepping up to slip an arm around Declan's waist.

He was so tense it was like wrapping my arm around a plank of wood. I squeezed his hip, tugging him against me, and he melted into my side. Better.

"You didn't get anything off the cameras at The Roost?" Gray asked.

"No, those are too far away to get a visual on vehicles driving by," I said. "They just cover the doors and windows right around the cabin."

"It was a mistake to only put cameras there," Declan said, "but I thought it was just kids looking for a place to party."

"No way it's just kids making off with over a grand worth of polycarbonate though. Not to mention my toolbox. That sucker is worth five grand with all the tools inside."

"I'm so sorry," Declan said. "I've never had problems like this before. I promise I'll compensate you for the loss."

Gray shook his head. "Let's make the bastard who did this compensate me."

"We should put a camera at all entry points to the property," I said. "If we can catch even his license plate on camera, we can give the sheriff's department a lead."

"Then I hope he comes back," Gray said. "Maybe I can be here when he does. You know, I could camp out in the Tree Hut for a while. Keep watch over there. It's got a good vantage point."

"Really?" Declan sounded relieved. "That would be a load off my mind."

"And we could stay out in The Roost," I told Declan. "We'd cover more property that way."

"Sounds like a plan," Declan said.

∿

Over the next week, we all operated in a state of high tension.

Each night, Declan collapsed into bed exhausted, then tossed and turned because he couldn't sleep.

He checked his camera feeds every few hours, and at least once a night, I found him out walking the grounds. Sometimes, I joined him on the patrols, knowing it gave him a sense of control in an unpredictable situation.

But I worried about how long he could go on this way without burning out. He still had to work all day—at least until I finished out my last few shifts at the Swallow's Nest—and I hadn't seen him tend to his garden all week.

Hudson had given me rides home, staying long enough to have a beer and check in with Declan, so I knew I wasn't the only one who worried.

Friday, the bed jostled me awake in the middle of the night. Declan sat on the edge of the mattress we'd placed on the bedroom floor of the Roost, fabric rustling as he kicked off his shoes and pants.

I reached for my phone, squinting at the display to read the time: 3:30 a.m.

"Hey," I rasped. "It's really late. Or should I say early?"

"Sorry." Declan scrubbed a hand over his face. "Didn't mean to wake you."

"I don't care about that. You need to rest."

"I can't relax," he admitted. "Every time I close my eyes, I think, what if he's out there right now? Then I check the cameras. Then I think, what if he's just outside the range of the cameras?"

"Declan, there's a possibility he won't even come back."

He groaned. "I know. I just can't turn off my brain."

I knelt behind him and wrapped my arms around his shoulders, hugging him from behind. "I'm worried about you."

"I'm sorry," he said softly. "This shouldn't be your problem."

I drew back. "Are you kidding? This is my life too, right? I may not own the B&B, but you said—"

He turned and kissed the protest from my lips. "Yes, of course. I'm sorry, love. I just hate that this is infecting your life, too."

I smoothed his hair back from his face. "I signed up for this, Dec. There's no other place I want to be."

"That means a lot."

"Good. Lie down. You're going to stay in this bed and rest, even if I have to tie you down."

He chuckled. "I'm not into that kinky shit."

I guided him down to the mattress, wrapping an arm around him so he couldn't sneak off on me.

"You're not too old for a spanking, so don't push it."

He remained still, but he practically vibrated the whole dang bed with tension. I rubbed his shoulders. Damn, they were tight and hard as a rock. I kneaded until his flesh warmed and his muscles softened, then slowly made my way down his back.

When I squeezed his glutes, he startled.

"Shh, relax." I moved my hands to his thighs, working his quads and hamstrings. "I'm not trying to dick you down."

His laugh was heavy and slurred. "Might not even notice if you did. So tired."

"I know, sweetheart. Just close those eyes. I'll check the cameras for you, okay?"

"Mm."

He exhaled, body slack and heavy, and finally slept.

And that's when the camera alert finally went off. I lunged for the phone, checking the stream, and sure enough, there was a truck passing by the camera at the entryway.

It would drive right by the Tree Hut, so I grabbed my phone and called Gray.

"Yeah?" he answered gruffly.

"He's here." I checked Declan's camera. "Look out your window."

There was a rustle of bedcovers shifting, then the rattle of blinds. "I see him."

"I'll have Declan call the sheriff."

"He might be gone by the time they arrive," Gray said. "I'm going out there to detain him."

"Gray, that might be dangerous—"

"Call the sheriff and get him out here ASAP then."

Click.

He'd hung up. I turned to see Declan awake and alert. He held out his hand. "Give me the phone. I'll make the call."

I handed it off and reached for my clothes. "I've got to get out there. I don't want Gray handling this guy alone."

"I'm right behind you," Declan said grimly.

I tugged on my shorts while Declan talked to the sheriff's department, then raced outside. Without the camera feeds on Declan's phone, I had no idea where our trespasser might be. I headed toward the Tree Hut, since that's the last place he'd been—and the place Gray was most likely to have intercepted him.

There were sharp voices coming from the middle of Declan's garden. I veered left, heading toward the two man-shaped silhouettes. As I watched, one took a swing, the other ducked and lunged, and then a full-on scuffle ensued.

Shit! Who knew how dangerous this guy was? Even if he was a petty criminal, he wouldn't want to be caught.

I poured on the speed, barely noticing when I passed too close to a rosebush and a thorn tore through my calf. I reached the scene just as Gray wrestled the perp's arms behind his back, pinning him to the ground with a knee.

"You okay?" I gasped.

"Fine." Gray grinned wolfishly. "Caught me a vandal."

The guy squirmed. "There's been a misunderstanding!"

I crouched down, eyes widening when I recognized Bruce Ford. He ran a fishing charter about ten minutes south of town. He used to work with my father.

"Bruce?"

"Cash! Thank god. Will you tell this man to get off my back? Please. My arms feel ready to snap."

Gray eased up the pressure, though he didn't let go. "You know this guy?"

"He worked with my dad back in the day."

My phone rang with Declan's number, and I picked up. "Hey, we're in the garden. Gray has him pinned down, and I know who he is, so even if he gets away, he isn't getting away with anything."

"I didn't do anything wrong!" Bruce shouted, bolder now that he wasn't pinned like a bug.

"Be right there," Declan said.

By the time he arrived, sirens sounded from the main road.

"Bruce was just telling us what he was doing here," I said as Declan arrived.

"I was just out for a walk," Bruce said.

"So why did we see your truck on camera?" I asked.

Bruce faltered. "Yeah, I mean I, uh, was just out for a drive, and then I saw this great garden, so I decided to get out and enjoy—"

"Bruce, you live half an hour away, and it's four in the morning. Try again."

"You can't prove anything," Bruce snapped as Declan slipped away to wave the deputies over. "A man can be outside!"

"This is private property, sir," a deputy named Wade said.

Luckily, Gray had released Bruce when the deputy cars arrived and was standing there looking menacing but innocent. I'd hate for him to get hauled in for tackling the guy for us.

DJ JAMISON

"Well, I didn't realize that," Bruce said. "I apologize. I'll just leave."

Wade shook his head. "I'm afraid it won't be that easy. We're going to have to take you in for questioning in a series of vandalism and thefts on the property."

Bruce swallowed hard, and I could see by his expression he was scared shitless. This was our guy. There was no doubt in my mind.

"Why would you do it?" Declan asked Bruce. "You've got a business to run just like us."

He scoffed. "My business is in the shitter, not that anyone gives a damn. You've got plenty of family money stashed away. We're nothing alike, you and me."

Deputy Wade pulled the cuffs off his belt and read him his rights. After he put Bruce in the back of his car, he tipped his hat at us. "We'll get to the bottom of this. Don't you folks worry. Get some rest, and I'll check in tomorrow. You can let me know then if anything else was disturbed tonight."

"We've got camera footage too."

Wade nodded. "Send me anything that'll help the case against Bruce."

"Deputy," I called as he turned away.

He paused next to his car. "Yes?"

"I don't think Bruce would do this on his own. It doesn't make any sense."

"Sometimes men just get angry and desperate. In my experience, crime hardly ever makes any sense."

CHAPTER THIRTY-FOUR

Declan

"Babe, wake up. The sheriff's calling."

Cash sat on the edge of the bed beside me, holding out my cell phone. I wiped at my bleary eyes, trying to clear the sleep fog from my brain.

I could swear I'd only just closed my eyes, but the bright sunlight filtering in through the window suggested hours had gone by.

After the deputy left, it had been damn near five a.m. Cash, Gray, and I had gone to the kitchen to make a pot of coffee and speculate about why Bruce would vandalize my property.

He could sell the supplies he'd stolen, but why damage The Roost at all? It didn't make sense. And I didn't care what the deputy said, there had to be *some* reason for it.

An ugly suspicion started to form, a pit in my stomach that said I knew the answer if I really thought it through. But the adrenaline from the confrontation dropped, and I started crashing hard. Cash had sent me to bed with a promise to wake me if there were any updates.

"Declan?" Cash prompted when I was slow to wake up. "Do you want me to take the call?"

"No," I rasped, reaching for the phone and bringing it to my ear. "Hello? This is Declan."

"Declan, sorry to disturb you. Sounds like you had a busy night," Sheriff Roy Minnis said with a chuckle.

"We did. I assume that's why you're calling?"

"Yeah. We checked Bruce's property. Found the exact number of polycarbonate sheets you reported stolen along with an industrial toolbox full of tools. Didn't even have to get a warrant. The dang fool had it all sitting out in his yard in broad daylight. We're getting it all documented, and then we'll release the property back to you."

I exhaled noisily. "That's great news. Thank you."

Cash leaned in closer, and I angled the phone so he could hear the other side of the conversation too.

"Once we told Bruce what we found, he was more forthcoming. Says he was hired to do the vandalism. The theft was just for his own benefit. His business took a hit from a new competitor across the lake. He's been struggling."

"Hired by who?" I asked. "There's no one around here who'd benefit from it. The resort is my only competition, and they're doing great."

Not to mention Skylar would never do that anyway.

"Bruce didn't have many details," Sheriff Minnis said. "He answered an online ad placed by a company named Second City Acquisitions. They arranged everything via email. Have you heard of the company?"

"Nothing comes to mind," I said.

"It could be a false name to hide the identity of the perp, but if you can think of any connections at all..."

"Second City is a nickname for Chicago," I said slowly. "I got an offer from some developers based there. They wanted to tear down the B&B and put up condos. I turned them down. But I researched them thoroughly after everything that happened with those shady guys and the resort. They go by the name 360 Views, and they have projects all over the world. I don't see why they'd want the B&B badly enough to resort to criminal acts."

"It's worth checking out anyway," Sheriff Minnis said. "We'll give you a call to let you know when you can retrieve your stolen property. This is almost over."

"Thank you. I appreciate that." I hesitated. "What will happen to Bruce?"

"Well, I don't know. He's cooperating, so most likely the district attorney will offer him a more lenient deal. Restitution to pay for the damages, probation, maybe a little jail time. It won't be too long, most likely. I know that may not be much comfort—"

"No, it's more than enough. Sounds like Bruce fell on hard times. I just want this to end so we can all move on."

"I understand," he said. "I'll let you get back to your day. If you can think of anyone else who'd want to target you, let us know. We'll look into 360 Views to be sure they're not involved."

"Thank you."

I hit Disconnect, frowning to myself. Something wasn't adding up. Yes, 360 was in Chicago and they'd offered me a development deal, but I'd had no contact with them. Every step of our deal had been negotiated through Nate.

My heart stuttered.

He wouldn't...

"Declan?" Cash asked. "What is it?"

I swallowed hard, remembering the suspicions that had tried to form before tiredness got the best of me. They were back now, far too clear to ignore.

319

"I think..." I shook my head, unable to say it out loud. "I need to make another call."

"Okay," Cash said gently. "Do you want me to leave or..."

I latched onto his wrist. "Stay, please. I'm going to put it on speaker phone, just in case... Well, just in case. Don't say anything though. Just listen, okay, and confirm for me I'm not being paranoid."

"Okay, sure. Who are we calling?"

"An old friend in Chicago."

I brought up Nate's contact and hit Call. I was pretty confident he'd answer because after his apology text—which came not long after The Roost vandalism—he'd called twice to just *check in.* He hadn't pushed for the development deal, not after our first fight, but he'd dropped hints it would be there when I was ready.

Nate didn't give up easily, so I wasn't surprised he was like a dog with a bone. But he'd seemed to accept that he couldn't force my hand.

Or maybe he'd just decided to force it another way?

The phone rang twice.

"Hey, Declan!" Nate sounded happy to hear from me. "How's it going out there in the boondocks?"

"It could be better," I said.

"Oh?" He sounded concerned. Either I was wrong about Nate, or he was a damn good actor. "What's going on? Maybe I can help."

"We've been having a rash of vandalism out here," I said. "Some supplies and tools were stolen last week."

"Shit, man, that's bad luck, but it's not too late to sell and get rid of all those headaches."

"Yeah, about that..." I said. "We installed cameras, so we were ready when he showed up again last night. We caught him."

"Oh yeah? Well...that's good then."

"He was hired by someone in Chicago."

I let the statement drop between us. I glanced at Cash. His eyes were narrowed, jaw tight. Obviously, he understood my suspicion, and it was taking all his restraint not to jump in.

I squeezed his hand, and he squeezed back. He had my back, however this talk went.

Nate broke the silence with a nervy laugh. "Why would anyone in Chicago care about vandalizing your property?"

"Good question. I was just sitting here wondering the same thing, and the only connection to Chicago I still have is you and 360."

"Shit, you think 360 is behind this?"

"Not really, Nate. They're too big to care about this one little deal." I took a breath and forced out the words. "I think it was a bigger deal to you, though. Right?"

"Me? You think I'm behind this?"

"You brokered the deal. That meant a payday for you. It must have been a big one too, because you just couldn't let it go, could you?"

"Jesus Christ, Declan, I can't believe you'd accuse me of something like that based on some semantics bullshit. And after everything I did for you. I'm your *only* fucking friend because no one else wants to be around you!"

Cash leaned toward the phone I held between us. "Declan has plenty of friends, asshole. *Real* friends."

"Who the hell is this?"

"I'm Cash, his boyfriend."

"Ah, the reason he backed out on me. Let me guess? You wanted him to keep the B&B so he could take care of you. Is Declan your sugar daddy now?"

All Cash's *daddy* jokes flitted through my head. I repressed a hysterical laugh. The image Nate was trying to paint, the gaslighting he was trying to do, was ludicrous.

Cash met my eyes. "I'd gladly let Declan spank me anytime he wants."

"Jesus, Cash," I grumbled.

"But our relationship is built on trust and mutual respect. I'm guessing you don't know much about that, Nate."

Nathan scoffed. "Sure it is. Declan, don't let your dick lead you, man. You need to do what's right for you, not what will please some piece of ass."

Nate clearly had no idea I was graysexual or he might have tried a different argument.

"Even now, you're still trying to sell him," Cash said in disgust. Then he winced. "But I'm supposed to be staying out of this. Sorry for interrupting, Dec."

"That's okay," I said with a tight smile. "You're not wrong. Nate's first priority is always closing a deal."

"So the fuck what?" Nate growled. "Selling that lakefront land would have made us so much fucking money. I put my ass on the line to make it happen, and I was counting on that deal to go through. Did you even think about that before you backed out on me?"

"I didn't formally agree to anything," I said. "I told you not to rush me."

"Well, I didn't have time to wait around!"

"Why not?" Cash asked.

Nate went silent.

"It was you then." It was no longer a question. "You hired Bruce to vandalize the property and get me to change my mind."

"I never said that."

"Maybe not, but I'm not stupid," I said. "I let you play me

for too long. I thought you were actually my friend, or I might have put this together sooner."

"I didn't play you," Nate said. "I proposed that deal because you were unhappy there. I *was* being your friend."

"But something changed. When it came down to money or friendship, you chose money."

The pause that followed was its own kind of confession.

"I think I better call my lawyer," Nate said.

"Probably," I agreed.

The line went as dead as our friendship. I sat there, mind reeling as I replayed every interaction we'd ever had through a new lens.

Nate stopping by my office to bring me a coffee and chat about my work. A chat that always led to market trends, current speculation, and my latest data analysis.

At the time, Nate had validated my work. But now I could see it for what it was.

Nate used me to get a competitive edge over other brokers. He cultivated a relationship with me, but it was always about work. Even when he'd reached out to me here over the years, it'd been to casually ask my take on the markets or to float the idea I might want to come back to the city.

Why didn't I see him for what he was?

Cash rubbed my arm, interrupting my internal spiral. "Are you okay?"

"I feel so stupid."

"Don't do that," Cash said. "Nate betrayed your trust. He's the asshole here."

"And I didn't see it."

"He's good at pretending. That much was obvious to me, even in this phone call."

"If I hadn't closed myself off to everyone, if I wasn't so isolated..."

Cash cupped my face. "Listen to me, Declan."

I met his gaze with difficulty, eyes burning and throat tight.

"Nate was a piece of shit, but you've got real friends now. You've got me. You've got Hudson and Fisher, Brooks and Skylar, and Pop—"

"I've got Hudson, but the rest are your friends."

"Remember how you said Kat was part of loving me? That we were a package deal?"

"Yes."

"Well, so are my friends. They're all your friends too, Declan. And you're not closed off and isolated. You're warm and loving and worth so much more than someone like Nate will ever understand. We've *all* got your back."

I didn't doubt him. Not after the way Gray stepped up last night. Not when Skylar never once protested I was poaching one of his best employees.

His friends had greeted me like one of their own at the cook-out, but even before I dated Cash, they'd always welcomed me as Hudson's friend.

I'd been the one holding back—and I was done doing that.

"I guess deep down I knew that Nate wasn't the same kind of friend that Hudson was. Or even Mimsy and Pipsy, you know? People in Swallow Cove are just different."

"We're wacky but lovable," Cash joked.

"More lovable than I ever imagined."

"Aw, you're just saying that because you're obsessed with me."

I laughed, loving how he could always lighten the moment, even a serious one like this.

"I guess you've got me all figured out."

He shrugged a shoulder. "Why else would I love you so much? I only do that to people who really deserve it."

"Why does that sound more like a threat than a promise?"

Cash grinned. "Well, I can be a lot. You'll have to put up with me."

I leaned in to press our foreheads together. "It's a burden I'll happily bear."

Cash kissed me softly. "Good. Now, call the sheriff and tell him what that asshole did. No one fucks with my man and gets away with it."

I smiled grimly and hit Call.

Part of me had known something was off with Nate and this deal for a while. He'd reacted too strongly to my calling it off. He'd tried to apologize, tried to make nice, but it had never really rung true.

I should have realized he was behind the vandalism. Maybe I hadn't *wanted* to see it. But now that I did, there was no going back.

Cash rubbed my back, reminding me I wasn't alone. Never would be again.

I drew a breath. "Sheriff? It's Declan. I've got a new lead for you."

CHAPTER THIRTY-FIVE

Cash

"Treehouse B&B, this is Cash speaking."

"Cash?" The voice on the other line was confused. "I thought you worked at Swallow's Nest Resort. Did I call the wrong number?"

I chuckled. "Nope. I used to work there. But now I help... run this place."

My brain still tripped over the knowledge I was no longer just *helping*. I managed this place. Declan made it official the moment my shifts at Swallow's Nest ended.

I had a title, a salary, and an invitation to add my name to the deed anytime I liked. Maybe I would eventually, but there was no rush. I didn't need a piece of paper to understand that Declan was inviting me to share his life.

"Oh, that Declan is a sneaky one! Good for him."

I recognized Pearl's voice now that I heard it.

"Good for me too," I said.

She giggled. "I'm happy for you two. I was just calling to see if he'd be coming by the Outdoor Market this week. I wanted to give him some strawberry preserves as a thank-you for sharing his delicious fruit with me!"

"Should I be jealous?" I joked.

"Oh, you!"

"Delcan's busy outside right now, but I'll tell him you called."

"Perfect! Thanks, lovey."

I scribbled down a message then slipped out the back door to watch Declan out in the garden. He was kneeling in the dirt, looking relaxed and happy.

Finding out Nate had betrayed him had hurt, but knowing the vandalism and theft would end was a huge relief. Gray and the guys had gone to pick up the greenhouse supplies, and they were continuing construction.

Not a minute too soon either, because Gray had decided to go back to Riverton and his foster brothers. He was going to finish out his responsibilities in Swallow Cove, sell off most of his belongings, and drive home.

Home. It was a funny word that still caused a pang in my chest.

My phone rang, and there was my mother on Caller ID as if she knew I'd been thinking about her. I'd only seen her a few times since we left home—mostly in passing while we both worked at the resort.

I'd asked her for space, and she'd respected my request, but I couldn't put her off forever.

I took the call. "Hey, Mom."

"Hey, Cash. I, um, wanted to call and tell you that I drove your dad to rehab this morning."

"Oh." My heart fluttered, then sank. What was I even feeling? I should be happy Dad had gone to get help, but we'd been here before, hadn't we? I'd told Mom he needed to go back and yet...it didn't mean he'd get better this time.

It didn't mean anything would change.

"I'm trying," she said softly. "I know it might be too little too late for you. I've tried to do the right thing for your dad and you kids both, but I know I made mistakes."

I swallowed. "This doesn't mean we're going to come back. I have a life here now. I'm managing the B&B, and I really can't do that from somewhere else."

"You're an adult, Cash. Of course you don't have to come home."

What she didn't say hit harder than what she did. "You want Kat to come back?"

"She needs her mom, especially at this age. I promise you that I'm going to put her first from now on."

"And when Dad comes home from rehab?"

"He already knows that he has to make it work this time. You kids come first. I made that abundantly clear."

Declan looked up from his gardening, catching my eye. His forehead furrowed, and he climbed to his feet, dusting the loose soil from his knees. Even from across the yard, he could tell something was wrong. I'd never had a connection like that with anyone else.

"I'll talk to Kat," I told my mom, hoping to wrap up the call.

"Thank you," Mom blurted. "I've missed her so much. Missed both of you."

"I won't make her do anything," I warned. "And even if she goes home, if Dad pulls more shit, she's coming right back here. I've got a B&B, and there will always be a room for her."

Maybe my name wasn't on the deed, but Declan was letting me run the B&B. Hopefully, he wouldn't mind me using that as leverage.

"I understand," Mom said, sounding chastened. "I'm going to do everything I can to make sure she's happy and safe in her own home. But I'm glad she has you. No matter what, I know

Kat will be taken care of. You've looked out for her, looked out for both of us, more than you ever should have had to, and I'm so sorry I let you shoulder that burden for so long."

My eyes burned, and I blinked hard a few times as Declan reached me and wrapped an arm around my shoulders. He didn't say anything, just held me, a solid support at my side. Someone I could always lean on, even if I hadn't been able to lean on my parents.

Mom had done her best. She loved us. If she had any blame in this, it was that she was too loving, too forgiving to take a stand against Dad. But she was trying, so I tossed her a bone.

"We've missed you too. Maybe you can come out for dinner this week, and we can all discuss it."

"Really?" Mom sounded surprised. "That sounds great."

If nothing else, I could finally make arrangements to get the rest of our stuff out of the house. Kat and I had both been avoiding it because we hadn't been ready for another confrontation, but we couldn't stand still, unmoving forever.

It was time to figure out what came next. Plus, it'd be nice to stop wearing the same damn clothes over and over. I was a colorful guy, and I needed to express it through more than a handful of outfits.

We said a stilted goodbye. It was going to take time for our relationship to heal. While I'd lived at home, I'd been so angry at my father that I'd never processed my mom's role in our situation. She'd enabled Dad.

But then I had too, hadn't I? By staying and supporting the family, I'd allowed it to continue as much as she had. We'd both done our best in a crappy situation, though. Maybe it was time to focus on the future.

"You okay?" Declan asked.

"Yeah, just a call from my mom. She's sent my dad to rehab."

"That's good, isn't it?"

I nodded. "If it works, it is. There's no guarantee it will. Hell, I don't know if I want to see him again, even if it does. Is that awful?"

"Not even a little," Declan said. "You feel what you need to feel, love. No judgment here."

"And if Kat doesn't want to go back there, I sort of told my mom I'd let her stay with us...indefinitely. Is that okay?"

"Of course it is," Declan said. "This is your home, which makes it her home, too. She always has a place here. If your parents fight it, we can get a lawyer. Whatever it takes."

I pulled his face to mine for a soft kiss. "What did I do to deserve you?"

"I believe you harassed me into loving you."

I laughed. "I can be very persistent."

"Yes, you can, but I'm so glad you came crashing into my life. I can't imagine a future without you in it now."

Declan smiled at me, and this expression was so warm and full of love it was miles from the resting bitch face that he was known for. It was the real Declan, the one he'd kept tucked away, guarded behind walls of surly indifference.

This kind of smile was rare and only for me, but that only made it more precious.

"You know," I teased, "with the B&B fully renovated, we can book a lot more guests."

Declan grimaced. There was the grump I knew and loved.

"That's...good," he said, looking as if he'd bitten into something sour.

"Mm-hmm." I slung my arms around his neck. "Maybe we should move out into The Roost? You know, it's a lot closer to the greenhouse and my introvert can hide out away from other people until—mmph!"

Declan kissed me so hard he nearly knocked me off my feet. "You're perfect, you know that? You have the best ideas."

"I know. It was my idea for you to love me."

He pinched my ass, making me yelp, then kissed me again.

I could get used to this life, this man. The rest of the world might see his resting bitch face, but all I saw was the love of my life.

EPILOGUE

ONE YEAR LATER

Declan

"THESE TOMATOES ARE JUST GORGEOUS," JUDY NASH SAID, picking up two bright-red romas from my table at the Outdoor Market near the marina.

"They're delicious too," Pearl put in from the vendor's spot beside me, where she displayed her jams. "I bought a crateful to make my tomato jam. It's never tasted so good."

"Ah, well, the greenhouse allows me to control the conditions so much more," I said, brushing aside the compliments. "And Mimsy's help getting set up out there has been invaluable."

"Don't sell yourself short," Judy said as she picked out cucumbers, squash, and onion. "Hudson's told me how hard you work out there, and it shows."

"I love it," I said simply.

That was an understatement. Since devoting my life to the greenhouse, gardens, and landscaping at the B&B—while Cash covered the hosting responsibilities—I'd found a fulfillment I didn't know possible.

I was living my dream—a life I couldn't even conceptualize until Cash came along with his limitless fount of optimism. He'd changed everything for me.

Beside her, Ansel tugged at the bill of his Weekend Hookers hat, clearly impatient. "Will you stop fondling the man's fruit?"

Judy slanted an unimpressed glance his way. "Really, Ansel?"

"What?"

"Do you even *listen* to the words coming out of your mouth?"

While they bickered, I boxed up Judy's selections, then checked the time. I only sold for a few hours in the morning. I had no desire to stand out in the summer heat all day. Folks had learned to stop by early if they didn't want to miss out.

"Tell Hudson to call his mother when you see him," Judy said as she put the box of produce into Ansel's arms, the old man grumbling about lugging it all the way home. "We're overdue for our family dinner, and these romas will be perfect for my pasta sauce."

"I'll tell him tonight. We're meeting up with some other friends."

Judy smiled. "Good. I'm glad to see you coming out of that shell of yours. Cash has been good for you."

"Yes, he has."

I'd never be an extrovert or have a flair for small talk, but when I'd chosen to stay in Swallow Cove—when I'd acknowledged the true connections I had made here—I'd finally embraced it as my home.

Nate's betrayal still stung. It had come out in court that he'd been in debt up to his eyeballs, but I couldn't find it in myself to forgive him. Maybe because deep down I knew he hadn't been a true friend, not like the ones I'd made here.

I cleared out a few minutes after Judy. She'd bought nearly

all my remaining produce, anyway. I gave the two leftover tomatoes to Pearl and one carton of strawberries to Ruth Marie, so
she wouldn't feel left out. The women were competitive, and I
didn't want to give them any more reason to snipe at each other.
Then I drove Cash's battered pickup—a purchase from Gray
when he left town—back to the B&B. My aunt's antique Ford
was tucked away in the garage, reserved for date nights and
other special occasions.

The property looked better than it had since my teenage
years spent with my aunt, when I'd needed to escape the reality
of being the only gay boy in a conservative school. Swallow
Cove wasn't *liberal*, by any means, but it was a fresh start where
I could share—or not share—what I wanted of myself.

That was probably when I'd started holding parts of myself
back. The failed relationships over the years, guys who couldn't
accept me for who I really was, added to it. By the time I took
over the B&B in Swallow Cove, I was closed up tighter than
Fort Knox.

Sometimes Monroe and I speculated about why Aunt
Millie gave me the B&B instead of dividing it amongst us.
Monroe had her own business and roots where she lived, of
course. But we figured it went deeper than that.

Millie knew this place was my special retreat.

Maybe she'd hoped I'd open up over breakfasts with guests
—or maybe she'd just given it to me so I'd have a place to hide
away when I needed. Either way, I was damn glad she'd
inspired me to leave my job in the city and try something new.

And now I could look out over the grounds and feel closer to
her than ever, replaying the memory of her showing me her
plans for the B&B just as soon as she found the money.

"A greenhouse, Declan. Wouldn't that be lovely?" she'd
said. "We could have fresh vegetables and fruits year-round.
And imagine if we expanded the balcony outside the Treehouse

Suite? The Roost needs a modern kitchen and bathroom, maybe with one of those jacuzzi tubs..."

We'd put one of those in, and Cash and I had enjoyed the hell out of it. For me, sharing baths and showers was just as intimate as sex. I loved feeling close to Cash. That was the most important thing. Occasionally, our dicks got involved, and that was good too.

It was Cash's heart that attracted me most, though, and it always would be.

I parked the truck and headed into the main house through the kitchen door. A clamor of voices trailed out from the great room. I headed that way, easily separating Cash's voice from the other two.

"The Rusty Pub is a local favorite, so don't tell anyone I told you or I'll be in trouble," Cash said, a playful lilt to his voice. "I'll be there tonight with some friends, actually. It's a low-key place to get a good beer. The Swallow's Nest Resort has some fine dining that's great. The Savory Swallow is where a lot of folks go for fancier cuisine, but it's a bit snooty and overpriced."

"We're not really in the mood for fancy, are we, Tru?"

"Nah. We didn't visit a lake town for that."

Cash's eyes creased up as he grinned. "Good. No one's ever accused me of being fancy, and I would *hate* to disappoint."

The two men exchanged a look.

"Cash," I scolded as I reached them. "Your flirting filter is turned off again."

"What? I didn't..." He paused and laughed, running a hand through his dark hair, looking more gorgeous than anyone had a right to be. "I didn't mean *me*, as in you'd be in the mood for— I meant the B&B, me as a host, but not..."

"Keep digging that hole," I teased.

"Ugh." He grabbed a handful of my shirt and tugged me

close enough to kiss. "I love this guy." His eyes held mine. "Only this guy."

"We figured that out on our first day here," Truman said with a smirk. "Those heart eyes wouldn't fool anyone."

Cash grinned, not the slightest bit embarrassed. "Good. I want everyone to know I'm Declan's boy toy."

I shoved him back a step. "Don't start with that Daddy crap again."

He laughed. "But it's so fun to see you glare and get all surly. You hardly ever give me resting bitch face anymore."

I shook my head, eyes rolling up. The man exasperated me. Damn, but I loved him.

"I'll let you all make your plans for the day," I told them. "I need to check on a few things out in the greenhouse."

Cash turned back to Truman and Lyle. "Oh, make sure you check out the Master Bites Food Boat if you get out on the lake today."

"Master Bites?" Lyle said with a laugh. "That's almost as bad as Glazed Holes."

The two guys were from Granville, where Fisher had family. We'd started seeing a trickle of guests from there, won over by Fisher's tales of how awesome our quirky lake town was.

Late last year, Garrett Rafferty and his boyfriend Kevin, the prettiest guy I'd ever seen—who also performed as a drag queen across the lake during their visit—brought their family to the B&B. Cash had dragged me to the show, and I had to admit, Sassy Solo was impressive. All the queens were, but there was a special energy to Sassy's stage presence that really captivated me.

So much so that Cash teased me all the way home, pretending to be jealous and offering to wear lace for me. I told him to wear anything he wanted, but all I needed was him.

Garrett's grown son and daughter—Darren and Emily—had

also come along, along with their partners. They were all close in age to his boyfriend, so that must have made for an *interesting* situation when he started dating Kevin. But they were such a loving couple I was glad it hadn't stopped them.

Not like Cash and I were exactly close in age either. I just didn't have any kids running around. I tried to imagine it and shuddered. *No, thank you.*

Not long after the Raffertys left, an older gay male couple had booked with us for a weekend. LeRoy and Eugene spent most of their time out on a fishing charter, but they must have had a good time, because a few months later a little family of three: Hunter, Clark, and a kid named Toby, who was eleven or twelve years old, turned up.

By now, we were used to seeing Granville folks visit. In fact, we jokingly said that Glazed Holes were a part of the booking fee, and they always brought us a few treats. Good thing too, because we were all becoming addicts.

I left Cash to his work and set about doing mine, meeting up to help him turn over a couple of rooms near the end of the day before showering and dressing for dinner. I wore my usual button-down white shirt, though I paired it with jeans these days.

Cash was more casual, in a pale blue shirt that stretched across his chest, snug enough to show his body's form, red basketball shorts, and flip-flops.

"Did you call Kat?" I asked Cash as we headed out.

"Yeah. She might come stay this weekend. She says Dad is getting on her last nerve." He shrugged. "Rehab may have dried him out, but he's still a miserable bastard."

I winced. "She can move in more permanently if she wants."

He smiled faintly. "She knows, but she and Mom have gotten so much closer in the last year. If Dad steps out of line,

Mama Bear isn't gonna put up with it. Not at the risk of losing her baby girl."

I chuckled. "Well, good."

Cash nudged me. "But thank you. Knowing she has a place to go makes all the difference. She'll never feel trapped again."

I pressed a kiss to his temple. "As long as you're both happy..."

His smile widened. "Oh, Mr. Sullivan, you make me *very* happy. No worries there."

I laughed and decided we better leave before Cash got other ideas.

Hudson waved us over as soon as we entered The Rusty Hook. They'd pushed two tables together. Now that all the friends were coupled up, the group had doubled in size.

Tonight was a special occasion, Brooks's two-year anniversary with Skylar. He'd wanted us all to meet up here, where the two had first met and fallen in love back when Brooks bartended and managed the pub.

Everyone had turned out.

Fisher sat so close to Hudson he was practically on his lap, while Poppy sat on the edge of her chair with near perfect posture, her platonic partner Jasmine, from Hot Buns, beside her. Once she became part of the group, they'd folded in Danny and Abe, as well. Danny *was* actually in Abe's lap, not just close to it, with one arm draped around his shoulders. Sawyer slouched in his chair, ballcap over his curls, though a few spilled out. He'd hooked an ankle around Ash's calf, sending him a playful smirk when he thought no one was looking.

Cash approached the table, shaking the box of Glazed Holes we'd gotten from Lyle and Truman when they arrived in town. "Delivery from Granville!"

Fisher's eyes lit up. "Who's here?"

"Truman and Lyle," Cash said. "Do you know them?"

Fisher pursed his lips, eyes growing distant as he thought. Then his gaze latched onto something by the door. "Oh! Yes." He stood and waved an arm. "Guys! Come over here!"

A glance confirmed that Truman and Lyle had taken Cash's advice to grab dinner at the pub. They approached us.

"Fisher, right?" Truman said. "We met at a barbecue at Garrett's place, didn't we?"

"Garrett, who's with the drag queen?" I asked.

They turned surprised eyes on me. "Yeah, that's Kevin. We're good friends, actually. They told us how great their B&B stay was, so we had to try it out."

Cash snorted. "Declan is obsessed with Sassy Solo."

"I am not," I protested as they all laughed. "Sassy's just very impressive on the stage."

"That better be the only place Sassy is impressive," Cash muttered.

"I'm sure Garrett thinks Kevin is impressive in all sorts of places," Truman said while Lyle shook his head with a fond smile.

"I mean, he'd have to be impressive to snag his best friend's dad, right?"

"Best friend's dad," Cash said with a delighted laugh. "That's almost as bad as what Fisher did."

"Good, I think you mean," Fisher said with an unrepentant grin. Then, for the Granville guys' benefit, he added, "My dad doesn't like Hudson."

"Didn't like," Hudson clarified. "He likes me now."

"Eh..." Fisher waved his hand in a so-so motion, then broke off with a squeak when Hudson pinched his side.

"We didn't mean to barge in," Lyle said. "We'll leave you all to your night."

"You're welcome to join us," Skylar said with a kind smile. He was always the sweetest, most welcoming of the friend group. Not that they weren't all nice, but there was just this genuine empathy in Skylar. He really, truly welcomed everyone.

"That's all right," Truman said. "We came on this trip to spend some time alone. We hang out in groups just like this all the time back home."

"Which is great," Lyle put in quickly.

"Just not what you're looking for on this trip," I added. "We understand. Enjoy your evening."

Cash and I took the two remaining chairs while Lyle and Truman found a quieter corner alone. They seemed like nice guys.

Cash nudged me. "You're better with people than you think you are."

"Not really," I said, amused. "I just know how it feels to want to escape."

"Do you want to escape now?" Cash asked, seeming serious.

I smiled at him. "No, love. I'm with you, so I'm good."

Fisher grinned. "Dang, you two are so adorable. I never thought it'd happen."

"Not in a million freaking years," Sawyer put in.

Cash shot him a glare. "Thanks a lot, man. I appreciate all the faith you had in me."

Hudson chuckled. "Well, to be fair, Declan didn't think it would ever happen either."

I shrugged. "Glad to be wrong on this one."

Cash leaned in to kiss my cheek. "Wasn't gonna let you get away."

Brooks sat forward and clapped his hands. "Okay, as happy as I am about this love fest, there's a reason I invited you all here tonight."

We glanced toward him and Sky.

"It's our two-year anniversary," Brooks said, turning to look at Skylar. "When we met in this pub, I was just this dumb guy who thought he was straight."

Skylar smiled. "No, you were a sweet guy who thought he should protect me from my big bad ex. Which I appreciated."

Brooks shot him a rueful grin. "Well, obviously, I didn't stand a chance once I got to know you, Sky. You were just everything I didn't know I needed."

It wasn't like Brooks to get this mushy in front of the rest of us. Possessive, yes. Touchy-feely, sure, sometimes. But sappy? That was more Fisher's purview.

Brooks slid to one knee on the floor, and Skylar gasped.

Ah, it all made sense now.

Brooks reached into his pocket and withdrew a gold band. "Skylar Addison, you've become the center of my universe. You opened my heart up to not just you, but all the friends and family I have and made my life so much—"

"Yes," Skylar blurted, dropping onto the floor to pepper kisses all over Brooks's face.

Brooks laughed. "I didn't get to ask yet!"

Cash slipped his hand onto my thigh and squeezed. I threaded my fingers through his, my heart expanding at the idea that this could be us one day, promising to love each other forever. My heart was already his. A ring would only be a symbol, but a nice one.

"Okay, ask," Skylar said impatiently.

"Will you marry—"

"Yes!"

"Me?"

"Yes, yes, yes."

Ash whistled sharply. Fisher and Poppy clapped, shouting congratulations. Sawyer was on his feet, rounding the table to hug Brooks.

Over the cacophony, Cash leaned in and murmured in my ear. "Does this mean we have to give them the Glazed Holes?"

I grinned. "Afraid so. But I imagine there will be a lot more in our future. These Granville folks just keep coming."

"Fine," Cash said with a mock pout, "but when I propose, don't be surprised if I use one of these doughnuts as the ring. It'll forever be associated in my mind now, and I'm *starving* for it."

He managed to make it sound so ridiculously dirty that I laughed even as my stomach flip-flopped at the implication.

I leaned in, meeting his eyes with a pointed look. "Not if I ask first."

His eyes widened in surprise. "I was just kidding..."

"I'm not," I said. "You're the most amazing man I've ever met, so damn sweet and supportive and—"

"Don't forget impossibly sexy."

"So sexy." I paused. "And a great cuddler."

"The highest of compliments from you."

He was teasing me, but he wasn't wrong. It was the highest compliment that Cash accepted my love in whatever way it expressed itself.

I dropped my voice, letting it purr in the quiet space between us, knowing it'd drive him crazy.

"I'm never letting you go. You're mine."

Cash pounced on me, kissing me far too aggressively for a public setting. Three coasters flew across the table, nailing us in the shoulders.

"Trying to get engaged here!" Brooks said.

Cash turned to them with a cheeky grin. "Sorry, man. You're not the only sappy fuckers here."

Poppy shook her head. "God, you're all ridiculous." She sent a smile Jasmine's way. As an aro-ace, Poppy wasn't *in love* with Jas, but she did love her and rely on her like her other half, so in way, she'd found her happy ending too. Then she surprised us by saying, "I call dibs as Skylar's best woman!"

"Only if I get to be Brooks's best man," Sawyer said.

"What? But I'm his cousin!" Fisher protested.

"Exactly, he's stuck with you, but he *chose* me."

They immediately began arguing. Brooks and Skylar exchanged a wide-eyed look. "Uh, I think I'll get another round of beer," Brooks said. "Apparently, our wedding is going to have a *lot* of best men—"

"And women," Poppy put in.

Skylar smiled at her. "I wouldn't have it any other way."

"Don't worry, Fish," Cash called. "You can be my best man when I tie the knot with Declan."

All the friends' heads instantly swiveled toward us.

"Are you..." Hudson asked.

I shook my head. "This is Brooks and Skylar's night. We wouldn't get engaged right now. But someday...yeah." I turned to Cash. "If he'll take me."

"I'll take you tonight, baby," he said with a saucy wink.

The friends all groaned. Brooks went to order a round of beers. Poppy leaned across the table to start planning colors and flowers and all sorts of wedding details that made my head spin. The rest shouted over each other, talking and laughing—sometimes insulting—one another.

I never thought I'd be so happy in a loud, noisy group like this. But Cash's hand was on my thigh, my anchor, grounding me and making me realize I was one of them now.

Part of Swallow Cove and all its wacky characters.

At home. At peace.

And in love.

ALSO BY DJ JAMISON

Swallow Cove

Dock Tease: I've been in love with the man my dad hates for years. He resists because I'm young and a virgin. But I'm not giving up. I'll find a way to lure in my man.

Pretty Buoy: After leaving my toxic ex, I flee to Swallow Cove, where I meet Brooks Riggins. He has a surprising protective streak. When my ex turns up, Brooks offers to play fake boyfriend, but our kisses feel all too real.

Knockin' Boats: Ash and I were once friends, but that was before he took our rivalry a step too far and moved in on my girlfriend. I hate the guy. And thanks to our jobs, I can't even avoid him. Ash gets whatever he wants, but he won't get me.

Rom-Com Reboot

Sexless in Seattle: After my parents died, I took custody of my kid brother. I've got no time for romance. But when my bro decides to post on a social media site and play matchmaker, everything changes.

You've Got Male: Carrying on my great-uncle's little record store means everything to me. Too bad a big-box store is opening on my block. The owner, Chase Fox, is too friendly, too smooth--too *flirty*. My only comfort is the new friend I recently met online...

Legally Brawn: I'm devastated when my boyfriend dumps me to find someone with brains as well as brawn. I go to law school to change his mind, but it's my best friend Jordan who makes me review the evidence. Verdict? I've been pursuing the wrong man.

Rules We Break

Don't Date A DILF: As a teacher, I live by this rule. But when matchmaking drives me to fake date Hunter Rhodes, resisting this man may be the one test I can't pass.

Don't Mess With The Ex: I've lived by one simple rule for the last twenty years. But when Laurence Kensington III shows up to tell me we're still married, we'll both be put to the test.

Don't Bang Your Stepbro: I'm not one for rules, but not hooking up with your stepbrother is kind of a no-brainer. Until I wake up with him in a Vegas hotel wearing nothing but a wedding ring.

Games We Play

Two Truths and a Lyle: When our friends use a party game to drop a truth bomb that my BFF and I are in love, the drunken kiss that follows opens my eyes to feelings I never thought possible.

Never Have I Evan: When a party game reveals I still have my V-card, it's embarrassing. But when the sexy new guy in town wants to coach me in the art of flirtation, it's game on.

Truth or Darren: When I push my ex-girlfriend's brother too far with a dare, I'm the one to pay the price. A very sexy but utterly confusing tongue kiss with a guy.

7 Minutes in Kevin: When my dream man steps into the closet during a make-out game, I jump at the opportunity to get my hands on him. It might be a terrible idea, but how often will I get a chance to kiss my friend's sexy dad?

Mistle-Joe Kisses: A bit of mistletoe sparks an amazing night between coworkers. But will the prickly office manager Augustus bend his rules for love? A Games We Play/Rules We Break cross-over novella.

Thrust Into Love

Swiped By My Dad's Best Friend: Cooper is a frat boy, general screwup, and...Daddy's boy?

Matched By My Rival: Simon is an ex-football star, a bitter rival, and...falling for the enemy?

Tapped By My Roommate: Ethan is a shy geek, newly bi-curious, and...propositioning his gay roommate?

Sexted By Santa: Christian Kringle is a college professor, reluctant Santa, and...fake dating his neighbor?

Marital Bliss

Surprise Groom: Caleb is shocked to learn his family could lose Bliss Island Resort—unless he can pull off a marriage of convenience with an investor's gay, go-go dancing son.

Wrangling a Groom: Wyatt and Diego made a childhood pact to get married one day. But they grew up, life got messy, and young love wasn't enough. When Diego visits the ranch, they have one more chance...Can they get it right in time to fulfill that marriage pact after all?

Nobody's Groom: A sexy ranch hand and a naïve country boy ignite each other's tempers—and passions—in this bisexual awakening, cowboy romance.

Faking a Groom: Avery Kinkaid has been repressing his deepest urges for as long as he can remember. But when his father pushes him too far, he's ready to call his bluff. All he needs is a groom, and his first love is the perfect man for the role of fake fiancé.

Hearts and Health

Heart Trouble: Nurse Ben Griggs is leery of trusting his heart to anyone, let alone a thrill-seeking patient, but he agrees to a series of dates, if only to prevent more injuries!

Bedside Manner: Zane Kavanaugh is still recovering from a traumatic coming out, but he finds himself drawn to the calm, collected, much *older* ER doctor who treated him.

Urgent Care: Surgeon Trent Cavendish returns to his hometown—and his first love. Xavier isn't the kid he remembers, but a sexy man in lace *and* a competent nursing student. And neither version of the man is going to make it easy for Trent to find his second chance at love.

Room for Recovery: When Beau is bullied, teen heartthrob Wade comes heroically to his rescue. But their growing attraction won't come without painful truths.

Surprise Delivery: A thrill-seeking doctor teaches a workaholic administrator how to live in the moment before the responsibility of a baby arrives, and in return he finds love after loss.

Orderly Affair: A bi-curious orderly explores with a geeky lab tech, but between Ian's reluctance to come out and Callum's annoying ex, they'll have to work for their HEA in this hookups-to-lovers romance.

Operation Makeover: A cute but insecure X-ray tech and a gorgeous hairdresser join forces for a makeover that brings them both a love they never saw coming.

Rapid Response: A firefighter discovers a new side to his sexuality with a bossy male paramedic. Their chemistry is red-hot, but Sean will have to come to terms—not just with his attraction to a man, but with his desperate need to please.

Holiday Romances

Grinch Kisses: Griff is a festival planner who has lost his love for the holidays, but that all changes when his sister brings him an unexpected gift, one that is tall, brand, and handsome...

Yours for the Holiday: Remy loves to hate his brother's best friend. Or maybe he hates to love him. Either way, sparks fly when the two share a room during a holiday vacation.

All I Want is You: One kiss under the mistletoe destroyed a friendship. Will another Christmas kiss remake it into something better?

Want more?

This is just a sampling of my books. See my full catalogue

ABOUT THE AUTHOR

DJ Jamison writes romances about everyday life and extraordinary love featuring a variety of queer characters, from gay to bisexual to asexual. DJ spent more than a decade in the newspaper industry before chasing her first dream to write fiction. She's spent a lifetime reading and continues to avidly devour her fellow authors' books each night. She lives in Kansas with her husband, two sons, one snake, and a sadistic cat named Birdie.

Made in the USA
Monee, IL
21 February 2025

12417041R00208